THE
SWORDSMAN

By
David McLeavy

MONTAG

Dedication

To Mom — For always encouraging my passions, no matter how impractical.

To Logan — That one day, when you're grown, you will take this book from the shelf and read a passage once in a while and be proud of your old man.

And Ashley — For believing in me when I did not believe in myself, and for loving me unconditionally. I couldn't have done this without you.

I

PLEASANTRY

1

They went out north into the wetlands with their blades still slick from murder, barely able to carry their plunder so weary were they from a long cold morning of death. As they moved the sound of sheathing weapons and rows of boots harrowing the marsh and a wet cough elsewhere cut the silence of the predawn, their human noises faint and then growing, as if signaling the birth of something foul from the amnion of this place where all else was dead.

They paused before long amongst a row of salt shrubs to rest, overlooked by the lightening sky. The remnants of the evening faded there into the horizon, the last ebbing glimpses of pale starlight driven back by the gathering day. Some of them tended to their wounds during that time, or rinsed the blood from their faces and hands with muddy backwater as they watched the dawn break, speaking not a word. Then, when the morning was upon them at last, they continued on, appearing in the pale dayglow as undead awakened from the sphagnum. Behind them, the wreckage of a hansom, the remains of their victims and the spoils not worth carrying faded and then were gone, washed from sight by the mist as if they never were.

Earnald Avers stayed back from the rest of the group, as if distancing himself somehow absolved him of what they had done. Until moments ago, he had battled a surge of panic and revulsion that had nearly overwhelmed him; now all he could think of was escape. The idea of it consumed him, forcing all other thoughts away as he stared at the backs of the other men marching ahead with their tattooed heads bowed and their hands on their weapons.

Escape. The word felt alien, though its foreignness did nothing to dilute the singular nature of his new goal. He *had* to get away; it was as simple as that. Nothing else mattered now.

He scanned the marsh as they went, looking for an obvious path, some route away from the other highwaymen, some sudden opportunity that might reveal itself. There *must* be a way, he told himself in his most childish parts. But was it childish? It felt as though what he wanted was right there, so close he could smell it, obscured by a tangle of cypress trees and some thickening fog and nothing else: freedom from these men and the horror he had just seen. Maybe he could point at the sky as the last dark of night ceded to the day, calling out a warning, and then, while the others were distracted, he could pick a direction and run until he collapsed. Maybe that was all it would take.

Sure, and you'd be dead before you made it ten paces into the marsh.

The certainty of that thought sat like a stone in the center of him; no one left the clan of their own accord once they had been accepted, especially not the likes of Earnald Avers.

A man named Carver looked back at him over his shoulder as they plodded forth, his eyes narrowed, the tattoos on his face inked with lamb's blood and ash into the shape of tridents and meaningless symbols encircling his ear. Earny kept his gaze downturned in response and rubbed at the remains of his left eye through its patch until he was sure the other man had looked away again. The move was not just for show; his ruined eye itched him terribly in this damp weather. The gnarls of tissue and dead nerves hidden there were a record in bas-relief of violence done to him years ago, committed by a man he could hardly picture now. If only the ever-present irritation had left along with that memory. Had there been a single day since where that old wound hadn't tortured him? He could not remember one.

They continued their silence as they navigated the heather and the sedges and the reeds, the smell of blood and decaying plant matter and a dead animal somewhere rank in their noses. At one point the company sent scouts ahead and behind to ensure no one approached, the men who went chosen for their woodsmanship, which was fair at best but better than the others, and as one they crept into the fogged distance making no sound. *They must be getting jumpy in their old age*, Earny decided. He wondered how far they would go before they grew bored and turned back; until this morning he might have placed a wager on it.

When the scouts did reappear they were salt-white and stir crazy, the rumble in their stomachs audible as they neared and their trousers wet to the thighs from trawling the fens. Nodding that all was clear, they fell back in line. Earny watched their manner and their expressions, thinking it was just as likely they had stolen a nap as surveyed the area.

"Keep movin', ya bastards. We need ta get at least near tha riverbend 'fore we stop," said a voice up ahead. Without argument, the men obeyed.

The day drew on as they marched through the slate grey land and the fog eddying around them. Further north, the marshlands would give way to drier plateaus and the thicker forests of the Shodan, though whether they headed there or somewhere else, it made no difference to Earny. Anywhere was better than this forsaken place.

"What plan've ya? North through Pleasantry?" asked one of the men. His name was Gaur, but Earny thought of him as the Turtle.

"We turn west at tha river's divide. Bigger towns out that way."

"That's twice the walkin' for fuckssake."

"Yar but four times the people, sure. Need ta sell what we've got, 'less you wanna carry it round the rest o' yer life."

The Turtle shrugged and admitted he did not.

When they felt safe, they bivouacked in a crook of the Hunter River and set about binding the rest of their wounds and cooking up lunch. Earny chose a spot far from camp to keep watch, and he stood there in the cordgrass matting at his face with his shirtsleeve. That same panic welled up again, threatening to drive him into the river or through the trees or straight into his company with his weapon raised for even the barest chance of escape. The feeling was overpowering, surging from some primal place inside him he did not know existed. He went so far as to take a step forward and wrap his fingers around the hilt of his basilard before he stamped the urge down again, leaving a swirling hot ball smoldering in his chest.

"Anyone ever tell you ya move like a bird s'bout to die, Earny?" a man named Fensely asked, laughing as he picked at his teeth with a twig. Earny looked at him, expressionless, then moved further away and gave no response.

The air was colder near the water, the chill carried outward by a thin spray shed from the seiche like dead skin. Earny crouched with his cheeks wetted by it and watched the waves bend into ripples the branches and the peat submerged there and the fish milling above. How long had it been since a summer day? More than a year if he had to wager. The churning whitecaps of the Hunter River should be fit for swimming by now, but in this ceaseless pre-winter those black ripples were cold enough to shock a man white and lock his muscles until he drowned, affording him no more regard than the dead leaves drifting across their swell. The endless drear infecting every inch of this land made Earny miss his years back in the Lower Vale, when the sky did not hang so pale and stark above the passing days and the world was not so utterly dark. There had been life amidst the sorrow and the death then, birdsong everywhere in defiance of the encroaching cold, a sound almost forgotten now, and there had been blooming flowers, too, in thin patches and only where the flora was hardiest, but still common enough. Missed most of all was the scent of fresh freckle berries and chilled summer wine, sweet and tart and refreshing all at once, brought down even to small villages like Pleasantry by the peddlers from Eastfield. But never again, his heart told him. Those things and their like were as vanished from the ken of mortals as the souls his company had slaughtered this morning.

He lamented this and was only half-looking when something moved in the band of fog south of them as it drifted incurvate and aimless along the horizon. The dark shape, whatever it was, had looked man-sized or greater as it emerged from the gloom briefly before being swallowed whole again. Earny wondered if it was an elder deer, or perhaps a black bear, though neither were common

here. Bears did not often wander so far north, not near the marshlands, and when they did it was to forage and find new habitats and
they were not territorial. Elder deer at times ventured to the edge of
the Thresh when pressed by starvation, though what living vegetation
they hoped to find in this rotted wetland he could not imagine. He
supposed animals did not consider things so far.

Nothing else stirred again, and Earny stared after the movement
once it was gone until his vision defocused with boredom. *A slippery
mind*, that's what his departed wife had once called it with affection,
Keeper bless her.

Focus, Earnald. Something's out there and you don't know what.

Muttering to himself, he rose against his stronger urges and
mounted a blackened windfall, grunting as he heaved himself up, and
from that higher vantage point he scanned the distance once more.
Still nothing stirred on the horizon; the water bleeding outward from
the mist rumpled and smoothed in time with his breathing, holding
trapped within it a murky semblance of the sky and the ragged field-
work of the distant mountains. That ancient stone rose black from
the horizon like the scutes along the back of some reptilian titan,
rippling and plunging itself into the mist standing at the edge of the
world, soundless in its enormity. Earny knew there were hulking creatures called Misties that walked these woods now and then, said to
appear astride a viscous Mist that gave forth from the earth or some
infernal place, but Mist was distinct and bore telltale signs and he saw
no indication of such things now.

He glanced back at Raef, their leader, called Big Old Ugly when
he was far out of earshot, and found him engrossed in skinning a
cony away from the camp, his eyes unfocused and mad. Blood splatters on his tunic and trousers had begun to dry to a dull black in
places, and between his boots thrust into the muck like a row of con-
gregants stood the chattels he had claimed from this morning's raid.
Whether the blood on his clothes belonged to the cony or something
else, Earny did not know.

"Earny, you havin any of this slop?" asked Fensely. He held out
a ladle steaming with brawn and mushrooms and something else
unrecognizable.

"That's my mother's recipe," said someone. It sounded like the Turtle.

"Remind me to give her a solid one to the face, then."

"Better to make her eat it. Grow some eyeballs on her ass."

"Or worse places."

The rest of the men laughed; even their mirth sounded predatory.

Earnald Avers sighed.

Then, as if led to him from the ether by unseen hands, a vision of the girl from this morning washed over him.

He looked away with his mind's eye.

No. Go on. Think of her. Pretending it didn't happen doesn't make it so.

The voice was right, and so he did.

She had been young, traveling by hansom through the forest not long before dawn. The men escorting her were green, their estocs bright and un-notched, their helms fresh from the smithy and polished to a shine better fit for ceremony than warfare. Men like that were too zealous, too enthused for their first errand abroad, their blood always at a pitch and their want for battle clouding their senses, all of them no doubt eager to show the world and perhaps the young lady they protected that they were indeed fighting men to be taken seriously with a long, glorious career before them.

Now every last one of them lay dead somewhere in the mud.

Earny had not partaken in the slaughter—he had never been the fighting sort, even when the enemy was deserving. After the last man's throat lay open and emptying, they had dragged the girl screaming into the forest away from the slain soldiers, her bare feet pale and digging at the mud and the leaves and flocks of muddy globs splattering her dress and her pupils black saucers shining with the bright burning life that always flared when death approached, as if the fuel of the soul must in whatever timespan be consumed before the end.

Earny had forced himself to look when it was done, to witness her slender outline prone in the mud like a doll with blood crawling her thighs and her gaze skyward, seeing nothing. What untold future generations had been rubbed from existence by Raef and his bloodlust? A thousand years of them, maybe. No one would ever know

now. Of all the parades of murdered souls marching black-eyed and bloated through the halls of Earny's memory, this contingent was the worst: seeing that girl robbed of everything she would ever have had changed him, leaving him hollow inside the way a tree throw leaves a gape in the earth.

Would anything ever fill that emptiness again? He did not think so.

As if responding to Earny's thoughts, a man called Dorn produced a slender severed finger from among the jewels in his satchel, the knuckle bent lazily as if indicating the eastern forest. After a moment he poked the finger into the ear of the highwayman beside him and grinned.

Earny bent down and emptied his lunch into the river.

"Earny's taken sick."

"Probably that fucking stew."

"Maybe he's a milky after all."

"What's a milky?"

Dorn cackled with the rest and rocked like a child and replaced the finger in his satchel. No conscience or humanity appeared behind his dull stare; his idiot eyes might as well have been marbles for how much wit they shone.

This is who you call your clan. This is who you've chosen as your circle. You've no one to blame but yourself.

The thought nearly made him wretch again.

When he was sure he would not, he wiped at his mouth and stood straight, still swaying. A redtail caught his eye and fluttered away as he did, singing into the mist all the while. He watched it rise, heading for the fog in the distance. Then something else appeared there again, still shapeless, blinking in and out of sight. But it most certainly *was* there.

"Boys…" said Earny, his voice a raspy whisper.

The mist parted and now the black shape lay closer.

"Boys, I think someone's coming."

"Mind yerself, Earny. There's naught a man for hefts either way."

Earny splashed into the first inches of the Hunter.

He saw it then: it was a man, a wide-brimmed hat sunken low on his brow, the felt blacker than night and creased lengthwise, a long duster that looked awfully hot draped across him like a cape. Strapped across his back and jutting skyward was a long, slender sword, its white hilt gleaming beneath the daylight; it jostled with his every step as though as eager to press forward as its master. He was tall, a head and change taller than Earny, and even from a hundred yards his eyes looked clear and bright and easy to spot, as if they were lit from the inside.

"There's definitely something coming!"

Mutters erupted. *Is it Misties? Naw, couldn't be. If it was Misties, we'd be eaten already.*

"He's almost on us!"

Earny turned, already aware that Raef was rising, for when that much man moved you'd be a witch to hide the sound. Raef's mace, gaudy and impractical in a smaller man's hands but deadly in his own, rang like a chime as it scuffed the ground and settled onto his shoulder. In a half-drunken dance his posse eased into position behind him, eyes clouded by stout but feigning alertness. Some of them bore pistols—of varying quality, to say the least—and Earny knew from the cold light in their eyes that they were eager to train them on prey more stimulating than kinder goats and brush rabbits.

Than helpless young girls.

The approaching man halted twenty paces away with a tuft of mist swirling at his feet. Earny opened his mouth to speak, searching the murk of his thoughts for whatever words might keep the dark man's sword in its sheath. He was silenced before he could make a sound when a hand wider than his head clamped across his shoulder. "Why d'nt ya keep yer lizard's tongue in yer face before you start a rumble ya can't finish, Earny," said Raef, his voice hushed. The clan leader was seven feet tall, a wide-jawed man with large walnut eyes better suited for a bear. A filament of scar tissue divided his face crosswise; it looked phosphorescent in the daylight.

He stepped past Earny to face the newcomer, spat tobacco, and stood there swaying with his hands cradling his mace like an infant. "Welcome there, feller. How do ya?"

"Stand true, yon stranger, and with thanks," said the man with the sword.

"My, isn't this the to-do? What look ya for?"

"I am looking for a town called Pleasantry." The dark man's whisper cut the cold air and sounded clear to Earny even from a distance

"What business ya got in that shithole?"

"The sort I'd have the mayor know in confidence."

"Come now. No secrets worth keepin' among fellow travelin' folk," said Raef, the deep lines of his face drawn up.

"Are you the mayor?"

Raef threw back his head and howled laughter. "Well, now. Yes and no. 'ppreciate the estimation."

"Make your answers plain. I've not much time."

Raef propped himself on his mace with both hands. "I'm known to be plain as men come, if ya can believe it." He looked back at his men, his eyes aglow with something he found amusing but that Earny could not decipher. "It's a shortcomin' o' mine, might say."

"If you've not seen anything useful to me, I'd as soon move on."

"You got the talk of a Northerner. Whereabouts ya hail from? Up the way of Dunnharrow, methinks. If any o' tha like of ya survived that mess."

The dark man pursed his lips in the manner of a parent irritated by their child. He looked about to take a step forward when Raef held up a hand. "We've got a bit of business with ya, 'fore ya *move on*, as ya say."

"I'd not trouble you more. The day is late and I've not crossed a bed or warm meal for a long time, friend."

Raef shrugged. "That's a shame, friend. You'll find just that up in town. But 'fore ya get ta all that, ya got ta mind tha levy."

"Levy..." The dark man's tone was humorless.

Raef gestured to his clan of inbreeds and thieves and murderers as though making a fair point. "Yar, to keep with tha town's high standards and such. Somethin' yer like to fathom with yer fancy talk and lordly way about ya."

"Has any other stranger passed this way of late?"

"Not a one. We don't get ourselves too many wanderers out these parts. Same folk day by day. If there was, I'm not rememberin' 'im."

"You would remember," said the man with the sword. "He stood as tall as yourself, strange violet eyes, if you paid any heed, robed in white. He calls himself the Cleric."

"Can't say I recall, stranger," said Raef. "Familiar to anyayoo fellas?" he asked of his men. The mass behind him of shaved and tattooed heads and greasy ponytails gestured with overwrought denial, and Earny read in the dark man's shifting posture that he was not amused.

Raef turned back to the stranger. "Care fer some drink? Nothin' but poison out tha way ya came. A parched man's a senseless man."

A smile crept onto the dark man's face which might have been pleasant had it reached his eyes. *Odd* was the best word Earny could think to describe it. "Thank you, but no. I will leave you to your day. Good will and fortune."

He took a step forward, and as one the Clan of Raef drew together, some of the men whirling their weapons clumsily in drunken flourishes before recovering into a semblance of a fighting stance. A dull ringing hung in the air for a moment afterwards, the hum of an oversized, misshapen tuning fork.

"Now," said Raef, scraping his heels through the mud as he began to pace. "As I said, we're toll collectors of a sort, and…who's be think of it, here ya are come wandered onto our bridge."

When the man with the sword moved at last it was so sudden that a palpable force of surprise washed over the band of highwaymen. They surged closer, weapons thrust before them, but the man with the sword paid them no mind as he reached into his satchel and withdrew a tin box full of small, round leaves. He rolled one into a tube and placed it in his mouth and chewed.

"That Boon?" asked Raef.

The man with the sword held the tin out, proffering it. "Care for some?"

"There's else I'd rather have o' you."

"You'd offer terms?"

"Call it a proposition."

"For crossing your bridge..."

"Mhm."

"A large bridge to cover with just twelve men. I wonder if any more worthy of your efforts are slipping past while we dawdle," said the man with the sword. As he spoke, he closed the tin of Boon and disappeared it back into his satchel. There was a finality to the movement that unnerved Earny.

As if responding to the same, Earny saw Raef's thick fingers, dangling near his thigh, twitch and drum the smears of lignite there and the blood spatters they obscured.

"Enough. I'll make it plainer since ya got a bit of wit in ya. We'll let ya pass for that bright shiny piece you've got strapped there," said the clan leader, nodding towards the man's sword, which Earny could see now was hilted in some sort of bone scrawled with tiny incisions.

"I have my own terms. Beneficial for us both. Let me pass, and you will all have breath and mind five minutes from now," said the dark man.

That's it. He means to kill us all.

A tense silence grew. For that long moment, undercut by the slap of the Hunter on the river rock around them and the call of the redtail still circling above, Earny prayed a sudden case of good sense might seize Raef, that it might drive him away and so banish them all to the marshes, unmanned but alive to begrudge it. But instead Big Old Ugly stepped forward, his mace slung low and to the side, gripped now in both hands. "You're sure o' that offer?"

The dark man nodded. Still the smile; twisted; cold.

"Okay, then."

Then the clan leader brayed the nonsensical battle call he himself had devised, and his posse sang dissonant accompaniment. Earny, no more a fighting man now than he was this morning, served two purposes on most days for the Clan of Raef: to negotiate terms with their enemies, and to sound the battle cry when those negotiations were at an end. Robbed of those duties by his master, he could only fall back, his mouth hanging, his eye wide, his hands loose to his sides and all of him useless while the men with whom he had lived and looted charged ahead with battle-mad eyes, reassured by their numbers and their bravado that no harm could ever befall them.

The first of the posse, Benjii Soamfield is what he called himself, reached the dark man, who seemed to...*teleport*. Or something. Earny wasn't sure if it was magic or not. There was no hint of motion, no coiling first, no wind up to the punch. He was standing still as stone with an axe arcing towards him one moment, and then he was standing two paces to his left, his sword in his hand, and Benjii had no head anymore. Blood erupted from the stump of his neck and his axe continued its downward swing lifelessly, cleaving the mud. Benjii's corpse fell to its knees and then to its chest as his head rolled away into the Hunter.

Raef sidled behind him, that mace, which was heavier than a good-sized child, shredding the air with a whistle. The dark man leaned away with inhuman balance and the mace swung past, disturbing his hat but little else. Then he trapped Raef's arm—it was all so casual, like he was dismissing a servant—and sliced the clan leader's thigh open to the bone. Raef howled, dropped his mace, and staggered back, clutching the bloody ruin of his flesh, then keeled headlong and lay screaming in the bushes, blood squirming between his fingers.

Earny stared, all notion of fighting wiped from his mind, immune to the blind rage or stupidity or inbreeding or whatever it was that kept the other clan members going instead of running.

Three men—one was William the Herder (Earny knew him since he was seven years old and blowing up the hind ends of dogs with firecrackers)—swept in, broadswords gleaming. The dark man with the sword ducked and parried and struck, his movements closer to a flowing black fluid than to a man. A high-pitched whine accompanied every curve he drew as etched steel severed flesh and tendons and bones, and William the Herder's days of fire-cracking were over as his torso split open from shoulder to gut and blood sloshed from his mouth and pooled in the underwood where he lay gurgling.

Porrin Sal, his half-eaten hock forgotten, thrust with his blade, and the dark man side-stepped with insouciance, his sword flashing skyward—*Keeper save us, did he do that backwards?*—severing Porrin's arm at the elbow. He glided away then and left the highwayman grasping at his red spurting stump and wailing into the forest.

A man named Franky Cope drew his throwing knife not two paces from where Earny stood gaping like an invalid, sized up and threw, but the dark man must have smelled the smoked porter on the highwayman's breath because he twisted Porrin's head askew then with a *snap* and killed him just before Franky's knife sheathed hilt-deep into his death stare.

That old steel glimmered again and again beneath the impassive gaze of the sky, dancing to the rhythm of some unheard war drum to which the dark man's very existence was counter-melody. Earny receded to a tree before he realized he was moving, his basilard slipping from his fingers, any sense of self-preservation gone. All he could do was watch.

One more halfwit approached bearing a pistol. It was Carver, who Earny had watched strangle an old woman in her bed for the piece after she had refused to sell over in Haretown a while back. It had belonged to her late husband, she had told him, discovered in the dark crags someplace where the dregs of men whose bones were now dust still lay undiscovered. Carver didn't much care for touchy bullsnot triflings (his term) like that, and he had taken the gun once his murder was finished and never again mentioned the old lady or how her eyes had bugged or how the veins in her neck had ruptured and bled beneath her skin while she strained to hold onto life.

Carver propped the pistol now on his opposing arm to steady it, one eye closed, and sought the dark man's head between the sights.

The man with the sword seemed to sense Carver in his peripheral, and without hesitation mounted Porrin's severed hand across his boot and kicked it forward. It drew a beeline through a rolling eddy of fog and Porrin delivered a right hook from the grave, snapping Carver's head back and sending his pistol shot thundering astray. He was trying to claw his way back to his feet, fingers slipping through the wet leaves without purchase, when the dark man's hand whipped outward, firing a long thin silver spike twenty feet and through the back of his head.

At last one man found the sense to run. It was the Turtle. He was thirty paces into the forest when another spike glimmered and speared his throat. He fell plashing pleas for his life into the misty air.

The dark man grew still then with the same suddenness with which he had begun, blood wriggling down his sword, mist dancing around him. The bodies of his foes lay strewn about like broken dolls, the sum of their lives rendered moot by his blade. He looked perturbed with the situation, as if someone had just finished his last bite of stew without permission. Frowning, he stepped over and around the bodies, retrieving his spent silver spikes. When they were all accounted for, he turned towards Raef.

The leader of the slain highwaymen threw up his hands, eyes white with terror. "Please don't. You can go, fer the love in it. It's... I—"

His mouth snapped closed as the dark man planted one mud-crusted boot against his chest. "Where is Pleasantry?" he asked.

Raef pointed a jiggling finger up the road. "That way. Three or four hefts. Ya can't miss it." He looked a child afraid of a whipping; it was the way that Earny would remember him forever. "Who... Who are you?" he asked.

The man with the sword regarded him.

"My name is Donovan Maltrese."

Raef was still processing the name when Donovan's sword flashed and lopped off his head with a lightning sweep and slid sheathed in a single, smooth gesture.

Then Earny saw those stark green eyes and knew that his turn had come. To his surprise, as he found his feet, he realized he was possessed by a strange lucidity.

Better than wetting himself, he supposed.

He tucked in the front of his tunic, flattened his hair as best he could, adjusted his eyepatch, and said, "Make it quick, if ya please."

Donovan Maltrese stared at him. "You're more of a man than any of your compatriots. Good will and fortune."

And with that, the Swordsman drifted on into the mist in the direction of Pleasantry, noiseless as a shadow, vanishing just as he had come.

2

The Hunter farm lay two or three hefts out from Pleasantry, a third of the way to Eastfield, a smaller town, less established in commerce and civility, which was no small feat. To the north rose the mist-shrouded silhouette of a switchback, and beside the farm's outskirts ran the road called the Drudge, and where that muddy tract terminated none in these parts could say. Perhaps at the end of the world, a place to which Jana Hunter suddenly felt a strong desire to venture.

She looked now at the family plot and recalled long summer days as a child, the sun high and hot and relentless, leaving the fence and the house sunchalked and driving the Hunter family to the river and, as evening drew on, to bonfires at the town square and then to sleepless nights with her brother spent naming every star in the sky. Now she had twenty summers behind her and the river ran cold always and there were no more fires and this place felt more like a prison.

A prison from what, though? There's not much world to escape to, girl.

The thought stung, yet she accepted it. The cities were gone as far as travelers told, wiped from the earth as if they never were by Misties or by these new creatures known as Blood Demons, though from what characteristics that moniker was begotten no man seemed to know. And with the cities, Kolendhar and Dunnharrow among them, the Swordsmen and their High Lord had perished, whatever peace promised by their efforts now ghost calls on the evil wind that blew through this countryside and would never leave.

Here, though, within earshot of the trickletalk of the river, what did such tales matter?

The Hunter Estate (she grinned as she thought of it as such, as well as how Dad went out of his way to assert that they were of no relation to yonder river) lay unvisited for long stretches, isolated yet never lonely. Men came calling on occasion, eyes bright, clad in their russet finery, their buckle boots polished to a dull sheen and bouquets of primroses thrust before them like weapons. The long felting-session chitters of Pleasantry women racing their needles against the looming winter chill relished dwelling on Jana's denial of such men. Good for them.

But there was also *him*, neither here nor there, the man with the violet eyes who had stayed but a night and changed her deep, maybe forever, if she grasped the meaning of the word.

When she tried to conjure up his face in her mind, all she could see were those piercing eyes hanging in the dark, staring into her and through her, and his smile: that brilliant, horrible smile. A flash of it streaked through her mind and curled her stomach.

Three moons gone now she remembered waking in the deep night with gooseflesh on her arms and a chill in her breath. She had eased out of bed, her toes curling back against the cold plankboards, her arms hugged around herself, drawn without thought directly to the window facing the old shed and the Shodan Woods. There had been no palpable attraction to that spot; it had just *felt* right, some irresistible beckoning there from the dark of her mind or perhaps voiced by the night itself.

He was looking right at her when she leaned onto the sill and peered out, a white specter with glowing twilight eyes bearing a gnarled staff helmed by a curved blade that lay half cloaked in fog. It *had* been fog. Certainly not Mist. Never Mist here.

His voice had thundered in her head like he was standing beside her shouting, yet he never moved. *Come to me, child*, it said.

And she did. Like an obedient dog on a tether, she stepped out into the night, the cold blast of wind on her face ignored, the aching hardness of her nipples barely noticed, the crunch of frosted grass between her toes but an echo of a memory that seemed someone else's. The moon peered through the haze like some perverse celestial onlooker as she reached him, and it was here that her memory was most vivid. It had been like standing before the Keeper to await judgement, she thought, but somehow different, as if judgement had already been passed, as though she was awaiting execution.

He had reached out with a pale hand that sprouted long, slender fingers—*Piano players hands, he got 'imself,* is what Mum would have said if she could have managed to speak in the presence of this man. Jana could not, and when his hand touched her shoulder an electric jolt had lanced through her body, leaving her chest heaving and a warm throb between her thighs that bled a moan.

Come with me, is all he had said. And she did.

The hours in the shed afterward felt so distant, like she was recalling a perverse bedtime story: his thin, hairless body atop her, writhing, those wan and narrow lips whispering words of which she now had no recollection, whatever form they possessed reduced in the aftermath to a droning warble that thrummed inside her memory. It all felt so filthy; she wanted to scrape the inside of her skull to rid herself of the sensation. She had always dreamed of what making love to a man might be like, well past the age when her childhood friends had settled down and begun plopping out whelps, but this was not her chance to find out. He had *fucked* her until it hurt, used her like a doll and then thrown her aside. But never against her will. At least she didn't think it was; that was what made it all the more awful.

When he was done, he had left her with one last clear memory: his fingernail, a scaled and tawny thing as long as her nose, tracing a path from her shoulder to her heart. At his touch, white fire had flared within her, kindling in her chest and coursing through her body until her pores felt as if they were leaking smoke. She remembered screaming and arching her back in agony while he hovered over her, smiling that ghoulish smile. Then it was blackness through and through.

When she woke in the morning, still in the shed, she was sure it had been a nightmare. But when the ache between her thighs whispered otherwise, she had tugged down her tunic and *it* was there, beginning where he had touched her and spreading from bosom to neck, spidery and evil. The little girl within Jana begged it to be a rash, or even a case of hertweed, for folks survived that plague now and then, but she knew well it was something else, something infinitely wicked that was now a part of her.

She snapped from her trance and ventured a look beneath her shirt, examining the defacement the violet-eyed man's invasion had wrought, and then covered it again. Even now it throbbed with a heat that might have been physical but bore also a vague sense of guilt. She knew at once that her plan would be to keep it hidden and wait for it to mend. Until then, she would reassure herself that there was no sinister man who visited in the night, and she would do so as long as needed. While she was at it, she'd deny Misties or any other such wickedness that lay beyond the unflappable palings of the Shodan; right now there was mom and dad, the farm, peace and quiet, and Cory.

As if summoned by the thought, Cory appeared over the hill with Dog scampering beside him, the lithe spaniel's fleshy salmon tongue dangling and gamboling and spraying saliva from the corner of his mouth. *Keeper save us, how I wish he'd name that forsaken mutt something else.* Cory was eight years old and full of piss, though his gaze held a dark and mature edge no one his age should bear hint of, let alone be full.

She arranged at the lee of the rise near the shed a broad downy duvet with stones at the corners, the needlework courtesy of one Mum Hunter. There were times in years gone when these outdoor meals would take place far from the Estate, by the flat stones of the east riverbank or atop the promontory to the south or beyond if their legs felt peppy. Now the fog kept them huddled close to home. The Mist had never come near here, although she had mistaken normal fog as herald to the grim monstrosities called Misties on some nights (just as she had *that* night, the one that did not exist). Where there was Mist, there were Misties, and where there were Misties no one sane would linger.

She stretched across the quilt and breathed deep the gelid air and savored the soft touch of afternoon breeze on her skin and the million small hairs it stirred and just stared at the sky, tousling her hair absently; it shone even in the gloom, golden and fine and tied back in a ponytail. She was taller than her mother, and long runs through the valley beneath the star-spackled sky and hard days of toil with the cattle and the corn and the wheat and the plow had molded her legs and arms into a shape she supposed men found desirable. Her skin was a deep shade of tan, nearly umber, and if anything physical might be her pride it was that, for too often Pleasantry women seemed content to store themselves in their hovels nursing and knitting and making a hermit's life. To Jana that life seemed the Maw itself, to reduce a life's worth of possibilities to a pair of sore teats and a score of children shambling about gorging on your hard-won food while you slipped to bed hungry.

Is that what you and Cory are to Mum and Dad?

She sighed and knew this was not so and felt guilty for entertaining it.

Such thoughts had never crossed her mind as a young girl naive to the black inclinations of the world, during the years when she did not fear sundown, when she had stolen out of bed while her family slept and navigated by starlight to Grampy's house (again, no relation), who even then had been over ninety years old. He'd be awake no matter how late she arrived, seated on his porch with steaming hot Boon tea in one hand and his gnarled cane drawn across his lap. She would pick dandelions or lilies or roses if she could find them along the way and appear to those kind old eyes with a bouquet wrapped in cord, and he'd smile and squeeze her cheek and tell her to have a seat. Some nights they would just sit and watch the black trees standing and swaying like a congregation of drunkards against the moonwashed night and they'd say nothing past hello and goodbye. Other times he'd tell stories, most from his fighting days, and he'd whisper of bloodshed and love and loyalty and betrayal and a thousand of life's faces that Jana knew must exist somewhere but could not discover for herself.

Perhaps tonight would be the time to see him again after all these years. She could bring her young brother as well, maybe inject the rascal with visions of things grander than shoveling manure and shucking corn.

No, she caught herself. *I can't risk letting them see what he left on me.* The people of Pleasantry, as they were, would cry witch and string her up and burn her alive at the first glimpse of her gift from the stranger in white.

She broke out of her thoughts as her stomach growled beneath her folded hands. "Dad, if dinner takes any longer I'm going to start going gray."

Her father's gravelly voice grumbled from behind the fretwork: "Would you be patient, for the love in it? Can't rush a masterpiece."

Her dad was a farmer (though a fighting man once, said the dirk he kept stowed in a bronzed mahogany trunk near his pallet), as was his father, and yet there was no lack of joy to be found in milling grain or furrowing good black earth to hear them tell it. Was it arrogant of her to hold distaste for that simple life? She couldn't figure if she considered herself above such things or just outside of them.

Cory somersaulted towards the quilt with Dog at his heels and rose with a scrawny oak branch thrust forward like a fencer. "Fight me, Jana, fer king and your booty."

"Say that again and you'll get your eyes knocked out of you."

Cory twirled his stick and spun to stab an imaginary attacker, then discarded his weapon into the woods. Dog, yapping, bolted after it. Jana patted the spot on the quilt beside her and Cory took a seat. "Have ya seen Mum since she got back from town?" he asked, wiping reddish, oily curls of hair back from his face. He was fairer than any of them, pasty as cream and peppered with freckles.

"Yar, I saw her come back with an onion and some cider from market. Why don't you make yourself useful and go help your father, Stink." She almost slapped her forehead. *Yar.* Talking like a forsaken highwayman or one of the old-timers.

"You're the woman," Cory said with a mischievous look. "'Less somethin's changed. Why don't ya go inside and stir somethin'?"

"I am gonna get you, Stink. I mean it this time." She laughed and jumped to her feet, running after him. He twisted away and danced back and forth, but she had long runner's legs and trapped him easily and they fell laughing. She squeezed him tight and ground her knuckles into his scalp until he begged for mercy.

"All right, all right. Settle down, it's time to eat," said Dad, a long loaf of bread and an old crock in hand, Mum behind him balancing a small tower of wooden porringers. Father Hunter eyed Cory. "You oughta be ashamed. Yer sister would never've been caught like that.

Avoided a lifetime's worth of spankings, ya did, Jana. I could never catch you."

"I never even bothered tryin' to catch ya," added Mum.

"Yeah right. Jana's never done a rash thing in her life. Bag of boring bones she is," said Cory, jamming a playful elbow into Jana's ribs. She punched his shoulder but said nothing; her womanly place still ached with the guilt of something more rash than they'd believe.

A sudden chill settled onto them, so subtle in its approach that she did not notice at once. She hugged her arms around herself while her father scooped steaming ladles of stew into the porringers and passed them around. When she looked down there were raised bumps along her forearms, the peaks of something rimy crawling inside her. Her teeth began to chatter something fierce, dicing plumes of her breath which were now visible. "Feels like winter's coming early," she said.

"Pretty soon it's going to start coming Midyear and last almost till winter next, I'm afraid," said Mum as she arranged her sundress and plopped down.

"How was town?" asked Jana. "Is Grampy well?"

Mum laughed. "Grampy's gonna outlive us all, mark my words. He's doin' fine. But don't ya go wandering off to visit him, ya hear? Buncha wild-eyed zealots they are, likely to skin ya as shake yer hand."

"Hush it, Mum, it's not that bad," said Jana. "I ran into a couple of boys on the Drudge a week ago. Said they're putting up a new bell tower since the one they've got now is rotted halfway to hell."

"Watch your tongue, Jana," said Dad. "And never mind what those boys say. They've been talking about re-doing this and that in Pleasantry since I was chasin' your mother's skirt, and every time they get geared up to do it, they remember they're going to have a hard enough time putting food in their bellies to waste time on trivial things like that."

"What's... triv-ull?" asked Cory.

"It's half tha people you'll meet in the world, boy, so get ta learn it well," answered Dad. That seemed to be enough for Cory, who returned to poking at his stew with his spoon.

Mum scooped up a mountain of the meaty, steaming fruits of her kitchen toil and was halfway to her bowl with it when the sound began: a roar so deep in pitch Jana felt it more than she heard it. It echoed into the leafless trees hemming the Estate, and when it had faded, Mum's hand was quivering and dribbling stew onto the duvet.

Jana's mouth ran dry. Beside her, Cory stared unblinking into the Shodan. "What is it, Da?"

It boomed again, closer, deafening, loud enough to stir ripples through the Hunter family's meal.

Where's Dog?

Then she saw it.

A cold wave crashed over Jana. The thing she feared most, that formless portent of creatures from beyond the lands walked by men, the thing she had convinced herself a hundred times beneath the oilblack watches of countless nights would never cross her land, lay ahead now, three hundred paces out.

How could they not have seen its approach?

Jana armed at her eyes, the little girl within her vying for attention, hoping to wipe away the vision before them. But now she was certain of it.

The Mist had come, and it was almost upon them.

3

Rosaline. *My dearest Rosaline.*
The Swordsman fought the picture of her face as it danced in his mind, incorporeal but bound with great weight, close enough to smell but just far enough to escape should he reach for her. Gone forever was that warmth, that unearthly smoothness, that sparkle of depth and intelligence and mischievousness, gone to that place in the Black along with so many others he had loved; perhaps it was akin to the place from which this new part of him had spawned, where the Cleric trotted merrily along with a progression of demons dancing on his coattails to songs of death.

My sweet, sweet Rosaline...

He looked away from her face, which hung in every shadow at the corners of his sight, and forced his eyes to the road. There was blood, drying now to a dull black, on his hands and drizzled about the hilt of his sword. Likely it caked his duster and chest plate as well, but he could not see it against those black folds and scrawls.

He felt his sword prod his back, as aware of it as of his arm or his fingers, and was never impeded as it bounced with his step or dug in when he turned.

Orin. His only keepsake survived from home.

You bear the Cold as well. Ever at your side, ever waiting, it is. That comes from home, too.

He ignored the thought with measured precision and thought instead of the metal digging into his skin, of that ancient bone. What would have stopped an average man in their tracks to reposition a strap instilled Donovan with the comfort of an embrace; indeed the only thing he'd miss more than losing an arm or some fingers would be to lose his sword, the one companion he possessed or required, the only one he could trust in this forsaken world.

The early morning glow gave way to a grey midday light as Donovan maneuvered a particularly muddy stretch of the Drudge, and he was reminded of the high walls of his home, cool stone stacked skyward by a thousand years of dead men. For a moment he considered this and recalled the different feel of the air, of the world itself in those lost years. He wondered if the sensation was fancied or real, then decided it was the latter. So much had changed since his last moments inside that keep far to the north that he felt like a specter divorced from the mind of its dreamer, cursed to roam some foreign land that might be a reality to some but a nightmare unending to himself.

Not far from the truth.

The road from where the bandit corpses were being picked to the bone by crows winded through the Shodan like a brown snake slithering up the mountainside. The fog was thinner here, barely visible in places, and that was good; the last thing Donovan needed now was to encounter anything more consequential than a gang of strongheads with stolen liquor on their breath. Men like that and other denizens of these forests were at most inconveniences to him, but the Mist carried things with it that made even a Swordsman's heart beat a little faster.

The dead highwaymen behind crossed his mind again for an instant, and then those thoughts turned to smoke that would never coalesce again. Death was entwined with him, always present, either in the moment or just beyond the horizon, and long-forgotten were the days when it fazed him. When he killed, the Swordsman still felt something deep, deep inside, like the faintest echo of a pebble thrown into a vast canyon, but it faded quickly, most times before he even noticed it was there. He supposed that made him dead inside. In that case, what exactly was he doing? Why force one foot before the other across all the disease and evil stricken lands of this shell of a world when he could just as easily find a nice clearing somewhere and fall on his sword?

Rosaline is watching, still. She knows your mind.

That was why, he supposed. The thought of entering the Black to find her gazing on him with disappointment, or worse, dismissal for the weakness he would have shown by leaving this life unfinished, stayed his hand. That he had caught himself weighing the notion at all filled him with a sense of shame.

Would you ever be capable of actually doing it? If so, you are going mad.

But what was madder than hunting a man Donovan had seen neither track nor cloak scrap of since one last glimpse weeks ago from a great distance, when all that had been visible was the wink of a fire and the feel of those horrible eyes aimed his way? What drove him with such certainty now? He knew the answer even as he considered the question: the low voice; that was what shamans called it, the phantom consciousness that breathed and thrived somewhere between hunch and imagination.

The Cleric's stink is still there. That is not your mind at play.

He was suddenly as sure of this as he had ever been about anything. A smile eased onto the Swordsman's weatherworn lips, a smile that felt as out of place on his hard face as a breast would have on his forehead. The utter certainty that defined him, lost for days he now realized, was back. It pulled his shoulders square and straightened his spine as it filled his body. The glimmer in his eyes returned, the one his friends, in a life that seemed ages ago, would have called this his steeliness—others, his obsessiveness. They could call it a donkey painted orange if they liked, but that impulse had driven him on this forced march hefts beyond where those same comrades would have fallen on their faces dead from exhaustion.

How far now? How long ago since Kolendhar?

It occurred to him that he no longer knew how many days he had been marching. Then again, what did it matter? It was all a part of the *endless push*; that's what Master used to call it.

That does sound glorious, doesn't it?

Donovan paused in the middle of the road as the wind carried a sound to his ears that perhaps a wild animal might have perceived, but certainly no man. He turned casually; footfalls whispered much to his trained ears: how their makers carried themselves, what equipment they bore, how well they moved, balanced, breathed, how heavy or thin they were, how long they had been a woodsman, how old they were, and a thousand other nuances. The man approaching was gaunt of limb but with a soft, exaggerated pot belly, bore a weapon he had little idea of how to wield, fancied himself a woodsman but in folly, and moved like a drunken monkey.

Donovan watched the mist, not bothering to reach for his sword. Moments later, a man appeared over the hill, limping and jogging and wheezing, and for the first time in a long while, the Swordsman was surprised.

"Wait, sir! Please wait! I beg ya!" shouted the man as he dashed along in the mud. An invisible stick or a slick spot must have obstructed his path because the man's feet slipped out from under him seconds later, and while he hovered in midair the Swordsman wondered darkly if he would land on his head and snap his neck and let the universe be done with him. But instead, the man rose, mud dappled across his face, and ran stumbling the rest of the way down the hill.

"That's far enough," said Donovan. He saw now it was the highwayman he had let live.

The one-eyed man squatted on his haunches, wheezing. "Please... Wait fer me, sir."

"I'm short on time. Say your piece."

"Th... Praise be fer sparing me. I owe ya my life."

"You don't. Go along with your business before I change my mind."

The highwayman rose to his feet and proffered his hand. "I'm Earnald Avers. My boys called me Earny sometimes. 'Fore ya killed 'em all, that is. But that's what I wanted to talk to ya about."

The Swordsman turned his back on the one-eyed man and continued along the road. "Go home, Earnald Avers. Have yourself a drink and a night in a warm bed. Farewell."

Earny watched him go, resignation in his eyes, then followed regardless and said, "Never in my life have I seen such a thing as what ya did down yonder. Was like the Reaper 'imself come grabbed up some steel and made mince of the best fighters around like it was easy as breathin'."

"If those were the best fighters around," said the Swordsman, "then Keeper help mankind if ever there is a war to be fought."

Earny contemplated this with little success, then returned to his original trajectory. "I want ta learn from you. I've lived this life too long, out on tha road doin' wrong by folks, making'a nuisance of myself to society. I wanna reformate into somethin' honorable. Never in my years have I met a man who seems so full of mastery of his... fighting...self, so to speak. Please!"

That's certainly a way of putting it.

The Swordsman stopped again to face Earny. The look in his eyes drove the highwayman back a step. "Listen to me. Men of your ilk and line are the way you are for a reason. The universe doesn't make mistakes. I could hand you over my sword and train you for fifty years and you'd still be cutting pieces off yourself and would as likely fall off a rock and die of fright on the way down as slay an enemy. So I'm going to make this plain: turn around, go somewhere that's not where I am, and never let me see you again. If ten more seconds pass before this is so, I will change my mind as I said, for I am already regretting my decision."

Earny's face twisted with something between terror and disappointment as he began to backpedal. "As ya wish, Lordship. If ever ya should decide to tha contrary..." The Swordsman took one step forward and already Earny was headed the other way, sprinting up the hill faster than a mouse with eagle talons behind it.

When the bouncing basilard and mop of hair was lost behind the horizon, the Swordsman turned and continued his march, barely glancing at a decrepit wooden sign informing him that the town of Pleasantry, population one hundred and fourteen, was just up ahead.

4

Jana sprinted through the Shodan, dragging Cory by the wrist, hot sweat swimming over her face and lips as her moccasins crunched in the forest bed. Cory's skin was white as the sky overhead, his face and hair drenched in blood that was not his, his whimpers incoherent and soft. Nothing had touched him, but he looked a massacre.

She took no conscious note of any of this. Her body may have been running hard, but at the moment the young woman named Jana was crouching huddled in a dark recess somewhere, legs tight to her chest, pitching back and forth and wondering dumbly where all this blood had come from. Her legs levered and pushed and she ducked and veered and leapt without thought, some automaton remnant bearing only a vague resemblance to the human form from which it was crafted.

The world barreled by, soundless save for their footfalls and the pounding thrum of her heart.

He's covered in blood, but it's not his.

This time the thought jarred her mind awake. The next was worse: the sweat on her lips tasted *coppery*. She stopped abruptly. Cory stumbled past, sprawling facedown. She didn't see him; she wouldn't have noticed the Keeper himself standing beside her now. Blood slithered in spirals around her fingers, suffusing her palms with rust-red pools. Her eyes turned to the splatters flecking her tunic like a butcher's apron, to the carmine shreds of hashed flesh inching down her thighs like slugs.

She bent over and threw up her stew.

Cory lay in a crabwalk, pupils like black coins, nostrils flared, a shell of the boy who twenty minutes ago had been gallivanting about the forest with Dog.

Jana steadied herself and swept Cory into her arms. He buried his face against her neck just above her scar, and even that wicked defacement now seemed the ghost of a dead time lost in the faded distance. Her only clear recollection was of the thing that had appeared from the forest, featureless in her mind's eye, followed by their Mum's corpse unfurled upon their duvet like a turkey, their supper mingled with her insides, and then Dad brandishing a bread knife—his dirk was still stored inside the house—and screaming for her to run. And she had. Keeper save them all, she had.

"Are we safe?" asked Cory, trembling.

"I don't know. We have to keep going," she said, brushing his tears. "It'll be okay. Dad'll be all right. He'll meet us in town." The words felt hollow; Dad was being devoured as she spoke, a hundred yards from where he had been born.

She scanned the forest to avoid the thought. The Mist was everywhere. They were surrounded by it. How far had she come? In what direction had she been headed? Panic bubbled up but she stamped it out. If Dad had stood between her and the house, then she must have turned and headed straight into the Shodan, which would be west. Nothing here looked familiar, and she knew most of the surrounding woods like the lines of her face. They were lost.

Does it matter? Stay here too long and we'll be dead for sure.

She cupped Cory's face in her hands. "I need you to follow me. Don't let go of my hand, and don't look back. Promise." He nodded limply and she kissed his forehead. "I love you, Stink. It'll be all right. Come on."

And then they were off, Jana leading, following her gut, hoping she still possessed some vague remnant of awareness that was not yet numbed by fear, Cory struggling to keep pace.

The Mist remained thick as they sped into the deep of the Shodan, and Jana chanced slowing as the ground grew rocky and the evenness of the leafy floor gave way to a broad monocline and, below it, knife-shaped slate. Soon they happened on a footpath, one that few traveled from the look. They tracked the path as it twisted downhill, threading a narrow pass peppered with bone flinders before widening again where it merged with a road broad enough to accommodate a carriage. If this path was meant for trade or royalty, then it must be bound for civilization, and around here civilization meant Pleasantry. Maybe the universe was attempting to compensate for their run of bad fortune. *Here you go, children,* it said to her. *Sorry about your parents getting eaten. No hard feelings.*

She considered as they ran what she would do once they arrived. Keeper pray it high and low, the folk of Pleasantry were as terrified of Misties as anyone, although they kept no defense but a large shelter called the Hole to bury their heads in and a watchtower in the center of town. The latter would be manned by whoever was drunk enough to spend the day thirty feet off the ground. None of those dullards could help her. Perhaps Grampy or mayor Tomson could.

She looked at her brother then and those desolate eyes made her throat clench up. He was her responsibility now. Forever. The word sounded false in her mind; until now, forever existed only in bedtime tales. Somewhere, in her more childish parts, she waited for her father to appear behind them and call out that it was safe, that he had bested the huge demon with his butter knife and quick wit, and that they should come home and bury their poor mother before the crows got her.

The crows got them both, Jana. Anything left over that the other thing didn't eat. They're scarfing them down like a roast.

A roar flooded the forest then, stopping Jana dead. She stood grasping Cory's hand, breaths baking in her lungs, soaked in sweat and gore, tears pooling in the corners of her mouth, and stared. It had come from the trees directly ahead. The creature (it *was* the same one, wasn't it?) could very well be stalking up the road to head them off. Up that way, a long procession of trees scaled a steep ridge and then disappeared down the other side; to Jana, it seemed a giant mouth waiting for them to run in unawares.

"What do we do?"

She looked at Cory and realized she didn't know.

The roar boomed again, closer, and the hairs on Jana's neck stood straight; it sounded like it was just over the ridge. The Mist was thicker now, asphyxiating. The creature would have them in minutes if she didn't do something.

Clenching Cory's hand, she hooked right, off the path and into the forest, maneuvering the rimrock to a sloping ravine. Just beyond lay a natural stone revetment crowned with a wall of scrub that stretched as far as she could see. She vaulted a toppled oak and somehow Cory managed the same, and together they lost their footing and slid to the bottom of the ravine and lay there as the pebbles and debris settled about them.

The silence after crushed everything flat; the whisper of the wind crept, emotionless, past their heaving chests and bloody faces while they stared into the blank sky and waited.

When Jana regained her breath, she rose to all fours and peered back towards the road. Nothing, no hint of the creature, and suddenly the Mist seemed thinner. *Isn't that what happens when they leave?* That's what Grampy had told her years ago. As far as she knew, Grampy was the only person who had faced a Misty and lived, thanks, as legend said, to a deft stab of his short sword.

"Is it there?" asked Cory. He was still pale but seemed to be thinking right again.

"I don't see it," said Jana as she watched the trees. A breeze swept over them, rattling long-dead branches, but nothing living moved, animal or otherwise, that she could distinguish. When she was convinced nothing would appear, she crept down the ravine and crouched beside Cory. "How ya doin, Stink?"

Cory didn't answer. She reached to brush his hair from his face, stopped as she saw her fingers quaking and bloodstained. She clenched her fist to hide them. He didn't seem to notice, thank all that was good. She wanted to console him, to tell him everything would be all right, that she would not allow anything else bad to happen, but she couldn't bring herself to lie. The best she could manage was a forced smile which he didn't return. That would have to do for now.

She spotted something farther along the ravine that sent her heart fluttering. "Save us! I know this thing," she said, indicating the wall of brush. "This leads down to Branner's. At the edge of town. You remember?"

Cory nodded. "Mum used to say it was unnatural, a bush getting so big so fast." His voice sounded tinny and brittle, and Jana watched the thought of their mother grow into pain in his eyes. She wrapped him in her arms and held him, rocking like Mum used to when they came home with a scraped knee or woke from a bad dream. But this wasn't childhood silliness that could be cooed away. Somehow she knew she'd never again trouble over those fleeting ills that seemed the world entire for their breadth, only to be forgotten the next day as new imaginary adventures arrived.

Never again.

She watched the ravine while she held him, waiting for something to materialize from the Mist which still lingered in the distance, but she distinguished no sound or motion and at last her nerves settled.

She ruffled Cory's hair. "Come on, I'll race you to Branner's. Whaddya say?"

He looked at her for a long moment without responding. Then, as she was about to speak again, he interrupted her. "Are you gonna take care of me?" His voice was shivering exhale.

The tone of his words, the unfettered sadness in them, caught her off guard. She fought the quiver in her jaw and poked his chest. "You know I am. We're gonna take care of each other from now on." He smiled faintly and nodded, and that was the last she ever saw of her kid brother.

Enormous claws the size of a man's torso smashed through the wall of brush, the stones of the revetment tumbling and splintered branches bursting outward in a plume and raining leaves and shattered bark. They clamped onto Cory's shoulders and yanked him backwards through the hole, his body contorting at an unnatural angle, his feet flailing. He began a cry that ended in a horrible wet sound as he vanished into the darkness.

Jana started backwards, white with shock. A scream was boiling in her chest when the blood erupted through the brush, geysering as if a hundred arteries had been opened at once. It engulfed her face, smothering her. She fell to her back, the bite of that warm lifeblood stinging her eyes. Yet still, she watched the hole, unblinking. The thing hunched just beyond; she could see one massive shoulder hitching and plying beneath dark threadbare cloth as the noise of disintegrating bones and tearing sinew was replaced by the distinct sound of chewing.

"Run, Jana," she told herself in a whisper that barely escaped her mouth. She didn't listen, still transfixed on the creature that was dining on her brother's corpse. Her mind was gone completely now; the husk of Jana Hunter inched away, hands and legs jouncing, a tendril of drool dangling unnoticed from her lips. Then another roar reverberated from the dark ravel of scrub before her and she knew the beast was nearly finished with its meal.

"Run, you stupid bitch!" she screamed, and at last her body responded.

She wheeled and flew down the path, keeping to the brush, and prayed the Keeper that the creature behind her did not follow.

5

The town of Pleasantry was older than anyone could remember, older than any piece of writing, which was rare to find these days, could tell. Some of the buildings were newer than others, and some folk remembered back when Cole and Tilda Forrester had built their hut on the hill during a snowstorm, and Grampy even recalled the ramshackle tower at the crossroads when the lumber was freshly hewn and still being erected, the warning bell atop gleaming like a gaudy hat, which in those days signaled incoming marauders and not evil things born of the Darklands. Then there were other places, buildings that looked and smelled ancient, fashioned from materials unknown, shaped by mysterious craft into intricate corridors and planted in the muck. They once had been fragments of a greater whole, judging by their shapes and layouts. Now they were relegated to hovels. Grampy thought they must be left from the old days, before the Shift, when mankind ruled the skies and the waters through some magic lost to time. Those aged structures had huddled there where trees grew no longer and resisted rot, resisted time and wind and sun and hail, and watched while their builders vanished, as their cities crumbled, leaving this flimsy shell behind. Still, there slept a dim hope, unwhispered by any but held by most, that one day things might be better, that there might be light at the end of all this shadow.

Hope.

Hope was one thing that Grampy had little use for. He was a hundred and nine years old, and he had seen so much of life repeated that just one thing was certain: things never got any better. Not in any permanent way. Bitter talk from an old man, yet in the most secret recesses of his soul, worn thin by the years but strong enough still, he knew it was true. Not that it prevented him from enkindling a deep and constant joy, or from anticipating each new day. With these long years beneath his belt, a man might expect life to grow drab, that he'd become eager for the end, but if Grampy had learned nothing else during this protracted existence, it was that savoring a day you didn't die never became old.

He sat on his porch now, his thin knees crossed, his cane, made from shucked bleachleaf, farmed from the southern Drudge forty-eight years ago, bouncing in a rhythm against his thigh as he watched the milling townsfolk go about their day. He sipped his Boon tea and marveled, as he often did, at how little a man required to survive. He had his shelter, a rickety adobe thing with rough-hewn vigas, and he still grew his own food in a small garden. Now and then the more gracious folk would bring him strips of cow meat from the market. He was a charity case for his antiquity, though he wouldn't argue that; cow meat was his favorite. He'd had a family once, but they were long gone, lost to the hertweed sickness that had run its course through Pleasantry aways back. He fancied his grandsons would've been married by now and seeded more younglings to entertain him during his twilight years. That would have been nice. Yessir. But the Keeper had other plans for them all, and He wasn't someone you could debate. It was for the best, he supposed; the last thing an innocent child needed was to be born into this damnable world rife with things unspeakable.

With the things from the Mist.

Grampy shivered.

The Mist Dwellers had appeared in small numbers at first, creatures of myth, frequenting tales carried on the backs of drunks and highwaymen. But then common folk began to glimpse them, too, first on the Drudge and along the hardpack trails crisscrossing the Shodan like spiderwebs, and then on their doorsteps. Grampy had been brave—or foolish—enough to confront one and live, more by fortune than skill at arms. Good fortune had always clung to him, parasitic, keeping him from the Black where his family and friends no doubt awaited with a vat of Boon tea and an oven that magically filled itself with cow meat for the rest of eternity. And wouldn't that be finer than another day in this mudhole?

Grampy sighed deeply.

Ah well. No need to let that thought ruin a perfectly good day.

He watched men trundle past with sacks of grain hefted over their shoulders. A lone bird—a Rustie, if his mind still had any edge at all—called out into the windswept fog, at once soulful and empty, its cutting note echoing into the switchback beyond the town limits. To Grampy it was a lonesome sound, one that echoed what lay in his own heart. Folk thronged here, there, some missing eyes or fingers or arms, others deeply scarred by hard years growing life from this dead earth. Along the splintered palings of a fence, a young girl toyed with a stone and a twig as though they were dolls, her face streaked with filth, the skin below as colorless as the sky. Grampy frowned and prayed her pallor was a symptom of the endless cloud cover and not something more serious. There were no healers to be found here.

The thought made him reflect on the many local children that had been lost of late, though not to sickness, nor were the young the only victims. First had come word of the dead, men and women along with the children, happened upon in their homes or in the forests, some missing limbs or even their faces, others eviscerated so thoroughly it was difficult to distinguish them from animal corpses. Then the tales began, yarns spun by traders and hunters who frequented the Thresh, naming the new creatures responsible Blood Demons. Most of Pleasantry called it nonsense, a common proclamation by townsfolk who knew nothing and yet by some imaginary measure considered themselves worldly. Grampy, however, was not so hasty. When men from all over converged in this backwater town, their paths never before crossed, all spilling nonsense of the same particular shade, he reckoned it was prudent for a man to pay attention. And when there was a total consensus about said nonsense, well, then a man had best open his ears and forget what he thought he knew, which was no simple task; people clung to their beliefs as though they might starve without them, comforted by their familiarity, often in defiance of the truth. This open-mindedness was a defining ideal of Grampy's mind, one that had kept him alive when so many others in his life had perished: listen to those deemed lunatics and heed their warnings. Sometimes they were right, and the rest of the time erring with caution had few drawbacks.

"Do ya right today, Grampy?" asked a boy's voice from off to the right.

Grampy craned his neck with a series of cracks and pops and squinted into the distance. "Who's that trampling mah daisies? That be you, Thunderfoot?"

The boy, years shy of shaving, stood at the foot of Grampy's stoop with his knuckles on his hips. "Ya callin' me large in tha waist, codger?" he asked with a smile.

"Callin' yer blur large, Keeper help ya."

"It's me, Collin."

"Yar, yar, Jaynor's son. I could smell tha roast spice on yer hair from a hundred yards. Out with tha years go the eyes, mind ya, but the nose only gets keener till ya keel. Boy of yer age should have his feet planted against the assault of time from the get-go, methinks. So keep yer head of ya, cozy?" *My Keeper and all the Blessed Blood. Can't hide the age in my talk one bit.* Not that he possessed the inclination; one other thing old age provided, which a man appreciated if he had his head on right, was to give a big achey one about approval. If folk didn't care for your tune, they could go stick it in a trough and blow.

Grampy adjusted as his right buttock was beset by pins and needles. "What can I do ya fer, young master. Quick before I fall asleep on ya."

The boy's smile broadened. "Dad wants to bring Mum a patch of lilies and wanted to know if ya have some to spare."

Grampy mulled it over. He did indeed have a patch of lilies left of which he was quite fond. He had intended to nurture them outdoors until full winter came, then pick them and bring them inside and feed them firelight and keep them watered, applying whatever innate skill he had inherited from his parents that preserved plants long past their prime. *Dad and Mum. I do by ya right, I hope.* Grampy's eyes and smile might be described by his neighbors as boyish, no doubt with some exaggeration, but the memory of his childhood seemed downright ancient even to himself. He had been an adult and advancing in years almost as far back as he could remember. Images of his youth brooded in the fog, sparing him fleeting glimpses of what had been. Maybe that was best, too; nothing gets a man keen on the now like forgetting the before.

After a calculated pause, Grampy said, "And you think yer tha one got tha right to take my hard-earned lilies to yer Da, pray ya?"

"Yessir," said the boy without pause, rocking on his heels but unintimidated.

People in Pleasantry knew Grampy too well by now. He couldn't even pull one over on the children anymore. He attempted another dramatic pause anyhow, then smiled his gnarled smile and gestured with a liver-spotted hand. "Go on, pick 'em yerself. Tell Pa Jaynor I say fine day. Mind the roots, hear me?"

The boy's face brightened. "Oh, I will, Grampy. Thank ya!" he said and sprinted off around the back of Grampy's hut, a spade in hand that must have been tucked into the waist of his pants or concealed in his boot, or maybe it was in his hand the entire time and Grampy had missed it because he was old as the dirt itself. Oh well and shuckatees on that. Wasn't that what the boys in the fourth division used to say?

The sudden urge to stand struck him (it was generally a scheduled event that he had to work up to), and he strained upright and kept his weight on his cane until he could lean on the porch rail. Something had caught his interest through all his pontificating, a shape that even at a thousand feet had struck his old eyes as out of place. The approaching man looked tall from here, dressed all in black, and that was the first sign of warning: men in black were not to be trusted—unless that was their only pair of britches, pray it. The hat didn't help, giving him the look of one of the wooly Wildermen from the South Vale that grilled up pig guts and smoked stinkgrass. He moved with a smooth deliberateness more natural for a borecat than a man, his eyes noting every weathered recess of the town and every move of its denizens with a practiced air that belied familiarity with peril and the training to survive it. But those things weren't what troubled Grampy the most.

The man was wearing a sword.

That by itself might not have been enough to stir his gut into a froth, but that wasn't all. This was a sword unlike any he had seen in years. It wasn't the sort a bandit might have lifted off the wreck of a carriage, or from the body of a fallen soldier, and it certainly wasn't the sort a local blacksmith could forge for a few cattle and some Boon. This was a sword someone wielded only if they were of a line that had always wielded it, or if could best the man carrying it and take it from his murdered hands. And not many could, Grampy wagered. Maybe no one could. That blade was titanium folded over thousands of times, etched with acid. He knew this without being able to see it clearly, just as he knew the handle was whittled from bone and carved with the story of its bearer's lineage. He knew this all from the second bit that snapped up his attention: the man looked *right* carrying that sword. And not many would.

Grampy's knees were already aching and he was tempted to sit down and finish his tea, which he had placed aside and now craved, but something kept him upright as he watched the dark man with the sword stride into town like he owned it. Others began to notice as well, a brewing curiosity overtaking their attention in waves, leaving mouths swung open dumbly and vacant eyes struggling to comprehend this sudden unexpected event that had upended their world after years of rote.

Whatever this man's purpose was, every bone in Grampy's body warned him that the people of Pleasantry, despite their fascination at the moment, were not going to like it one bit.

6

Pleasantry was what Donovan expected, down to the shit-looking muddy road and the gaunt, red-eyed, shaggy faces that peered out through the sashes and from behind barrels and over the spots where they had stopped their work mid-stitch or shovel-load or hammer-swing to gawk. It matched the impression he had built from nothing in his mind down to the rotting wood siding, the shoddy shingles missing from rooftops at intervals, to the odd mixture of Old and New that mingled here. Over yonder was a building placed well before the Shift. And there was another and yet another. These people likely had no idea what it was they lay their heads in each night, or drank and ate and made children in. To them, it was simple luck, a little less labor required to make a place inhabitable. In a way he envied them.

He walked at a steady pace up the main road—the only road, likely—that divided the town in half. A vague bridle path and nothing more. To his right, horses jostled and nickered near a well coping, their unshod hooves clopping, their reigns rasping against the hitching post. To his left, three boys climbed a split rail fence and watched him without blinking. One held a broken stake and raised it overhead in salute. Donovan fought the urge to draw his sword and salute back. *Still a child*, said his old master from years past. *Still just looking for the glory of it all.* He gave the children the benefit of a slight nod and then looked away.

"Is he a Swordsman?"

"Couldn't be"

"How'd you know one if ya saw 'im anyway?"

"He's one. I'll bet my cattle on it."

"Not a real one."

"Every a-one of 'em been killed back at Dunnharrow years gone."

"What ya talkin' about? Dunn-who?"

"Quiet, I think he can hear us."

And he could. No matter how far apart in hefts and cultures, people of all cities and villages said the same things when they laid eyes on a Swordsman.

He knew without looking that a crowd had begun to trail behind him, far enough to turn on a coin if need be and run, close enough to stretch their necks until then and soak in the sight. Here and there men left their horses half-shod and women lost track of their ovens and left their pies to burn.

Yes, always the same.

Every town he visited greeted him like some traveling circus, a spectacle to behold and distract. He used to conceal his passage through such places, where simple folk stamped out their meager livings in emptiness, but no longer. They always found him out, no matter how deep in the sand he buried his head. Towns, even ones this small, possessed too many eyes and too many mouths apt to let slip secrets.

In the center of town was a laddered wooden tower, perhaps thirty feet high, with a rusty old bell caked in verdigris drooping from its sagging crown as if with half-asleep indifference. A man atop the tower watched Donovan with interest, and in the back of his mind the Swordsman heard a dull warning: if anything was going to happen in a small chunk of backwater land like this, it would be while the lookout was staring at the newcomer with the shiny sword and not at the forest.

He paused near the crossroads, feeling filthy and exhausted and sore in a thousand places, but at the same time rejuvenated. He filled his lungs with the local air, which felt close and contained and lacked any sense of the outdoors. It wreaked of manure and brimstone and firewood, but there was goodness there, too, dried meat and fresh bread and spices and Boon and a dozen other pleasures. But through the applemud and the cinnamon and the dirt and the pine and the pungent odor of unwashed men long at work lay something else, infinitely more interesting. *It* was here, sure as the brim on his hat,

unmistakable as the shape of a woman or the caw of a crow. It called to his every sense, stoking the fire in the center of his being.

The Cleric had been here, and recently.

Whether the man had sought the comfort of a bed and a woman or passed without a glance at a distance was unclear, but it mattered not. That Donovan was still on the trail, and that the Cleric's residue was strong enough to rouse his senses was enough. The *itch*, that sense of the man he sought, always at the very periphery of an awareness Donovan could not name, ever-present, grew overwhelming in anticipation.

A gentle tug on his finger drew his attention outward. Two girls stood fidgeting at his feet, no older than four or five. One peered up at him with striking blue eyes, thin locks of golden hair framing a round, pearlescent face, the jewels of a lineage fit for royalty. She grasped his dirt-encrusted forefinger, her skin smooth and fragile, his thick with callus, worn, dark with a tan.

"Are you a Swordsman?" she asked.

The faintest tick of warmth inside him.

"Are you going to save us, sir Swordsman, sir?" asked the other girl, smaller than the blonde, eyes like chestnuts set within the large hollows of her face. Her lips were cracked and her skin was the color of milk hinted with yellow. If ever a place was ripe for a case of hertweed, it was here.

He extinguished the warm feeling inside with the same numb calculation his enemies found themselves privy to in the moments of their death, and then pulled his hand away, leaving the girls to stare after him.

They were forgotten moments later, his thoughts returned to his quarry. That smile crossed his face again, foreign on his hard features, parting his lips and baring his teeth like some untamed animal.

Today might just be his first good day in a while.

A very long while.

He was still thinking this when the screaming began.

7

Jana heard a scream grate the air. It was a horrible, mindless sound that would have made her grab Cory and dive behind the nearest bush and stay put until sunup. What in the Black was it? The sound of a kitten being murdered, maybe, shrill and strident and stabbing. It may even have been a madwoman screaming—could only be that, she thought—for in a healthy mind people possessed a seal that prevented the body from producing such a howl.

Her feet pounded the forest floor. She had lost a moccasin somewhere and her bare foot was deeply sliced; the blood between her toes turned every step treacherous. Was it her blood? Or was it Cory's? No, it could not be Cory's. His death was from a nightmare; the most vivid one anyone had ever had, perhaps, but still just a nightmare. The one thing she needed to fear was dying in her sleep; she had heard folk say as much, that if a person passed in a dream then their body would die, too. She would have to keep moving then if she ever wanted to wake up and eat Mum's applemud and warm herself with Grampy's Boon tea. She could almost taste them now.

The creature hunting her was larger than anything she had ever seen, yet it moved in silence, flowing over eskers and gullies and leafy outcrops like a dark wind. It was almost upon her; she knew this without looking back. She could feel the bulk of the thing bearing down, its jaws widening.

The trees cleared suddenly and she was in a field. The screaming still thundered in her skull, but now another sound joined it, one that snapped her awake: a bell was tolling. She knew in that moment, rendered suddenly vivid by the anxious call of that ringing, that the screaming was coming from her. Her throat burned with it, her voice

diminished now to a cracked and raspy thing that barely escaped her mouth before being swallowed up by the Mist.

The field ahead seemed to elongate as she galloped forward. In the distance, at long last, lay the dark huddled outline of Pleasantry, its adobe huts and sturdier houses and its bell tower rising from the fog shroud like a small, frightened animal. She had no idea if she would be safe there; all she was knew was that she had to get there. Even if she died a moment later, she would get there. It was close, so close she could smell Grampy's flowerbeds.

She was straining to make out Grampy's hut when her footing gave and sent her tumbling. Her breath exploded from her chest as she struck the ground full-force and rolled prone. She lay there, the field whirling inches from her face, her breasts heaving against the grass, and her legs would not move.

You're almost there. Pull, damn you.

And somehow her arms did move. Fingers gouging the wet earth, grasping fistfuls of grass, she dragged herself onward. When she looked up, some people had gathered at the edge of town and watched her with blank expressions. They made no indication they would help.

Of course they wouldn't.

Her anger flared. She attempted to stand, only to fall to her knees. Then some deep cord of strength within her, bound by a single stubborn thread, snapped and she collapsed, eyes fixed on the crowd who were about to watch her die.

Damn every single one of you to the Maw.

But no, she couldn't be angry at them. She would have stood back and watched, too.

The roar that washed over her next resounded across the plain. She used the last shreds of her will to roll over and face the thing that was coming for her, and there she heaved forward and knelt in the grass, a sanguinary ghoul drenched in sweat, tears carving flesh-colored trails through the grime on her face, and watched as something taller than a house emerged from the forest and bore down upon her.

8

Grampy's days had stretched long upon this earth, and never had he felt it more than in this moment. He had seen a dragonfly eat its own tail, watched a man fend off a pair of hungry wolves to save his family only to catch his foot upon a stone seconds later and roll off a cliff to his death. He had seen people love and hate and steal and murder and chide and confide and partake in all manner of acts which the nature of man affords, only to arrive here, now, where not one damn thing transpired before his old eyes on any given day to garner the slightest notice, let alone bewilderment.

Today was the day that claim was laid waste.

He struggled down the footpath from his house to where the people of Pleasantry stood watching the stretch of field that terminated at the Shodan. They parted for him, ignorant of anything but the horrible spectacle ahead. Any other day they would all be underground in the Hole already, the doors bolted (Grampy wondered if that flimsy thing could even *slow* a Misty, should it put its mind to opening it), praying to the Keeper. But something was different today. A sort of lunacy had settled in, and it held their gaze transfixed.

Grampy inched to the front of the crowd and saw that there was a girl kneeling in the field, young from the look of her, covered in blood, just watching the forest like a fool. Then came the roar, a sound he knew too well, and without thought he hobbled forward as fast as his old legs would carry him. "Come on," he cried. "We've got ta do somethin'!"

He was ten steps out when he looked back at them, his puckered skin straining over his bones. Not one of the inbred swine-loving dunny-crunchers had budged an inch. The people of Pleasantry

48

beheld him with an empty stare, frightened cows all of them. "Do ya forget tha lines that brought yer seed into being, ya simple folk? Do ya forget what men did and gave to get ya to yer shitty lives in yonder muck? I can't carry her myself. I beg one, come do right by me now!"

A long silence. Exchanged glances drenched in apathy. Uncertain grimaces. Still no one moved. It was as though he addressed a rank of statues and not living breathing caring folk. Grampy's runnelled lips settled into a frown as he gathered his strength. "So it be then. Hold it in yer hearts what ya did this day till your graves, I beg ya," he told them. And, with that, he started again towards the girl, his breathing already labored, his legs already burning with effort.

He kept his eyes on her huddled shape as best he could, straining to make out her features as he struggled closer, and it only took a few steps for sudden realization to settle in him: the girl was Jana Hunter.

What in the Keeper's breath is going on?

With renewed fervor, he moved towards her as quickly as he could manage.

He had closed half of the distance when the Mist Dweller emerged from the forest. At the sight of it and the roar that followed, Grampy flailed, losing precious balance, and crumpled to his back.

The Misty stood twenty-five feet tall, a broad, sinuous monstrosity wrapped in a black cowl that kept its face in shadow. Its claws were massive, rippled with black scales as hard as armor. Its nails, as thick as a man's forearm, extended like scythes from its fingertips, each long enough to cleave a torso in two. Its robes, tattered and hole-ridden, flowed across its frame on the gathering wind. The Mist arrived behind it, pouring from the forest, edging near the creature's feet, which were bundled in thick black rawhide straps. It drew a sword from its back, twelve feet from hilt to tip, serrated, crude and black, and stalked forward.

At last, the people of Pleasantry were awakened from their shock. They turned screaming, tangling and stumbling over one another, trampling the eldest, pushing the children aside, the shelter of the Hole their lone sane thought.

Grampy struggled to all fours and reached for his cane, his back throbbing as though he had been struck, but he couldn't

reach it. Keeper save them, he just couldn't. He watched instead as the creature glided towards Jana without haste, as though the terror of its approach recouped half the trouble of chasing her so far, for Jana's family lived out away from the Drudge where no Misties had been spotted before. Grampy clamped his eyes closed and thought of what she must have lost to have arrived here, and then opened them again to watch the end. The end of himself, too, most likely.

After the display his fellow citizens had just given, he felt no particular urge to go on living in this world any longer.

* * * *

The Misty drew near, towering above Jana, and even from this distance she caught a glimpse of teeth that were thin and long and sharp as knives; rows upon serried rows of them vanished upwards into the cowl where no face could be discerned. Blood and saliva dripped in ropes from its mouth and pooled between her ankles as she sat immobile and watched its sword rise until it was above the creature's head; it hung there in the cold for what seemed an eternity.

Jana held her breath and waited to join her family.

But she would not. Not yet, at least.

The Mist Dweller hesitated, then withdrew. Jana followed the Misty's hidden gaze and saw now that Grampy was there on his haunches, lacking the strength to stand. He wasn't looking at her; he was staring back into town.

The people of Pleasantry, insane with dread before, had halted their flight. As one the crowd made way for the figure who held their attention, Misty and man alike. He carved his path through them, curved sword dancing, its bone hilt bright and almost alive, its inset jewel glimmering.

He stepped forth from the townsfolk and onto the field, duster trailing back, hat tugged low. He passed Grampy without a glance, but his presence must have infused the old man with some extra reserve of strength for he was suddenly able to rise.

The man with the sword halted by Jana's side, plumbing the depths of the Misty's cowl. The creature took a step closer and the ground trembled now beneath its weight (by choice, Jana wagered, after the noiseless chase through the Shodan). She looked from the man with the sword to the creature regarding him, viewing the scene as if from a great distance, every sound muted and echoing within the vast chasm of her shock and exhaustion, and could only watch.

* * * *

Grampy watched as the Swordsman stopped and looked up at the Mist Dweller, his body language betraying no emotion. The creature's massive sword remained aloft, although something in its angle now spoke of uncertainty to Grampy's eye. A gust of wind rose, ruffling those great robes and whatever dark anatomy they contained, and all the while the Swordsman did not yield, did not sway, did nothing but reach for his sword, the blade of his ancestors, forged in the Cold Flame five thousand miles from here in a time forgotten by most. As he drew it forth the blade rang into the trees and the sky, a calling chime to summon all who had come before, those who had lived and trained and served and died to make him who he was. He held that relic of metal and spirit aloft where it gleamed in the diffuse light, and when he lowered it to his side the people of Pleasantry seemed to have forgotten about the Mist Dweller, so drawn were they to the glister of that steel.

When the Mist Dweller returned its sword to its hold, it was without notice. It gave Donovan a last regard, as if chagrined, and then returned to the forest, bereft of its dessert, and vanished into the Mist.

The silence after thundered louder than any roar could.

Soon after, another sound filled the air, utterly foreign to most in this forsaken place, a sound no one living save Grampy had heard in Pleasantry until this day, in this moment, and it was they themselves who made it: the people were cheering, running, children with their arms thrust into the air, men and women clapping, smiles of relief on their soiled faces. They converged onto the field, the call for courage past now, and surrounded the Swordsman as he sheathed his blade.

9

Donovan could not help but let pictures of his home emerge as if surfacing from a deep black pool, each as intangible as a wraith but planting an ache in his heart. Those withered and bloodless faces from the past glared at him, then receded back into the dark of his recollection. The sound of common men roused to action by a thing so facile as a symbol, be it the man or the blade he carried, was once music oft-heard within the walls of Kolendhar, and yet here on this sodden plot it rang alien. The gleam in the mindless eyes swarming him now declared that everything the world had so far denied them now lay within reach, for here stood a Swordsman and his instrument and how else could it be? These villagers would approach him as though they were old comrades and embrace his hand and grasp his shoulder and invite him for drink and food or even a night of fierce lovemaking in exchange for the comfort of that hope, yet Donovan knew in his marrow that they would never find here that which they sought.

He looked on the girl who had begun this. She was young and beautiful somewhere beneath the mud and sweat and blood. She didn't look injured, and that was fine for he would not have taken time to heal her otherwise. Her mind was in need of much mending though, and this was obvious at a glance: her jaw hung loose like an invalid and her pupils had all but swallowed her irises. More than that, there was an emptiness the Swordsman had seen too many times, the look of someone who has just lost everything.

He had looked that way himself, and not so long ago. Nothing could treat that wound save time.

Tempted though he was to wonder about the creature from the forest, the nature of its response to him, or if it had any relation to his quarry, Donovan willed himself to focus on his original purpose instead. The mind was a hoarder of threads and details and tangents, accumulating its stock subtly, ever gathering and insatiable. Those collected details would crush a man beneath their weight if the mind was given too much leeway to roam, and so he had nurtured the habit of culling them mercilessly. Rosaline would have chided that his unimaginative nature was a side effect of those habits and that it made him terribly dull, and the look in her eyes as she said it would have set his insides ablaze with desire.

I miss you so much.

He extinguished that thought as efficiently as he had all the rest. Donovan didn't know what exactly he expected to find in this place, but *something* was here. He was sure of it.

Sparing the girl one last dispassionate glance, he headed back into town without further rumination, the parade of villagers behind him gleeful as they followed in a herd.

* * * *

Jana had been waiting for the man with the sword to open his mouth, to reach down and ask if she was all right, to offer her water, a wet rag, to do anything besides turn away. She started when a hand did touch her, and the feeling in her heart then brimmed so with relief and love she felt she might burst. Grampy hunkered above her, and even though it must have pained him fiercely, he knelt and wrapped his brittle arms about her shoulders and gave Jana what she craved more than food or water or shelter: he embraced her tight and just held her to his bony breast.

She melted against that paper-thin body and wept.

"Is there anyone else comin' after ya?" he asked, but in his eyes she saw that he already knew the answer. Blinking back tears, he grunted to his feet and took her hand. "Come on, child," he said, his voice strong and warm and fragile and ancient all at once. "Let's get ya clean and by the fire."

She stood and found her breath still thin and fast and her legs unsteady. "I can't go yet," she told him, and when Grampy looked at her with one bushy eyebrow cocked, she added, "I want to talk to him." She nodded towards the Swordsman.

"Forget that wag fer the now. It'll do ya right to get yer head before ya go abreast the likes of him. Come on," he said, offering his hand again. She took it, reluctant, but she was still staring after the Swordsman and his parade while Grampy led her up the footpath and into his house.

* * * *

Donovan Maltrese watched the girl and the old man go.

"He *is* a Swordsman, save us!" said a feeble voice in the rear of the mob.

"Sent here to take care of the Misties!"

"I'd wager my flock on it, stand true," said another.

"Who leads you?" asked Donovan, already weary of it all.

The villager he addressed pointed and drew Donovan's gaze. The man who approached looked sturdy, though not in a threatening way, more parts oak tree than beast. His eyes were red-rimmed, his face a maze of canals and hollows and crow's feet that drew up as he managed a smile; his skin could have been a barber's strop. He kept his thumbs tucked into his pockets as if he might break out in a folk dance at any moment, which was about the most absurd thing Donovan could imagine given the weight the man seemed to bear on his muscled shoulders. He unhooked one of his thumbs and proffered the attached hand. "I do. Name's Tomson. Pleased and blessed to look on ya."

Donovan embraced his hand. Tomson had a grip like a vice, not little to do, he suspected, with an attempt to show this Swordsman-or-whatever-he-thinks-he-is who the real man was in this town. But as Donovan examined Tomson's visage he saw no pretense, even in the deep parts. Perhaps this be a rare case of a prudent man possessed of some principle. If so, he was a diamond in the dunny river. "Stand true, friend, and with thanks," the Swordsman said as if he was addressing court and not a man dressed in burlap and rabbit skins. "You can call me Donovan." After a moment he added, "I need food." Might as well get to the core quickly and be done with this place. *Sometimes expediency is found by beating around the bush*, Master whispered from the back of his mind.

"Ya don't waste time, do ya," said Tomson with a broad grin. Donovan saw then exactly what had led the folk of Pleasantry to put their faith in their leader. That smile was unimpeachable, the sort politicians worked to contrive but that only true character could manifest. Donovan found himself, normal reserves aside, trusting this man.

"I'd talk with you as well afterwards. I've scant seen a deer for forty hefts and my belly's aching of it," said Donovan with a smile he knew possessed none of the traits he saw in Tomson's.

Tomson patted Donovan's shoulder just as five other men had done between the field and this spot, though this gesture bore none of that disingenuous nature and the Swordsman knew it at once. "Come then, Donovan. My wife cooks the finest dewdrop stew your tongue will ever meet, and we've got stout to match."

Still talking, they headed towards one of the buildings that was old, left to Pleasantry by ancient, unknowable dream figures, those enigmatic men who had lived before the Shift, and this gave Donovan pause. Perhaps not everyone here lacked regard for these places that had survived time unfathomable, weathering storm and war and more so that a nomadic rabble could stumble upon them and stake claim to what would one day be Pleasantry. Tomson seemed like just the sort to consider such things.

As soon as he stepped into Tomson's home, Donovan realized that he was right to consider the man highly and, for the first time in recent memory, he felt at ease.

A small iron stove warmed the room, the door to which was open, baring a dock ash grate and chopped oak aglow within; without, the firelight scuffled with the dim sheen of a nearby window. The walls were crafted from oversized bricks common to these ancient buildings, their color once a rich cream perhaps, now bleached and cracked by time. A quilt lay draped across one wall from corner to corner like a tapestry to disguise the damage. A cherrywood chifforobe hugged the bare east wall, a fine lacquered thing with fluted edges. Atop a small table nearby were clay pots and vases, fired and painted bright blues and greens. A brown bearskin rug covered the center of the floor; one look at Tomson told Donovan the beast was downed and skinned by none other.

As soon as he neared the dining room entryway a flurry of scents assaulted the Swordsman that drew grumbles from his stomach. Each alone would have been enough to start him drooling; combined they formed an orchestra for his nose. "Smells fine, whatever it may be," he said, mad with hunger.

"Smells a sight less than it's gonna taste, I warrant, so watch you're able to leave once you get used to it," Tomson said, jovial about it all. He offered a seat in the eating space to Donovan, who unstrapped his sword and propped it nearby. The fire in his legs that lay disconnected most days roared up from his boots to his hips as he settled. Too much marching for any man. *And how much more ahead? When does it end?*

A woman, just as Donovan imagined a Pleasantry housewife would be, entered the room then. She was small, almost two heads shorter than Tomson, with round rubicund cheeks and big brown eyes that gleamed above a smooth smile. She wiped her hands on her apron (which bore a sister image to the quilt in the living area, this one of a range of mountains and a lake hemmed by pines), and offered them. "Pleased and blessed. I'm Mary," she said in a voice a register too deep for a woman.

"I thank you for your courtesy, friend Mary. Call me Donovan," he said carefully. To what degree formalities here applied to women he had no notion.

"Relax yer bones, Sir Donovan," she said with a pixie's smile. "We're all family here."

Donovan bowed. "Better to err with caution. Calling a spoken-for woman *ma'am* cost me a drop of blood six months gone," he said.

"That's the sort of thing makes you wonder if people even deserve surviving, think ya?" said Tomson with a frown.

Donovan nodded; he was thinking just that. Five angry brothers and a would-be lover had fought for the mortal damage to that lass's honor. A bunch of inbreeds lucky to still be alive as far as he was concerned. How could a single person be so sharp and yet once grouped with a pack become so dim?

"I hope you brought an appetite. I was making extra anyhow but it turns out two aren't comin' as told, so it's two bellies-full for ya, sir Donovan."

"Just Donovan," he replied, reaching for the comforting feel of his sword. She smiled and did something that was cousin to a curtsey, and then vanished back into the kitchen.

A quiet moment passed as Donovan studied the wall while Tomson poured them mugs of stout. He handed one over and took a seat across the table. "You come from beyond the Vale, do you?" Tomson asked.

"Far beyond," said Donovan.

"What news of Kolendhar then? We've not heard a bird fart since two winters past," he said, then added, "Hope such country talk doesn't offend your ears."

"My ears are not so pristine, mayor, so don't trouble. There is no news from Kolendhar. I have not been there for two winters past myself," said Donovan, aware that his face was growing ashen.

Tomson looked displeased, but changed course without follow-up. "Why did the Dweller leave when it saw you?"

"Dweller?"

Tomson's cheeks reddened. Donovan realized then that perhaps, despite his imperturbable demeanor, Tomson valued Donovan's opinion of him. "Forgive us, I don't know the word you might use for them. Here we call them Mist Dwellers. Or Misties, if you're a highwayman or a farmer."

"The thing in the forest?" asked Donovan. Tomson nodded. "Some men call them Shades. As for your question, I don't know why it left."

"You don't know, or you won't say?" countered Tomson. Sharp and on point. "You would have fought it if it came to that, wouldn't you?" Tomson's tone had changed now and it set Donovan back on watch. Something beneath that question stank of obvious guile. Speaking the roundabout was not Tomson's strong suit, it seemed.

"I'm looking for a man called the Cleric," Donovan said curtly, without transition. He described the Cleric as he always did, a towering man with a scarecrow build dressed in flawless white that stained not a drop no matter what swamps and bogs and deserts he traversed. His eyes seemed chiseled from amethyst and sat back in a bony face with high cheekbones that stood like watchdogs to either side of his long sloping nose. His smile made a man feel as though bugs crawled their skin, and the long staff he used to walk was headed with a blade sharp enough to cleave trees, should he feel so inclined.

Tomson didn't need all the details. "There was a man here that looked the way you describe. He didn't use a name, though."

Donovan felt that familiar electricity fly through his veins. He leaned closer. "How long ago?"

"Maybe two, three days gone. Who is he? Some sort of killer holy man I reckon, by the look of his staff."

When he realized Donovan wasn't going to answer, Tomson crossed his legs and arms and studied an indistinct point on the floorboards at his feet. When he spoke, his tone was distant. "I heard stories of the demons from the Old War when I was knee-high and full of piss. My daddy used to say they were left over from the Shift, came when whatever man did to himself that got him buried in nine feet of dunny had run its course, then kept up rampant-like ever since. I even got a book about it all buried somewhere. No writer's name on it, but it talks about the place beyond the Black. Call it the Maw, maybe. Could all be a bunch of shim sham by my estimate, though with all that's been happening lately who really knows? Even your friend the Cleric spoke of it like it was doctrine. And you know, now that I think back, a few days ago wasn't the first time I saw him either. He was here before. Midsummer, bout a year and four months gone. Scared the balls off some of the fellas in town. To me, he just seemed like any other charlatan with drama in his nose. And you know what? It wasn't much later that the Dwellers came calling, either. First time in years. Everywhere except in town itself for some reason."

"How much later?" asked Donovan, intrigued.

"Weeks. The first to die were the Hamiltons, farmers who lived out north, a couple of hefts away from town. Found nothing but entrails."

Donovan thought hard on this. A connection between the man he sought and the creatures who came with the Mist? Baseless but fascinating. They had appeared now and then throughout history, never for long and never in numbers. Not like it was now. "Did the Cleric ever mention the Dwellers?" he asked Tomson as Mary re-emerged with trays of food.

"He said they were an omen from the Keeper. That we were being punished for the sins of the old world. I would've told him to shove a rag in it, but I'm not the sort to start trouble where it's not needed." He leaned forward to take a deep breath of Mary's stew. "My, my, sweet Mary, you're the life in me." She smiled at him and winked and went back to the kitchen to fetch another batch.

Donovan tasted a spoonful and learned something new about Tomson: the man was not one for hyperbole. It was the best damn thing he had eaten since the foodmasters from the Northern Vale had fed the royals last Sun Festival more than ten years gone. He let the spices linger on his tongue until he felt soaked in their flavor, then swallowed and ate more with fervor. While he gorged, Tomson said, "Your man stayed at a place in town his last two nights here. Called Shag's Inn. Not what you think, though. The name, I mean. He was the only customer there, like as not, not that it matters a wink. It don't cost Shag a thing to keep it open. You might want to go see fer yerself. Still no one there."

Donovan nodded, gazing into his stew. Tomson sized him up, said, "You know, we could use a man like you 'round these parts."

"I'm not good for much in the way of building a town."

"But you are good for fighting. I can tell just watching you move that you know how to kill. And that Dweller was afraid of you, or at least wary. I don't know any other explanation for it." He shot a glance at Donovan's sword; even a gesture so small was enough to put the Swordsman on edge. *Like a wolf and its endangered cub.* He made no show of this as he took a hearty swig of the stout, loving the burn as it went easy into his gullet. "I've seen swords like that before," Tomson continued, "A long time ago. You *are* a Swordsman from the north."

Donovan frowned. These comments always came. He had learned to wait it out, like loosing a child to sprint to and fro while tethered to a clothesline until they were too weary to cause a nuisance.

"The world was once a glimmering gem compared to what it is today, or so the stories go. And your kind were able to unite the peoples, give 'em hope and such. Is this not true?" When Donovan still did not answer, Tomson leaned forward so fast that he could have landed a blow. "Those creatures have eaten our flesh. Man, woman, and child. And I don't see a reason for them to stop. Unless we stop them."

Donovan finished his stew, unperturbed by Tomson's outburst. "I'm not for hire. I have my own matters to attend to."

Tomson stared at him, intense for a space, then relaxed and eased back into his chair. He was about to speak again when the drum of approaching footsteps cut him short. Louder and louder they grew until the front door burst open. A young man spilled in, dressed in rags, chest heaving. "Mayor! Mayor, come quick!" His voice was so thick with urgency that Tomson rose and followed without question.

Donovan, less concerned, stole one last taste of Mary's stew, and then strapped on his sword and stepped out after them.

Outside, the town was chaos.

10

Dozens of fingers, all hard calluses, and deep grime, hefted Jana into the air. A shriek waned at her lips as her body went limp and the throng below gathered vigor. Tomson knew exactly where they were taking her: the Old Tree, where supposed witches and others were immolated, excising depraved forces, at least in theory.

Purified through agony, pray it true. Haven't had a good burning in a while. Town's due. Tomson considered this as a waking person might ponder their fading dream.

The mayor followed the young man, Dumprey was his name, down the hill from the house, the Swordsman behind, and watched Pleasantry's denizens shriek and cavort. The girl was hefted over their heads, flaccid as a gutted spindlefish. She let out one harsh cry—the most awful, wounded sound Tomson had ever heard—and then didn't move again. *Passed out cold, more 'an likely.* He frowned at his fellow townsmen. From smiles to murder as quick as the wind changed. They'd kill him along with the girl if he intervened. Taking solace in impotence seemed compelling for the now, given the looks in the townsfolk's eyes, shame him for thinking it. He almost accepted the thought and turned his back—might as well mourn the poor girl and be done with this business. Then his father whispered to him from the Black that he and his ancestors didn't live and die to breed no half-assed coward sonnovabitch.

Put that in your bowl and burn it, Tommy. Get your tender movin'.

"Stop this!" Tomson said as he charged the crowd. They didn't listen, or maybe they couldn't hear him through the throb of their panic. Shoulders and elbows clipped him as he pushed forward. No sooner did he clear one mass of unclean bodies than another swallowed him whole with the girl still thirty paces away. "Stop, I say! If ya love me, then stay it. I beg you!"

"She's got the Reaper in her!" cried a voice in the crowd.

"Burn it out! Burn it out!"

A flux of movement crashed into Tomson, knocking a hot ball of wind out of him, and now the anger he kept caged most times woke and there was no holding it back. He used the full of his size and strength to carve through the crowd, plowing past men with a growl, leaving a heap of them in his wake. "Stop this madness now. I demand it!" As his deep voice echoed into the air and faded, at last the residents of Pleasantry snapped free of their murderous ardor and faced him.

He reached the men who held Jana and took hold of their arms, grappling for her release. Robert Mullville, potter and jack of lumber and amateur bowman, let go her ankles, still in the throes of whatever madness this was, and whipped one scrawny fist about towards Tomson's head. Tomson (he'd swear later not a thought of it struck him prior) reached out and caught Mullville's punch in his meaty palm, twisted him around like a child, and crushed him with his forearm. Mulville dropped whimpering to his knees, his nose gushing blood. He did not attempt to rise. At last, the few folks still stirring a ruckus shut their damnable mouths and listened.

Tomson motioned to his deputies; only young men they were, and barely that. They looked scared clear out of their minds, but to their credit, they swallowed their fear and bucked up when called. Tomson pointed at Mullville. "Put him in the Hutch. Let him think about things for the night." The boys nodded and pushed forward from the wings. Mullville struggled upright, a look half-bemused and half-frightened on his face. The boys secured him with rope and dragged him away.

The men holding Jana eased her down, eager now beneath the fire of Tomson's gaze. Tomson offered one stocky arm for her to grab onto. The girl looked weak but unharmed. To the crowd, he said, "What has this girl done to deserve this?"

"She has tha mark o' tha demon, Tom!" a woman wailed.

"She's gonna turn into one of 'em!" said another.

A villager who Tomson did not know lunged forward from the flock, and eight doughy fingers grasped Jana's threadbare tunic. One sharp tug and it tore, exposing an olive-skinned breast. The folk nearest fell away signing themselves, and a few of those fell prostrate like penitents.

Infecting the smooth tan of the girl's skin was a ropy scar, its tendrils so deep a purple that it appeared black in this grim light. It grew from her collar bone and crawled her torso, insectile, branching into horrible, wiry tributaries which terminated at her stomach and the crest of her shoulder. The shape reminded Tomson of teeth set in a monstrous jawbone, or a mutant millipede burrowing its multi-eyed head into her flesh. His stomach froze in his chest and his spit dried up at the sight. It took him a moment to recover his wits and pull the girl's ruined tunic over her exposed skin, and while he did so he felt as if he had just sunk his arms to the elbows in leper flesh.

"She has to burn. It's tha only way!" said a man close to Tomson. Tomson had no response. A thousand possibilities had been expected when he first laid eyes on these crazed dullards; the last—aside from daisies sprouting from their rears—was that he might side with them. The Change was riding up on the Hunter girl, and fast if that mark be the Blood Disease. Dwellers were one sort of bad; Blood Demons were of an ilk even worse, the kind that visited in darkness without warning to swallow life out of folk before they knew they'd been attacked. Worst of it was they were neighbor and friend the night before, human as ever there was.

Before Tomson could recover, eager hands clawed forth from the crowd, again capturing hold of Jana's body and heaving her upwards. She watched Tomson during this, eyes deadened by pain or guilt or resignation. The dirt-mottled sea of hands ferried her towards the Old Tree, where her pretty young face and soft body and supple breast would turn black and stink the air until they were reduced to ash.

You can't let them do it. For all that makes you a man, you can't!

The thought rang clear and harsh in his brain. With renewed abandon, he threw himself into the thick of the townsfolk. "No. Stop, I say! Let her go!"

"Get away, Tom! You know this is how it hasta be," cried one man, barring Tomson's path with an arm thick from hammering steel. Tomson shoved it aside and dove ahead.

"There are other options. We'll send her south. This is not our way!" Tomson pleaded. If someone had asked him yesterday if he'd ever beg for a damn thing in this life, Tomson would have told them to go hang.

You never really led these men, Tom. No more than a tail leads the dog it grows from.

He, who knew himself as a man of fairness but also of flaw, had been shown for the figurehead he was, something to reach for when prayers waxed intangible and the Keeper felt distant. Little good all that was now. Bloodlust compelled men far more than principle.

He was lamenting this when something dull and heavy cracked into the back of his skull. The world flashed white and then red and the sky spun around until he landed on his hands and knees with his breath run out. Clods of hay and mud blurred and swayed beneath his fingers, doubling and tripling. When he touched the back of his head he felt warm blood oozing from a gash. Dazed, he watched the townsfolk disintegrate into a bleary fog, and that, as the fishers down the Mire far south said, was that. The girl was lost. And it was his fault, as much as he'd convince himself otherwise.

That thought still echoed when a loud *ding* thundered into the bleak autumn sky. At the sound of its piercing knell, every last person in Pleasantry froze where they stood, their zealotry broken. Tomson's vision refocused, his hand clamped against his leaking scalp. Now he could see Donovan Maltrese standing at the peak of the bell tower, sword drawn and gleaming, a black creature unnatural crawled from the bogs to scrutinize them with harsh demon's eyes.

The bell, as old as it was, was sturdy and bore average wear, yet with one strike Donovan's sword had cracked it open like an egg.

* * * *

"Let her go," the Swordsman said.

"We can't! Ya know we can't! She has tha demon's breath in her!" someone shouted.

"Indeed she does," said Donovan, "but she'll not be one of them. Not soon enough to concern you."

"We can't risk our children!" screamed one house maiden, her apron drawn up from the mud.

"And you won't," said Donovan, as calm as a man ordering a drink at a saloon. "I will take her with me when I leave this place."

"Then leave now!" people cried.

"He can't leave now! We need him to fight tha Misties!"

"We don't need more demons here. Leave!"

"I'll leave soon enough," said Donovan, filled with disgust. A half-hour ago, these folks were cheering him as if he were the Keeper's servant. Now they wanted him gone, and were it not for his sword they would string him up beside the girl and set him ablaze just to be sure. Master was right about them. All of them. They could burn for all he cared.

He climbed part way down the tower's ladder and then leapt to the ground, black mud spuming from beneath his boots. The crowd parted as he made his way to the girl, who was lowered now onto weakened legs. She watched Donovan approach through a curtain of tears. "I am not here to harm any of you," the Swordsman said, thinking that he would take any of their lives without hesitation as he spoke. "I have my own business and the girl is now a part of it. I will be gone by midday tomorrow and I will take her with me. If anyone objects, we can settle it with the sword."

At that, all muttering hushed. The low call of the wind danced on the dead boughs watching, wizened and misshapen, from above.

"Would any come forward?" the Swordsman asked.

These folks are dense. Best to be clear.

No one would. Donovan took Jana by the arm and she set her weight against him. Without a word, he peeled away her tunic and inspected the scar beneath. The Blood Disease was in her, not as these simpletons feared but in a way far worse, one with which the Swordsman was intimately familiar. Wearing a deep frown, he led her away from the gathering of black looks and muddied glowers and towards the inn, Orin still dangling nimbly from his fingers.

Tomson trudged behind them looking drained and saddened. Not one glance did he spare his fellow townsmen. Their gazes shied away from him as well; Donovan suspected that they knew, as Tomson no doubt did, that something had broken today that would never go back together.

* * * *

Grampy watched them all from his porch. Strong a codger as he was, stopping a young girl drunk on impetuousness was beyond his old means. Will was quite a thing, not to be bridled, so he had sat out here, tawny feet rocking on the rail, face crinkled like old parchment, and he had watched. Keeper bless 'em, it had managed to work itself out all right, yes indeed. Not near as bad as it could've been. But in the hot twist of his gut, Grampy held the notion death still danced on the horizon for all of them, wearing a demonic mask and shaking its rain stick and howling to the heavens that the end was nigh.

Oh yessiree. The sweet, cold end was nigh.

* * * *

In the distance, away from the events in town but close enough to hear all, three other men looked on. Upon fleeting glance, they could have been farmers or blacksmiths or any of a hundred things, but a closer look betrayed them as something else.

The leader stood a head taller than the rest. He surveyed the town square with a soldier's keen eyes and reached for the pendant dangling from a lanyard looped around his leathery neck while he pondered long and hard. Ahead, the odd play by the bell tower was coming to a close. He studied it all with deep thoughtfulness.

Oh, but how that stern kneel-before-me look in the Swordsman's eyes raised his blood.

The man's pendant, gilded and cast in the shape of a lion's head, shone in the ashy afternoon light as if to say it shared his thoughts; be that the case, it must think this Swordsman—despite fancying himself lord of the land with his lavish northerner's blade—needed to be put in place. And he, the leader of these strongbacks, called Creel by his friends, known in the valleys and mountains about this town as the Lion, felt he was just the man to do the placing.

Bet your life and stock on it.

He motioned to his two companions and, without a word, they drifted away from town and slipped into the forest.

11

The inn was yet another vestige of the old world, built of white-washed hemlock and hemmed with dead bracken. Its walls were rotted and peeled for stretches baring underwork the color of poultry, and the dentil above was bowed and missing in places. No doubt infested with Grinders (or whatever name they bore here), Jana wagered. Grinders were relations of termites, only five times the size and with a penchant for flesh when wood became scarce. She thought of Lee, a man Grampy had once escorted through Raistland when she was a child. Passed out on stout, Lee had, and Grampy had left him to his slumber only to discover him the next day with a hole the size of a peach burrowed through his cheek. Lesson learned, sharp and durable.

Your family's dead, and you're cursed. Oh, and the town wants to burn you alive.

Those thoughts seemed far away, unreal. Everything about her seemed removed, fogged, as though she was trapped within a stained-glass prison and could barely discern the world without. She knew she should feel anguish, but right now Jana Hunter's insides were simply numb.

When they stepped into the inn's foyer, Jana's first thought was that the air smelled of lilacs and burning hair. A pair of flocculent feet, crossed at the ankles, bopped atop the counter to an inaudible rhythm. Shag peered up at them over his toes, a rotting tome entitled *The Cat and the Fungus Tree* folded over his lap, and Jana marveled at the survival of any sort of book in this forsaken place. Shag's glasses were thick as a man's thumb, and they hunkered on a fat beet of a nose. His eyes sat a little too close together and a little too far back in his head, and they blinked incessantly; looking at him there was dizzying. Jana focused on the harsh creases of his brow instead. "Can I help yer there, mefellows? Oh and is that you thar, Tomson, lad? Scant seen a bite of ya more a year then I kin count on a hand, bless ya. What brings the sword bearin' like here?" he said, bubbling with excitement.

The man's accent was thicker than Grampy's, thicker than anyone Jana had heard for some time. It was the talk of folk three or four generations gone from civility. *There must be a picture or two in that book of his. Not a chance in the Black he can read a single word.*

"This is Donovan, Swordsman from the north. And this here is Jana, of the Hunter clan."

I am *the Hunter clan now.*

At this Shag bolted upright, his book tumbling to the floor. He placed his hand on his hip in an outlandish flourish and bowed deep. "Pleased and blessed, I am, fine sir. Honored to look on ya."

Donovan nodded. "No need for that, friend. Stand true."

Shag kept his bow a moment longer, then turned to Jana. "Pleased. You look a stitch familiar though I can't place ya. How can I aid yar fine folk at this hour? Needin' a room? The finest for hefts have we, pray it."

Tomson began to speak, but Donovan quieted him with a soft gesture. "We do, indeed. With one request. There stayed here not long past a man. Tall, violet eyes, dressed in white, carrying a weapon difficult to misremember."

Shag's face went sallow. "Yar, I reckon that face'll look'n me as I put a foot 'n'the grave, Keeper save. Wickedest fella I've set these eyes on. Haven't touched a speck in his room since he left n'the early morn. No mor'an two night he put up his bunk under my thatch, blessit. Why n'the Black would fine folk as yar seek such unholy filth? I'd best burn the room before givit to ya."

Jana watched this exchange over what seemed an infinite expanse. In her mind she was still holding Cory's hand, his skin warm and rough from summer days spent hoarding flatrocks and thorny brambles. She was pulling him through the sullen chill of the Shodan, nearing the forest brink where the crouching skylighted smokestacks of Pleasantry waited to greet them. Soon they'd be headed back to the farm, where Dad would be grumbling of pesky Misties and their dreadful timing and mum would be stirring a broad crock of summerwine pudding till its aroma flooded the Drudge.

During all of this, somewhere in the distance, voices were chattering about something or other. One of them was familiar. What was his name again? Oh yes, Tomson, who was saying…

"Did he cause any trouble when he was here?"

"Not in of tha way thon jack fossywart youngins are spreadin' at the burial place this season, and no pinch the sort a bandit or harrier might be like to put upon ya. No, sir, nothing o' the like. This was a horn worse'en that, wager a thumb." His eyes turned murky at the thought.

"What sort of trouble?" asked Donovan.

Shag woke from his trance and then returned to the fascinating adventures of the Cat and his nemesis, the Fungus Tree. "Nothing worth mentionin', I'll say. Best ya go now, 'fore the sun sits too low. Things creepin' round when shadows get long, bless ya. Begone Tomson, though I love ya. Even'the thought is too fierce fer me."

The shakes took him then as he fumbled with a page. Donovan and Tomson waited out his fit, but his look drew Jana forward; the particular shade of gray his skin had turned was familiar, as were those tremors, which she knew began at the base of the spine and shuddered up to the neck like a spout of arctic water. *Oh yes. I know it. As well as my own hands. This man, this Cleric, whoever he was, planted that infectious seed everywhere he went.*

She laid her hand on Shag's and it stilled. The man was much older than she had first appraised; the verve and frankness of his look belonged to a much younger man. "Y-you. Yar've seen tha damned fellow, too, ain't ya. I wager I'can still see tha stink of'im growin' round ya like a bog cloud. Not that I'd compare somethin' as pretty to a bog, mind, but more akin to, say, a rose… No, that's not it. Ah, forget it. Important bit is, I look in'those pretties and I know ya seen what I seen to the letter, an'it wasn't a man by a hair or bush."

"No. He wasn't," Jana agreed. She felt Donovan look at her sharply from the edge of her vision, but he said nothing.

Shag turned to Tomson and The Cat and all his Fungi landed on the floor again with a *thunk*. He grabbed hold of Tomson's sleeves and drew him close. "I'm sorry, Tom. I'm so sorry. I beg it. Forgive me."

"What are you asking forgiveness for, you old buck?" asked Tomson.

"Fer not tellin' ya sooner that somethin' from tha Maw climbed out wit'its own two claws and came ta yer town dressed as a healin' man. I knew it, and I knew thar was not a thing a one of us could've done of it, wisp and whistle. But I shoulda told ya of it anyhow. Forgive me."

A smile eased onto Tomson's weathered lips. "I would've liked if you'd told me, t'is true, but I knew anyhow. The more right of it is that there's nothing any of us could've done. That might've changed now, let's hope. Donovan here came to town looking for just this man, and if anyone within a thousands hefts of Pleasantry is to deal with such as this Cleric, I'll wager it's him. So get off your knees and let's take a look at where the bastard slept, can we?"

Shag's eyes brightened and he labored to his feet. The reality that was Donovan seemed to strike him for the first time now and he eyed the sword, the hat, the boots, and everything in between with a child's wonder. "Now... When you say yer a Swordsman, do I take it to mean a swordsman? Or a *Swordsman*, pray ya? First is common as herp on a whore, but second is like a shootin' star burnin' red, so word is."

All eyes turned to Donovan. "Let's take a look at the room," he said.

"Of course, yer Lordship, sire, sir. This way. You kin come, too, Tom! Hold yer nose, beg. The evil stinks mighty up thar."

He led them with giddy energy to the dusty old stair in the rear of the inn, and the steps there groaned beneath their weight as if ready to buckle. Jana fixed her attention on the stairwell walls, which were unlike anything she had ever seen. Strips of pinewood as thin as her wrist sat together in staggered patterns, the creases between planks never joined the same way twice, all stained and lacquered and broken by columnar plaster molds. It was old work, partly in disrepair, with sections that bellied and sagged, wracked with mold and thick gray dust. Still, it all looked so...solid. There were some who conjured their own paint in Pleasantry, and new houses were still built from time to time, but never with such craftsmanship. It was all too perfect. Perhaps there existed hulking machines which prowled the earth in times lost, dicing trees into perfect skinny strips only to slap them together with precision and slop there a coat of seraphic sealant which had survived until its makers were dust. Then behold! Shag the wily appears and makes camp. It's all for a reason, pray it.

You are beyond silly, girl.

Making light did little to avert a sharp pang: she saw now Cory's eyes, Mum's, Dad, each as she remembered them best, smiling and eager for a hearty supper together.

She clung to those images.

Then the smell struck her.

It was detectable as soon as she cleared the last step, only it was her heart and her mind rather than her nose that discerned it, a saccharine essence folded into a thousand tiny knives spearing her from the inside. But it *was* a smell; it seeped from the sagging paper of the walls and the ancient grit of the floorboards, so thick she could almost see the skeins of gaseous emerald death writhing in wait outside the door at the end of the hall. *Come closer,* she thought she heard it whisper. *Come breathe deep of me, and join us in the depths with the rest of yours.*

"You can feel it hard, kin ya, Swordsman?" asked Shag. Donovan nodded, stony as ever, but the crease of his brow told Jana he, too, felt the burden of the Cleric's residue. "It gets worse closer ya get. Not everyone can feel it, mind. Betsy Callahan swept up and turned the bed after he was gone. I asked her if any o'the sick'd squirmed her up and she gave me a look like I were a banana tree, blessit. But you can'all feel it true, so say yer eyes. Brace tight now. Here we are."

The energy emanating from the door inundated Jana as they approached. Her body responded, each breath threatening to drown her in the wickedness their eyes could not see but their minds could. The scar on her chest throbbed and ached and blazed; worst was the churning warmth that throbbed between her legs before growing into a wetness. She mashed her thighs together, sickened.

Damn you for this. I'll feel a blade sink into your guts if it's the last I do.

And then they were at the door.

What lay within felt anticlimactic. The room was plain save for the skill of the woodwork, which was worn but still spectacular. The double bed was a late addition and looked like it belonged in Pleasantry (probably crafted by Troy Spence or his father). A burl walnut night table crowned with white marble held a twin wick oil lamp, and snug to the wall lay a tallboy engraved with ash swirl veneers which were burned black. Silk flowers here, an old Courier's Horn hung from nails there. A troupe of wooden effigies frozen in time stood watch on the bay windowsill. Of all these things, most striking was the intangible: the feeling of evil, overwhelming a moment ago, vanished once they crossed the threshold.

Donovan stood in the center of the room, turning a full circle.

"It's gone, whatever it was," said Tomson.

So he did feel it, too.

"When did he arrive here?" asked Donovan.

"I'd say an hour past sunfall. Sauntered in from the forest edge. Not wit'the look of crossing the Drudge, pray ya. Notta spit. Pearly as a baby's first tooth. Nor a drip of sweat or a hair out of place on that one. *Unnatural* is all I'll call it, reckon. And... I might've had a toucha stout 'n me, but Keeper save, I saw my own front door slam shut behind him on its own."

Donovan nodded, distant. He walked the perimeter of the room, tracing his fingers over everything.

"What do you think?" asked Tomson.

"I'm not sure," he replied. "Did anything happen when he left in the morning?"

Shag shook his head. "I heard 'im more than saw 'im. I was tendin' tha kitchen 'n I caught a flash of that damnable staff or spear or both he carries about, and next I know he's gone. And I tell ya, Keeper pray, I *felt* him go."

"I believe it. He wasn't even here and I felt the last of him go just now," Tomson said, hooking his thumbs in his pockets. "I don't think you should stay here, Donovan. I know you've more of the affair in your head than I so I'll go with your word, but something in me says no matter how much you know of this Cleric, layin' in a bed of his stink won't help one way or another."

"I can feel him close but I can't point to his direction, as far as he is..." answered Donovan, trailing off, stamping at the floor with his bootheel. Jana peered closer at this and noticed now a blister the size of a coconut there at his feet charred into the planks. She held her tongue and hugged herself, gooseflesh rigid on her forearms.

"Are you sure ya won't take a room down tha hall? Even tha room next over! Close enough ta get tha feel but not so close you wake up wit'your pits smellin' th'like of it!" Shag clasped his hands before him as if in prayer.

"No. We'll stay here tonight."

Tomson's frown deepened. "As you say," he said at last. He took Jana's hand. "You'd best stay at my house. The wife'll fix you up with something good to eat, make you feel a sight better."

"No," said Donovan. "She'll stay with me. But... If your wife decides to bring some of her cooking this way, I'll not be one to deny it." The faintest curve touched his lips; Jana expected that was as close to a smile as the Swordsman could manage.

Tomson looked like he might argue, but the burly mayor just nodded instead. "As you say. I'll leave you to it. Good night."

Jana listened as he headed downstairs. Shag backed from the room soon after, and then she was left alone with this Swordsman from an older and nearly forgotten world, one who knew the mind of the man she wanted to kill now with all her heart. The Cleric was at the center of this; she was sure of it. That this all should take place days after his departure could be no coincidence. To the Jana Hunter who had died earlier in the forest alongside her kid brother, no one could have said the thought of doing murder might yield such comfort, but now, in the grim cast of the fading day, the thought cutting the Cleric's breath from his lungs seemed like a fine idea to her. Just fine.

"Have you eaten?" asked Donovan.

"No."

He drew back his coat and produced a leather satchel which contained half a bread loaf which he tore a piece from and offered. She nearly took it from his hand with her teeth and it was gone in seconds. His hand trembled as it withdrew. "Are you scared of me, too?" she asked. *Always a lip on you, there is. One day I'll catch ya, then you'll be in fer it!* whispered Mum from the depths of the Black.

Donovan took a seat on the bed. "If ever I was to fear a thing in this world, it would not be a little girl bearing a scar and a smug grin, I promise you."

She wanted to fight back, but her spirit was gone. She sat against the wall with her knees pulled against her chest, fighting the tightening sob in her throat. Donovan reached back into his satchel and produced a clay mortar and the bud of a purple flower, which he placed in the mortar along with oil from a dropper and ground into a paste with a pestle. When he was done, he kneeled beside Jana. "Brace yourself. This will sting." He gave her no time to do so as he applied the paste to the wound on her foot, which had been cleaned but needed new dressing. She let out a cry and clutched his shoulder. When the hot streak of agony burned out she released him and he wrapped her foot with a length of bandage. "That will throb till sunrise but will heal in days," he said, standing. After another look in her eyes, he added, "You should cry if you feel the need. It helps."

His gaze lingered on the effigies by the window as he drank long from a canteen. Then he kneeled to look under the bed, and then pressed his nose to the mattress and inhaled deeply.

"Yer brave for doing that," she said.

Donovan stood and unstrapped his sword, propping it by the bedside. His look went cold. "Where did you get that mark?"

Jana's jaw quivered. Tears warmed her eyes, but she held them back. "I don't know," she lied. *You're no good at that and you know it.*

"Then how long ago did you notice it?" Donovan asked flatly.

She fought the grief. It was no use. Tears swarmed her sight and she bent her head and wept against her kneecaps. Donovan sat and watched until those sobs shrank to whimpers, and he hadn't moved when she looked up again. When he seemed satisfied that she had regained control of herself, he asked again, "How long?"

He knows you're a liar. Better just stick to the truth.

"After one of the Dwellers touched me," she lied anyway. *Why can't I just get it out and be done with?*

He leaned forward, one rough hand wrapped tightly around the hilt of his sword. "Tell me the truth, girl. There's no good that talking the roundabout here will find you."

Jana felt like a child suddenly, like her hand was forearm deep in the applemud mix, scooping free a mouthful, and her dad had just walked in on her. What even was her goal? She realized that she had none beyond the death of the Cleric; her thoughts now marched along famished and listless through the badlands of her mind without guideposts. Why even deceive this man? He might take her with him if she could earn his trust. Perhaps the straightaway was best to grease those wheels. *Yer thinkin' too hard of this, woman. He's right and you know it. No sense falling an oaktree with a butterknife.*

"It happened before the Dweller came, I reckon," said Donovan, interrupting her thoughts.

She nodded. It hurt to bring back the memory. She could still smell him, taste the blight of his scarecrow lips, feel his ghoulish fingers against her breasts as he thrust himself into her under the thick cowl of the night.

"What did he say to you?"

She looked at him sharply. "How did you know?"

"You wear his scent like a cloud. Did he speak?"

She nodded. "He told me..." She thought hard and now she could make out some of his words. "He told me not to be afraid. That I already had evil blood in me and that it only needed to be awakened. He said he wasn't doing anything to me that the Keeper hadn't already decided on. And he said I'd be reborn, perfect, a god on earth."

Donovan's eyes lit up. Zeal glowed behind his face. "He touched you there and the mark grew?" When she nodded he said, "Did he tell you where he was going?"

Her lips tightened in response. What if the Swordsman meant to save her until all that could be gleaned from her mind had been reaped and then he would dispose of her by the roadside or leave her to burn? What then? *How would that straightaway work out for you, silly crust of a girl?*

She steeled her gaze and did not answer.

"You'd be a charred pile of flesh and bone right now were it not for me. You owe me answers."

"You saved me for yourself. How do I know you won't kill me when you're done with your questions?"

"You'll have to trust my word. I would not have your blood on my sword for any measure."

"Because I'm a woman?"

"You're not a woman anymore."

"Then what am I?"

"Something else."

The tears returned, but this time she crushed them. She would not be weak before this man of strength. "He said he was going to Pal Myrrah."

Donovan looked caught off guard by her sudden directness. "Did he say why?"

"No. He didn't speak much. That was all he said." Her eyes turned downward like a beaten dog. When she looked up again the Swordsman's hands were shaking and palsied. He interlocked his fingers and gritted his teeth and Jana thought she could hear a soft grunt deep in his throat. A moment later a spasm overtook him from legs to nape.

"What's wrong?" The words sounded more akin to the wind than her voice.

The Swordsman recovered after a time. A drop of sweat skated the bridge of his nose and he wiped it with his sleeve. "If that is what he said, then Pal Myrrah is where we will go as well," he said as if his fit had not happened.

"We?" asked Jana.

"You bear the Cleric's mark. These Dwellers are drawn to it like a sea monster to chum. They will hunt you wherever you go until you Turn."

"Turn into what?"

"You are alone now?"

The memories clamored. Dad chasing her with a wet towel across the sedge near the Shodan. Cory huddled with her by the escarpment on the far side of the Drudge, exchanging riddles.

I will not weep. I will not.

"Yes," was all she could manage. "My family is dead. All of them."

"The Cleric was at your home?"

She nodded.

"For how long?"

"Just one night."

"You woke up with that mark after he made love to you…" It wasn't a question. A detached fog gathered in his eyes.

Jana felt the burn of shame in her chest. "Yes. If you call what he did to me making love."

Donovan stroked his chin, leaned back on the bed, and set his boots against the footboard. "Would I be foolish to expect you to stay the night without trying to run?"

"Where would I run to?" she asked. It was true. Close to this man was safe as she could hope to be. No one from town would dare cross a Swordsman, no matter how drunk or foolish they were. Donovan looked satisfied by her answer and closed his eyes.

"Why are you looking for him?" she asked, not yet ready to be alone.

"Why does anyone look for anything?" he said with no irony in his voice.

Seconds later his breathing deepened and she knew he was asleep. She remained on the floor, the ceiling staring her down, the machine-hewed floorboards pressed to her soles. She considered trying to sleep and, as the relentless gloom of the day faded to a murky dark, she lay on her side and closed her eyes. Once she thought she heard the plankboards in the hall creak as though someone approached. *No. There's nothing to fear here, Jana. Nothing but yourself.*

She frowned. She sighed. She slept.

12

After watching the Swordsman rescue the girl Jana from the village rabble and head towards the inn, Grampy had limped home for some much-needed rest. Short bursts of activity softened by copious naps; that was how he liked his days. Now, as evening drew close and the last light of day faded, Grampy stood in the center of his hut contemplating the monumental event of lowering down onto his knees.

His old prayer pillow, purchased from a peddler along a road that skirted most of the southern end of this continent (back when Grampy was but a young buck, too full of gusto and too lean on sense to know his toe from his pecker), waited for him on the dusty pine floorboards with what he perceived to be a touch of grumpiness. Grampy closed his thin fingers into little fists—they looked like oversized flesh-toned prunes striped with spider veins—and held his breath as he eased first one knee and then the other onto the pillow. At once pain shot from his hip to his toes and he nearly fell forward. When he found his balance, he clasped his hands near his waist, his burlap nightgown draped and gathered across his small body, his long nose bulbous and painted orange by the candlelight. The flames from those candles danced down the wick before him, and across the trestles and the vigas black shadows flickered in and out of existence. Models for life, candles were: never stop dancing till you're out of wick. Grampy liked that one. He might have just found his new motto.

All the same, he got the notion his wick was just about burned out.

The man who had sold him the pillow was probably dead of old age by now, as was the woman who fashioned the candles at which he now stared. The world around him was headed for the hills, see ya and thanks for coming. And why not him? What use could a codger like he be to a world run amuck with hotheaded man-children and beasts from the Maw? Folk would say not much, short of discourse and the occasional fart of wisdom.

But maybe, just maybe, he could still be of use.

If not, the Keeper'd see his damnedest try tonight.

Sometime between when the man who had made pillows crossed his path and the end of his wandering days, Grampy had picked up a thing or two, knowledge mostly, bits he had never spoken of to a soul. One of those things, which may be about as reliable as a barn made of dunny, was called Warding.

Twice a year he'd cast it, once at Harvest and once at Sowing. It was an old ritual, judging by the dusty and cobwebbed feel of the words, but there was comfort found in things that had survived so long; ask any of the folk who paid him regular visits when their days grew especially long and hard. Sowing was months away, and Grampy had no knowledge of the lifespan of his efforts, or if they were even worth conjuring more than once, but given what had happened today, he had decided that an extra Ward or two wouldn't hurt anyone. First thing was first, however.

He bent down with a sizable groan and produced a small, flat stone, blood red and polished to a mirror shine. He wrapped it in his old fingers and held it to his forehead and reached with his mind into the earth just below him, seeking the energy he sensed there. He tapped into it with practiced ease, his old mind adroit still if only with work of this nature, and that energy trickled into him like stout from a tap. Grampy's eyes, which had seen more years than any three of his neighbors combined, remained closed but became aware of a dull blue aura; it felt like a big warm hug. From his wife, maybe. Yes, that was how he envisioned it, a nice, tender embrace from the love his life, gone forty years now, remembered as if he had seen her this morning. He allowed the sensation to soothe him for a time and then channeled it outward. He envisioned that brilliant blue light spreading beyond his hut, beyond the crossroads and the bell tower and the mess of hovels and swine and cattle, all the way to the edges of town. There it stayed, a perfect pulsing sphere of translucent energy whose purpose was to keep out...something. Evil in general, maybe. Whether it was the Warding or the Swordsman that had kept the Misty clear of Pleasantry today could not be known for sure, but Grampy was going to do his part regardless.

When the Warding felt sturdy enough to stand alone, Grampy relaxed and opened his eyes. That sensation in his heart remained, a cozy heat which he nurtured and savored. The whole world might be going to the Maw, but this old man was going to do his worst to ensure this dunnycake of a town, his home now for decades, would be as safe as could be.

Now if he could only figure out how to stand up again.

13

*T*he raw chill of winter air swept in from the massif in howling sorties. The ebbing sun trundled forth, weary, leaving a cast of long shadows to veil the blackened city walls. Ramparts rent and crushed. Archer's towers half crumbled into ashy boreholes below like hungry maws. Waiting for a repast, maybe. Once children's laughs had echoed in the air here. Once there was bustling market chatter in the streets and the rhythmic clack of wagon wheels maneuvering the cobble and crowd. Now only crowsong and the crackle of distant brushfire could be heard, faint and dying alongside other sounds: black talc skittering beneath the portcullis nearby, muddy water splashing idly below the drawbridge without, working southward to the Bend before joining the sea near Raistlin.

Donovan trudged through the detritus, the glint of the bloody sunburst riding his weary back. His sword danced between his shoulder blades in drunken sways. In the cool shadows that swallowed him, the carved bone hilt of his blade looked like a serpent peering over his hat, one jeweled eye unblinking. The smell stung his nose; decomposing flesh; burning privet; spoiling ration. His footfalls echoed into the courtyard, once a gathering place, now a columbarium. Massacred soldiers littered here and there. Donovan kept his eyes on the street beneath his boots. A patina of evil on every other sense; it felt slick and revolting. No need for it in his eyes, too.

She is here. I can feel her, even amidst all this sorrow.

But she was sorrow incarnate, his personal sorrow, the light under which all else fell, the darkness that filled his heart.

Somewhere up ahead, he would meet her again at last.

He wasn't sure if he yearned for it or dreaded it. He thought of turning away, tail between his knees, and running until he fell dead on the road. Better that than to face her. But the thread that wove his fabric was spun of principle, no matter how much he wished otherwise, and so he pressed on.

He reached the end of the courtyard where the road branched to either side of a massive stairway carved from white granite. At the top a grandiloquent dais bore skyward, crowned with a matching balustrade. In the center stood the Keeper as sculpted by the king's finest artisans. Marble robes draped his powerful arms, transfixed forever in wind-billowed elegance. His broad fingers clutched a nameless tome to his breast. His other hand reached skyward, palm up, as if anticipating a drop of rain. At his great feet lay Donovan's destiny. His all. He pushed towards it. Twisted limbs and ruined faces stared at him from every direction with sightless doll's eyes. They were dead because of him.

Because of him.

The steps seemed to stretch as he climbed them. The sun was gone when he reached the dais, snuffed into a smokeless smolder beyond the buttes in the west.

Ever to rise again?

Did it matter without her?

He knew not.

He straddled the top step with his eyes closed. The wind blew unobstructed here. It traced the hard lines of his face and left his lips dry. For a moment just the cold dankness of moist air under his coat, down his shirt, in his core. He opened his eyes at last and saw her, beautiful beyond measure, serenity itself. Her porcelain skin shone in the gloom. Her thin fingers interlaced, posed against her stomach. Her white gown drawn and gathered like swells of tundra. The stone table beneath her, detailed with runes. The mahogany halation of her hair. The silver circlet set upon her recumbent brow.

So peaceful.

Dead leaves scattered before Donovan as he approached. They sounded like large insects scuttling. Every movement was an exercise in agony. At last, he stood over her. He did not reach for her. He did not think he deserved to. The wind died and the devils and gods warring in the skies left them to be alone at last.

Rosaline. My dearest Rosaline. What have I done?

Her lips lay parted at their center; she looked like she was sleeping. He reached for his sword and unstrapped it. Only near her did it feel alien. With her close, he had no need of it. He tossed it aside. Hands pressed to the hard stone of her eternal bed, he leaned near, savoring her minutiae. Every lash. Every pore.

I miss you. So much.

He savored her, said his goodbyes, and then turned to go.

Three steps before he turned back.

He needed to feel her. Just one last time. Keeper save them all, he needed *to.*
Pivoting on his heel. Approaching one strained step at a time. At her side
again. His fingers hovering above hers. He brushed them, careful, as though they
might burn, unsettled by the cold within what was once so warm. He unclasped
her hands and held one. Cold but so smooth, still so comforting. He would give all
of himself to feel those fingers alive and tender on his face.

I did this. I lost you. I'm so sorry.

He drew her close. His lips near hers. Afraid to kiss this husk of what he
loved. Familiar still with her closeness despite the deathcool within. He leaned to
kiss her.

Just one last time. I don't deserve it but grant it anyway. I beg you.

His lips touched hers. He held her close as if she were the only thing keeping
him from plunging into a great chasm. And she was.

He was still thinking this when her eyes snapped open. Obsidian eyes, pupil-
less. Her lips opened, baring serrated teeth as sharp as razors. Her nails grew to
claws before he could react, and they skewered the flesh of his back and pinned
him. He tried to scream. It emerged garbled and wet from his gorge as her teeth
sunk deep into his throat and tore free his windpipe in a brilliant burst of blood.

14

The crisp exhale of the bay window embraced Donovan's body. He heaved upright and stared into the room. Staccato breaths burned in his throat. When his wits returned he groped at his sweat-soaked neck like a drunkard fumbling for his flask. No terrible notch in his flesh. No deep ruts from keen claws. Nothing at all but adagio cricket song and wafts of chimney smoke in his nose.

Just a dream?

If so, it had been more vivid than any he'd had in years. But no, it could not be. She *had* been there. He had stood aside her corpse as true as his hat lay next to him now. Every speck of him said this was so.

Keeper save us, could that have been a dream?

The footboard stared at him with ambivalence as he cleared his mind as best he could. When he felt sharper, he began to sift through his senses for peripheral details, a habit from childhood: the cold drip of sweat pooling in the dip of his jugular notch (*aim your downward thrust or arbalest bolt there, young Donovan*); the knitted bunch of the quilt beneath his body; the deepening sense that something was wrong.

He almost dismissed the last. *The mind is weak and flawed, Donovan. Much is not as you see it, and even less is how you remember it. Keep this ever in mind.* And he did. But this did not feel like paranoia.

Right now he was sure there was someone else in the room.

His eyes, still groggy, combed the shadows. The floor where Jana lay earlier was empty. The powder burn left by whatever godless ritual the Cleric had performed here stared up at him like a black, lidless eye. Donovan cursed himself. He'd been stirred from sleep by the beating of fly wings on a heavy breeze before. How could she have left without waking him?

85

Your mind truly is dying. You know that's why. The Cold is coming.

His hand drifted to the bedside without thought, seeking his sword, finding only air where it had stood when he first fell asleep. He peered over the edge of the bed. It wasn't there. Someone had come into the room, taken the girl and his sword, and they had done it without a sound. Slipping past a Swordsman, somnambulistic or not, was nigh impossible. And the person who could would not go far. He'd probably stay—

"Don't you move yer fair tender, lord, if it's yer life you value," said a voice from just past the footboard. Donovan stared hard into the darkness and saw his intruder at last.

I didn't even hear him breathing.

The man sat on a cherry pressback that was tilted to the wall, one deerskin-booted foot propped across his knee. He was a heap of coiled muscle and sinew, stubbled and leathery. A fierce chin thrust forward from his face, misshapen at birth or perhaps broken and improperly healed in the past. A thick black mane draped smoothly over powerful shoulders, a tight braid of it on the left side, corded at the end. He toyed with the gold lionhead dangling from his neck and smiled in the shadows.

Donovan angled his body a single degree and immediately came the *click* of a pistol hammer easing back. "You should drop that thought right now 'fore yer little honey snatch gets a knife in her."

Donovan froze.

"Good. Now let's have us a talk here, shall we?"

"Where is the girl?"

"First worry 'bout yer own self. Leave the girl to me," said the man as he settled back, pistol still trained. Donovan watched and listened; just as he knew the fool on the road was harmless halfwit, so he knew this was a man to be reckoned with, practiced and without the need for dumb luck or superior numbers.

(The Cold is coming. It's waking.)

The feeling, dormant for days now, appeared without warning. Donovan stilled himself against it, muscles slackened, fingers feeling naked without his blade. "What do you want?" he asked.

"Tell me somethin' first. Where're you from, stranger?"

"The North."

"From Kolendhar."

"There is no Kolendhar," said Donovan, too harsh and short. Now would begin the Game, something Master spoke of often, for it was a dark pleasure of his: the moments before violence where men pitted their skill of countenance and discourse against one another in a flurry of ego-laden stratagems. Whether this man was a simpleton like the rest of his villagers would yet be seen, but somewhere in the nameless dark of Donovan's instinct he sensed the ever-growing face of the Cold skulking closer, a red-eyed demon bracing to leap forward and overtake his mind. But it would not, not this time. Even if it would be useful, he would not let it. Let death come first.

"And where, pray-tell, did it venture to, friend?" The man with the lion pendant's finger gyrated against the trigger like a lover. His eyes glowed of something faint yet zealous.

"Destroyed, from within and without," said Donovan. Even as he spoke the truth his mind rejected it. His home. *Her* home. In his heart, he felt as if it would still be there just as he remembered it: the royal guard awaiting high up on the battlements with the king's standard swelling on a summer wind above their gleaming casques; the peal of silver trumpets mourning the dead but rejoicing the return of the living; the king on his gilded throne surrounded by the Black Guard. And her. It could all burn but for her.

(She's gone. It's coming.)

"Well, that's not a thing I'd expect to hear. And the ghosts 'n yer face tell me it's all the truth, too," said the Lion, thoughtful. He adjusted his gun, always pointed at Donovan's heart. "I'm known as Creel in these parts. Some know me as the Lion. Remember the names, you'd be well to."

The Lion. And here I thought I was making light of the man. He'll do it for me, it seems.

For some reason, the name made him think of his old friend Shadow.

"Now I hafta know. What's a Swordsman, who to hear it is without king or country, doing splashing around through the Drudge and come to a town like this just in the nick to scare off a Misty?"

"You'll have none of my business and I none of yours speaking this way. Put down the pistol and we'll talk like men."

"I have a feeling the pistol and yer feelings fer the girl are all that's keepin' us acting like men, pray it. She is a sweet piece of honeyloaf, I do say. And I'm the only one that's had a taste of it, mark me."

Not the only one, I'm afraid. Donovan smelled the lie of it anyhow. The man, Creel, may be a killer, but that did not put him above pettiness. "Was it everything you hoped for?" he asked.

"And then some. Yer a dirty pecker, you are. Now I say again: what business've ya got here?"

"Creel. I need you to take heed. You managed to get this far upon me and that is no easy task, so I praise your skill. That said, now is the time to listen to reason."

"A fat wad of ego the man's got in 'im there. Sneakin' up on you was a pinch easier than most, lost in whatever night terrors yer conscience was givin'. Now, are you gonna tell me or do I need to ask harder?"

"My business is my own. That's all you need know."

The Lion looked set to fire his weapon. After an effort he said, "Tomson's taken to you like a whore to a gangbang. That's just fine, pray ya. For all that's loved I cherish me a good fighting man well as the next. But there's a line too far fer anyone to dandy over, like of a Swordsman or not. And when I see me a man who stares down a soul-eating demon and wins, I see me something unnatural as the things gone ripped the Hamiltons to bits and ate their guts. And I also see me a man who needs to get 'imself out of town no later than tonight. And he can take his bitch demon cocksucker with him, fancy?"

"You don't want to do this, friend," said Donovan. "Give me the girl now and go on your way, and we can forget this ever took place. I'll be gone by midday or earlier. You have my word."

The Lion threw back his massive head and roared with laughter. "Yer forgettin' yerself now. Swordsman without a sword. What's that make you?"

The Cold swam inside Donovan's body. It was gaining strength, rending his muscles, soaking his vision red. He fought it back down. He could not let anyone see what he was. Not even this man.

Keeper save me. I beg it.

"Is it true what they say?" asked the Lion. The curiosity in his voice sounded genuine. "I heard of you folk. Swordsmen. Bred and trained for more years than a man kin count fer just the sort of unpleasantness been takin' holda the world as of late. And first sign o' the Misties you all tucked an' ran. That true?"

Donovan stayed quiet. It was all he could do to keep the biting Cold at bay. He was brimming with it. Any second now it would overtake him. It had waited for this; it was these moments when he lay vulnerable that it chose to rear and charge, some dissociative beast buried in his depths.

Stay back, I say. I do not need you.

"If it is," Creel continued. I find the whole of it a damned riot. Like buildin' a wall to keep an army out, then opening the gate fer 'em when they arrive."

"Where is my sword?" Donovan asked, a whisper. A hint of what grew inside rode his voice.

If Creel heard it, it did not seem to affect him. "Oh, I have it somewhere safe. Mine now. 'ppreciate it all. Always wanted me a Swordsman's blade. Never thought it'd be so simple to come by. Now, are you ready to march clear of this town or nay?" He leveled the pistol and leaned in, his eyes glistening in the dark like blue-hot coals.

"Take me to the girl and we'll leave together," replied Donovan, his body clenched tight.

Control it. Control it.

You do not rule me. You will never.

(It's coming.)

Creel nodded, cracked and peeling lips parting into a mongoose's grin. "Of course, yer lordship. Of course. Come with me."

He motioned for Donovan to rise and he did.

When they were in the hall, Creel paused, chuckling.

"Is something amusing?"

The Lion nodded, his smile fading. "You and yer ilk. All pomp with fuck all beneath it. That's what got you and yours killed, methinks, every last of them. At Dunnharrow and Kolendhar." When Donovan had no response, Creel continued. "I know yer type. Swordsman or drunk in an alley, makes no difference. The look in tha eyes tells it so, men the like of ya. Bet ya got someone ya cared for killed dead as these walls with yer cowardice. Maybe that's why yer dreams torture ya so."

Donovan stopped. "What did you say?"

"You'll have time aplenty to figure it on the road away from here. Move."

Donovan felt his body snap taut on its own. His fists clenched. "Tell me again what you said." He knew well already, yet the dark awareness within him yearned for any hold to grasp onto and leverage against so it might clamber up from his depths and take control. One more shred of insolence from this man would provide just that.

Creel replied with a sharp downward strike. The butt of his gun cracked into Donovan's skull and the Swordsman landed on his knees, wheezing. "I said move yer ass, Swordsman. Now."

It's here. There's no escaping it.

(Please no)

It's here.

The Lion watched Donovan gasp for breath, then grow silent and rise. A smile creased Creel's thin lips. He opened his mouth to speak, but whatever thought lay on his tongue was lost forever when Donovan turned to face him, eyes glowing red in his skull.

* * * *

The night air was dank and crisp beneath a lightless sky. Reaper's Moon, they called it. This was the time for it anyway; nothing was visible through the cloudy cerement cowling the world. For years Pleasantry had been cold and overcast and grim more often than not, yet for the past few months it was somehow more so, the cloud cover endless and the chilled air clinging and penetrating and never driven back by spring. Maybe the whole world was the same way. Vance did not know.

He stood in the moonless and starless black with Roger at his side and the girl gagged and hogtied at their feet while they waited for Creel. The glow of their lanterns crept into the field of catclaw ahead, tracing the scree to the northeast where the rocky terrain rose and became mountains in a steep skyward slope that was blacker than the sky. The lone guard atop the bell tower was fast asleep, his snores audible from here, and every so often a cough or chuckle could be heard from one of the hovels nearer to where they stood. Otherwise there was no sign of the townsfolk; at this hour they stayed ensepulchered in their huts, Tomson included. Nothing to fret about there; a well-fed man with a woman beside him was a man well occupied.

Vance eased his gaze from the mountains to the curve of the captive girl's thigh, partially bare through a tear in her trousers, the revealed skin smooth and tan. It was a runner's body for sure, firm and muscled just right, probably the finest his eyes had ever savored. Keeper pray, men had killed for less fine a bounty, and it was hard not to reach for her. He put his hand on the knurled leather handle of his mallet instead.

"What in the bloody fuck is taking so long?" asked Roger as he rocked on his heels.

"You bitch like a bird on her jam rag. Hush it," said Vance. Roger kicked at the girl and she squirmed and cried.

"Don't touch her."

"Why not? We're just gonna kill her anyway."

"No, we're not."

"Who says? You really think Creel's gonna take these two and pat 'em on thar asses and wave goodbye? Yer outta it."

"She's got the Taint in 'er. Don't want to be touchin' no matter what he's gonna do," said Vance. He ran his fingers through his hair; it was soaked with sweat despite the cold. They stood in silence as a low howl of wind rose and fell.

"Maybe the Swordsman got 'im. If thar was a tougher man 'an Creel it was that one. With his crazy eyes. Creel shoulda let us go fer 'im together."

"You woulda woke 'im up with a fart and we'd all be dead," said Vance. That *was* what would've happened, too.

The Swordsman's blade lay at their feet, thrust for half its length into the earth, its scabbard away in the field somewhere. The sword and its Drakkenbone hilt teetered in the breeze, the inset gem glinting. Vance stared at it longingly, wanting to draw it free and run. A blade like that would fetch him a farm, cows and all, in Raistlin or the like, he wagered. Maybe he could bring the girl, too, have a fine piece of tender to dip his wick with. *That* would be the life. Done and done.

He smiled, suddenly aware of the rot that had taken half his teeth, then felt the smile fade as his sense of loyalty overcame him. He owed Creel his life, and even if he didn't, he considered him a friend. And friends didn't steal each other's bounty.

Why do I have a conscience again? Remind me, pray it.

"You think he's gonna be a few more?" asked Roger.

"What does it matter?"

"Think we have time to take her over to the Hutch and break her in?"

Vance looked at him. He almost said no. *When in the Keeper's gray and trodden earth will you ever have the chance to hump a heap of ass like the one laying before you right now?* He weighed it out, then nodded. "Fine. Me first."

"Why do you get to go first?"

"Cuz I said so. Look out fer me."

"Hurry, would you? Fer the love of it all. If you get to it and I don't I'm gonna cut off yer nuts and nail 'em to yer elbow."

"Yer a poet, Roger. Bless yer mother."

"Fuck off."

Vance grunted onto his haunches beside the girl and lowered her gag. "You're gonna be needing that mouth a yers, pretty." Jana thrashed and kicked and pulled away from him. He struck her hard backhand across the face and she stopped. Blood filled the space between her lips. "Fight and I'll knock you cold and do what's comin' anyhow and then you'll have a throbbin' head well as a sore cooch. Now come here." He threatened with his hand again and she looked at him through her tears and then lay still. Then he lifted her into his arms and headed towards the Hutch.

"Isn't Mullville still in the Hutch, Vance?"

"Maybe he is. So what?"

"You gonna do all that with him watchin' and droolin'?"

"I'll do it in the back, all right? Shuttup for the love of it."

He took her into the gathering dark, the wind rising and causing the leafless trees overhead to thrash. When he was still just visible in the lantern light, something else moved in the grass, and Roger turned to where he heard the sound. "That you, Creel?"

Vance stopped and looked back at him. "What was that?"

Roger frowned into the darkness. "I heard somethin'."

"Creel?"

"I don't know, damn you. Come back here."

Vance cursed under his breath and headed back, Jana curled in his arms like a child. "Everythin's always gotta be ruined 'fore a man gets what he deserv—"

A grumble sounded from beyond the lantern light, and Vance felt the blood drain out of his face. He dropped the girl and stood frozen, lip quivering, gripping his mallet until his knuckles turned chalky. The sound of the wind made it difficult to discern any other noise. "Roger, what was that?"

Roger's face looked drawn. "Let's go."

"What about Creel?"

"You care that much?"

"That wasn't a Misty, idiot. Probably just a dog or somethi—"

Something large and dark hurled itself forth from the night and bowled Vance over to his back, powerful and smooth of motion, red eyes ablaze and its insane black hair rippling on the wind. It buried its teeth into Vance's throat and tore it open in a detonation of blood that looked black in the dim lantern light.

* * * *

Jana watched the man called Vance die, his neck twisted at an impossible angle, his empty eyes fixed on her. A scream built in her chest that could not pull free. The creature hovering over him savored his blood with a growl, then turned its burning glare towards her, hunger and instinct and something else wild and unknowable in its eyes. Realization swept over her: the creature was no creature at all. It was Donovan. He looked at her with blank hate, pupils and eyewhites swallowed by the demonic glow in his skull. Splatters of blood wound from his purple lips and over the strong cleft of his chin to soak his tunic. Another inhuman growl rolled from his throat as he turned away from her and towards Roger, who was racing towards town.

Jana tried to follow Donovan's movement in the dull light—he was so fast—and watched him draw his sword from the muddy earth, closing the distance to Roger in the space of a breath. Roger was yelling for help with his arms flailing when Donovan's blade whirred and cut a filament-thin line through the back of his neck. Roger's corpse dropped to its knees and landed face down in the scrub and poured blood onto the mudclay. It twitched and then lay still.

The Swordsman's hunched body bucked as a spasm overcame him. A fount of blood deluged from his throat, followed by a metallic *cling*, and Jana squinted to see in the dark, searching for the source of the sound. She found it at last: a medallion in the shape of a lion's head, made of gold, slick now with blood. Then Donovan set his gaze upon her and stalked forward, blood dancing the tempered edge of his sword, boots squishing in the viscera and mud, teeth working back and forth.

"Donovan. It's me," she said. Her voice quivered. He did not respond, but only crouched and held her by the throat, sword high over his head. She screamed as—

* * * *

The world stormed and stretched like a dream as Donovan held the snarling beast down. It gnashed up at him, eyes slatted and reptilian, long fangs drooling venom over its scaled face. It writhed, chomping inches from his hand. One bite would be his death. He felt the creature kick its legs out and strain to strike.

He must end this quickly or it would be ended for him.

He aimed the tip of his blade towards its throat and doubled his hold. The demon screeched fell consonants into the air, words from some dead tongue hidden in a throaty wetness. Yellow ropes of poison flew from its mouth and wetted Donovan's cheek. He brushed them aside, hoping the beast's spittle was not acidic, and then moved to end its vile life as—

* * * *

Jana held Donovan's wiry forearm with her last heave of strength. "Donovan, please! It's me. It's Jana." No recognition in those blazing depths. The sword levered forward, its needle-fine tip opening the slightest hole in her neck. A thin line of blood trickled forth from it. She gasped, mashing her back into the ground as if it might give way. "Donovan. It's me. You remember me. I know you do. You saved me. You saved me. I know you remember…"

Donovan's body tensed, arm coiled.

"Donovan, please!"

Nothing in those empty red orbs betrayed understanding or empathy or recognition, and Jana knew then that she was going to die. After everything she had survived, after all she had lost, the end of her story lay not in some far-off place with the Cleric slain by her hand, but here in the filth of Pleasantry, awash with the howling wind, killed by a Swordsman's blade.

And then, suddenly, Donovan withdrew. He slipped away from her before she could register the direction, his movements inaudible against the lowering call of the wind. He stood tall against the featureless night and drew his blade across his arm, carving a bloody line and screaming. His cry ripped through her, vicious and droning, until she was forced to look away. When it subsided she saw he was lying on his back, soaked in sweat, gasping for air. His eyes were human again. He sat up at length and dabbed at his face and lips with shivering fingers. When he saw the dark red remains of his victims crawling there, he stared at them without understanding for a moment, then emptied his stomach onto the field.

"Donovan?" she asked, her voice low, afraid that too strong a call might bring the demon back rather than the Swordsman.

He didn't answer.

"Donovan, please…"

He responded at last. Matting his mouth. Still bloody. He rose and severed the rope that bound her ankles and helped her stand, and it seemed to take every last bit of his strength to speak. "Come on. We have things to do before the villagers rile themselves up," he said, his voice cracked and weak, though his usual stony tone had returned.

Then Jana watched him glide noiselessly into the night. She hesitated before following him, tiptoeing over the corpses of her kidnappers, too afraid to turn and run from this thing that was not quite a man.

15

Donovan tore the bedsheets into strips and used them as rags to soak up Creel's blood, which had pooled in the hall and crept under the door to their room. Shag slept in the office behind the main desk, an empty bottle of stout clutched close, *The Cat and the Fungus Tree* open beneath his slavering mouth. Almost done reading, Jana noted distantly. He stirred, then returned to snoring as she eased the door closed.

Jana knew the Lion by reputation; by all accounts, he was not a man to be trifled with. Stories of his exploits in Eastfield and Pleasantry and beyond had made their way to the Hunter farm over the years, all of them overlooked by Tomson as far as she knew. Having met Creel now, she was sure the mayor had turned a blind eye to them because there was nothing he could have done about it anyway. The Lion was not a man you could best in a fight, or so the farmers and highwaymen claimed, so when Creel returned from other towns with sacks full of Boon or gold or weapons, no one dared ask where they came from or how he had happened upon them. By all accounts he would stay outside the town proper when he visited Pleasantry, holed up in a commandeered hut that was once home to the Smithson family. More than one tavern brawl had been attributed to him and his unbridled temper, and when the occasional wagon shipment or shiny bauble or town miscreant went missing, Creel's name was whispered nearly as often as the highwaymen who staked out the Thresh. But more than anything, Jana knew that Creel was a man that few in Pleasantry seemed to like, and for good reason, she wagered, given the company he kept.

She supposed none of that mattered now though.

Creel's corpse was near headless. His neck lay attached by threads of sinew and a slat of splintered spine. Jana tried not to look at those gaping eyes that would never blink again. They had been calm and confident eyes, right up until demon Donovan had ripped his head from his shoulders. Poor Lion.

What would stop him from doing the same to you?

When she lay to rest earlier she had felt safer with the Swordsman than she would have anywhere else on earth. Now she watched his every flinch like a frightened animal. She would need to get away the first chance she found. There was nothing else to it. Misties and the crazed witch-hunting simpletons of Pleasantry seemed mild compared to the ruthless bloodlust she had seen in the red glow of those eyes.

They wrapped the Lion's corpse in a shroud fashioned from a spare blanket, and Jana watched as Donovan dragged him to the edge of the forest and laid him to rest, covering him in willow branches and earth. He piled a tomb of stones about the body so the branches would not be disturbed, inspected his work expressionlessly, and then headed back. Then they did the same for the other two men. When they were finished, Jana wrapped her arms tight around herself and breathed deep of the muggy air. "I feel dirty."

Donavan raised his shoulders in an almost imperceptible shrug. "You learn to live with it. We'll tell Tomson of their deaths as we leave. They have the right to know." He trudged away into the night. "Come," he said over his shoulder when she did not follow. "I won't harm you. I swear on my father's soul, Keeper save it forever." When she still did not budge, he turned and held out his hand. "Please." The word carried not the usual tone of command he tended; there was a sadness there that ached her heart. Feeling as though her life lay with this decision, she forced herself along and took his hand. It was callused and cold.

Together they returned to the inn, their foul work motionless beneath the sod in the gray forest behind them.

* * * *

When they were settled in their room with Donovan again on the pressback facing the window and Jana on the floor against the bed, the Cleric's black mark between her heels, she raised the nerve to speak again. "You were going to kill me, weren't you?"

"I wasn't myself," he said. His sword lay across his thigh and bounced lightly as he raised and lowered his heel.

"Then what were you?"

He didn't answer. His eyes were glistening and unblinking.

When it was clear he would remain silent, she said, "Why are you looking for this man? I need you to tell me."

"I hope you're used to not getting your way."

"Then I'll be gone before you wake up in the morning," she countered, blood flushing hot on her face.

"If you run, everything wicked will be drawn to you as I said. If you truly believe yourself to be in more danger by my side, then by all means leave. Truth of it is, the only light at the end of this for you is with me. Questionable as it might be." Though he was still looking out the window while he said this, it was the most he had ever uttered to her in one breath and it took her aback.

"How do I know what happened out there won't happen again?"

He faced her then, reached beneath his coat, and drew a six-gun. It was well-kept, in better condition than any she had ever seen, with a grip trimmed in fine snakewood. He smacked it into her hand and then returned to his seat. "If you see me do anything like that again, shoot me in the head. Three times, if you can manage." She stared at the pistol like it was a creature that might bite her, weighed it with a flip of her hand, and took a moment to accustom herself to its feel between her fingers, which seemed frail next to its metal bulk.

"You were having a nightmare when they took me. I'm surprised you didn't wake up." She wondered how on edge he was; it might not be the best time to lean on him. *He's here telling you he'll protect you on the same night he slept through a break-in. You have all the right.*

"You should have called for help." His voice was as cold as his callus, through and through.

"I did." It was the truth; she had kicked and screamed his name and beat her fist against her kidnappers and not once did Donovan stir. "You just lay there sweating and muttering to yourself."

"Then you should have helped yourself." At last a hint of emotion. She preferred him angry to lifeless. He breathed deeply as if to center himself. "What did I say?"

"It was *your* dream. You should have been paying attention."

A gleam in his eye, dangerous for sure. He reeled it back and stepped to the scorch mark at her feet, tracing his fingers over it in a circle. Then he reached into his satchel and drew forth a wineskin full of white powder, which he spread across the black area and wiped with his palms until it was an even spread of the same diameter. When that was done, he sat cross-legged and folded his hands and stared at his work.

Minutes passed, and when nothing happened Jana said, "What are you doing?"

"Waiting."

"For what?"

"You'll see. Quiet now."

The part in her that her dad would have called the Mule dug in, ready to fight, but she managed to let it go and sat in silence.

They were still for what seemed like hours. When she was just about to nod off, Donovan leaned forward, excitement in his eyes. "Did you see it?"

She stared at the smooth mesa of white granules at her feet and saw nothing. "What am I lookin' fo—"

"Shh!"

He reached into his satchel again, this time producing a small shard of quartzite, which he polished on his sleeve and held above the center of the powder. Then he dipped the tip of the quartzite a fingernail's length deep and held it motionless there. Soft mutterings grew, breathy and unintelligible, from his lips as his eyes folded closed in concentration. He kept the quartzite still during this despite the slight sway of his body—it looked as if it had been thrust through the floorboard for how moveless it remained. Then, when the incantation was complete, he eased his hands from the shard and brought them back to their original folded position, leaving it to somehow stand vertically on its own. One more soft word that sounded like *ranata* to Jana's ears and the shard began to spin. She stared at it, jaw slack, all thought of demonic Swordsmen or would-be rapists or dead family gone. All that was real was the light.

It coruscated from the center of the shard, brilliant streaks lancing through her vision. She closed her eyes but it was no use; the light might as well have been needles sticking through her eyelids. The pain caromed around the inside of her skull and she fell over with a cry. A glimpse of the shard told her it was moving by inches, still spinning, still erupting with its blinding glow. Behind it, Donovan's face remained expressionless, his fingers interlaced, his lips forming dark syllables as he called to whatever force had been summoned to do his bidding.

Then, at last, the glow faded to a soft orb and dissipated. The shard, which had reached the edge of the powder, wavered back and forth like a drunk before toppling over.

Jana's muscles ached as if she had just exerted great effort. She pushed up to a sitting position. "What in the Black was that?" she asked. Her voice sounded as weak as her body felt.

"Of all things, it is magic I fear most, I promise you. But that was the one bit I've learned. I pray I never need call it again."

"What did you do?"

He nodded towards the powder and she looked at it. A map had been carved into the powder by the shard. Mountains and forests were delineated in fine detail. Through the center, a thick line curved and wandered. Donovan pointed. "When the Cleric was here, he summoned magic to see something. His destination, most likely. What I did was call back what he found. This is the path his powers drew for him. To Pal Myrrah, perhaps."

He withdrew a leather-wrapped journal from his satchel and a quill, which he dipped in a small inkwell, and sketched the shard's map. The scrape of the nib against the parchment mesmerized Jana as she stared. When he was done with his sketch, Donovan climbed past her and lay on the bed, this time with his sword across his stomach, hand on the hilt. He tilted his hat over his eyes and didn't say another word.

"What are you doing," asked Jana.

"Sleeping. You do the same. Tomorrow we leave."

"I can't sleep on the floor. You should take the floor."

"Sleep well, princess. There won't be a bed under you for a long time, so get used to it."

He snored a moment later.

Anger ignited within her at the sound, strong enough to make her body shake. The feeling was as repulsive as it was familiar. At least this time it had reason to appear, even if its intensity was misplaced. At times her anger erupted for no cause cause at all, forcing her to blame it on something, anything, to save face. Often that something had been Cory, much to his frustration. Those sourceless surges, appearing unbidden and lingering for far too long, made her question her very nature. *You've been that way since you were in swaddling clothes, Jan,* said Mum in her mind. *Just one of those peculiarities.* That was certainly a word for it. Whatever it was, it was an aspect of herself that she hated, and one she could not best no matter how she struggled. Could something so vile be a permanent part of her, built-in from birth, never to be mastered? It *felt* like it existed outside of her, as much as the trees and the rivers and the birds.

She took a deep, centering breath.

No, she would not believe her anger was some essential element of her being; it *had* to come from somewhere else, some trauma she had suffered that was blocked away in a hidden grotto within her mind. People didn't just wake up and feel angry enough to break bowls and beat pillows without good reason, did they?

Get used to it...

In her mind's eye, she leapt at the Swordsman and grabbed him by the shirt and told him in no uncertain tone that he was never to speak to her that way again or he'd regret it forever. But no, that would be to waste this feeling. If, in all of the madness of this day, one comfort had come to her, it was that her anger, in all its unpredictable burning glory, could be aimed somewhere at last, directly at the man in the white robe. Right between his two hellish eyes.

She spent most of the night at the window, watching the dark draw of the forest and the mouth of the switchback beyond just visible in the black from this height. In her mind, she saw armies of malformed creatures sweeping across the flatland with honed shivs and women's skeans gripped loosely in clawed and misshapen fingers, each of a single thought and purpose: to sink their blade deep in her flesh and drink of her blood.

Or worse, to welcome her home.

II

THE PILGRIM ROAD

1

The pilgrim called Daley Rogen entered the grove with a collection of dry tree branches in his arms and a stalk of wheat between his teeth. The autumn air broke cool in waves across his cheeks, moist with the promise of a burgeoning storm. Beneath his feet the brome crunched and cracked and the sound rang crisp and pleasant in his ear. The air was light, yes lord, so very light; his body, rotund at best, felt light; even the branches in his arms felt light. A light day, yes it was, and rejoice it! At long, long last the fire-breathing heathen of a bitch woman was too far behind to lash at them with her acid tongue; at last the uncertain gloom of ten nights gone was near a close; for yes indeed, fair children, the Keeper's own garden, the last refuge of the White, the greenest pastures this side of Garland, the resplendence of the town called Pleasantry, which Daddy Wormach had told Daley of in his youth, lay two dozen hefts away, a featureless apparition some-where beyond the great scarp just to the north. It was far enough of a trek to intimidate him if he gave it a moment's thought. He didn't, instead applying his mind to arranging the campfire stones just so and building a pyramid of branches from his harvest.

As he worked, Daley heard a sharp clang of pots behind him and knew that Ellica was readying for dinner. He found her kneeling on a rolled blanket, her dress gathered close, looking like a nesting hen. Her bright smile warmed him. Nothing too beautiful was she by the reckoning of the masses, but to him she was the most stunning pixie in the world, a waif once stricken with the hert and scavenging the Harrows, now a picture of femininity. Keeper had blessed, that was certain. Blessed and prayed it true.

He went to her and kissed her neck and she drew him close with her thin fingers and rubbed her nose against his. "I can't fer tha life in me think of the name o' that song Mum used to sing during Harvest. Do you recall?"

"What was it about, fairest?" asked Daley as he fixed the last branch just so and leaned back to regard his work.

"Somethin' to-do about rabbits and a coyote and a hut made o' rock out in tha forest."

He whistled a tune and her face lit up. "That's it. Run of the something or other, I think."

It took Daley a few goes to light the tinder. When it was smoldering, he poked it beneath the firewood and stoked the growing flame until it blazed into the night sky and painted the trees and the stones and the scrub. Then he rubbed his hands above the fire and took a seat beside Ellica.

"I still can't believe what you said to Moriney," she said with a smile.

Daley nodded, his fingers interlaced across the bow of his stomach and his feet crossed at the ankles. "Way I look at it is this," he said. "There's two things a man needs to do when confronting a wicked bitch of a stepmother, no disrespect intended, my finest dear."

"None taken."

"One is, be respectful, all bitch-name-calling kept aside, mind. Two is defend his honor. Problem is sometimes the two o' those things don't quite mix, as I know you've reckoned," he said.

"You never told me what happened after ya said all that."

"Do ya care to listen?"

"What else am I gonna do but stare at bloody trees and grass while the stew simmers?"

Daley crossed his arms. Since growing into manhood, it had become his philosophy that just the right amount of pomp rang like music in women's ears, and so he pushed out his chest and said, "Well I'll tell you now, seein' how we're on the brink of Pleasantry with no more secrets to keep, wife-to-be. That was when she told me I was either gonna get back in the kitchen and scrub up or I was gonna be limpin' along the road without a home."

Ellica chuckled; it rumbled thick and hearty in her breast. Mannish, one might call it. He loved the sound anyway.

"So then..." he trailed off for effect.

She took the bait and leaned in. "Go on."

"So then I asked her if dad saw her limpin' like she just got fucked by an oak tree when she came home from Marshal Winter's place."

She erupted in laughter and he joined her. "Oh my good heart, I shouldn't be laughin' at that," she said, and then proceeded to laugh with him until they were sweating and teary-eyed.

Soon after the stew was ready and Ellica poured them servings. Daley nearly sunk his face into the broth and inhaled until he could feel the spices from the West End tingling the back of his brain. Fineness this was, made solid. "Go on, you labored over it," he said to Ellica.

"Watchin' you take the first bite is the love in it for me, Dales."

So he did, and they ate every drop, and afterward they lay by the fire under a quilt Ellica made during Harvest, holding each other in the brisk night. Daley thought of making love to his woman without speaking of it, but the thought of laying naked in the cold wet pine bed with Keeper knew what crawling up and about their nooks made his skin itch all over. Any plans of passion discarded by that prospect, they lay in place and stared at the dying flames for what seemed like hours, sleepless but content. Embers rose, silent and aimless, towards the clearing in the trees overhead, their leafless boughs encircling the black waiting mouth of the sky like teeth. No sound was audible beyond the *snap* of the tree sap in the fire, and to Daley the lack of animal and insect sounds here was unnerving.

The moment the awful chill closed its fingers around them, they both shuddered, bumps rising on their arms, but did not move.

"What was that?" asked Ellica. Her jaw jittered as the words left her mouth.

"I'm not sure," said Daley, rising and stoking the fire back to life and scrubbing his hands over it. It did no good; whatever this cold was, it was in their bones now.

Daley stepped to the grove's edge in a show of courage, and now the feeling of eyes on him, peering from the black, was unmistakable.

"It's probably the breeze, foul may it be. Or an animal. Small, I hope," he told her over his shoulder. "Let's get to sleep. We need morning behind us and fast."

Ellica nodded, but her gaze remained vacant as it combed the shadows beyond the firelight. Warmth crept its way back into them as they lay back down, Daley with his fingers in Ellica's hair, her with her bottom scooted against him and her eyes distant as they watched the campfire dance.

My how that does feel fine as can be.

That thought lay solid and sure in Daley's mind when he spotted the shape standing motionless at the hem of the forest.

He choked on a gasp and faltered back. Ellica, who had been halfway to sleep, woke confused and swept her hair out of her eyes. "What is it?"

Daley's hand raised like a marionette's, clunky and imprecise, and he pointed.

There in the trees stood something shaped like a man. Or was it? If it was true, he was the biggest man Daley had ever seen; judging by the tree beside him, Daley guessed his height to be seven and a half feet. In the gloom of night the man's silhouette was barely visible, and the only details Daley could see were the wicked curve of a spear-like weapon and two narrow, ghostly eyes peering from the crypt of his shadowed face. A robe, gathered and flowing, hung from his shoulders, and when a soft breeze wound through the grove the robe remained still, as though it was a carving rather than cloth.

"Hello there, stranger," Daley managed. "How do ya this fine cold night?"

The man in the robe did not move or answer. Daley thought he could spot motion within the clawing dark where the man's face should be, but he couldn't be sure of it. "It'd be nice to address a man greetin' ya, fine sir."

The man in the robe still did not move. It took everything Daley had to stand tall and keep his voice level. "You gonna talk, or are ya lookin' fer trouble, tell it?"

"I overhead the story of your stepmother," came a voice from the darkness, as quick as a snake's lunge; smooth and soporific, enthralling and inescapable, it poured into Daley's ears as if the man's lips were but inches away.

Daley stared with his head cocked and his lips ajar.

"As they say in the wild parts of the country, a whore's a whore even whilst dressed as a nun," said the man in the robes.

A horrible cold sat in Daley's stomach, and the man's tone was so dissonant with the air he exuded that Daley kept two fingers on the hilt of his dagger. "Heard all that, did ya?"

The thin white scar of the man's smile cut the shadows.

"Glad you kin see reason then. Always a good omen in a man, isn't that right, love?" Daley said without looking at Ellica, who he knew was not listening. "You headed for Pleasantry, then?"

"I've just passed through, in fact."

"That bugger Tomson still head there? I've heard he's big as a bear, that one. Where ya headed?"

"Northward. On the tail of the wind, you could say."

Those *eyes*, pray the Keeper. They weren't looking at him or through him; they were *consuming* him as if he was a fat, roasted Daley-steak. He wanted to run more than he had ever wanted to do anything in his life; the fear burned so fiercely that he considered leaving Ellica behind in a mad dash, curse him to the Black for thinking it.

Reason with the man. Keep things from escalating, Dales.

"We're lookin' to be married. Hopin' to find a place to settle down there. Grow some crops and kids, Keeper pray."

"Well, that sounds just fine. Plenty of space in the world. Nothing but."

"Pardon if I come 'cross as daft, but I've got ears pretty well regarded and I didn't hear a lick of you coming. Where exactly did you snake in from?"

"Delivered from darkness, and barely so. Much like you. Or maybe we have not escaped it fully after all. You feel it lingering as well, don't you?" said the man in the robe.

"I gotta say, fella. Yer a man who can confuse with yer back and towards."

"You've a keen mind in you, Daley Rogen. I can smell it."

Daley shriveled up inside at the sound of his name passing between those thin pale lips. "How long you been sitting watchin' us? Bit of the creep that is."

The man stepped forward suddenly, leaving his staff behind and gliding closer to the fire, which lighted the high rise of his cheekbones and the deep sink of his eyes, those violet stones pooled in the cavernous sumps of his skull. His fingers, bony and knotted, drew back his robe with inhuman grace. The firelight shied from the man's face as if that energy, weightless and shapeless and misunderstood by men, was as frightened as Daley. "Let me ask you," the man in white said. "Do you know why it is said only the dead know peace?"

"You have a habit of waxing stupid in front of strangers?"

"Dance and dance, my friend Daley. It does no good. Answer."

Daley gripped his knife tighter. "You playing games?"

"Never games, my friend."

"You gonna leave in peace after we have our little talk?"

"I was planning just that."

Daley thought it over. He felt like a boy of seven or eight at Studies. Keeper this and Keeper that, love the White, embrace it, the Black is nothing, blah blah. "Because life's just one big tribulation till yer done. Keeper takes ya if you do right and there's yer peace."

"Do you think that choice belongs to Him? Does peace exist only in His presence?"

Daley felt a slick coat of sweat between his palm and his dagger. He slipped it an inch free before he knew what he was doing. The man in the robe either didn't notice or, as Daley was more certain, did not care.

"The truth of it is, and this may frighten you, that there can be peace without death. If you can find someone to give it to you."

"I don't know what yer talkin' of, friend, but I'm not sure I like the feelin' you give out."

"Please," said Ellica suddenly. Daley realized she hadn't budged an inch since the man in the robe revealed himself. "Please leave us as you found us. I'm beggin' it."

That smile again. In the firelight it was somehow more unnerving.

Daley worked up every last bit of courage he could muster. "We didn't cause any offense, stranger. You go on yer way and everything'll be just fine."

"I intend to. And it will be. You're right."

"I mean it," said Daley. His dagger slid free with a tiny, unimportant ring. From the corner of his eye he could see the tip dipping as his hand shook.

The man in white gestured with his gnarled fingers—a movement so slight Daley nearly missed it—and like a puppet strapped to a bucking ass Ellica's body snapped straight, arms pressed to her sides. Daley tried to call out, to run, but he was shackled now by an unseen force. It felt like *skin*, like physical hands clamped onto every inch of him, as though corpses had burst through the earth to hold him fast.

Another gesture and Ellica glided forward, her toes dragging in the dead pine needles. Daley couldn't see her face, didn't *want* to, to know the truth of it. Keeper save their souls, he didn't want to.

"Shh. Shh. Be at peace," said the man in the robe. That smooth voice seemed all that existed while he spoke, and then as it dissipated into the flutter of the surrounding trees the world seemed to reconstitute in its wake. He gestured once more, the movement yet again so slight Daley thought he might have imagined it. "Be at peace…"

Ellica was not at peace. She screamed, a sound of pure agony. The woman he loved's arms convulsed, her breasts heaving, her back undulating. The *snaps* of her delicate frame twisting and writhing filled the clearing and stamped the fire crackle mute. Her body lunged forward, her screams deepening, wet and guttural. In horror, Daley watched as her fingers and arms elongated, a bony hump forming beneath her dress, splitting the fabric from her back. Back and forth Ellica of Wrestlertown thrashed until her clothes hung in tattered shreds from a hunched and mutilated body.

Then, at last, she straightened and stillness held the grove.

The man in the robe regarded his work with an artist's satisfaction. He took Ellica's face in his hands as if she were a child. "Peace…"

Daley tried one last time to escape, but his legs and arms would not respond. All he could do was stare as his once-lover lunged for him, her red canine eyes aglow, her serrated teeth glinting. A sharp flame of pain flushed through him as she sunk those teeth deep into his chest and ripped backwards, extracting his blood and his life with one violent lurch.

Daley Rogen's final scream drowned in a wet gurgle.

The trees swayed and the fire burned, undisturbed.

All the while, the man in the white robes watched with a smile.

2

Tomson wore a deep frown as he listened to Donovan's tale. Jana stayed away, hunkered in the corner, thinking that maybe this wasn't such a good idea after all. She had heard much about the mayor of Pleasantry, most of it complimentary, but she hadn't spoken five words to the man in years, and her feeling was that they were all going to be thrown in the Hutch along with Mullville to rot and starve for a few days. After that, who knew what would be brewing in this half-barbaric town.

When Donovan was finished, Tomson stared at his folded hands, deep in thought. "That boy Creel has been trouble since he was five years old sticking nails on chairs with broach sap during Studies. Never like to hear of the violent sort of death, I don't. But if fate had it out for one a tha folks hereabouts, it was that one."

"Was he known in these parts? He seemed to think he was," said Donovan.

"Known enough. The sort of man who's got friends in the hills, if you catch my meaning. I'd watch myself."

"Do we owe requital?"

"Not to me, Donovan of Kolendhar. And not to Pleasantry. I've not spent much time with Jana there, but I knew her father and her stock and I believe my ears when I hear tell those boys had rape and murder on their minds. But all the same, I'd appreciate knowing where they're buried. Not keen on who'd attend, but a man deserves a funeral no matter what he's done with his life."

Donovan shook his head. Jana imagined the look on Pleasantry's collective faces when they unearthed men ravaged by a wild beast rather than an angry Swordsman's blade, spine-sliced Roger aside. This lie would come back to them. She was sure of it.

"In the forest somewhere. They've had their funeral, and it was a quiet one."

Tomson seemed to be all right with that, grim as his face looked. He took Donovan's arm. "Luck to ya, Swordsman. I still count you as a friend. You two are welcome in my home any day."

Donovan nodded, and in his eyes shone a semblance of gratitude mixed with what Jana perceived as feigned indifference. Without a word, he motioned to Jana to follow as he passed her on the way to the door.

* * * *

Grampy stood on the edge of his porch with his aged hands resting on his cane. His skin felt frail and dry as he took Jana's fingers and pressed a small tin into her palm. "Take it with ya, girl. My secret stash."

"What is it?"

"Open and see."

And she did. Inside were aged and dried Boon leaves, about half a tin full. "I can't take this," she said with a smile, tears fighting their way up.

"Might as well be givin' ya my soul ripped from my chest, girl, so don't argue or I might just change my mind, pray it," said Grampy. His voice, creaky and wonderful, wavered as he took hold of her shoulders. "How's yer mind?"

"Numb," she said immediately. That was the best word for it. She felt numb, inside and out.

"That's it lookin' to do best by ya. Mind ya come back from that place when time's past. It's hard, Keeper knows. But remember yer folks love ya still and need ya ta move on."

She nodded and hugged him tight. He felt frail enough to break.

"Oh! Nearly let it slip my greasy nog. Stay put now!" he said, and then hobbled back into the house. It took so long for him to struggle through the door that Jana wondered if it might be tomorrow before he reappeared. But in moments he did return, shambling awkwardly, his hand cupped to his chest. "Hold yer hand out, Jana Hunter." She did, and he held his fist above hers and let dangle a small pendant looped onto a thin metal chain. It was shaped like a tree, molded from silver, and it looked as old as Grampy himself. "What is it?" she asked.

"Belonged to my wife. A long time past," he said. "Couldn't find a ring to save a mule so I sold my shoes and bought this from gypsies near two lifetimes ago."

"This I can't take. Keep it," she said. Her heart ached.

"Now you listen, girl. Since you were small enough to bounce 'pon my knee I told ya I would see ya married one day. Half tha reason fer it was to give ya this as an endowment. But Keeper knows where yer headed now, and I'm startin' to smell the end comin'. If yer to have this, I wanna put it in yer hand myself while I still have tha strength to do it."

She looked into his eyes, which were soft sky blue and more full of life than men a third his age, and she thought of what those same eyes had seen and how different the world must look to them now than it did to her. She took the pendant from his shaking hand and hugged him again and held him tight. "You're the only family I have anymore. I'll come back soon, I swear."

Grampy nodded, but his eyes said that he did not think it would be so. "Good luck to ya, girl. Keeper bless."

She looked back once over her shoulder and saw the old man, standing shorter than her by a head, raise his hands and his cane overhead in farewell. *That's gonna ache him for days.* Then she turned back to the road and told herself that she'd see him again one day. *Course you will, Jana. One day soon. You'll see.*

The people of Pleasantry gathered to watch them leave with looks of disgust and hate. Muttered curses made their way to her ears. She tried to ignore them.

"Good riddance, demon."

"She better not come this way again, pray it true."

"Paul Tubbs and the boys were gonna take care of it if she didn't up this morn."

Donovan waited at the edge of town where the Drudge picked up and cut through the Shodan. Jana clasped the pendant around her neck and set it just so.

"Ready?" asked Donovan.

She nodded. "Can we stay on the road? I don't want to see my house."

The frown he generally wore turned farther downward. "We'll see. Come on."

Much was on Jana's mind, things she would have spoken of in a time now lost. Strongest was the feeling this place seeded in her, one of safety, as mad as that sounded given what had almost happened. A voice told her that some sort of force was at work in Pleasantry, keeping the worst of the world out, for the Dwellers and Blood Demons often attacked homes at the farthest reaches of this region, hers now among them, but never the town itself.

Never Pleasantry itself.

But that was roundabout of the self-deluding kind and bore no weight on their journey, and so Jana Hunter said nothing as she fell in behind the brooding Swordsman. Together they headed towards the forest, the hilt of his sword nodding against his back before her, his hat pulled low on his head, that great duster sweeping out behind him.

Jana gave Pleasantry one more look, and then it was consumed by the trees in their wake.

3

Jana followed behind the Swordsman until late daylight spilled from the cloud well atop the dim and distant mountains into the pocked arroyo land northwest of Pleasantry. She knew this part of the road as well as her backyard. To her right lay the big redwood stump where she and her brother had once staged junk plays, and fifty steps beyond that was a mossy boulder scurried over by rainwater most of the year before it froze to rime in the winter. She had sprained her ankle near that boulder once when Cory was five, and he, mighty Cory, slayer of imaginary foes—all four feet of him—had held her hand the whole painful way home.

Torturing yourself, Jan? Great. Keep up with it.

She knew it but didn't care. At least it made her feel something.

Donovan stayed ahead and never looked back. The click of his equipment and the wet sounds of his boots in the mud were his only conversation. Jana's fingers crept inside her tunic and traced the Cleric's scar, that clammy, ropy path that felt like it wasn't a part of her. But it was, oh yes. Somehow she knew that vile thing, which felt like an massive centipede burrowing beneath her chest, wasn't going away any time soon. What exactly it was doing there in her depths, well, that seemed to be information the Swordsmen felt no compulsion to divulge. A part of her was convinced that no further threat lay at the end of this road, that the scar would not grow outward and inward and consume her in some nightmarish way. The rest of her knew better. There were times already when she felt something wrong, as if a critical element of her body was being nudged off balance. To what end? She prayed that Princess Jana on her redwood stump was right.

Nothing to trouble over at all, sweetheart. You just rest your little head right down and take a nap and you'll feel better when you wake up.

Her hand brushed the snakewood grip of the six-gun Donovan had given her. It bounced on her hip with each step, the length of rawhide looped through the trigger guard and across her shoulders. Her ripped tunic had been sewn hastily with mismatched thread, but the sleeve was still torn and her shoulder lay bare and it made her feel naked. When Donovan had first told her to wear the gun like that, she had asked him if it might go off. His answer was to stare at her like she was a child and laugh his odd laugh and then walk away. She still wasn't sure if that meant yes or no.

The iron chamber felt cold through her pant leg, like an importunate child jabbing her and whispering, *Still here! Might hafta blow a man's brains clear soon.* She watched the back of Donovan's head and wondered if she really could, all things at a point, put a bullet through him. She decided that she wouldn't like it, but should demon Donovan reappear with bloodlust on the mind and that feverish glow in his eyes, she'd do it without hesitation.

The silence of her companion gnawed at her as the day drew on. The sun was hunkering on the horizon when she finally broke the quiet. "Are you just going to march along there and not speak?"

"What do you want to talk about?"

"Where are you from?"

"The North."

"Kolendhar?" The name of the fabled city felt weird on her tongue, thought of often but rarely said. Caer Kolendhar, home of the Swordsmen and more, the last bastion of mankind's scarce regality and sophistication and culture. Whenever things looked too dark and grim for the folks in Pleasantry, when the air smelled more rancid than usual, when shoes disintegrated and bellies ached for the fortieth day straight, hope remained that somewhere in this foggy shithole of a world the folks at Kolendhar were fast at work fixing up the future. That no one Jana had ever met had *been* to Kolendhar never arose during these motivational talks; discouraging details were easy to overlook when it came time for survival.

"Forget Kolendhar. There's no one there to help anyone now," said the Swordsman.

"What do you mean?"

"Exactly as I say. Don't fall too far behind."

She hesitated and then followed, not liking what his tone implied. "That's not true. Grampy told us the stories about Kolendhar were real."

"Do you trust him?"

"Grampy's too cranky to bother lying."

Donovan chuckled; that weird, throaty sound.

"Tell me what happened to you. How did this begin?"

"When we have space to breathe. Now is not that time. Keep up, now."

He hastened his pace and didn't speak again, and Jana stopped herself from pressing the issue. As much as she owed him her life, Donovan the Swordsman was no doubt the most irritating man she had ever met. Mouth closed and face red, she turned her attention to the ground passing below her and fantasized about socking him in his dense all-knowing head, or perhaps pulling his arm off and beating him with it. That would be fun, blessit true.

When Donovan stopped again she nearly ran into him. "What is it?" she asked.

He turned full circle, head tilted as if smelling the air. He faced the forest and watched it through squinted eyes. "It's that way?"

Jana looked around and recognized where they were at once. *How'd you manage to dull yourself so deep you didn't see your own plot approaching, girl?* "Yes," she said, swallowing a hard sob; Mum lay somewhere to her left in a bloody tangle of entrails. Dad, too, more than likely.

Donovan nodded, eyes still leveled ahead, and then proceeded into the forest towards the house. When Jana realized what he was doing she gave chase and took him by the shoulders. "No, wait!" The desperation in her voice surprised her. He turned to face her and his glare made her recoil. "Please don't make me go there."

"I have to see, and I can't leave you alone."

"I can't. I really can't," she said. And she meant it. She felt like she might crumble from the inside. In the back of her mind she was aware of the scar throbbing, rhythmic, as if it held a pulse.

Something odd happened then. Donovan placed one worn hand on her shoulder, more tender than she would ever have guessed him capable of being, and squeezed. "It'll be all right. You can stay near the fringe. But I have to go. Be strong, girl. You have it in you. I can see it," His eyes did not waver. "All right?"

It took every bit of whatever strength Donovan thought he saw for Jana to nod in agreement. Then they were off into the Shodan, the Hunter Estate visible through the clearing ahead.

* * * *

Her first thought was that the place smelled different.

As the planks of the old shed peered through the trees, Jana felt any hope that this place could ever be her home again slip away. The Mist was gone, off to whatever grisly vault the Dwellers bided within when they were not slaughtering helpless children and loving parents. That was all well and good. If they could smell her as Donovan insisted, they'd be back soon. The only thing worth bothering over was the present. Jana knew that whatever happened, looking towards the lee of the knoll just east of the house would not be part of it. That was where the picnic duvet lay, stained with cold stew mixed with blood and flesh, her Mum's beautiful eyes (if Misties left the eyes— for all Jana knew they were the tastiest bits) gazing skyward until the crows came or the earth reclaimed her.

No, she would not look at it. Not even a glance.

Moments later she looked anyway, her gaze drawn to that massacre like a fly to putrefying meat. She thought—it could be her mind doing a dance on her, now—that she could make out the white corner of the duvet towards the western edge of the knoll, but that was all. The fear in her stomach turned to stone and sat stubbornly under her breasts with its arms crossed and a difficult expression on its face.

A stubborn rock with a face and arms. I've gone clear mad, Mum, clear and straight into the deep of it.

From here she could review her entire life in flashes, from toddling near the clothesline in the backyard to pouring a stockpot of cold water onto Cory's head by the larder. Each memory brought tears that anger fought away. Time to dig in and bite down, as Grampy was fond of saying. *Bite down hard girl, or no one's gonna respect a thing ya do in life.* And so she did.

She kept a wide berth as they traced the perimeter of the field, pausing for Donovan to crouch near the windrow and smell the hay. When they stopped again he said, "It happened in there?" He indicated the shed. She nodded without looking. Again she felt that ache deep in her womanly place. Her anger doubled up in response. "Did you see him leave?" Donovan asked.

"No. I told you, he was gone when I woke in the morning."

"Will you come in with me?"

She shook her head. If the man in white's stink wasn't reason enough, she'd also see the picnic site on the way out. "No, I can't."

Donovan looked like he might argue, instead said, "Stay where I can see you. I'll only be a moment."

She watched as he eased open the shed door. The hinge squealed—Dad had meant to fix that this week—and then the Swordsman disappeared inside. When he was out of sight, the growing sense of watching eyes put Jana on edge. She ignored it and stared at nothing until her vision blurred and her mind quieted. She waited.

When the Swordsman reappeared his hand was easing from his sword. He nodded as if to ask if everything was all right, and Jana nodded in return.

The south end of the house opened onto a porch, overlooked by a fanlight that Dad had fashioned himself. That had been just last summer, and how everlasting and wonderful life had looked back then. Once-white lintels held the roofing in place, peeling now, never to be touched up again, lest some industrious stranger wandered by. Maybe they wouldn't mind cleaning up the mess by the knoll, too.

Does making light of it ease the pain? Fool of a girl.

The voice inside her was right: with every unsaid quip, her wounds opened a little more.

"No sign of your father," said Donovan in that way he had. *Yer Dad's dead somewhere, too,* his tone mocked. Jana nodded and kept her eyes downturned. As they walked she could smell a hint of Mum's stew hanging thin in the air and her stomach grumbled. Never again would there be a brisk summer night enjoyed with her family. Nevermore would there be feasting and laughing and games played together. Never. The word had been hard to comprehend when she was a child; her few years of maturity beyond that hadn't helped much. She had always thought of Cory as so much younger than her, as naive and unworldly, but truth told he hadn't been far behind her. Had he been childish? Yes, she supposed, but his nature was the sort a man held into maturity of his own accord. A feature, not a shortcoming, Dad had called it. The thought brought with it some more nevers: Cory would never see manhood, never enjoy a family of his own, never find a woman to love, never do anything ever again.

Never.

Jana decided she hated the word.

Donovan stepped onto the porch and looked in. "Keep your six-gun ready."

Her fingers hesitated before she brought it to her breast and pointed it skyward.

"Have you fired one before?"

She shook her head.

"Keep it pointed up like that unless you mean to kill something. Be ready for it to buck when you fire. Hold your breath right before you pull the trigger. And don't waste bullets. I only have a few left." He seemed to realize his words were sliding right through her mind without resistance. "If you need me, call out."

She watched him enter the house and tried not to blink.

* * * *

You stand the line before the Black, at all times its breath on your neck. This is where you thrive. This is where instinct serves you. This is where death awaits, dealt from you. Mayhap to you. This is your home.

The Hunter residence was more barn than house. Wool mattresses stuffed with hay lay between what might have once been stables. The larger, to Donovan's left, sat elevated to knee-height on a redwood frame. Plain, but nice enough. A night table to one side of the bed with dancing intaglios and a marble top looked out of place. Fine cabriole legs. Scavenged from the Shodan or somewhere else, to be sure. Atop the marble were trinkets: a figurine of a bear, three miniature casks, and a stack of hollow coin-sized metal discs. At the edges of these were a hundred evenly spaced points, like malformed cogs. Something had once been written across the top of each, but was worn off now. A pile of old shoes, most hole-ridden, lay here, rusty tools mounted on the wall there—more remnants from before the Shift. A stuffed bear with one eye. A blown glass candelabra with half its arms shattered. In every corner things were stored and stacked. One thing was apparent: The Hunters were hoarders.

In the opposite stable lay another, smaller bed. There was no third. One for the parents, one for the kids to share. Donovan stepped lightly across the dustcaked floor, which creaked despite his best attempts at silence. At the far end lay a sooty hearth with a bronze kettle depended from above. Not used much, from the look. The window on the west wall allowed in a bar of sun, leaving the rest of the place in shadow. A swarm of dust churned up on its own below the window, sudden enough to set Donovan on edge. He watched it settle before he moved again.

Electricity pulsed in his veins; in all truth, it had from the moment they arrived here. He was close, so close he could smell the fetid stink of the man. His every morsel (even the Cold, watching from the back of his mind) knew it. Was it simple excitement? No. There was something else, too. Sadness, perhaps. This place, as much as he thought it barely suitable for a horse, had been home to the girl as Kolendhar had been to him. It was too easy to forget that. He let the thought linger until it stayed put in his mind. Would he still be human if he rid himself of empathy? He wasn't sure. Keeper knew, he was afraid to find out.

He noticed the sound just as he was returning from his thoughts: *Tap. Tap. Tap.*

Fingers ready on his sword, he moved towards it. Already his mind was at ease, its place of rest, its home position, frozen in readiness. His senses spread out, drenched in the details around him, aware of every spider, every fleck of dirt, every birdcall, every aroma. No matter how often he fancied himself master of his mind, the training always taught him otherwise. *You are not a man, Donovan. You are a sum of all that has come before you, ever changing, ever shifting, at all times accruing and shedding. Take heed of what the past says.*

No need to remind himself; he could no more avoid the past than he could will his heart to stop.

He spotted the source of the sound from fifteen paces away: something dripping onto the first step of the loft ladder. He crouched beside where it pooled and dipped his finger in. Blood. He already knew this, had known it from across the room, but went through the motions anyway. A man couldn't smell blood from that distance. That was impossible.

The loft steps creaked as he climbed. The rest of the Hunter food store lay here, serving as a sort of scullery. Corn husks strewn about like shed snakeskin. Trampled slices of tomatoes and grapes and, between those, blood pools an inch deep. He stepped from the ladder and his boots splashed in it. Across the walls, once whitewashed, were bloody fingerprints and peeling gouges, as if someone had been dragged about and had tried to grab ahold of something. A table by the window in the rear hosted an assortment of cutlery. Half of a melon rotted in the fading light, never to be eaten.

Donovan sloshed to the center of the room. One of the corpses must have been eviscerated here; the bowels of an entire adult body would be required to fill a room with this much blood. There was no sign of any flesh, at least that he could recognize. Consumed as likely as moved, he reckoned. He frowned into the puddle beneath his feet, a lead ball of certainty settling in him. Before he had time to question it, he was crouching. His fingers dove into the bloody mess at his feet, probing. Hay. Stone. Then something round and solid. He extracted it from the gore and wiped it clean. It was a coin, two inches across, marked with runes. A triangular hole in the center peered up at him. Of all the small treasures the Hunters had left behind, Donovan knew this one was not theirs. This came from something else.

Him.

He knew you'd be here. He left it for you. He wants you to follow.

The realization took his breath away.

For so long he had thought himself the hunter. It had never entered his mind that his mission might be just as the Cleric wished. Could it be so? He wanted to believe it was impossible. The Cleric's ideas about the matter were clear from the beginning.

That is what he wished you to think.

No. He might know Donovan followed, but he feared it. He must know the fire raging in the Swordsman's heart.

He knows it. That is what he wants. He's stoking it now, as you dawdle here. Stoking it from afar and laughing.

Donovan frowned at the coin. It stared back indifferently. Well enough; at least something could bear witness to his sour look.

If he had been downstairs when the noise from the rafters began, or had he not been enthralled by the Cleric's coin, or had Jana stood beside him to keep him focused (or distracted; sometimes they were the same), he may have noticed the figure above as it descended, serrated claws thrown wide, keen razor blade teeth bared. Ask the folk at the Kolendhar Temples about fate and they'd happily spout sermons detailing all the ways the Keeper's mechanizations knitted happenstance and randomness and intent and action and inaction together into a perfect cosmic symphony; Donovan's nature, as unromantic as Rosaline had claimed, kept him from investing in such thinking. So while the elders might look at a pile of shit and see the meaning of life, what happened in the next fraction of a second was, to Donovan, not luck or the Keeper's smile but the summation of a lifetime of training.

Somewhere between the moment the creature plunged towards him and the delivery of its strike, a switch threw within the Swordsman. That switch, a hair-trigger like that of Jana's six-gun, lay ready always when his mind was present. But it was in moments like these when something else, the Cold, maybe, kept watch instead with honed eyes, ready to activate it. Not a trickle of his scrutiny was turned anywhere but inward, pondering the coin and the Cleric and these last months of his life one second, and in the next the slightest register of... something... Perhaps the displaced air skimming the hairs of his neck as the creature's sinewy body plummeted towards him, or the ghost of a shadow barely perceivable in the ashen dark near his boots—if any knew the answer, it was not him. But Donovan Maltrese would not have time to contemplate this until after his body stooped on its own and tucked into a roll while the creature's claws cleaved the air inches away.

His sword was drawn before he was upright. The thing before him could once have been human, although it was difficult to say. Its face was misshapen and elongated, like a melted wax statue, and the flesh of its chin bunched and wrinkled about its throat and shone there with a coat of saliva, which seeped from between long spicular teeth. Its claws, if that's what those ossified blades were, seemed to be extensions of the finger bones rather than nails; they were soaked with blood that had dried to a dull maroon. Its eyes were white-less and iris-less, two glistening blood red orbs with catlike pupils staring, unblinking, from their centers.

Before he could ready himself the creature lashed out. Donovan's sword flashed and whined, parrying, discharging sparks that died like drowning souls in the blood at their feet. Faster than any human could move, the creature swept away a counter-attack and slashed downwards with grotesque hands, and as Donovan evaded he caught the scent of the beast's breath. Not much in this world could disorient the Swordsman, but something in that awful scent was *familiar*; that was the only way his mind could sort it. The stench rocked him off-balance and his defenses opened for the space of a breath. It was long enough; the creature threw itself towards him, bowling him over. Donovan was aware of his feet leaving the ground an instant before the barn wall disintegrated beneath the force of their impact, and then he was falling, splinters and silage raining about him.

White agony flowed through him as he struck the ground and tumbled to a halt, and there a bright pain blossomed in his shoulder. He struggled to rise, but his body was unresponsive, and for a moment he feared he had broken his back.

What a glorious end that would be for you. Ripped to shreds while sprawled out in the tomatoes and the carrots and the mud.

Then the iron in the holds of his mind braced once more, willing his body to obey, and he strangled the pain before it could overtake him. He rose to a kneel, his duster draped behind him, his hat aside somewhere, leaving his hair free to blow back from his face.

From forty paces he heard the creature's feet adjust against the second story plankboards, heard it push off in a fierce leap, watched its unblinking eyes seep blood as it landed in a fluent crouch before him. In the red burst of the dying day the creature's claws appeared more like daggers than parts of a living thing, its fangs more like narrow ivory brands than teeth. The demon took one ponderous step towards him and hunkered with its claws cocked back, its doughy face drawn up in a snarl.

Donovan kept his eyes on the creature's as his fingers probed the ground for his sword. He spotted it in his periphery, halfway between him and his enemy. Resolve grew in the Swordsman then; if a race is what it came to, then a race it would be. As a boy he'd been fast, once made fun of as lanky and uncoordinated, later wiry and precise to a fault. But the boys he had defeated at the festival races two cycles gone were human (and some clodhopping, to boot), and not curls of savage energy like this thing before him.

Before he was ready, he saw that his time was up. The creature charged—Donovan blinked and it seemed ten paces closer—and then the Swordsman threw himself towards his blade, the battle cry of his forefathers roaring from his lips. Even as he made his first stride he knew he was too slow; by the next, he knew that he would die here, that his warrior's life and all its pain and sacrifice and discipline would be squandered in a futile skirmish—or a trap; he would never know now. The creature was upon him by the third step, and Donovan felt his eyes close on their own as he bent forward, never slowing. His last thought was of Rosaline: he imagined her waiting for him, her arms open, and a sense of calm filled his heart.

At just about the moment he expected to die, a sound like a thunderclap echoed into the switchback. The sound came so unexpectedly that Donovan's feet slipped forward from under him and he slid to his back with his wind knocked out. He looked up in time to see the creature collapse face-first, its bulk spun fully around, bright blood spilling from its shoulder. It wailed and cawed and growled and rose grasping at its wound, blood slopping between its claws.

Jana was there, standing just beyond the creature's hulking form. She watched it turn to face her, six-gun thrust before her, a fire in her eyes.

Donovan's voice broke as he called to her. "Shoot it!"

The creature watched Jana, its breaths labored. Blood crawled from its eyes; the damn thing was crying blood.

But Jana did not fire again. Her finger crept away from the trigger, the resolve in her face draining, and her jaw swung loose as her eyes turned suddenly vacant. In all his years, Donovan had never seen the fight drained from someone so fast.

She took a step forward.

"Dad?"

And suddenly the entire world flipped onto its head. Donovan could almost see it, the ghost of a man he'd never met, the warm smile and kind eyes and callused hands of a weatherworn farmer who had loved his land and his family and especially his oldest child, a girl named Jana Hunter.

Jana's fingers trembled and the gun lowered.

Donovan rose to a crouch. "What are you doing? Shoot it!"

She didn't seem to hear him.

"That's not your father anymore, Jana," said Donovan. *And what difference does knowing that make?*

(It wasn't Rosaline, either.)

A tear traced Jana's cheek. Her breaths burst short and labored from her chest. But she wasn't moving. Keeper save them all, she wouldn't be able to aim fast enough if the thing went for her.

"Daddy, I know you're there. I know you can hear me. Please," she said, her voice rasping. "Please…"

For the barest moment Donovan thought he saw the creature's body unclench, its claws lowering, and he wondered if perhaps it could hear her somehow in the depths of whatever devilry was at work here. Then, without warning, it sprang, its claws positioned to remove Jana's beautiful head from her neck, and the Swordsman knew he would soon be next.

But something in Jana Hunter, who Donovan decided had not until this moment squashed a bug or skinned a rabbit in her life, stepped forward, raised her hands, and set her aim true. She screamed and levered back the trigger and cordite blew a round out faster than any eye could follow. The report thundered into the sky, and Donovan watched as the rear of her father's head exploded into a cloud of blood and grey matter. His body landed with a *thud*, crumbling into a twitching ball with a fleshy hole the size of a fist flapping against his nape.

Whatever reserves kept Jana standing gave out then and she dropped to her knees. Donovan regarded her and thought of his father the last time he had seen him, colorless and stone-faced, laying in an open tomb and deluged with rose petals, and of the hunger for human contact that had burgeoned within himself then, never to be assuaged.

When the Swordsman rose to his feet, he intended to take Jana into his arms and hold her to his chest and whisper that things were all right, even if they weren't. Nothing was all right anymore. Not one bloody thing. But instead he stepped to his sword, which he flicked up to his hand with a deft shift of his toe; Shadow, the captain of the Black Guard, had been fond of that flourish. "Stand back," he said quietly.

Jana did as she was asked, her eyes abandoned of comprehension. She faced the broad tract of the Shodan, still on her knees, and did not turn towards her old home again, even when the Swordsman held the blade of his ancestors on high and removed her father's misshapen head from his demonic body.

"Come on," he said, his rough hand outstretched.

"I can't," said Jana. She was as hollow as he had ever seen a person.

"We need to go. We'll camp soon and rest, but we must move."

"That was my father."

"I know."

He thought she might stay kneeling until her strength ran out and then lay wherever on the plain she might fall and remain there until she died. But somehow that girl, who he had thought a weakling and a fool but in folly, followed his lead away from the Hunter Estate with a haunted look behind her eyes, and together they navigated the forest and returned to the endless muddy stretch of the Drudge.

4

Jana looked up at the black wash of the night sky and the starlight fighting it, like shards of diamonds speckled across a great velvet canvas. She thought of how her dad used to take her out to Peddler's Reach, a narrow and tall crop of rock south of the switchback where the night sky was all they could see. There they'd lay out on blankets and make shapes from the stars until sleep took them, lulled by cricket song and the dying crackle of the fire. She tried to make shapes now, but all she could see were dark creatures glaring hungrily at her, or dead bodies with questioning eyes staring forever downward, wondering what had happened to their truncated lives.

Those thoughts and more staggered through her mind unchecked, and she watched them go by without taking full notice; though she sat now by the fire in a clearing a heft north of her old home with Donovan the Swordsman from Kolendhar, she might as well be back in the field watching a monstrous reconstruction of her father leap towards her like a bloodthirsty borecat. Watching and killing. She could still sense the trigger against the pad of her finger, could still smell the powder of the expended cartridge, could still feel the heat of the muzzle against her thigh as her arms dropped loosely to her sides after the killing round had been fired. At the same time she watched her father on Peddler's Reach smile and point at a cluster of stars just as his head burst open like an egg, spilling his brains onto the rocky floor.

Goodbye, Dad. So long. Oh, and there's an elephant.

The Cleric's scar felt hot and swollen beneath her tunic. Every time she shifted and her clothes moved against its insectile outline she had to force herself not to scratch it. Somehow it looked worse now than it had even just this morning. What she would not give to be able to pull her skin off like filthy clothes and burn them and start over again. And there was something else, too, even more revolting: pray the Keeper it was just her mind run amuck, but every once in a while, when her attention was elsewhere, she thought she could feel the scar *move*, as though it was wriggling beneath her skin. She had considered telling Donovan this twice now, and each time had decided to keep to herself. The last thing she needed was to act the fool in front of that one, the Swordsman whose existence she'd have doubted a few days ago, and who was now her only friend, if a dubious one.

Better stop the complaining, brat. One's better than none when it comes to friends.

She supposed that was true, even if her singular friend just *had* to be a high and mighty Swordsman who would run her through as soon as look at her. Those in need were those without choice.

The long pastoral stretch of fog-shrouded land about them should have been peaceful and reassuring to her, the slow weave of the meadow grass in the wind soothing to watch and the Maidenhair flitting above it and behind it all the dead, clacking branches of trees that were less hardy. When she was a girl, long before the Misties reappeared to hunt the families on the outskirts of Pleasantry, it would have been. She recalled again the times when she had wandered the Drudge alone at night, younger than Cory had been when he died, not a care in the world beyond what her imagination conjured.

Now you could be eaten between your dining room and the jakes.

That people still held on, fought, tried to settle and build a life, and that children yet were born into this world was a testament to either man's infinite durability or his endless stupidity.

"You look like you're trying to figure out how to build a fox from bird parts," said Donovan without looking at her. In his hands was the coin from Jana's house, which he had been toying with and studying without comment since they set up their shoddy bivouac. Its bronze verge glowed in the throw of the fire. The Swordsman gave it one more good look and then placed it away and massaged his wounded shoulder.

He offered no other conversation, and Jana felt a trace of annoyance. The man had plucked her out of Pleasantry and dragged her through the Shodan without sharing a single detail about the Cleric or what would take place when they found him, and yet still he dare lay there with his smug two-classes-above-thee look and his condescending eyes and not even talk to her like a fucking human.

She kept all this inside as she said, "Three days ago I was sitting by the larder with Dad talking 'bout traveling east, where he heard tell a city existed. We'd all go together. Even Dog, if we could get him to walk a straight line without chasing jackrabbits." Her voice sounded soft and even. *Buncha crock*, Grampy would have called that. Tears tried to climb to the surface and betray her, but she stamped them down. Truth told, she had no time for them; controlling her rage was about all she could manage. "Now they're all dead. And I killed them."

The last felt like a lie as it left her lips. But was it? Did Donovan himself not say the Cleric's mark would draw the wicked near? To her and those around her. To Cory.

"The thing you killed today was not your father anymore," said Donovan. His tone always danced that line between insult and compassion and it drove her crazy.

"Then what was it?"

"A Blood Demon," he said, lip curling with distaste.

"How could my father have become that thing?"

Donovan shook his head. His hat lay to the side and his hair was drawn up in a ponytail, which suited his face. He might even be handsome if she let herself see him that way. He kept his sword balanced on his thigh, inches from his fingers, ready for a fight, maybe with her if she pressed him. "I'm not sure."

The silence after his words felt thick. She fought it away, comforted more than she'd admit by conversation. "When you find him, then what? Will you kill him?"

"I don't know if he can be killed."

"What, then?"

He turned to her, his eyes flashing brilliant green even in the warm clutch of the fire, and then faced away and did not answer.

Jana felt the Mule dig in. "I want to learn to fight," she said. And she did. She wanted to learn to kill. If even a Swordsman feared the

Cleric, then little Jana Hunter was a long, long way from ever hoping to do this murder herself. But she would. Keeper witness her thoughts here and now, she would stand over his corpse and smile.

"No you don't. You want to get out of this alive. That means keeping your wits and staying your course. Not fighting."

His tone stung. Every time he spoke, she felt more like a child. "You never thanked me for saving your life," she said, meaning it to be sharp.

"You should not look for thanks yet. At least not until we see the end of this. You could well grow to regret it."

"You talk like you know everything, but you hardly know a damn thing past your nose when you're not looking down it."

"Next to a child like you, I may as well know everything. Now close your mouth and go to bed." He never looked back at her. The worst part was that he didn't even seem angry.

When Jana was six years old, she would gather small glass bottles scavenged during her sojourns into the arroyos near the house, left by passing travelers hailing from places where such things could be crafted. She had spent that entire summer collecting them, her dad's satchel slung low over her shoulder, empty on the way out, sometimes two or three bottles in it by nightfall. By early autumn they had filled the cubby over her bed, dusted and rinsed and arranged just so. She had planned to give them to her father as a birthday present, for Dad loved his trinkets nearly as much as he loved his children.

All would have been well were it not for Lana Preole.

Lana was an ill-tempered child with hair the color of rust and crisp blue eyes that saw much and cared for little—except wreaking havoc on Jana Hunter. It took only the barest hint of the bottle collection's existence to compel Lana to action, and the youngest Preole had snuck onto the Hunter Estate the very next day, her freckled cheeks no doubt flushed and bulbous with laughter, her eyes empty and dead.

When Jana returned home that night, she discovered her bottles had been crushed into a pile of sand.

Her reaction had been first quiet sadness, then red hot anger.

The time between then and her arrival at the Preole house was a crimson blur. One minute she was standing over the debris, and then Lana was on her back sobbing while Jana pounded a closed fist into her red-haired head again and again until she sprained her wrist doing it.

That was the first time the rage had visited her as far as she could remember.

It was worse now.

She leaped at Donovan, slapping and swinging, blows connecting to the head and the throat, taking hold of his shirt with white-knuckled fists. He grabbed her by the shoulders and held her in place, expending little effort in the process, which only enraged her more. She continued to kick and lunge, launching clumps of dirt and pine needles into the air. From somewhere came the sound of tearing cloth.

When her anger subsided, he looked at her. "Are you finished?" He sounded genuinely curious. Reluctantly, she conceded. He watched her with a parent's disappointed frown as she sunk to the ground, and then examined his torn tunic.

Then she saw the scar.

Keeper save us all, it's just like mine! The thought was half exciting and half terrifying. "You have the same mark as me," she said. It was true, only his was much larger, a terrible growth that encompassed his chest and encased his shoulder in a veined and twisted spaulder.

He ignored her and worked his injured arm.

"Does that mean he made love to you, too?" she asked, waiting for him to hurdle the fire and plant a boot square into her smart mouth.

Instead, he took a seat and sacrificed a pine needle to the fire. "I'm afraid not. Congress is not a requisite for this disease."

"What's going to happen to us?"

"We are cursed," he said. Simple. He might as well be reading a recipe for pie.

"Like what happened to my father?"

He shook his head. "You'll start to go mad. People will look like monsters to you. Even children. Voices will keep you awake through the night for months on end. Eventually, you'll forget you ever saw another human being and you will live in a world of madness for the rest of your years, slaughtering beasts wherever you go, never knowing whether you just killed an innocent man, woman, or child, until one day you die or someone kills you."

At last Jana's anger vanished. The image of the Swordsman, blade in hand, mouth full of a dead man's blood, eyes aglow like smelters, burned in her mind.

"I must find him before that happens. Every day I lose a part of myself, and I don't know how much longer I can hold out."

"And this Cleric can stop this from happening?"

"I don't know. But I do know that no one else on earth can. So we go north, through the Wastes, to Pal Myrrah." His tone said in no uncertain terms that the conversation was over, and he returned to his reclined position, the strange coin in hand once more.

"What is that?" asked Jana, indicating the coin.

"I'm not sure. It's familiar but I can't place it. He left it for me to find, I think."

"Why would he do that?" she asked. The notion of the Cleric wanting them to follow in the most direct route possible enthralled her darkly. Something else was going on here that the Swordsman would not admit.

"I'm not sure," said Donovan. "We'll find out the hard way, come time."

Jana nodded and tried to be satisfied with that answer, wondering when that would be and whether she'd be ready.

* * * *

In the deepest dark of the night, she awoke with the Swordsman still fast asleep nearby. She was certain now her scar had moved; she imagined it exploring the nether regions of her body like some sarcous tentacle that crept and probed and then froze in an unassuming position whenever a prying gaze set upon it.

For some reason that idea didn't disturb her as much as it should have.

Donovan still slept—she thought so, at least—his breathing short but even, his hat pulled over his eyes, his sword cradled close like a lover. She wondered if that was all a trick to lull her into a false move so he might spring to his feet and clobber her senseless and tell it was all for her own good. She decided that was not the case, no more than it had been back at the inn when Creel had made his move upon them unawares. Whatever horrors gripped the Swordsman's mind in his sleep, then and now, they left little room for the real world.

Go to sleep, Jana. You'll be useless otherwise.

Dad's voice? Mum's? Her own? She didn't know anymore.

She tried to lay still and wait for morning, preparing for what must be done, praying she'd have the chance to do it without Donovan's meddling. She didn't want or need his help or his condescension; soon, either by the Cleric's death or by losing her mind to madness, she wouldn't need help with anything ever again. One thing was certain, however: if she was going to meet one of those ends, she'd do it on her terms. First, though, she'd see her family one last time.

She forced her eyes closed and hugged herself tight.

She saw her dad smiling at her as she drifted back to sleep.

She smiled back.

5

The Swordsman woke in the wan morning murk and bolted upright. The lightless chill crept under his duster and tunic and drew bumps as his eyes focused on the girl-sized imprint left in the hoarfrost. The girl, he saw now, was a touch knock-kneed and walked a bit like a duck; not something you'd notice if her legs were before you to distract. The charred framework of the pyramid he'd built from ironwood still smoldered, the back end of which had collapsed inward sometime during the night without waking him. Not hard to imagine the girl sneaking away then, for wherever his dreams abducted him to disarmed his senses and unhinged his mind. He felt such crushing disappointment in himself from this, from how far his mind and instincts and senses had eroded, that it took all of his willpower to stifle despair.

He aimed his attention at the footprints leading back the way they had come and knew immediately where the girl had gone with her light-as-dust steps. If he was already this compromised, this relieved of his hard-earned faculties and instincts, then he may as well abandon his quest now and spend the rest of his nights imbibing keffa and smoking spidergrass or whatever other spiritual analgesics he could commandeer. At least then he'd enjoy himself on the way through the Maw Gates, and perhaps he might hold Rosaline again, too, if only in narcotic fantasy. If all went well, his mind wouldn't know the difference.

Enough of that, fool, said a voice that wasn't his. The Cold's, perhaps.

He wanted to leave the girl to her devices and head northward alone. She would only slow him down once they reached the Wastes. A fighter that one was, almost to her detriment, but natural inclination could not replace hard-won wisdom and ability, and there was no time for him to teach her adequately. On her own she might still find a way to survive given no other choice, provided she stayed clear of Pleasantry. Leaving her behind would be the wise thing to do; he knew it and his low voice knew it.

He went so far as to douse the fire and take a few steps away from the Hunter farm, secure in his decision, already steeling his mind for the march ahead. But before he had left the clearing, visions of what might become of Jana Hunter should she cross bandits or Dwellers or worse snuffed out his apathy and stopped him cold.

He looked back at her footprints and held his breath.

Weak in waking as well as asleep. What purpose do you serve? Remind me.

It was Master's voice. The voice he loathed; the voice he yearned for even now, which he kept secret to all—sometimes even to himself, if that was possible. He flushed it away and strapped his sword across his back, comforted by its weight and motion.

Thinking himself a fool, he followed Jana's tracks into the forest.

* * * *

In the dim Golgotha of the Swordsman's memories, the moment shining clearest was of his father, standing atop a crest of soil, the corpses of a hundred peasants dead of hertweed spread before him like a rich child's unwanted dolls. He remembered standing in the dying amethyst twilight, the cold embrace of Year-End sneaking under his lambswool coat, and watching the fourth strike of steel on flint burst the torch into living flame.

His father held the torch overhead, muttered the Keeper's prayer—Donovan thought now it was for himself more than the slain—and hurled it onto the bodies below. The oil dousing the dead caught fire with frightening intensity, heaving yellow-white tendrils strong enough to singe young Donovan from thirty paces. He watched the bodies change from sick remnants of human forms to something chunky and coarse and black before his eyes.

One in particular held his gaze: a girl about his age. One instant she almost looked alive but for her ocher skin and unblinking bloodshot eyes, and the next she was enveloped by flames. Her hair went up first, its dull blonde tangle igniting into a brilliant orange; like watching pine needles burn, he recalled thinking. He watched her vacant stare and gaping mouth as they caved and shriveled.

His father trudged past, shoulders slumped and head down. The weariness in his voice was striking. "Pray them, Donovan. Pray them straight to the Black, Keeper will it. Pray hard, for your ancestors' sake."

And with that he headed back to the road where their horses waited, anxious, tethered to a lone banner pole flying the standard of the king. That was then, so long ago it seemed a picture drawn by another's hand rather than memory.

Now he emerged from the Shodan with that same reek of burning flesh and hair thick in the frigid air. Ahead, a towering plume of black smoke rolled into the cloudless sky, riding the wind towards sunrise. Below, the Hunter house and shed were in flames.

As Donovan drew near he saw things he would remember until his dying breath: the near-black remnants of mother Hunter's blood where her entrails had laid yesterday; the dark crust of hardened demon spittle where father Hunter's head spun after Donovan's cut; and, most of all, the image of Jana Hunter, amber hair light on a faint wind, who had all by herself gathered up the pieces of her dead parents and brought them to one spot, standing true with a makeshift torch moribund in her trembling hand while she watched her past collapse inward into flame.

Donovan almost came to her side to watch with her. Still that trace of something in him, the opposite of the Cold. He wanted to hate it; wanted to and failed. Instead, he wheeled and returned to the edge of the forest and waited.

Some moments in life were useless unless faced alone, and for Jana Hunter, this was one of them.

He found a fallen tree to settle onto and drew his sword onto his lap and traced the hilt absently, lost in deep thought.

* * * *

For Jana, the world swam in a slow, detached pirouette, devoid of substance or weight. In her hand, the torch, crafted from a shred of Dad's shirt and a fence paling, slipped from her blood-soaked fingers. She was aware—so barely that it was a stretch to call it so—of the hot lick of flame on her face, but the thought of catching a burn did not concern her. She was aware of the specks of blood near her chin and across her cheek, small as ant tracks, from where a piece of her Mum had slipped from her hands and splashed in the detritus, but she paid it no mind. The important thing was that she hadn't cried. Pray it and bless it true, she hadn't shed one tear. They wouldn't have wanted her to. Grampy was right about that. He was usually right.

Sheathed at her side was Dad's old dirk, left from his fighting days. It's flared boxwood pommel shone in the firelight between her fingers, the brass collet bracing its cap cold and wet with condensation. It was the only thing she had taken from the house.

She watched until the last of the flames burned out. When it was done, only a spread of floor, somehow still in rank, was identifiable, fanned vertically in a semi-circle that reminded her of a rowel.

She had rehearsed leaving in her mind, readying for the brutal hurt she knew she would bear. And she did. But, in that odd way life managed, there came also a modicum of peace. She wished Cory were here, alive if the Princess could have it, dead at least to return to the earth. But this was good; good in the only way it could be. Good as she could pray for until the Cleric's blood crawled the old steel of her father's blade.

As she turned back to the Shodan, she caught sight of the Swordsman. He watched her come, his stare grim and his mouth pressed into a neat, tight line. There was something in his eyes, though. Maybe sympathy. More likely disdain. But it could have been the first. It could have.

Without a word, he turned back towards the Drudge and she followed.

The ebbing smolder crawled skyward in wisps behind them.

That a Dweller would be crossing their path very soon did not enter her mind.

6

Jana stood twenty paces from a gnarled ironwood with her dirk's pommel gripped overhead and her eyes narrowed to slits. She measured her aim, breath held, body coiled, mind brimming with spiritual warrior-speak of the sort she imagined Donovan recited before battle: *Be one with the dirk. Feel its weight. Savor the earth. The wind. Feel the peace before the violence.* Abandoning that, she wound and threw so hard that a blast of hot pain burned in her shoulder. This attempt improved on the last: the dirk struck the tree pommel-first before clattering to the ground.

She supposed actually hitting the tree was a good first step.

"It's not suitable for throwing," said Donovan absently as he rolled some Boon into his pipe and lit it.

"What if you had to?"

"I'd never have to."

"You can't know everything that's going to happen in a fight. I don't care how *Swordsman-ee* you are."

"You can if your eyes are open and your senses are outward and nimble," said Donovan. Pipe jutting from the corner of his mouth, he stirred a pot of dewdrop stew and breathed deep from it, his eyes rolling back as though the rising steam was a drug. He had smuggled the stew from Mary's pot just before they left Pleasantry—with her blessing, he claimed—and two days on the road had done little to diminish its taste.

Jana rolled her eyes as well, readied again and adjusted her aim, compensating for the extra rotation she had seen last time. She hurled with a cry and watched the dirk *thud* against the trunk longways. She growled, more frustrated by Donovan's regard in her periphery than by her failure.

"The right tool for the job is half of it," he said with that faint curl of a smile that raised her hackles.

Jana retrieved the dirk, backpedaled, and threw. Then again. This time it tore a chunk of bark free but did not stick.

"Good thing I gave you a gun."

His chiding made her see red. She considered marching over and planting her heel into his smug grin; instead she snatched his spoon, the quickness of her hand surprising both of them, and swallowed a mouthful of stew, a more effective attack as the Swordsman was not keen on sharing. "Good as fresh," she said, hand over her stomach.

The Swordsman stared at her with mirthless eyes. Jana stared back.

Then, without a word, he rose to his feet and vanished into the forest.

"Where are you going?" she called after him, but he gave no response. The forbs and the waving leaves of the forest swallowed his dark form moments later. *Fine. I'll do better without you watching over my shoulder.* She'd be able to hit the center of his forehead without looking by the time he returned, and then they'd see what quips he had for her. Still, she worried he might have just abandoned her for good.

She kept to her practice until the sun burned hot behind the cloud cover and warmed the midday air, the moisture hanging there thick in her every breath. After countless tries and swear words that would have made her father blush, at last Jana managed to make the dirk stick, the blade piercing less than an inch into the gray runnels of the ironwood's bark. Donovan, of course, was nowhere to be found. That was for the best, she discovered, because after a few seconds the old dirk slid free and landed blade-down in the twisted rootstock, mocking her.

Donovan reappeared soon after with a brace of hares slung across his shoulder. "These are for you," he said, monotone but clearly grumpy.

"What about the dewdrop?" she asked just to prickle him.

"Not for you, princess. Be thankful for what you get."

"That's a shame," she said, easing onto her throwing spot, dirk grasped tight and high. "I was gonna trade you for some Boon, but you're past the need of it I see."

He plopped the hares down, frowning. "And where would you find Boonleaf? *Pray it.*"

"Yer starting to sound like a local. Better watch yourself. Might get lynched when you get home. Or fail a test of the written word, bless it true," she said, wearing a self-satisfied smile as she threw again without success. She saw Donovan ready a retort, then watched him clam up and turn to skinning the hares instead. "You shouldn't dress meat where you camp. Not healthy," she said, pedagogically as she could muster.

"That's a bunch of boar dunny. Who told you that? Your father?"

"Yessir."

"Meat's fine long as you keep the gizzard and such apart and cut the rest on metal rather than wood. Carrying juice-soaked timber is what will make a man ill."

"Whatever you say, mister. Always right you are, I've learned it," said Jana as she threw again. The dirk ricocheted off the tree trunk and spun into the scutch below. "What in the bloody fuck!"

"If you're so bent on throwing that thing," said Donovan, "try a loose grip. And stop thinking of where to release. Think instead of the target and let the bottom of your mind do the hard part."

The Mule wanted to argue and buck its hinds, but Jana silenced it along with her pride. *Enough with that. This is what you wanted from him, isn't it? Isn't a lesson worth the sting?* It was, she realized, even if it meant conceding defeat to a contest she could not name.

Her fingers eased as she found her stance, her breathing smooth, her mind clear of technique. With a deep, centering exhale, she reached out with her senses and tried to *feel* the target (she made that part up). Then a coil of energy, readied in her marrow and muscles and sinew, unbeholden to consciousness, loosed on its own the way a bowstring snaps forth, the dirk flashing in the sun as her arm whipped outward and her fingers eased, needless of command from her mind. The dirk whirled and its blade cut the air with a whistle and, where it had clawed into the old bark without purchase countless attempts before, this time it stuck true and held in its crags, swaying slightly with its momentum and then growing still.

Jana turned to Donovan with a smile she meant to be proud, but knew looked smug instead.

"Good," he said. "Now when you can do it more than one time out of a hundred, you'll be ready for anything."

Her smile melted. "You know, I've never in my life met a man as full of shit as you. Loose grip and all that can go right up your ass." She imagined burning a hole into his head with her eyes as she retrieved the dirk. The image was more satisfying than the stew the Swordsman hoarded. Ignoring his continuing half-smile, she returned to her throwing position, dirk held high, searching the unknown fathoms of her instincts for inspiration once more.

"Too tight again." He never looked up from his rabbit concoction.

"Fuck off."

"Your father would not be proud of your mouth, Lady Hunter."

"You didn't know my father."

"No, but now I know his stock. It's up to you to show it true. And your grip's still too tight."

She almost turned and threw the dirk at *him*, her vision awash with a fadeless red that overwhelmed her self-control. She faced towards him, saw him react almost imperceptibly to the motion, then at the last moment angled back and pitched her weapon hard at the ironwood. The dirk collided with the tree sideways, the boxwood pommel clacking against the older wood and pirouetting into the forest. Yet another misthrow that would see her killed in battle.

Her arms went limp and she marveled at the Swordsman, for he had done the impossible: in her mind, there was no Cleric, no dead family, no anything except her blood-boiling anger. "This is just fucking impossible any way you look at it. I've never seen someone throw a knife outside a bloody carnival. It's probably ju—"

"Listen…" he said, interrupting her. "Do you hear that?"

She studied the rawboned trees jutting upwards against the formless clouds and heard nothing but layers of birdsong and the click of dead boughs aroused by the wind. "Hear what?"

Donovan pointed and she followed his gaze. A large maple leaf flashed reds and oranges as it drifted towards the earth, slowed by a thick weave of branches and the warming late morning air. Faster than Jana had ever seen anything move, Donovan opened his duster, revealing a row of long, sheathed spikes. He drew one from its tubular clasp and let it fly without hint of effort or even a glance at his target. The spike traced a hard line to the maple tree and sunk halfway into the bark, the plummeting leaf impaled at the center.

He shrugged his injured shoulder with a grimace, then returned to preparing their meal. "Loose grip," he said without looking up.

Jana stared, mouth open, and never argued with the Swordsman about knife throwing again.

* * * *

Once the hares were in their bellies and the fire doused and scattered, they continued northward, keeping to the Drudge. The fog had receded during the early day, leaving the afternoon a semblance of clear. From a distance, it was difficult to tell fog from Mist without constant discipline and awareness, which Jana minded always. Her father's trick was to look for the edge of it; the outer wall of Mist was thinner than a man before it became opaque. At times natural fog appeared that way as well, though, so a cautious approach was always best. *Safer is livelier*, as Dad had liked to say. She realized that was the first thought she'd had of him without a deep pang, and that gave her some hope. Her ordeal at the house just might have begun to heal a wound she had thought would never fade.

"I've been thinking," she said as they navigated a stone run where the forest turned thicker.

"I hope you've not overtaxed your mind in doing so," said Donovan without turning.

She glared at the sword on his back as if the voice had come from it. "If that thing was my father, does that mean *he* was still there when the Dweller attacked?"

To her surprise, The Swordsman did not chide her or respond right away. After a moment he said, "I do not know the nature of whatever power the Cleric wields or its peculiarities. But my feelings say yes, he was nearby. For whatever that's worth."

"Does that mean he brought the Dweller, too?"

Donovan shook his head. "No man commands a Dweller, not even him. Though his power might have lured it. Who could know?"

He said no more, and Jana nodded to herself and decided that if all they had were assumptions, then she would assume this was entirely the Cleric's fault, Mist Dweller and all. His and no other.

They stopped only twice as the day wore on; the first so Donovan could dig up an applegum plant, which he separated from its root and stored in his satchel; the second when Jana's bladder felt so full she thought she might explode. She made Donovan wait near the overgrown path they followed and hurried behind the broadest tree trunk she could find, dropped her trousers, and squatted.

Then she heard the shouting.

It came from directly ahead. She tried to see the source through the thick scrub with her floodgates still open, and almost cried out when Donovan appeared behind her. He clamped his coarse palm over her mouth.

"Shh," he said with barely a breath. "Be silent and wait here." Then he headed for the sound and vanished.

Jana finished emptying herself and hiked up her drawers.

Damn him if he thinks I'm just going to wait.

Stubborn, stubborn Mule. The smart thing now would be to do as she was told, to wait by the road like a good girl, maybe draw a picture or find a doll to play with while she was at it.

She frowned, weighing her options.

Yes, the best thing to do would be to wait.

Six-gun drawn, she took a deep breath and followed Donovan into the scrub.

* * * *

She reached a break in the trees and stood beside the Swordsman and peered from the shadows into the upland beyond. Ahead was a small caravan consisting of three merchants—two men and one woman— who were in the midst of being robbed. The merchants were dark-skinned Raistlinders, dressed in garish cashmere robes too opulent for their own good. An assortment of scrimshaw pendants dangled from their necks, threaded by braided rawhide, and they clacked like castanets as the merchants cowered.

The woman stayed behind the men, a deep cerulean gown gathered behind her like rolling waves, her small arms frail but elegant beneath dolman sleeves. A water pearl brooch tied at her neck gleamed in the sun; that would be the first thing to go, Jana reckoned.

Their three attackers were as most highwaymen, all leather skullcaps and wineink tattoos and stolen jewelry, and they all of them bore flintlock pistols which were drawn and pointed. Jana watched the largest of them lever his fist full-weight into a Rastlinder's jaw, opening his lip and costing him a tooth.

"I told you to wait," said the Swordsman.

She moved past him, stepping quietly—silently, even—to the tree nearest the clearing in time to watch a highwayman club the standing male Raistlinder over with the broad side of his pistol.

Jana's gaze narrowed. "We have to help them."

"No."

She snapped him a look. "Why?"

"They should learn to help themselves. Otherwise, they should stay off the road," he said simply.

"You should because you can."

The Swordsman's eyes hardened. "Helping people like that does nothing for them or for me. Everything happens for a reason. Now come on."

He left then, as quiet as moonrise.

Jana watched him go. Teeth gritted, sure this was the stupidest thing she'd ever done, she uttered a quick prayer, kept her gun tight to her chest, and stole forward into the clearing.

"Get up," said the largest highwayman; a tattoo of a fish swam his arm. The brigand behind him snapped the woman's brooch from her neck with a sharp tug. One of his rings, Jana saw, was cast into the shape of a monkey. He and a third gunman hovered over the brooch and gawked.

An embroidered veil concealed the lower part of the female Raistlinder's face. In her soft gray eyes lay a wildfire of fear. "Get down with tha rest of 'em," Fishhead barked at her. She froze and did not respond and the highwayman crushed his pistol into her temple in response, sending her sprawling.

He had one mudcrusted boot on the carriage step when the crisp call of a pistol hammer stopped him cold. Jana stood ten paces behind him, settling into a wide stance with practiced quiet, her six-gun trained on his head. Inside her body, fear ruled and ran rampant; outwardly—she hoped, at least—she wore a calm and focused facade. "Get down from there," she said. Her tone was even. A good start.

Fishhead stared like she was the oddest thing he'd ever seen, but complied and eased back from the carriage with his hands on his hips. At first the other men did not listen, their looks more bewildered than fearful. Careful to keep them all in her field of fire, Jana wrangled the three of them into line with their hands raised and their weapons thrown down. "Now," she said, meaning to sound fierce, "head east. And don't stop till moon-up."

The gunmen erupted into laughter. "Missy…" said Fishhead. "Ya look lost. If you care fer it, we'll let ya go on yer way 'fore anything untoward goes forth here, pray it."

Mind yourself, girl. You expected a fight. Don't let them faze you.

She stepped closer, able to smell the man even from a distance. "Go. Now."

"Yer not tha killing type. But if ya want a lesson in how to use that pretty thing ya got, I'll be happy to show ya," said Fishhead, flashing a tawny smile. A chunk of red meat dangled from between his front teeth.

The man's audacity triggered anger in her, inching her towards that too-familiar red-soaked place Donovan so ably aroused. She stepped up to his fading grin and—she felt so detached from it all—thrust the pistol between his lips. They curled upward from the pressure. "Don't make me tell you again," she said, so softly only he could hear.

"All right, miss. Just as ya like. We'll go," he said, but still did not move.

Here it is. Your first blood. You gave him fair warning. The thought did not ease her dread.

Then something small and cold parted her hair and pressed into her scalp, and even as an exhale of rank breath broke on her neck she knew her mistake. A fourth bandit, hidden somewhere, had gotten the drop on her.

A thousand outcomes raced through her mind, all with one common thread: she and the merchants were going to die here. And still there was no sign of Donovan. The bastard really did leave her here. *Rot in the deepest stinkhole of the Maw, you fucker. Forever with your bloody self-righteousness.*

Her next notion was to put a bullet in Fishhead and be done with him, for at least she'd claim one of them before her brains splattered the caravan. But a quiet voice in her head (it sounded like Donovan's, damn him) said to draw this out. Wait. These were the sort that made mistakes. Frequently, she reckoned. She could get the upper hand if they underestimated her.

You're kidding yourself. You have about four minutes to live.

That thought rang truest.

Then the gunshots began.

The first bullet caught the newly-revealed fourth bandit in the leg. A crimson blossom flourished from his thigh and he dropped his gun and tumbled backwards screaming. The next shot whirred so close to Jana's head she could feel the breeze of its passing, and Monkey Ring's shoulder split open and blood ran onto the grass by his feet as he choked on a cry.

Jana faced the sounds, expecting Donovan, finding instead an odd-looking man about her height, thin-limbed but with a round crest of a stout-belly straining clear of his belt, gaunt face drawn up in concentration, an age-old six-shooter gripped loosely in his trembling hand. He stood beside her, studying the bandits with one shifty blue eye, the other covered by a patch. "You heard tha Miss," he said in a voice that bordered on ridiculous. "Now listen harder and move before ya get moved." Jana stared at him, unsure what to think. The man was braver than his befuddled features betrayed, whoever he was. Now if only he'd had the sense to keep the fourth bandit in his sights...

The fallen newcomer lunged for his pistol, plucked it up, and took aim. Jana saw this in time to watch the trigger lever back, the cranking of the gun's firing mechanism thunderous somehow against the quiet of the clearing. She thought of the lore professed at Studies insisting that a person's life flashed through their mind the moment before they died; it didn't. All she saw was the inside of her eyelids as she closed them and held her breath.

"Fein!" cried Fishhead, eyes bright with fear. He grabbed Monkey Ring and together they helped the one called Fein to his feet.

"So sorry, miss," said Fishhead with sudden and quite genuine repentance.

Jana watched as the four of them hobbled away, looking back only once. Before she had time to wonder what in the name of it had just happened, they were away into the forest.

Satisfied, her rescuer holstered his six-shooter and smiled a yellow smile. "Excuse the manners, my lady. I am Ea—"

"Earnald Avers," said Donovan from behind them, sheathing his sword.

Earny beamed. "Praise all that be true. You remember! Call me Earny if it pleases ya."

"Damn you, Donovan. How long have you been standing there?" asked Jana. He had saved her life again, and for some reason the thought made her livid.

"Long enough," he replied.

As they quarreled, Earny saw to the merchants. "You folk all right?" he asked in his queer, strident voice. They nodded and clasped their hands and bowed; Jana got the impression they didn't speak the language.

Donovan—begrudgingly, it seemed—produced his strange flower and ground more of his healing paste and applied it to their wounds. When they were ready to move on, the Swordsman told the merchants something in a language made of wet, guttural noises and throaty clicks. The woman responded, bent forward and kissed Donovan's forehead, whispering what sounded like a prayer, and with that they moved on, their carriage felloes jostling over the rocky upland on their way south.

"All that and he's tha one gets the kiss," said Earny.

Donavan turned towards the departing merchants. "They're on their way back to Raistlin. They have a long journey ahead." Turning back to Earny he asked, "How did you find us?"

Earny straightened, looking uncomfortable. "Well...see, the short of it is, Master Swordsman, sir... I've been followin' ya these days past. Since we met, ya see."

Donovan's mouth unlatched, a look Jana took much pleasure in. He measured Earnald Avers up and down. "You have been following me..." he said in a voice equal parts wonder and annoyance. Earny nodded. In his eyes lay such naive enthusiasm that Jana knew he was telling the truth. She could tell the Swordsman knew it, too.

"From quite the distance, mind, but followed nonetheless. Tracked a ways also, and lost you at one point till I saw the burning barn." At the last, Jana's eyes turned downward.

Donovan considered this for a space, then nodded. His odd, crooked smile appeared. "Fine work," he said. His tone still carried annoyance, but his words sounded genuine nonetheless.

Jana saw stars in Earny's eyes.

To Jana, the Swordsman said, "Come. We must go."

Jana smiled at Earny. "Thank you. You saved my life."

Earny's cheeks reddened. "Ah, lady, it was nothin' of the large sort. Glad to have been of service." She smiled again and followed Donovan towards the Shodan.

"W-wait, just one moment, please, if ya would," said Earny before they had gone far.

Donovan stopped short of the forest and pivoted back on his heel towards the one-eyed highwayman. The Swordsman's good will had already run out, Jana could tell, and he was looking more than just annoyed now.

"Sir and madam. If I could please have just one more bit of yer time. See, I've been privy to a lotta bad things in my day, but thing of it was, I've never partaken in any of it. Always the bystander I been, due to the safety in numbers it afforded, like of Mr. Donovan here crossing paths notwithstanding, blessit. But still, that absolves me of nothin' I know, and in tha Keeper's eyes I'm nothin' but a raking, murdering sonnovabitch just for being in the vicinity while others did what I would not. And so…" This part seemed hardest for him; the whole thing was touching to Jana in a way that was hard to name. "I'd like to come with ya, far as I can without being too big a burden. I know I asked ya once before, Swordsman, and maybe I don't have tha stock to wield a blade true as you, but least I could do is try and be better. No man ever asked a thing more frank."

Jana knew the look in the Swordsman's eyes, and it was not pleasant; when his voice sounded full of genuine warmth, she felt the urge to slap herself awake, for what else could this exchange be besides a bizarre dream? "If you can keep up, and if you can avoid making a nuisance, you may follow us to the Gestalt. After that, I'd beg you take leave for your safety." Earny's eyes lit up and his thin lips spread into the biggest grin Jana had ever seen. It faded as Donovan added, "But this comes with a request."

"Yes, lord. Anything!"

"There is a chance, and this may arise without warning, that an illness, a…madness…might overtake myself or Jana here. If it does, I'd trust two pistols over one to put us down. Or, in the worst case, you'll be charged with both of us. Keep your gun clean and oiled, but I can't promise you'll survive. Even at your readiest. Is this still worth it to you?"

Earny paused as if to process it all, which Jana could tell was hard for him, and nodded at last. "Yes, your lordship."

Donovan nodded. "Good. Come then, we've lost too much ground today."

* * * *

They hiked the Drudge until the blood orange sun spilled bright reds and violets into the darkening sky. They skirted the switchback, turning northwest, and thus passed beyond Jana's knowledge of Vale. The Swordsman kept to himself, footsteps nearly noiseless, eyes always watching the road ahead. Earny stayed silent as well, staring at the back of the Swordsman's hat in awe. The jewel set into the hilt of his sword kept a constant watch over them; the thing, silly as it might sound, looked alive—she wouldn't be the least surprised if it sprouted a mouth and called a warning to its master should they try anything unsavory behind his back.

They camped under a broad outcropping overlooking Moira Lake and the cordillera beyond to the west. Past that lay the Gestalt, then the Ven Mountains, and then the Wastes. And Pal Myrrah. The Swordsman watched the glint of moonlight skid the frisky, wind-blown surface of the lake with Boon Leaf burning in his pipe. Earny fell asleep at once; the man snored like a wood saw. Jana smacked him hard and he muttered and turned over, breathing easier.

As the darkest draw of evening set upon them, she sat beside Donovan with her legs hugged to her chest and her chin planted on her knees. She noticed his hands shaking, saw him clasp them together hard and grit his teeth.

"Are you okay?" she asked.

"I'm fine. Go to bed."

"I'm not tired."

"Do it anyway. You need your strength."

"I want to hear your story. About how this began. What happened between you and the Cleric?"

Donovan gave her a weary look. "Not tonight."

"Then when?"

"Don't ask me again. When the time is right you'll know more."

There was something in his tone, colder than usual. She frowned as she headed back to the bedrolls, stopped and said, "Do you think the whole world is like this?"

"Like what?"

"Dead."

He didn't answer right away. A deep drag off his pipe, followed by a slow smoky exhale that spiraled through the moonlight. "I've walked this world all my life, from the deep eastern valleys to the western beach, and I've never seen any different."

"You've been to the East?"

He nodded.

"Are there Dwellers?"

"No Dwellers, but other things."

"Like what?"

"Nothing pretty. A lot of Blood Demons. As of late, anyway. There are pockets where men huddle in fear, or fight on occasion but usually for the worst. They're divided beyond repair. That's the truth of it."

She wondered if he knew how deep her frown ran. Good thing the Hunter Clan had stayed home and not tried for the better life of the eastern cities; it would have just drawn out the inevitable.

"Do we have a chance?" she asked softly.

"No," came his response. No hesitation. "But that's never stopped me before."

For reasons Jana did not comprehend, the empty stubbornness of his voice made her smile.

"Go to bed," he said again, crossing his arms as cold lake air scaled the rocks and swept over them.

She did as told, laying near Earnald Avers, reformed bandit, and slept.

She dreamed of Donovan's glowing eyes as he hunted her through the shadows.

In the end, though, it was a Dweller's jaws that closed around her body until all was black.

7

They walked single file, looking worn and soiled and weary. The longest straightaway of the Drudge vanished into the fog ahead; once it bent westward they'd be off the road, according to Donovan. That part scared Jana the most. Nothing bad had happened on the road yet. She wondered if that was for a reason or just a run of good fortune. She suspected the latter, for what would stop a Dweller from besieging them anywhere it so wished? Certainly not the muddy sluiceways of the Drudge.

Twice they met travelers along the road. The first was a boy about Cory's age and his father, a scarecrow man with silver stubble and a hard limp. They saw the Swordsman and his blade jutting above his shoulder and pointed, hopeful smiles gleaming from their unwashed faces.

"Dad, was that a real Swordsman?"

"I believe it was."

"Will the people come? Will they fight?"

"No," said the father. "I don't think so. World's not ready for that."

And then they were gone, enveloped by the silken fog that could change to Mist at any moment. Jana wondered what their fate would be and prayed it would be long and peaceful. She suspected that was yet another fantasy from the Princess.

The second was a threesome of mendicants dressed in rags. At the sight of the Swordsmen, they all three of them genuflected, making the sign of the Keeper. The leader was a paunchy man with one milky eye and skin pocked deep with crow's feet and laced with spider veins.

"Master Swordsman. Do you come to call the people to arms?"

"The Demons are everywhere. Please help us. Please."

"We'll not survive scattered, Swordsman. The people will follow not themselves. But your kind... They may listen," said the last. A black viscous fluid flowed from his ear and had dried along his neck. He did not seem to be aware of it. Donovan met their looks with somber eyes and a tight grimace, but did not answer.

Jana dipped a run of cloth in water from her canteen and stopped to wash the man's face. When she gave him the cool cloth to keep, he told her the Keeper smiled on her. If only he knew the truth.

The three men watched them go. Jana and Earny looked back at them every now and then until they, too, became forgotten blemishes on the pallid distance.

Donovan never looked back.

* * * *

Why is he here?

Two weeks upon the road from Pleasantry and Donovan wondered this while he watched Earny work on ruining the girl's already questionable pistol technique. Frustrated, he looked instead into the Boon leaves drifting through his tea and sighed; it felt like the whole world hung on that sigh, with only him to move it. Adopting the ex-bandit flowed hard against his nature. Yet this was as Master taught, what the old tomes and long hours at Studies urged: trust the gut before the mind. The low voice. And the Swordsman's low voice told him this lumbering fool of an ex-bandit belonged in his circle. Perhaps the chance to *have* a circle played a part, too. How long since Donovan of Kolendhar walked this barren earth any way but alone? Not so long to forget the comfort of companionship, slow or naive may it be.

He stirred his tea with a rough, scarred finger. That reminded him: his stash of Boon was low—he'd have to barter with Jana for more. He had a good idea what she'd ask in return. The girl was predictable, too much so for her own good, though he had been the same at her age. More a sign of potential than flaw, he wagered. Yet back with the Raistlinders he had almost left her, truly and sincerely, Keeper pray for them all. Someone foolish enough to run a gauntlet like that deserved every measure of the lesson it served. But something had brought him back, a deep-running river cognate of duty that he had long dismissed as lost.

You should because you can, the girl had said.

The truth of this was irrelevant; its idealism moved a part of him he had inhumed some place unmarked and forgotten. It was a part that was childish and useless of course, now more than ever, but it felt good, pray everything true, to embrace it.

And damn everything, it only took a few days for him to start thinking in local-speak.

When they were done cavorting, Earny settled in on his bedroll, which was surprisingly well-kept, and smoked his pipe. Not Boon but something else—Donovan had no taste for it, judging by the smell. "Tell us your story," he said to the one-eyed man.

"My story, yer Swordsmanship?"

Donovan nodded.

"Says the man who won't tell us his," said Jana as she sat and carved lines in the ground between her feet with her dirk.

Donovan pursed his lips and looked sidelong at her.

Earny struggled to gather his thoughts, judging by the sweat beading on his brow, not noticing their exchange. After a long quiet he said, "My story's simple, pray. My da used to tell us the world got mowed over by something fierce and big and dark so long ago no one remembered it, and ever since people've been trying hard and fast to scratch a livin' off not much at all. Everyone fer himself, Da' said bout men. Got no need of seeing to the others and they got no inclination to see to you, Keepit and blessit."

Earnald Avers of Vale took a deep breath.

"People broke off, some held up with villages and such and kept civil, others went off the deep and started eating babies and killing themselves in groups, throwing themselves off ledges or slitting their arms open and the like. Somehow big groups here and there formed together, made Kolendhar, and the Swordsmen, as yer like to know, obviously. Thirty, forty generations ago that was, to hear it. That called to me most, ever it did. Sounded downright divine, like it was what we were all meant to do.

"He told me things were bad enough until 'bout the time of my great grandfather, when all the trees died and the fog settled in, akin to Mist he called it, but without the Misties. Only thing's that'd grow were in gardens, and then only under the best crop-raisers. Guess I was one of 'em, cuz my crop would come in season after season sure as you could wager the sun'd show up. Da' also said people used to see the Swordsmen everywhere. He said his granddaddy used to see them four, five times a year. They'd come settle disputes, make sure people's voices were heard, punish criminals, and take care o' sore spots in the world. Bred of fine stock, so it said, years spent finding the best mates to father the smartest, sharpest youngers who got trained in all manner of things. You can tell me if I'm wrong 'bout this, but I'd rather ya didn't, to be honest. I like the ring of it," said Earny with a bitter smile.

"Anyhow, by time I was a boy no one even believed the Swordsmen were around anymore, save everything. They said they been wiped out, or that they stayed in their castle now and ate and made it with princesses and had no need of common folk. I know there's royalty out there somewhere, people with gold and fine clothes and such, but I don't know where they come from or what they're the rulers of. Small stretches, I'd guess, where their family trenched in good and early and lesser folks harder up latched on for the ride afterwards. My family had a farm like Miss Jana here and that was that. Till a few years back, when hertweed took my wife and my daughter. I didn't know why not me, too. I used to hate the Keeper fer that, making me stay alive. I wanted to spite him, I sorta did. Spent most of my life 'fore that thinkin' of how to help people in this dunny world, and next I know He takes it all away."

Jana swallowed a lump as she listened.

"So I set out on my own, a vagabond, pray it all. Went from village to village, somehow didn't get killed by Misties or bandits or anything between. Started taking up odd jobs in the south Vale, Minderland, some other places where big groups'd gathered and called it a town. When I was old enough to be a man I was sick of that life, too. Thought about killing myself once or twice even, Keeper save me. And He did, sort of. He sent me Raef, who came to town one day looking for fresh faces. By that point I had been shot, beaten, stabbed once, and more, and if nothing else in this world reaches a man dense as me, it's that you're not good when yer in this game alone. Raef and his friends seemed strong enough, sure, so I tried to fit in with 'em. And that's how it began. We carried on a stretch, up and down Vale and sometimes beyond, raking and laughing 'bout it after. I laughed, too, in the beginning. Felt good to do as I wanted and spit in the Keeper's face. And it felt good to belong to something. I think it's possible to live yer whole life in this dead stretch and never know the like of havin' other people round you ta consider your own. We're all sort of just scrappin' here, aren't we? Making do. But we don't make do. We really don't. Cuz you can't escape the voice of yer gut."

Donovan nodded. *The low voice.*

Earny leaned back and puffed on his pipe. "No ya cant. So after years of holding onto that feeling, and that feeling of safety, foolish may it been, one day the push went too far, and Raef and the boys did something that…" Earny paused and swallowed hard. "That just… snapped inside a me. Couldn't close my eyes to it. Felt like I been rocked, I did. And then you." he pointed at Donovan, "You appeared like the Reaper come from the pages of the old times made flesh and suddenly it was true! It was possible to be this thing, this person who was bred and trained and stood fer what people should be doin' rather than squabbling over which piece of the shit pie they get. And I felt fire in me like I never felt before." His one eye was gleaming with passion now and Donovan felt moved in spite of the man's lanky movement and grating voice.

"And so here I am, with you, Master Swordsman, a place I never prayed I'd be since I was a boy. And like I said, I intend to make you glad you took me on as yer companion. Take that to the Black and hand-deliver it to the Keeper, pray it." He exhaled a cloud of smoke that hung in the air between them. "I'd say that about sums me up short as I can make it. Forgive me fer being long-winded."

Donovan watched Earny with something new in his eyes, something like respect. "You are forgiven, Earnald Avers. It is my honor and fortune to hear your tale. Keeper bless and pray it true."

A bright, hole-ridden smile grew across Earny's face, which he wore until he fell asleep.

* * * *

They set out again when sunup stretched skyward and the first indistinct notes of lonely finch calls rose from the cold, dead remnants of night. It was dusk again when they at last left the Drudge behind (forever if Donovan had his way), and with it all visible fruits of human endeavor. Now lay heft upon heft of wild forest that terminated at the Gestalt, a massive lake so wide it would take a month to encircle. Even by that course, their destination would be unreachable, for the mouth of the Wastes was a pass through the Ven Mountains no wider than a small farmer's field, with sheer cliffs hemming the lake that continued onward to the sea.

There was only one choice, and that was the Ferry.

The endless shell of chalky clouds had returned, bleaching away the powder blue sky and diffusing the now alien sunlight mere hours after it first appeared. When they camped again, Donovan threw an armful of branches into a pit and struck a spark onto the tinder ball and carefully lit them. He sipped the last of his tea and watched the flame undulate, in the back of his mind always probing the distance for the scent of the Cleric, if it could even be called it that. His sense of the man was more of an itch still, one that he could only scratch by pressing on. *The endless push.* All things true, he was weary of it—so weary that it took his every reserve to continue. He'd find the Black before he'd admit it, though.

His fingers caught a sudden bout of the shakes, spilling his tea. An abrupt flood of the Cold broiled from his gut and he bent forward, eyes bugged, choking on a gasp.

(It's coming. It's ready.)

Donovan clamped his hands together with a loud *smack* and bit down until his teeth stopped chattering.

You will not come for me. I will be rid of you.

(I am you.)

A brilliant flood of pain caught fire in his chest and seared him all the way to his fingers and toes. A scream coiled up that he barely caught with his teeth, biting it into a quiet gasp as he rocked onto his back and stared at the crown of trees above.

He didn't sit up until he was sure he could do it without stumbling, and when he looked at Jana and Earny he saw they were too lost in their child's play to notice him. Too lost to do anything if the Cold consumed him. All for the best, maybe, for Donovan knew in his heart that few—certainly not a young girl or half-daft brigand—would be able to put him down once his curse took him fully into its fold. And take him, it would. Better they be smiling when he ripped their lives away in madness.

"No, no, lady. Set your weight on the back foot, steady with the left, look down the sight. Hands clasped on tha butt like so."

"Call me Jana, for the love of it."

"Yes, lady."

As Donovan relaxed at last he removed his hat and tied his hair back in a ponytail. It was oily and full of filth. He sniffed his armpits; they smelled like the dead. Tomorrow they'd take turns in the Moira. Finding the Cleric would do no good if their stink struck him dead before they got some answers.

"Earny," said Donovan. When the ex-bandit turned to face the Swordsman, his eyes were filled with a timid joy that was so heartfelt Donovan could not help but pity the man.

"Yes, milord?" said Earny, hand still on Jana's, where he had been adjusting her technique. She removed it.

"Both of you. There'll be no hand clasping gun butts on my watch. Firing arm straight, cupped in the left to steady, ready for the buck. Go on."

Earny's smile broadened. "Yes, Lord! As ya say!"

Donovan nodded, settled back with his hat over his eyes.

Just before he did, he saw Jana staring at him, wearing a small smile. He returned it with a weary frown.

8

Jana dreamed of the Dwellers again that night. The dreams came vivid and merciless and felt like memories of a true event when she woke, which perhaps they were in part. In the dream there was not one Dweller or two but dozens, all with the taste of her flesh on their feral minds. They had come to finish what started on the Hunter Estate, hungry for the last rung on the family ladder.

Job's not worth doing lest you're gonna do it right. Right and through to the end.

Her dad taught her that. Who was to say Dweller mommies and daddies didn't sit their stubby demon spawn on their crenelated knees and whisper similar words of encouragement?

They stopped to bathe early in the day near a bluff that slanted hard down towards the lakeside. Donovan went first, leaving her and Earny to their devices at the side of the footpath. Jana caught sight of him through the trees just once, dunking his head and splashing his face, naked, and did not immediately look away. The Swordsman's body was covered in scars and bruises, not least of which was the Cleric's mark which matched her own, but his training had also left him well muscled and lean and her eyes drank deep of him before fear of being caught turned her back towards Earny's vacant grin.

The only thing that numbed Jana's mind to the shocking cold of the Moira was her scar. It looked larger already, now spanning from her collar bone to midway across her ribcage, and this time she saw it moving when she splashed water onto it. The very idea of that *thing* creeping through her flesh made her feel faint. What was this wickedness growing inside her? One night soon she would take the Swordsman by his ponytail and force him to tell everything, including whatever sordid story preceded all of this. She needed to know and he had no choice but to tell, for this was her story now, too, and he owed her at least that much respect.

When they were dressed and packed, Donovan crouched and drew in the silt. "We are here," he told them in his dry, emotionless way. "Out this way…" he drew a line perpendicular to their course, "lies the Ferry. There are others like it in the world, but this one is special for two reasons. One is that it leads to the mouth of the Wastes, which is surrounded by a high wall of mountains called the Ven. It blocks the way forward everywhere but for one pass on the far side of the Gestalt. Second…" he trailed off, gathering his thoughts, eyes turning briefly to Jana, "is that this Ferry is likely the charge of a Shade. Or, as you folks call them, a Dweller."

Jana felt a fist reach into her throat and squeeze her heart. "What do you mean it's the *charge* of a Dweller?" she asked.

"Misties don't have hide or ball of sense in 'em," said Earny. "Like animals through and throughout, them. They've a mind for eating flesh and prowling about but that's all."

"Then where do their swords come from, pray?" asked the Swordsman, eyes glimmering. "And their cloaks? They all of them wear cowls, no matter what reach of the world you find them. These are the ways of beings with intelligence and at least a rudimentary culture."

"They're monsters," said Jana through clenched teeth. "That's it."

"Well, be that true or not, what I can promise you is that one awaits at the Ferry, making sure none cross it," said the Swordsman.

"How do you know this?" Jana asked him.

Donovan's eyes registered the shiver in her body. His frowned deepened. "Much the way any tale comes to be known. Other men have witnessed it from afar and survived to write their stories down. We'll see if they are true soon enough."

"What do Misties care a lick whether anyone crosses a lake?" asked Earny, fingers tight around the grip of his old six-shooter.

"I'm not one who knows. But that does not change the fact that we must face it and seek its blessing to cross."

"And how do we do that, short of fighting?" asked Jana.

"With this," the Swordsman answered, holding the odd coin with the triangular notch. "I've not seen this or its likeness since I was a boy, but I remember it well now. It came to me as I woke this morning. This is *alai-bo*. A blood toll. Left for me though I'm sure it was, we'll use it anyway. We have no choice."

"A coin to pay a Dweller for crossing?" said Earny, as much to himself as anyone. He sounded amazed at the prospect.

"How do you know it will accept? How do you know it won't hold out its claws and wait for you to hand it over and then bite you off at the waist and save the rest for supper?" asked Jana, feeling her cheeks flush. She had no patience left for cordiality. This was utter madness and the Swordsman knew it.

Donovan rose. "I don't know, but I've faith, girl. Whether we find our way across the lake or find the Black together, we'll do it because we have no other course."

Jana stared at him. *Smooth as riverstone at all times, that one.*

"It's better than my original plan," he added as he strapped his sword across his back.

"And what was that?" asked Jana.

The Swordsman shook his head and did not answer; that was enough for her.

"Master Swordsman, sir," said Earny, his feet doing an anxious dance. "Do you still mean for me to stay behind once we reach the lake?"

The Swordsman mulled this over. Jana watched him through a sheet of panic. Facing a Dweller, mayhap traveling with it across the Gestalt rang so insane that her mind could not make heads or tails of it. And worse, every time her anger appeared to cut down her fear, the image of Cory, one minute bright and alive—albeit covered in blood—the next ripped through a hole half the size of him, body snapping backwards, limbs twisted inward, filled her mind.

"Something in me says no, Earnald Avers of Vale," said Donovan. "You are bound by no oath. Certainly by no duty to me. If you wish to come with us across the Gestalt, then my low voice says that is your decision." For once, Earny's smile was not full of boyish enthusiasm. He nodded, solemn, and looked at his toes for answers.

"We should move. When we're close to the Ferry, you two will stay within the forest and I will meet the Dweller alone. If all goes well, we'll be crossing the Gestalt by twilight of that day."

"And what happens if all goes to shit, Donovan?" asked Jana. Any other time the Swordsman might have dismissed such a comment, but she meant it now.

"We'll just have to hope it doesn't, won't we," he said with his cockeyed smile rising darkly. "Now let's go. Stay close to me."

He went and they followed.

Jana felt Earny's hand on her shoulder, tentative and soft. She turned to face him. The man looked scared half to the grave. "Do you think it'll be all right, my lady?"

"It'll have to be, won't it," she said, knowing that offered no consolation.

* * * *

For three hard weeks they marched, their conversation sparse, their gazes turned within. They ate and they slept and they marched again, and then repeated the exercise the following day, and the day after.

Earny had lost count of the days when the road they traveled dropped off at the sides into steep slopes overlooking a broad slate bight. Loafed upon its rise was a ridged monocline with all the ages of the world scrawled across its breadth. Always the world watched them, aged tree boles glaring like black slatted eyes from the depths of the forest; a lone blackbird perched upon a rock overhead with dead worm crusted at the corners of its beak, a look of endless surprise in its beady eyes.

After weeks of occasional but regular insistence, the Swordsman agreed to show Jana some rudimentary techniques to practice with her dirk. It seemed uncharacteristic for the Swordsman to concede so easily to anything, let alone to the menial task of training a young girl to fight, so Earny decided he must have an ulterior motive, whether it be forging Jana into a more able ally or simply staving off boredom. The Swordsman would work with her at night for a time whenever they made camp, demonstrating thrusts and parries and grips with his usual smooth expertise. He did not dig or tease at Jana as she attempted what he had shown her, and this caught Earny's notice as well: the Swordsman seemed to take great pleasure in tormenting the last of the Hunter family as a general rule, and it stood out when he restrained himself.

At the end of the next week, they plodded through the bleak curtain of endless fog without stop until midday. Earny thought of his posse (or ex-posse, now), still dead in the tacky glop of the Drudge several hefts south of Pleasantry. A few weeks ago Earnald Avers had had his life plan carved in stone and soundly in the midst of execution; it took just one visit from a Swordsman from Kolendhar (until that point considered myth, he'd emphasize) for all of that to be turned on its head. Now he followed the man who had killed Raef and his other companions—and who might have killed Earny, too, if the winds had blown that way—blind as an old dog tempted by the scent of fresh meat, only this meat was something abstract and unidentifiable, as was the pull which had brought Earny this far, first by tracking the Swordsman, then by revealing himself. The low voice, Earny had heard the Swordsman call it, lower than the gut, a voice that kicked a man this way or that for reasons he might never comprehend.

They stopped to rest when the featureless daylight seemed brightest. They ate toeleaf wrapped around gozen berries, an old tracker's recipe Earny learned from William the Herder, who was dead also from the Swordsman's deft cut. The Swordsman kept to himself, away from the others, and Earny dared not bother him. There had been a look in his eyes since the previous night, and it wasn't the peacekeeping kind.

During lunch Earny caught Jana staring into space and flicked an acorn at her and it tapped her forehead. "Gotcha," he said with a grin. He had never been more aware of the air passing through the spaces in his teeth as when he smiled at this girl. Jana looked at him sidelong as if to say stop being such a child, but smiled after and flicked an acorn back in retaliation, which he dodged. "I know yer scared," he said during the silence that followed. Jana looked surprised to hear him say it. "I am, too. And so's he," he nodded at

Donovan, "though he'd die before he showed it. No one in their right way'd be willing to face a Misty without their stomach running loops round their rear."

"Who says he's right in his way?" asked Jana.

Earny had no answer.

As they were readying themselves to push off again, Donovan held up his hand and shut them up.

Silence first.

Then Earny heard a distant sound, a high-pitched whistling that grew louder quickly—in the space of a half a second it became ear-piercing. Earny had no time to turn towards it or do anything except stand in place while Donovan performed his teleport thing again: one moment he was facing into the forest, hands at his sides, and the next he had spun all the way around with his sword drawn and turned downward. Somewhere in the middle of this, a loud *clang* echoed into the stark twists of the trees, and then a deep *thud* as a long silver spike, much the same as the one Donovan used to kill Carver of the clan of Raef, stuck halfway into an old oak and stayed there.

The Swordsman had cut it down midair.

Donovan watched the forest, sword held smoothly in his nicked and leathered hands, bright green eyes scanning the indistinct distance. "Show yourself!" he cried in a voice that made Earny quiver. "For your line, show your face!"

A long quiet stretched after. Then two men appeared; where they had been hiding, Earny could not say. They seemed to materialize out of the bloody fog like demons stepped home from the Maw. The first was a giant of a man, a block of tall chiseled muscle, bald head traced with involute tattoos and odd inky runes. Across his back was the largest sword Earny had ever seen (on a human, at least), a cousin to a claymore perhaps, but longer and wider. Its hilt was carved bone that looked akin to Donovan's. The second man was smaller, about Earny's size, with shoulder-length brown hair tied back in a topknot. He was either tan as the Black or of relation to Raistlinders, and his hazel eyes were flecked with gold. Across his cheekbones, he bore wineink scrawls like his fellow. His sword resembled Donovan's, and he kept his fingers wrapped around the hilt until he and his companion stood ten paces away. They both wore leather armor the color of charcoal, incised with intricate intaglios.

Donovan straightened and held his sword to his brow. "Stand true, yon Swordsmen."

"Stand true, and with thanks," said the bald one in a grumbling baritone. Then he smiled a smile that made Earny want to run for Pleasantry and dive into the Hole and pray the Keeper for his eternal soul. Donovan seemed to possess no such notion, and he stepped forward to take the bald giant's hand with a smile of his own. "It is good to see you, Goesef." He looked at the other, smaller man. "And you, Vine."

The one called Vine grinned and the tattoos on his brown cheeks danced. "Where goes Donovan of Kolendhar along this earthy tract, tell us true?" His voice pulsed with bright energy. Earny found himself liking this man better than the other.

"Northward. Towards the Waste."

"Well, blood and ash. You're mad to head that way," said the giant named Goesef.

"Tell me how you happened here? I've not had word from our kind in three years," said Donovan. For the first time, Earny heard true warmth in his voice.

"We've come looking for you," said Vine, plopping down upon a rock with his sword across his shoulders. "You're not easy to find, tell the truth. Methinks you don't want to be found. Am I right?"

"Why looking for me?" asked Donovan. He sheathed his sword now but kept his hands ready.

"You can relax yourself, Swordmaster," said Goesef. "Not for any reason you're thinking with your snake coil pose there." He laughed, thick and hearty. "We want to know if you'll head east with us."

"Why east? There's nothing there but ruin and Blood Demons."

"Nay, not true," said Vine. "Perhaps at one time, but now there's a city called Rend with walls to keep out Blood Demons and Dwellers alike. High walls, three times as high as a man. Closest thing we'll see to Kolendhar in this lifetime."

"Not to mention the closest thing to a clean woman. No insult intended, maiden," said Goesef, nodding to Jana.

"None taken."

"We were just about to give up on finding you when Goesef caught your trail back in the moor," added Vine.

"Why did you attack?" asked Earny.

"There's a lot of triptalk and roundabout these days. Easiest way to spot a Swordsman is to spot the man who moves like one," said Goesef, and Donovan nodded as if this was a good explanation.

"How many men within Rend?" he asked Goesef.

"An army's worth, now. If any creatures should get within the walls, we could bring five thousand blades to their fight in minutes. The other *Ko'tai* are seeing to the training of every man and lad. The price of admission, you might call it."

"Five thousand strong and trained, you say," said Donovan. Now his interest waxed genuine and he stroked his chin. "With a force like that, you could march, come need."

Vine laughed low and deep. "March on who, Donovan? We've barely put together a hold we can keep. The last thing the folk there'll do is march to war when they don't have to. Besides, no one would follow us. You know that well as any."

Donovan looked like he might argue, instead nodded with a frown.

Goesef straightened and adjusted his massive sword. "Well. That is our piece, then. Will you come with us?"

Donovan crossed his arms and thought hard. "I cannot, I'm afraid."

"Are you sure?" asked Vine.

"I am. And besides, what will you do once you are in this place, Rend?"

"We will enjoy what's left of life," said Vine. He had produced a small dagger and was whittling a chunk of wood into something Earny could not identify. "Enough years have been squandered in service of what has amounted to nothing. Master always said it would be so." At this, Goesef nodded in agreement.

Donavan crossed his arms over his chest. "We were overwhelmed and then we despaired. That was never what Master taught."

"Despair and wisdom walk the same line at times," said Goesef without emotion.

Donovan looked from one of his brothers to the other and shook his head. "How did our way become so lost?" he said, more to himself than anyone else. His words drew deep frowns from the other men. "Will you camp with us?"

Vine put his carving away into his satchel and sheathed his knife. "I'm afraid no, brother Donovan. Much to do and many to see. If you change your mind, you'll know where to find us. Rend is near the shore, just north of Hammershorn. Maybe our paths will cross again."

"Stand true, friend. Vigilance to the end. Strength till the Black we find," said Goesef, embracing Donovan's arm.

"Stand true," Donovan replied. Just for a fleeting instant, Earny saw something...*off* in his eyes. Yes, *off* was the best way to describe it. More was going on here than he could figure. Most definitely more.

The Swordsmen bid farewell to Jana and Earny and made their way due east.

The one called Vine turned once to look back at them all, and then they were gone.

9

A week after their meeting with the Swordsmen, after long days of marching ahead without variation, Earny broke off without warning from their short caravan and button-hooked into the woods—Jana almost thought of this part of the forest as the Shodan, but it wasn't any longer, was it? She was so far gone from her well-trodden homeland, small a patch as it was, she knew not what the natives, if such a thing in this barren stretch existed, called this particular collection of dolorous trees and phalanxes of sooty outcrops. She heard Earny's lazy, rhythmless trot behind her one second, and the next he was sprinting full out with no explanation. She wondered if it was dangerous for him to run like that, having only one eye and all. "Earny!" she called after him.

"I saw it! I saw it!" he yelled back without slowing.

Jana and Donovan exchanged looks. His eyes said it all. "No. We're not leaving him," she said, hands on her hips.

"I didn't say anything," said the Swordsman.

"I heard you think it."

"Put your magic to better use than that, Hunter'lue."

"Hunter what?"

He ignored her question and followed after Earny, who was just visible in the deep of the fog when she looked, gone a moment later.

They saw the sharp anvil of rock before they found their one-eyed companion, rising twenty feet high and jutting into the raw morning air like the prow of a half-buried ship. The surface of the rock looked slick from a distance, but as they drew near Jana saw that the rock itself was formed of a nacreous mineral that shone through the stark gloom. At the highest point, a broad white oak's arms stretched

173

outward as if praying for rain, its snaky roots splitting the stone from which it grew. The oak's branches, unlike any tree they'd seen for the length of their journey, wore a full coat of leaves, dull green in the pale light but green nonetheless. They played a papery song on a languid wind full of winter chill.

"Keeper save," said Jana, slowing. "What is it?" When Donovan did not answer, she looked at him and saw his bright green eyes wide as he stood abreast of her and stared as well.

"*Ji T'ai'lo*," he told her after a minute. "A Root Dragon lives here. I've not heard of such a thing since I was a boy. I thought they were a myth."

"What are they? And what in the name of it is that rock?"

"It's *ai'che*. Rootstone. Common rock made something else by the lacquer the Root Dragon secretes. It's what lets that tree grow," he said, nodding at the white oak. "It must have lived here a long time." The Swordsman did not sound much concerned, but Jana was. A dragon, from all bedtime accounts, was a giant monstrous thing that swooped from the sky and set you on fire with a sneeze.

"Have you ever seen one?"

"No one has seen one for as long as the tales tell."

"Are they dangerous?"

He shrugged and gestured with his hand as if to say, *What in this world isn't?*

Earny's scream shook them from their wonder. It was coming from the far side of the rock—*ai'whatever* Donovan had called it. They followed the sound and heard him again before they saw him: "Oh Keeper in the bloody Black and White of it all my skin pray it true. I found it!"

They hurried round to the foot of the talus where they discovered a grotto the height of a man leading into blackness. Jana kept her hand on her six-gun and shared a worried look with Donovan. "Earny, are you okay?" she called into the dark.

When no answer came, Donovan slid his old sword free of its sheath and took a step forward. "Answer if you ca—"

He was cut short as Earnald Avers emerged from the mouth of the grotto at a trot. Jana's first thought was that the Root

Dragon—whatever it may be—must be chasing him, and fell back a step expecting something bigger than a Dweller to come crashing through the stone and roar amber flames into the dead sky. When nothing appeared, she took a closer look at Earny and saw his hands were clasped at his waist, his lone eye wide with excitement, a childish smile bunching his leathery cheeks. "IfounditIfounditIfoundit!" he said, nearly slipping on the scree as he made his way down the talus.

"What are you talking about, Earny?" Jana was taken aback by the joy in the man's face.

The ex-bandit did not answer, instead hurried over to them, hands still carefully clasped, and held them out. Donovan recoiled from the motion, sword arcing around to a defensive stance. Jana slipped her fingers around her pistol and drew the rawhide off her shoulder. Earny ignored them and slowly cracked open his hands.

What Jana saw inside them she could not immediately identify.

It was a tiny creature, maybe six or seven inches from snout to tail tip, scaled and dragon-like if sketches Jana had seen, rare as they were, could be trusted. Its scales were white but rippled with all colors of the rainbow when it moved, and along its back grew rounded gray scutes that flexed with its movements as though soft. Tiny gray wings sprouted from its thin shoulders, drawn back and closed now; they wiggled and fluttered in a way that reminded Jana of a bird ruffling its feathers. Its eyes were the size of small berries and bore rings of blue split by deep onyx pupils that fixed on Donovan and then Jana in turn. *Intelligent* was the word that came to mind when Jana looked into those beady things. The dragon was looking back at her and mulling things over.

"*Ai ko'tai,*" said Donovan. His sword had dropped and the tip dug into the forest floor.

"Saw 'im flyin' by, I did. Pardon the sudden departure," said Earny, who might not have blinked once since he emerged from the grotto. He stared at the Root Dragon with a bright eye.

"I thought you said it must have lived here a long time. It looks like a baby," said Jana. She didn't notice how breathless she was until she spoke.

"This one's full grown, I think. Or near to it," said Donovan. He sheathed his sword and crept a step closer; it was the first time Jana had ever seen him look wary of anything. "They say a thousand men could live a thousand lifetimes without ever seeing one, and yet here it is before us. They say the Keeper's own luck smiles on the man who finds it."

"It's the most beauteous thing I seen in ma life," said Earny, who meant that judging by the sudden glassy look in his eye.

The Root Dragon took two small steps forward across Earny's palm, and Jana could see now the small black claws attached to its small toes. "Is it safe?" she asked.

"I've not learned the intricacies of their species. Only a handful of stories and legends," said Donovan. There was wonder in the Swordsman's eyes.

Jana started to take a small step forward when the dragon recoiled, winding into what looked like a defensive pose, eyes narrowing to slits, those black claws digging further in against Earny's palm. A low hiss, sharp and dangerous-sounding, escaped its mouth as its tongue flitted into the cold air. Earny fell back a step in response but managed to keep his hands aloft, though they quivered now.

Jana froze and shot Donovan a look, searching the Swordsman's face for his measure of the situation. She found no answers in his deep frown.

The Root Dragon lowered its head in a quick and aggressive jerk, loosing another angry hiss, and for the space of a blink Jana thought she could see dark, purplish veins, thin as thread, scrawling into the flesh of Earny's palms where the dragon's claws clung; it reminded her of the scar the Cleric had inflicted upon her. An overwhelming sense of dread filled her at the thought, leaving a burning tingle that climbed her back and neck.

Earny seemed not to register any of this as he said to the dragon, "It's okay, feller. Easy now. Friends, we are, I swear it." As if to make his point, he reached out with a trembling finger and gently stroked the back of the Root Dragon's head.

He's out of it. That finger will be gone in a moment.

The Root Dragon regarded Earny for a long, deliberate moment, then seemed to relax and raise its head back up. Its thin tail moved slightly to an unknowable, erratic rhythm.

Emboldened by its response, Jana inched carefully forward, and with an unsteady hand moved to stroke its head as well. The small creature noticed her when she was nearly upon it, turned and hissed again, snapping its small jaws in warning. Jana shrieked and jerked her hand away, holding it to her chest protectively. Out of the corner of her eye, she was sure she saw the Swordsman chuckling to himself. She resisted the urge to lash out at him for it.

"I wonder how old he is," said Earny as their new reptilian friend relaxed once more and began to climb his hand and arm, for its feet were apparently tacky.

"*Hae-leventy-forr centurs.*"

And they all shut up. The voice had come from the dragon, who was now perched on Earny's elbow.

"Donovan," said Jana, still staring at the creature. "Did the little white baby dragon just say something?"

Donovan nodded and leaned in. The Root Dragon watched him curiously. "Indeed it did. And a broken version of the Old Speak, it was. It says it's over a thousand years old."

"Keeper save everything true," said Earny. "How could it be?"

"*Saeya forn yungy toofalla,*" said the Root Dragon. Its voice was high and metallic and could have been mistaken for an odd bird call or insect chatter.

"He says he's still considered a child by his kind," translated the Swordsman.

"*Ifca nae soomi laal.*"

"But he hasn't seen another for as long as he can remember."

"Do you have a name, little friend o' mine?" asked Earny, tracing the tip of his finger along the dragon's white neck. It closed its eyes and tilted its head back with what Jana interpreted as a dragon-smile-of-contentment.

"*Alumoethongomanetuharuti,*" said the dragon.

"Alumo…" said Jana to herself. "That's more than a mouthful."

"Ruti! That was part of the name, bet yer stock. Heard it, I did!" said Earny with a grin. "That fine by you, fella?"

The dragon looked at him—it seemed to know common speak well enough—then seemed to shrug its wings and nod. "*Ruti.*"

"Can I keep him, ya think, Donovan?" asked Earny with all the naive enthusiasm of a young boy.

Donovan crossed his arms and thought it over. "A Root Dragon is not something you keep or don't keep. If it wishes to make our journey with us, then fortune smiles upon you for it."

"Why would it want to leave its home now if it has stayed here so long?" asked Jana. She found herself quickly becoming accustomed to the idea of a miniature talking dragon climbing around their once-bandit friend, more quickly than she would have expected; compared to her family being massacred and gone forever, fantastic creatures were easy to accept.

"*Aaaka loi. Sou lai tar elongua nufaar.*"

"It says it's been…" Donovan trailed off. "It's been years since I've listened to the Old Speak. I think it's saying it's tired of being alone."

"It's settled then!" said Earny. In response, Ruti crept up his arm and perched on his shoulder. "Got nothin' to pack, do ya?" Ruti flicked his forked tongue across his lips.

Do dragons have lips? She supposed she'd never know for sure.

Earny eyed the Root Dragon. "What dooya eat, feller?"

The creature didn't answer.

"It's taken care of itself for as long as my line has been recorded. It'll be all right with us for a few hefts, I wager," said Donovan. He turned back the way they had come. "We need to move. Tomorrow we meet the next leg of our fortunes. Let us be in good position to do it, and with time to rest."

"How far are we goin'? The little guy had trouble enough fluttering out to catch my eye. Don't wanna shock 'im by throwing him too far out in tha wide blue world, know what I'm gettin' at?" said Earny.

Donovan looked like he might reach forward to touch the small creature, but drew back when it pulled away from the slight shift of his posture. Jana wondered if it could sense what was wrong with him, with both of them, and if that played any part in choosing Earny of all people to be its caretaker.

"We go as far as we need to. The Gestalt isn't getting any closer on its own," said the Swordsman.

"You know," said Jana before she could think better of it. "Your stuffiness doesn't fool anyone anymore." Donovan looked at her with what might have been genuine surprise. "You let it slip too often, Donny of Kolendhar that is no more."

He gave her his driest sidelong glare, but said nothing as he forged westward again. Jana grinned in a self-satisfied way as she followed, Earny trailing far behind and narrowly avoiding trees while he whispered to his newfound friend.

* * * *

The Swordsman hunkered and watched the forest when they stopped next with only one thing on his mind: Earnald Avers should be dead right now. Four years ago, Donovan could have cut down an arrow loosed from full pull at a hundred feet without wasting a drop of sweat, but a few days ago, when the other Swordsmen had revealed themselves, he had nearly missed Vine's attack. It was half training and half luck that had allowed him to cut down that deadly throw before it ended Earny's life, something he could barely admit to himself, let alone to his companion whose survival had led to the discovery of what might be the last Root Dragon in all of existence.

The further truth of what had happened today was that it had been the Cold which had caused the lapse, at least indirectly.

For these past three days, hidden beneath a blanket of calm stoniness, Donovan was at war with the force the Cleric had introduced into him. Every minute, waking or not, was spent waging that war, firing psychic arrows from between mental merlons at an ethereal enemy who sortied and besieged from the dark of his consciousness. Even now his hands shook from the strain; he kept his thumbs hooked on his belt, or his fingers closed around his sword or satchel to hide it. The only way he had found to press the advantage was to cut the Cold off from the rest of him, much the same way he was trained to disconnect pain. Simple, that, akin to plucking a leaf from its branch, only this leaf carried something more precious than his body's ability to register damage: the place where the Cold had taken hold also kept his instincts, his training, and his battle-won skills. Without it, he was declawed and broken. It was only with the greatest effort of will and discipline that he had been able to gather every last scrap of ability he could muster and, with more than a little fortune, deflect Vine's purposefully slow and long throw.

For the first time in a great long while, the Swordsman felt afraid.

He watched as Earny held a leaf up to Ruti's small mouth. The Root Dragon took a bite, waited a moment for the taste to settle on his black tongue, then spit it out with a soft cough. "Don't like that, huh?" he said. Ruti shook his head.

Then, almost before he could brace himself, a hard, stark wave of the Cold blitzed the Swordsman, washing over his mind. In an instant, the world filled to the brim with creatures in every wooded nook, built of gory fangs and cinder eyes. He looked at Jana and Earny, who seemed devils to him now; even little Ruti looked a fiend ready to inject Donovan with poison from the black, hooked stinger now protruding from his tail.

Donovan hunkered and clasped his hands together with a hard *smack* and ground his teeth until he feared they'd turned to dust.

"Which way, Donovan?" asked Jana. Then: "I have to pee again."

"Why is it women feel the need to announce their fluids?" Earny asked Ruti, who ignored him and watched the forest with his strange reptile eyes. "Thousand years and ya don't get women, eh? Not surprisin'."

Inside his mind, Donovan was roaring with anger.

Back. To the rear, I say! You do not rule me!

(What did I tell you? I am you.)

I said back!

The roar came out as a stifled grunt as he stood straight and forced his hands to his hips. A deep breath steadied him, and just like that the Cold receded. Still trembling, he nodded northwest. He dared not speak; his voice would give his strain away.

They waited for Jana to finish her business, then pushed forward.

Earny said something about a column of fog he spotted rising through the trees ahead in the distance.

Donovan, incapable of considering this right now, pressed on and his circle followed.

* * * *

They made their way steadily through the thick of the forest, crushing through the forbs with their heads down, the late day sun oppressive as it scattered through the gloom of the growing fog. They spoke not at all save for Earny's whispers to Ruti, which the dragon would occasionally respond to, chittering back in its strange clicks and metallic notes that unnerved Jana with their peculiarity. She looked back over her shoulder occasionally to keep track of him, but more often than not the Root Dragon was out of sight. Earny did not seem concerned about his whereabouts, so Jana assumed Ruti was still somewhere on his person, perhaps in his pocket.

Their path crept up a mountainous area where the canopy overhead blocked more of the sky and the understory grew thick and more difficult to navigate. Donovan referred to his quick copy of the Cleric's map once, his tanned brow furrowed and a deep look of consternation in his eyes. He then hid it away again beneath his duster and did not refer to it again; Jana prayed he knew where he was leading them.

To a Mist Dweller. That's where he's leading you.

She had nearly driven the thought from her mind, but it returned in full force now. A flood of panic raged through her and spurred her heart until it drummed in her ears. She had allowed the Swordsman's plan to sweep her along, and she had accepted it in the moment as a prisoner accepts their death sentence, but now the thought of marching into the waiting jaws of one of the things that killed Cory no longer seemed the mandate of fate. All she would have to do is turn and run away into the forest and she would be free from this insanity—the Swordsman would not be bothered to follow her, of that she was sure. And so what if he did? At least she could find peace knowing she had tried, that she didn't mindlessly follow the possessed leader of their group to certain death.

Her thoughts were interrupted by a loud chittering behind her. She turned in time to see Ruti leap from Earny's shoulder and flutter away into the forest, clicking and muttering in his dragon-speak as he went. "Wait, where're you goin'?" Earny said, grasping after him.

Donovan grabbed him by the shoulder and kept him in place. "Hold, Earnald Avers."

Earny, eye wide with concern, looked as though he might not listen, but he did not move.

Jana watched as Ruti flew into the forest until he was a hundred paces from where they stood and hovered there. The forest grew still as the wind died. Then the bushes beneath Ruti began to rustle and shift, and Jana saw Donovan reach for his sword and Earny do the same. She put her hand on her dirk in turn, but did not draw it.

The bushes parted and a flash of orange and black darted from the greenery. A fox, nimble and fluid, slipped into view, its movements lithe and perfect. It paused when it saw them, ready to turn in a snap and vanish back the way it had come, but Ruti descended then and alighted on its back with a hiss that was audible even from this distance. The fox twisted away, frantic, as the Root Dragon sunk its black claws—Jana was certain they had grown by inches—through its fur and into its skin. The fox yelped and strained to move forward, its legs giving way. It collapsed onto its stomach where it lay writhing, Ruti attached between its shoulder blades. Jana watched wide-eyed as the fox's body contorted and shriveled and its fur, a moment ago a bright red, lost its pigment and turned to a dead grey as it fell in clumps to the ground. The revealed skin beneath shriveled in seconds, and Jana could see those same scrawling purple veins she had noticed on Earny's palms growing outward from where the Root Dragon grasped the animal's flesh. The skin faded to an ashen shade as the veins consumed it, the fox's body shrinking by a third as its eyes glazed over white. While its broken form rattled with its last moment of life, Ruti opened his small mouth and a fountain of pearlescent fluid flushed forth; it looked like the *ai'che* covering the tree where they discovered him, Jana realized through her horror. The *ai'che* accumulated in a blob roughly the size of the fox's body, and with one last hiss, Ruti released his quarry and burrowed headfirst like a snake into the viscous mass.

Nothing moved again for a time.

"Swordsman, sir," said Earny in a tense whisper. "What in the name of it is happening? What happened to Ruti?"

Donovan shook his head.

Then the *ai'che* mass began to contract, shrinking into its center as though being sucked up by an invisible mouth. Smaller and smaller it condensed, drawn back into the shape of Ruti's body, at first only in rough approximation, then growing in detail, revealing the contour of his scales, the ridges of his head, the curve of his eyes. Then the *ai'che* was gone, vanished into the folds of his scales, and Ruti lifted off again, hovering over the crumpled form of the fox. Satisfied with his work, he fluttered back to Earny's shoulder, looking aware and intelligent, but moving with an animalistic strangeness that set Jana on permanent edge.

"What in the bloody fuck was that?" asked Jana, her voice raspy with sudden fear. "Is he going to do that to one of us?"

Ruti seemed to look at her in response. His tongue flitted out of his mouth in a way she interpreted as antagonistic, but he did not respond in his strange dragon-language. Even Earny seemed wary of his small friend now, though he still smiled as the Root Dragon pressed closer to his neck.

The Swordsman considered what he had seen. "Let's go. We'll have to trust that our little friend here bears us no ill will. We'll camp once we've reached the lee of the mountain."

Jana stayed behind Earny this time and kept Ruti in sight for the rest of the day.

* * * *

The night was deep when the vague crumple of something thrashing against the wet bed of pine needles pierced the dreamless dark of Jana's sleep. Then came Donovan's voice: "Jana! Earnald!"

Jana's eyes snapped awake. She was upright before she could identify what had woken her. Then she saw the Swordsman laying like a frightened child, convulsing, teeth clenched and bared, eyes alight with fury.

"Come to me, both of you!"

They did as they were told. Ruti, who had been huddled on Earny's chest, scampered to the top of his head and peered down, looking more curious than afraid. Earny, on the other hand, looked ready to soil himself; his hand danced to the butt of his pistol and off again while he shuffled from foot to foot. Jana held her pistol ready and stood over the Swordsman, a shiver tracing an icy line down her back.

"Look in my satchel. There's a run of cord inside. Hurry!" the Swordsman hissed.

It was hard to turn her back on him, but she did and found the cord he spoke of.

"Bind my hands and legs to the trees. Do it now. And tie them tight, for your lord and your line. Do it now!"

She hesitated only a moment, and then she and Earny moved fast and in tandem. She cut the cord into sections with her dirk, then tied Donovan's wrists with a manger hitch the way Dad had taught her with cattle, with an extra loop and knot for luck. She saw Earny struggling and twice told him his knots needed to be tighter, but to his credit Donovan's legs were like wild animals, and holding them still was nigh impossible. When they were done they stood back and watched the Swordsman's body buck like an enraged bull. His eyes snapped open and Jana saw a red glow kindling in their deepest recesses. His voice was a growl, more parts animal than man. "Stand back, whatever happens. If you need to kill me, then so be it. Now back!"

Jana unloosed the rawhide from her shoulder and felt the cool snakewood grip against her sweat-slicked palm, held it at her side, and watched as the Swordsman fought his bonds until she thought his back would break. And then, faster than the beat of a hawk's wings, Donovan, Swordsman of Kolendhar, vanished and the

Demon, who had last sunk his teeth into Creel the Lion and his foolhardy men, appeared.

* * * *

The storm was back. It encompassed everything, a void of tenebrous clouds endlessly churning, filled with black eyes hungry for flesh. For his flesh. They were hunting him now, all of them, like wolves descending a dogie lost on a moonless plain. He had to get free, or they would have him. He took the rage, which burned from his chest with fury, and threw it into snapping the lines binding him. Two of the creatures were upon him, hunkered and insane, ocher claws scraping the ground, obsidian eyes glowing with hate, tusks coated with saliva as slick as oil wriggling over their lean predatory chins like worms.

Kill them.

(I cannot. I will not!)

Kill them before they kill you.

(Please don't. Please...—

—don't! Back I say!

(You must kill them. Do it now!)

Let me free! *he bellowed into the barren night and the roiling cloud bank above. His fingers, which felt full of an unbearable need to move, clutched at air searching for his sword. He tried to twist himself to the side, to close his teeth on the cord which bound him, but could not. He was captured. Any minute now the creatures would stop their gloating and move in for the kill. How long had they been hunting him? He couldn't remember, but it must have been a long time. He had been careful, so very careful. How had he been captured? In his sleep he guessed, for his temple throbbed now, from a blow to the head while he dreamed, no doubt. Somehow they had found him when he was most vulnerable and fell upon him with skill and cunning. Why they hadn't killed him at the first chance, he would not know.*

So they can see your face. So they can know your mind when you realize this is the end.

But Keeper save him, he would not find the Black without a fight, even if it meant tearing off a single piece of their flesh with his teeth the heartbeat before his death; at least he'd die with that satisfaction. Better than meeting the end of the endless push a victim tied like a virgin to be sacrificed. Better anything than that.

The creature closest to him raised its claw and he readied himself as—

* * * *

—Jana aimed the six-shooter at Donovan's head with an unsteady hand.

"What're you doin', Miss Jana?" asked Earny. Ruti hid behind his neck and peered around again, eyes wide and unblinking. He looked afraid now.

"Quiet!" she said harshly. She tried to steady herself, to keep the iron sight trained on Donovan's gyrating form, but it was hard. She thought of her dad, the way her bullet had exploded his skull, and then of Donovan in the rare moments he had been tolerable, looking on her with something akin to brotherly concern, or perhaps simple amusement which seemed both condescending and endearing. She considered ending the spark of this man with but a twitch of her finger and wanted to vomit.

You wanted to be a killer, Jan. Here's your chance.

Donovan's eyes flapped wide again and bored into her, fluxing a deep crimson light into the campsite. His lips had begun to foam, his teeth locked tight and revealed by the twitch of a snarl. Wave after wave of violent energy wracked him as he fought the cords with every ounce of his insanity.

Minutes passed like this, then an hour, and never once did Jana aim her pistol anywhere but at the Swordsman's brow; all the while his movements grew more frenzied.

Then the first cord snapped.

Donovan's right leg lurched free. It kicked empty air, and when he realized his position through the madness he strained upright, leveraging his boot against the scrub below. He spun halfway around, then rocked back the other way. A howl, which until today Jana would have sworn no human could make, ran screaming from his chest. Every hair on her body stood straight.

"What do we do?" asked Earny.

"*Oina ko-vey*," said Ruti. Jana wasn't sure what that meant, but she had the feeling they were all on the same page.

Donovan keeled to the side then with great effort and his other leg broke free. This happened so suddenly that Jana could barely lean away as he lunged for her, snarling, spittle flecking his chin. He snapped his teeth there like a rabid dog and never once blinked. Something cold and certain settled in Jana's stomach then, and she took aim between Donovan's eyes. Her finger inched back the trigger; in her mind, the noise of the hammer levering echoed into the night like the creak of a huge door hinge.

Moments before her bullet might have carved a tunnel through the malfunctioning matter of his brain, Donovan fell still with his eyes closed and the world went silent in turn. Jana realized she had been holding her breath and discharged it with a gasp. Earny had backed away twenty paces with his pistol drawn. He held it pointed somewhere in their vicinity, but didn't move or fire.

They watched as Donovan's long, nimble form hung like a masterless puppet, coarse hands turned palm-up, the muscles around his mouth disengaging, his shoulders relaxing until his body dangled and swayed on the cool evening breeze. His sword lay just out of reach to his right; in the chaos, Jana hadn't thought of keeping it away from him. That would have been a fine disaster if ever there was one. She flicked it farther off with her toe for good measure.

"What in the name of it was that, lady?" asked Earny, barely a whisper. "What exactly is he, Swordsmanship aside?"

Jana shook her head but could not speak. *He's just like me*, she wanted to say, but she knew her one-eyed friend would not understand.

"What do we do with him now?" The ex-highwayman's questionable aim was still trained on the Swordsman. Ruti paced from one of his shoulders to the other, looking from Jana to Donovan and back again. The small dragon looked enraptured by all of this human drama, as if this was the most interesting thing he had seen in a long time. A *very* long time if Donovan's translation of the creature's age was accurate. His wings shuddered and coiled to his back and his blue eyes sparkled in the firelight.

"What if he doesn't wake up?" asked Earny after a long stretch of silence.

"Then we'll have to go on without him. He drew a map that showed the way."

"And face a Dweller ourselves?" Earny's grimace would have been comical if it hadn't reflected her feelings perfectly. Facing a Dweller themselves. She had done it before and survived, which was better than her family and others had managed, but that was hardly a qualification. She found herself praying Donovan would wake, even if it meant listening to his damnable shit-eating tone day in and out.

"Would he really have killed us, think ya?" Earny asked her with such sadness in his voice it made her chest clench up.

She thought it over, then nodded. "Yes. I think he would have. And I would have returned the favor if needed."

Earny swallowed hard in response.

"He's fighting it now. I can see it. Curse it all, I can feel it. He's beating it down with his mind, back into the hole it wells up from," she said, watching the minute flinches of effort on Donovan's face.

When the Swordsman opened his eyes again they were back to their cold green selves. It took him a moment to find his bearings. "Did it take me?"

"You went out of yer mind, Master, sir," said Earny from afar.

"Are you hurt?" he asked them. Jana shook her head. A bitter look, and then Donovan went limp, still half-tied to the trees, and breathed deep of the night air. "Keeper save us. Keeper save us all," he said to himself.

Then he told her: "Tie me again."

"Why?" asked Jana. "Are you not all right?"

"I can still feel it on the edge and I'd not risk your lives on my ability to hold it back. Do it."

His tone left no question, so they did as they were told.

"If it comes again for me tonight, I want you to kill me. Do not hesitate. I won't be able to keep it at bay until I've rested, and if it goes much further I'll be lost. Promise me this," he said to Jana. She nodded and knew in her core that she'd do it this time without hesitation.

Then Donovan's body went lax and he hung suspended between the trees and did not move again.

They kept watch as he slept for much of the remaining night.

At one point Ruti crawled from Earny's leg and mounted the Swordsman's chest. Jana thought she saw the Root Dragon perch above Donovan's parted lips, tiny feet on his chin, and do something; what exactly, she couldn't say. But afterwards it looked like his breathing had regulated, deeper and calmer, and she relaxed at last.

"Do you think he'll stay asleep, Miss Jana?" asked Earny.

She shrugged. She had almost forgotten this part of him, or that this would be a part of her, too. And soon. "Maybe. I won't though. I'll stay watch. Get some rest."

"You sure of that, Miss?"

She nodded, so fazed afterward that Earny's awful snore didn't even bother her.

Despite what she had said, she fell asleep eventually, pistol laid across her belly, propped on a tree facing Donovan.

The night was cold and long and in the morning she knew they'd wake still afraid.

10

The Swordsman was still asleep when Jana waded up from the darkness of her dreams. She rubbed the sleep from her eyes and stretched, the land around her brightening from a grey pre-dawn, her pistol still in her lap. It felt dangerous there, and she looped the rawhide back over her shoulder instead as she stood and inspected the frayed ends of the cords where Donovan had yanked himself free and the knots they had retied out of them. What a night it had been for Mistress Hunter'lue of the Hunter Clan, sole proprietor of the glamorous Hunter Estate, now redone in an elegant charcoal trim.

As she tied her hair back, she saw Ruti perched on Earny's chest and preening his wing, if preening was the word for whatever such a creature did to its wing. When he saw Jana, he spread both wings wide and shook them, hissing and snapping his teeth at her. His tongue flitted once from his mouth, chiding, and the gesture lit a spark of anger in Jana tempered by a cool unease. The way the Root Dragon moved was unlike any living creature she had laid eyes on, both in rhythm and consistency; the motion just looked *wrong*, and it disturbed her understanding of the world. The Root Dragon, to put it plainly, gave her the willies.

Ruti narrowed his eyes and hissed again at her.

"Well fuck you, too."

Unimpressed with her retort, the Root Dragon turned and crawled to Earny's face and scraped at his chin lightly until he stirred and opened his lone blue eye. Earny mumbled something unintelligible and rolled drunkenly to his knees, not truly awake yet.

When Donovan woke he looked sick and pale and his eyes wore deep circles, their whites gone to red. She and Earny untied

190

him after reassurance he was himself, and the Swordsman ached to his haunches like an old man embarking on one last venture to the outhouse from his deathbed. Never had their stoic companion with the sword seemed so *mortal.* Jana understood easily how legends of the Swordsmen had arisen through the ages: their bearing and aptitude lay so beyond the mean that it was easy to forget they were flesh and blood and full of folly like anyone else. Even she had forgotten this, which made his fits of madness all the more jarring. After witnessing them firsthand on two occasions now, the truth was impossible to ignore: every time she looked at Donovan she saw her future. Only she, Mule or no Mule, possessed none of the Swordsman's strength, and so the Cleric's sickness would overtake her all the faster. If he had held out for a year or two, she would last maybe months, if that.

She mulled this over in a small grove hemmed by a dense thicket where she practiced the basic forms with her dirk that Donovan had shown her during their few begrudging lessons. She felt improved already, and the exercises burned enjoyably in her runner's muscles as she bent and thrusted and ducked and danced beneath the watching trees. She even took a few tries throwing the dirk again, this time sticking three of them (two really; the third wobbled and fell after about ten seconds). She wished she could practice more with the pistol, especially since her lone experience firing it involved ending her once-father's life, but they were low on ammunition and bullets were a convenience not easy to come by. So, instead of firing, she accustomed herself to the feel and weight of the weapon and to aiming by swiveling in place towards inanimate targets. When she was satisfied with her drills and her stomach was rumbling, she rejoined her companions.

They ate breakfast in silence. The morning was clearer than most, refreshing and brisk, and deep orange sun flooded into the forest through the overgrowth and dappled them with thin light. When Donovan stood he seemed shaky, but when Jana asked if he was all right he simply nodded and strapped on his sword, donned his hat, and said they should move out.

"Wait," she said to him as they were readying their things. "We need to talk."

"About what?"

"About how you nearly killed us last night."

"*Fa laey gouin cho-iq*," said Ruti with disinterest. He had climbed a nearby oak and was staring into its rutted bark for reasons unimaginable, his snakelike pupils narrowed to slits, his wings juttering with that impossible to predict cadence that unnerved Jana.

"That's what your six-gun is for. No surprises here, princess Hunter'lue," said Donovan. His tone said: *Stop nagging me, kid, if you know what's good for you.* It was exactly what she didn't want to hear.

"Will it happen again?" Somewhere in the last couple of days, she had gotten in the habit of leaving her hand ready on the grip of her pistol. It fell there now.

"Yes, but I will hold it off for as long as I can. You can set off on your own if you wish, but we both know how that ends for you," he replied coldly.

"Can the Cleric heal you? Heal *us*?" she said, stepping closer, into his space.

"I told you I don't know."

"Then what in the Keeper's name are we doing here, Donovan?"

"What would you have me do?" His eyes burned suddenly as he roared his response. He stood with his nose nearly touching hers. "Find a cave to live in like a beast and hunt men who pass by until one kills me? Or maybe you'd see me hang myself from yonder tree or put one of your bullets through my mouth to save you the trouble come time? And then what? What of you, Hunter'lue? Will you do the same when you wake one day thinking Mr. Earnald there is a giant spider come to lick your guts out? Or maybe you'll expect it of him? What say you, girl? Speak now or find silence in this for good."

She stood square to him, so angry she was shaking, her hand wrapped tight now around her pistol. She could not help but think of him last night, how those same eyes that looked into hers now with half-anger, half-shame had been all fury and savage hunger; of how those teeth had tried to bite the life out of her; she thought she could still see where the spittle had dried along his chin. "How far is Pal Myrrah?" she asked him. Her voice stayed steady somehow.

"I'm not sure. Many hefts, yet."

"Can you hold this madness back until then?"

The shame overwhelmed the anger in his gaze and he turned away. They watched as he stared into the forest with his hands on his hips and took deep, measured breaths. "I don't know," he said with a voice so full of resignation she almost couldn't recognize it. "But I'll tell you this…" He turned back towards them. "I will charge with my blade high into the Maw trying, Jana Hunter. With all I am and the stock that bore me, I will fight this war until I find the end, whatever form it takes. I swear on the blood of my dearest, it will be so. Will you take that answer?"

The earnestness in his voice, free of his usual pretense, knocked Jana off-balance. She relaxed her pistol hand and brushed her hair out of her face. "Yeah. That'll do."

The Swordsman looked at her for a long time, then nodded back.

"What in the name of everything sacred have I gotten myself into?" asked Earny, shaking his head. Then he broke out in laughter. "Went from crazy highwaymen to a coupla cursed folk hunting the Reaper. Only me, friends, only this Earny. Ha!" He laughed again and Jana couldn't help but smile too. Even Donovan's hard-lined face broke into his version of a grin, which was more of a lesser-frown. "You folk ready to quit your squabbles and get a move on?" the one-eyed ex-bandit asked. Ruti released the oak that had held his alien interest for the duration of their exchange and took his place on Earny's shoulder. Jana got the impression the Root Dragon had been sitting things out and waiting for the humans to work through their silly bickering.

Donovan nodded and touched Earny's arm. "You're a good man, Earnald Avers, despite the qualms you hold of yourself. Yes indeed. Let us go."

11

The forest floor rose steeply into a massif that cut the sky into a jagged umber crevice that would eventually spill forth the approaching eventide like a shattered astral container. The three humans and the one Root Dragon traversed the ever-moist scrub carpeting the col, wavering in the breeze like great cilia riding the breath of a large beast. All the while Jana repeated the night before in her mind, the moments with the Swordsman's head, hard as you like sober but still no match for a bullet, swaying this way and that beneath the sight of her six-gun. How whimsical fate was, yes indeed, letting a man of misfortune such as Earnald Avers of Vale find the world's last Root Dragon one minute, letting Donovan the Swordsman evade the Reaper's touch—courtesy of Jana's trigger—by a measure of moments the next. She wondered if Cory found fate's whimsy so entertaining in the dark clutch of the Black.

Donovan watched his boots as he followed the dead swale at the foot of the col. Jana wagered he had known the end loomed close these days, but that it was not until last night that the Swordsman discovered the madness rode his very back now, fangs opened wide, claws poised at his throat. One more attack and he'd be enslaved forever. Could that be his destiny? Both of their destinies? Could this endless trek be for a coda that might have come without the marching and suffering? Could people press their bodies so far to claim no fruit for their pains?

While they made their way, a great flock of birds wheeled against the lambent sky, wings full mast and eyes turned ever downward, awaiting repast. The travelers they watched kept quiet for the most part, except Earny, who was trying to teach common speak to his age-old companion.

"Eaaarr-neeee. Come on now, you say it."

"*Eue-lo-mee*," said the tiny white dragon. Even the way the Root Dragon pronounced normal words made her stomach churn.

"You can't teach an ancient dragon new tricks," Jana told him. "Especially when they've got dunny for brains," she added under her breath. She didn't know if Ruti understood her, but the Root Dragon shot her a look and snapped his jaws once with a *click* that made her flinch. One of these days she'd go too far with him and he would launch towards her and dig those black claws into her face and turn her veiny and grey like that poor fox, consumed and discarded.

"Buncha nonsense, that is, Mistress. Hope you don't mind me sayin' it," said Earny. He turned back to Ruti. "Suh-warrrds-muuhhnn. Try it now."

"*Swoeldz-miehn.*"

When they reached the mouth of the col they stopped and Donovan once again prepared them gozen berry sandwiches wrapped in toeleaf, which Jana was already weary of. She never complained, though, for she knew the Swordsman would see that as weakness and she'd die before giving him the satisfaction. Ruti sniffed one of the gozen berries, curious, and then wrinkled his nose and retracted. *You have good taste at least, Ruti.*

"He hasn't eaten since we found him," Earny pondered while he chewed. "Think he'll be all right?"

"When he's hungry enough he'll eat, if he's anything like me. I'd eat a pile of hay if the time was right," said Jana, wiping her mouth.

"I wonder what he likes. I'm gonna find out 'fore this is over," Earny said, holding Ruti up on his palms like a scullion displaying supper.

Jana frowned. Before this was over they might all be dead, with two of them mad out of their minds first.

Donovan halted their march and spoke, his voice calm and imbued with a gravity beyond his usual stoicism. "Listen well what I say now. Do I have your ears?"

His three companions stopped and looked at him.

"Do you hear that?" The Swordsman cocked his head and listened for a moment. Jana strained to hear anything beyond the odd Rustie call and the low howl of the wind. Then she picked out what the Swordsman was referring to, the ever so faint babble of water somewhere beyond the rocks. "We're nearly there. That runoff feeds the Gestalt barely a heft away. I've only heard tell of this Ferry on the backs of well-traveled scholars whose grandchildren were in the ground before it reached my ears, so I'll say heed this with an apple on the shelf as well as in the pie."

Jana wondered how the Swordsman managed to make even country nonsense like that sound profound. For some reason it made her want to slap his all-knowing mouth; instead, she folded her hands on her lap and stared with overwrought attentiveness.

"Like was said before, Dwellers possess some form of civility, if you'd call it such. They dress and make weapons and likely have a form of language, though to your ears or mine it would sound like not much at all." He finished his gozen berry sandwich and licked the juices from his fingers; the sight of it sent Jana's stomach spinning. "And then there are the coins. In the old books, there are but two accounts of men encountering Dwellers and living to tell of it. One was a mountain man who fought away a Dweller with a single lucky blow. That tale is not so helpful."

Jana's mind leaped, but she managed to keep the surprise from her face. *Grampy?*

"The second was the son of a lord who lived during the time of my grandfather. He lost a pursuing Dweller in the Mist at the expense of his company entire. But, rather than flee once the way was clear, he chose to double back and track the Dweller to its home."

"Wager a thumb and tumble me down!" said Earny. "Tracked a Misty? Misties don't leave tooth or print anywhere you can see. We've come upon their leftovers a couple times o'er the years, never seen a thing you could follow."

Donovan dug his bootheels into the dirt and leaned back. "Well if any could manage such a feat, it was this man. Tholpin, they called him, the man who discovered Boon Leaf they say and perfected the means to make it thrive, if the name rings familiar."

Nothing registered on their faces, so the Swordsman continued. "Tholpin tracked his way to the Dweller's home, a sort of holy ground as he described it. There were three other creatures present, waiting for the last to return. When it did, Tholpin mounted a ridge and watched through a spyglass. What he observed is what leads us here today. That we return now to what was is called *Naar*, the Ever Circle, the way of all. Tholpin saw the Dwellers, four in all, distribute coin in trade for meat and tools."

Meat. An innocent word before. Now it meant slain women and children. Jana shivered. How long had these demons hunted peace-loving families into the Black? How many widows and orphans made? How many sisters forced to watch as their brother was devoured? The red-hot anger, low burning the last couple of days, boiled up behind her eyes.

"Tholpin made it back eventually, but died soon after of gimpworm poisoning. But before he did, he drew a sketch of what he'd seen. And it was this." He held up the coin from the Hunter house that was. "This is what they use for trade. No man has ever slain a Dweller, nor injured one in any manner worth a tale, so when a man appears with such a coin in hand, a Dweller will know it was given to him. And if it was given, then he is to pass. And so you see," he rolled the coin across his knuckles before vanishing it, "our path is not mindless folly as you fear, Hunter'lue. Provided the stories are true."

"What if they're not?" asked Jana. "This whole thing stinks high and far. And what's the alternative if it doesn't work? Are you gonna let yourself get swept off into the deep again if the time comes? Hope when you're crazy and your eyes are glowing red you'll be a match for a Dweller?"

The Swordsman had produced his pipe while she spoke and lit it now, looking unconcerned. He drew a deep puff and exhaled it. "Do you still have the extra Boon your town friend gave you?"

"What in the Black does that have to do with anything?" She wanted to pound her fists into the ground, or better yet into his cockeyed dunny-licking half-grin. Instead, she stood and paced.

"I have no taste for tobacco or spidergrass, so I'd have some of your Boon, since you make no use of it."

"I'd take up the habit rather than give any to you. Answer my question." She put her hands on her hips and felt her face flush.

Donovan took another puff from his pipe. "Do not trouble, Hunter'lue. It will work."

"Beggin' all that's sacred, sir, but how exactly do you know that?" asked Earny. He was sitting crosslegged now and Ruti had climbed down his shirt and watched this exchange from his grass-stained knee. Earny stroked his nape.

"It must, for there is no other way, short of swimming the Gestalt, but from what's told there are things in those waters you'd choose a Dweller above, untold beasts that would lick clean your skin and drink of your blood and tend your broken body within a mucus sac to be digested alive over time."

Ruti hunkered down and flicked his tongue. "*Naal ti'vei.*"

Donovan nodded.

"What did he say?" asked Jana.

"In the Keeper's hands." Simple and without frills, like the Swordsman himself. He rose and finished his smoke and beckoned for Earny to come forward. "Now, Earnald Avers of the Raef Clan that was, I ask you one last time: your companionship is valued and worthy, but you owe no blood tie or requital. More the opposite, since Hunter'lue here obliges you her life."

"What in the name of it is this *lue* nonsense you've started?" asked Jana. It took all of her willpower not to leap at the Swordsman like she had the night of her final visit to the Hunter Estate.

Donovan ignored her. "On the far side of the Gestalt, I cannot promise what will occur. Pal Myrrah was in the old days a staging point for war, built on the skeleton of some structure left from before the Shift. Whatever reason the Cleric has to seek this place out, I feel in my bones his power will grow as he draws near to it. And should that be the case, I do not know where our," he indicated himself and Jana, "fates lie, let alone yours. So I say you: go whilst you can. There is nothing further for you to prove."

Earny stepped close to the Swordsman and bowed—damn it but the man looked comical even in his most honorable hour—and placed Ruti on his shoulder. "I 'ppreciate the estimation, I do, yer Swordsmansh—"

"Call me Donovan from now on, Earny. I may be stuffy," he looked at Jana, "but I'm still a man."

Earny tried the name silently on his tongue a few times before he said: "Master Donovan, sir. I 'ppreciate yer estimation, sure as my face is ugly. But that whisper deep in my gut you and I call the low voice is saying you and me've found each other for a reason, an' I don't think it was to wake you up with snoring or tie your ankles down during a fit." He gestured to his tiny scaled companion. "Finding this feller was part of it, methinks, but not the whole. Seeing how I've got nothin' to go back to short of digging in with highwaymen—which I'd shave mah nuts off 'fore I did, no offense intended to the lady."

Jana blushed and laughed. "I've said worse."

Donovan nodded in agreement. "I think Ruti would attest to that."

The Root Dragon moved in his jerky, unpredictable way across Earny's shoulder and stared at Jana with eyes somehow both blank and full of depth.

Earny turned back to Donovan. "I'm gonna stick with ya. I think it's meant to be so, if you believe that sorta thing."

Donovan smiled his dark, odd smile. "I do." His voice sounded solemn. "From here to the Maw, I certainly do." He turned back to Jana and held out his hand.

"What?" she asked him. All his kissy-posey with one-eye over there hadn't taken the edge off her mood.

"Boon?" the Swordsman said simply.

"Keeper in a bloody bag, Donovan!" she growled and paced in a circle. He did not retract his open hand. At last she faced him again and said: "Tell me your story first. The whole story. Then you'll have your Boon."

Earny looked from Jana to Donovan and adjusted his eyepatch.

The Swordsman withdrew his hand and frowned. "This way," he said. "When we reach the Gestalt, keep to the trees while I deal with the Dweller. Understood?"

Earny nodded, and Donovan took that as answer enough.

* * * *

The chatter of the runoff drew close faster than Jana had hoped. Secretly she had been glad for the distraction of the Boon conversation; inside she was screaming in terror. With each step her heart smashed hard and fast into her chest until her pulse thumped in her ears. When the first glistening ripples of the Gestalt appeared through the crannies ahead, she felt faint and almost keeled forward.

The Gestalt was the largest lake she'd ever seen, an endless sheet of liquid slate that breached the horizon before drowning in the Mist beyond. She thought she could discern the dreary stretch of the mountain wall on the far side, the divider between them and the next leg of their journey, if they made it that far. The stuff obstructing her view was Mist, she was certain of that much, for as she and Earny crouched near the forest edge she could already spot that unnatural boundary, thin as a man's arm-span, creeping closer to shore until all you could see was a towering luminescent bulwark reaching from earth to clouds.

Stretching from the beach was a gray dock fashioned from ghostwood. It protruded into the water like a fingerless appendage, perhaps probing for fish if she used her imagination, only it wouldn't be porter you'd find in those depths, Jana reckoned. In there *you* would be the meal, pray it true.

Bobbing and weaving near the dock was a raft as big as the foundation of a house, strapped to a lone bollard by a line of horse rope. A long, thin piece of wood, fashioned from an entire tree from the look, lay near the waterline. One end was wide and fin-shaped, and Jana realized what it was: an oar. It'd take three men to lift that thing, let alone use it. The panic stomping with spiked boots within her gut doubled its pace.

The two of them (three, if she counted the dragon) hid behind a stout ironwood, both with their six-guns ready, both wracked with shivers so fierce they would never hit a thing with them if they tried. Donovan gave them a look as he reached the threshold of the forest, then headed forth, still infused with that iron confidence that would have appeared as swagger on a lesser man. They watched the crisp silhouette of his hat and long duster slip noiselessly over the berm and to the lake's edge, sword sheathed, eyes searching the trees for movement.

"Do you think maybe it won't show, Miss Jana?" asked Earny. The man's voice, normally rich with childish enthusiasm, came out a hoarse whisper. Ruti scampered to his hand, which gripped a low branch with white knuckles, and peered out.

Jana, for her part, could not form words at all. Her lips worked and her chest pushed air out, but her mind could not turn it into anything intelligible. She closed her eyes and swallowed a taste of bile her stomach had wretched up. The fear drove her into the back of her mind, where she forced herself to think of summer twilights at home with her brother, of warm afternoons spent with her father in his work area when she was a child, studying his every move while she pretended to play. All the while, back in the here and now, she waited for the worst.

Donovan turned a circle near the soft lap of the Gestalt. Nothing moved but the tall tufts of grass swaying before him. Overhead, a flock of blackbirds took off and headed southward in a tight wedge. Maybe they were afraid, too; if Jana could fly like that she would've been gone long ago.

The Swordsman was halfway back to the forest when the first grumble shook through them all. Donovan froze, then eased onto his back leg, fingers dancing at his hip, eyes narrowed to slits. He turned to see the trees there thrash and divide, making way for the massive cowled creature spawned of an age immemorial as it approached, it's cascading gauntlet of horrible teeth hidden in shadow, it's razor claws curving forth from gray hands wrapped in titanic gauntlets. It bore its sword already, fifteen feet of black metal, squarish and crudely shaped but sharp enough to shear a tree in one stroke. It glided towards the Swordsman, footfalls silent as a spider's, tattered cloak fanned out behind it in a broad tail.

The world spun and Jana stumbled backwards. Earny caught her and drew her close and she clung to him and gasped against his chest. Cory's eyes appeared within her mind, full of sadness, massive jaws bisecting him at the waist; the vision repeated over again and again. She whimpered against Earny's vest and prayed the Keeper and everything sacred that the thing on the beach could not hear her.

If even a fraction of the fear pounding in Jana's head touched Donovan, the Swordsman did not betray it. He stayed moveless, that dark duster the color of coal wafting, his ancient sword banded across his back, not reached for, his broad shoulders relaxed. The creature regarded him, its hood somehow reading inquisitive to Jana's eyes.

Then the Swordsman reached into his satchel and produced the Cleric's coin and held it high into the freezing air.

For a long, terrible moment the Mist Dweller stood as still as stone and studied the Swordsman and his shiny trinket. When it moved towards him at last Jana nearly screamed to watch out, to run, to do anything but wait for the towering demon to skim soundlessly to him. But the Swordsman budged not an inch as the beast akin to those who had devoured the Hunter family halted near enough to breathe on him. It reached out with the veiny trunks of its fingers and delicately—oh so delicately, given its mass—took the coin from Donovan.

For a bare instant, Jana thought she saw the creature tense beneath its robes. She waited for an attack to come, clutching Earny's arm, and then heard the ex-bandit whisper for her to look.

Jana Hunter, last of the Hunter Clan, second bearer of the Cleric's accursed mark and first on the list to snuff his violet-eyed life into oblivion, gritted her teeth and threw every resource she could muster into facing the Dweller. She saw Donovan on the beach, sword still sheathed, watching the creature ease onto its oversized raft with the giant oar in hand. It found its balance, and then gestured with scythe-like claws as if to say, *All aboard!*

Donovan in turn motioned for them to follow.

"Come, lady," said Earny. His voice was still trembling. "Better go while luck's on our side, Keeper save."

Like the time between leaving her old home and beating the trouble out of Lana Preole, everything that happened next seemed far away and ethereal.

Holding her hand tightly, Earny stumbled from the forest and towards the raft, Ruti glommed onto his collar, Jana trundling behind like a drunkard pulled mid-sip from the tavern.

The Dweller reacted with body language that conveyed mild surprise as they appeared, then seemed to lose interest as they boarded the old wooden vessel.

Then, before she had time to fully embrace what was happening, Jana Hunter and her companions were off, sliding into the silent stillness of the Gestalt, a flesh-eating demon for a guide, an on-again, off-again bloodthirsty madman for a companion, and the fellow called the Cleric biding within his fortress of Pal Myrrah beyond the Wastes ahead.

III

THE ENDLESS PUSH

1

The man who called himself Shadow watched the mosquito circle his hand. It drifted in an erratic oblong path, perhaps considering in its low way which patch of skin would yield the most fruitful harvest. Its wings beat furiously as it did so, a blur in the latent heat of a dying day, the last breaths of the sun disappearing now beyond the rocky teeth indistinct on the velvet horizon.

Shadow watched and waited and smiled.

As with much in life, a wait now was worth the reward later (and often not too much later), and so it would be with Donovan of Kolendhar, head of the Order that was, upon his Master's leave, who approached even now with his bitch companion. Patience, yes, patience for all, for without patience men become beasts with but instinct to rule them. And wasn't that the point of all this?

He considered adjusting his weight as he sat cross-legged on the sandbrushed marble railing which overlooked the Wastes from the heights of Pal Myrrah, but decided otherwise, instead savoring the prickles and growing numbness in his backside where pressure had lingered too long. Letting things be, watching them, coming to understand them—these were all central to comprehending life. Too much time was spent fighting that which existed only to aid in the first place. If battle was the goal, then that time should be spent burying steel in another man's flesh, not fighting one's own demons.

Shadow still wore pieces of his Swordsman armor, for the dark leather plates and their scrollwork ever reminded him of what had come before, as well as what he had traded for this precious lot. The body beneath the armor was long and wiry as a borecat, though not as tall as Master's, gemmed with blue eyes which saw much and judged it harshly. His narrow face and high cheekbones appeared ghoulish to himself in the mirror, but women thought otherwise and many a night had found him warm pleasures with little effort beyond showing up in the right place.

He glanced at the concubines, three of them, asleep now in his bed, all with a film of passion sweat still moist on their skin, all destined to wake tomorrow sore and spent. Making love was much like battle, Shadow had come to realize, and he had natural aptness for both.

The muted call of boots drumming on stone echoed from the hall outside, drawing his attention. The keep was bustling these days, though with what Shadow could not precisely say. Master kept his cards close, even around his right-hand, whom he trusted with enough information to be functional and never more. Shadow sometimes wondered if others elsewhere in this very fortress knew different facets of the same wicked gem, carrying out vague tasks with half-explanations, trusting in their supreme commander to conduct their toils into a single fine piece of music. He supposed they were, but he didn't have to like it; in point of fact, he hated it, hated being treated like a simple retainer when objectivity said he was indispensable. For where, pray it to the Black, would Master find another trained as him to do his bidding without beginning again from scratch?

The mosquito's path drew closer to his arm, fine-as-hair legs drooping lazily, its long drinking tube—the proboscis, Shadow thought it was called—aiming for the ripest plot, its oversized middle legs, which he knew were called tarsus, dabbing at invisible points in the air. Still he watched, waiting, all the while contemplating the approaching Swordsman in the back of his mind, his kin for all purposes, perhaps the only other left who shared Shadow's unique skill set. And that perturbed Shadow a great deal. Why should they allow to live the man who was perhaps the lone threat to their mission? But Donovan's continued existence was as Master saw fit and so, like a well-reared child, Shadow did as told without question, at least outwardly. Inwardly he had his own concept of what would take place once Donovan discovered the next leg of his quest, and though the Master might be displeased at first with Shadow's initiative, by the end he would heap praise; praise of the sort that gained a man power.

At last, the mosquito set down. Shadow watched the creature's small thorax gyrate, its veined and speckled wings oscillating, its weightless feet shifting.

Eater and eaten, everything in life was, down to the smallest participants in this empty, pointless game.

Shadow eased his breathing and relaxed his muscles, felt his heartbeat slow in response, a parlor trick of which few at Kolendhar had ever found the knack. The mosquito seemed to appreciate this. It took its time, scrawling a path of concentric tingles about his arm, choosing its meal with care; Shadow empathized, for the satisfaction of waiting until the moment was *just* right was one of life's great pleasures. Yet also he wondered if such a creature possessed senses of pleasure beyond the mechanical. After all, were insects not simple things run exclusively on what men called the low voice, with no higher mind to diffuse their instincts?

He watched as the mosquito at last dipped its beak-like mouth-thing into his flesh.

Life of pure instinct seemed opposed to the natural path of man, yet was that not what Master declared ultimate happiness? In a way, Shadow supposed it was, if you defined happiness by a meeting of all needs. This mosquito required blood and air, and it possessed both right now. That it was minutes from its death meant nothing. He wondered if it could feel anything like fear once death entered its awareness. He reckoned not.

Eater and eaten. The Ever Circle.

He forgot the mosquito momentarily, happily engorging itself on his essence, and considered what he must do next: bide while Master laid his plans out for Donovan, then follow as Donovan executed them. Simple enough were it any other man, but if Shadow's battle-scarred years had taught him even one thing, it was that complications always arose when dealing with a man of this... *Caliber* was the word, though he wished it wasn't. And what of the Swordsman's companions? Not worth the worry, he decided. The girl the Master cared for in his incomprehensible way and would be tricky, but the other was useless and could be discarded.

But Donovan.

Oh, dear Donovan, how long this has been coming, and how savory it will be.

The very thought raised bumps on his arms, but did not disturb his small friend who was now almost full.

Somewhere in the Wastes a bird called; it was a dry, lonesome sound, perhaps cried by some poor creature who had lost their mate. He wished he could tell it not to worry, for nothing lives long in the Wastes, especially not alone.

Eater and eaten. Speaking of which...

He watched with interest now as he spied the mosquito, its proboscis still sheathed in the rough grain of his arm, beginning to twitch.

Years ago, when the threat of the Dwellers grew dire and Blood Demons had first begun their hunts, Shadow had made a decision never to become the eaten—or at least never *just*. Not in this lifetime. *Alamast* was the name of the poison mixed in his veins, deadly even in trace amounts, the sort old-world courtesans might have laced tiny knives with to prick the neck of a noble in the pale watches of the night. Building immunity was one task, but infusing one's blood with such a lethal mixture, well, that was something altogether different, something which rang pure to this once-Swordsman. Daily dosage was required to maintain an ample level of toxicity, but that was fine, just fine, for more frightening than dying from a lack of *alamast* was the thought of a Mist Dweller or other maneater's teeth crushing his life out without knowing retribution. At least then the eaten had one last chance to be the eater. Shadow hoped, in some dark place he kept mostly ignored, that one day he might find the chance to enjoy that satisfaction, perhaps when his days grew too numerous and his great flame but smoldered anyway, to rest assured that whatever thing consuming his life was swallowing its death as well. That would be a fine way to find the Black.

He watched as the last of the mosquito's primitive nervous system went haywire, its legs bucking twice and then failing, its body no longer possessed of the strength to withdraw from his skin. Then it was dead, still protruding from him like a gangled flag, staring blindly with its gridded eyes.

At last, Shadow reached over and flicked its corpse into the night.

He rose, smiling into the dusty pink sky and the fold of clouds that hung there, and then headed past the soft moans of the concubines, who writhed in their sleep as if reliving what he had done to their bodies, and out into the hall, towards the Hold, where he would brief his men on the approach of Donovan the Swordsman and his band.

2

The wide ghostwood raft crossed the mirror-calm of the Gestalt. The Dweller's outsized oar dipped into those Stygian depths in time with Jana's heartbeat, splash-less, each stroke near silent. From shore, she thought she had comprehended the breadth of this dark inland sea, but now, as hour upon hour smiled and waved on its way past, she realized she had underestimated it. The late morning of their departure had drawn fast into afternoon, now headed for a musty dusk darkened prematurely by the asphyxiating Mist traveling alongside them.

The Dweller seemed mostly disinterested in its cargo. Its nightmarish bulk twisted and worked beneath its tattered rags, focusing diligently on paddling them onward at a rapid pace. Those long claws, kin to those which had ripped asunder small Cory, clacked now and then as it adjusted its grip on the oar, making Jana shiver; it felt as though someone had their hand thrust down her throat and was rattling her spine. Sometime during the day her fear had simmered from panic to a low burn, bearable now but not low enough to rest. She stayed caddy-corner from the creature, one hand on her pistol, the other on the pommel of her dirk, and kept a close watch. She thought of the six-gun, its fine snakewood grips warmed from her palms, the grooved chamber still cold from the lake air, and realized if she did have to put this loud death-maker to sudden use, it would be on herself.

At least then she wouldn't have to watch those hellish teeth chomp into her guts just before she found the Black.

* * * *

Donovan, too, watched the Dweller with a keen eye. At first, he thought he could read signs in the creature's thewy build belying an attack, but when the thing kept to itself during the hours gone, the Swordsman settled into a watchful ease. As the inky stretch of beast-infested water glided below them, he began thinking of home, something he rarely afforded. Home that was once but nevermore, leveled from within and without by the man he now hunted. Of course, there was more to that story, oh so much more, which he had not yet shared with his companions. He wondered if he ever would, for its bearing on their roles in this junk play was negligible. Yet he felt as though he should tell them, that he owed them for their trust, which they gave freely despite his affliction during this nightmarish crusade. Then his other side, not the Cold but something of close relation, spoke up. His sense of duty was nonsense, it told him, for these two were parts of the whole who had shunned him and his Order, who had betrayed and murdered his friends, and who now, when the days grew darkest, sought coddling from someone—anyone—possessed of more strength than they. As he had told Jana, helping the weak upset the natural order of things; to believe otherwise was naive folly. *Let them help themselves*, his old master had once said, not long before Donovan's terrible scar was born. *Let them help themselves, because for you to aid them is to prolong their necessary death. Nothing more.* Yet in the quiet of this cursed lake with his silent companions, the words of the people he had left in his dust called to him from the black of his memory:

Will the people come? Will they fight?

I don't think so. World's not ready for that.

The starving peasant father trudging the hard-packed curve of the Drudge was right, more right than even he realized. The world was not ready for that. The only thing the world was ready for was being left to its devices, each man for himself, letting nature and the Keeper sort out who would survive. Donovan knew in his heart self-preservation was all that mattered in this game. Even the girl, hapless as a babe, was collateral in his tale of revenge. *Yes, call it what it is. Revenge for what he has done to you and yours.* But not yet; waiting for the moment to be just right was required—and would call on every last inch of Donovan's hard-earned discipline to achieve.

But it could be done, yes, and it would. Bet your stock on it, as the country folks say.

But he could not ignore Jana's small voice either: *You should because you can.*

* * * *

As the day drew on Donovan took advantage of the last hours of light to show Jana how to care for her six-gun. He dissembled it and laid it across a black terry cloth, which he kept in his satchel, oiling each piece and cleaning it, then letting her take a turn. Well and good she learned to do this on her own and practice until habit formed. The last thing he needed was a misfire when the madness of the Cold took him fully into its Siren arms.

He could sense the Cold watching, petulant now, no longer flaring in his skull but skulking in his depths, maybe keeping his low voice company, whispering soothing words to make it lull and ready it for one last push that would topple his mind for good. Let that happen if fate willed it, but not on this forsaken raft on this unholy water (though with grim fascination he did wonder what the Dweller's reaction to his madness would be; likely they'd all die at its sword).

He looked harder with his sharp eyes to observe the thing of many names that lived in the Mist, admiring its blade in the process for its sheer utilitarianism. No frills, no etchings, no family lineage worked into the hilt, just simple leather straps and perhaps ironwork for the blade, which was unpolished but honed with skill. It had no need for a sheath but rather attached to the creature's back by means of an intricate bracket system that snapped closed and was released by some method he could not understand. The Dweller seemed to purposefully keep its back pointed at the lake to hide its exact workings, which he understood; he'd do the same were their positions reversed.

They huddled close to the edge of the raft, which had no railings and felt precarious. Earny inched over as the day grew late and said under his breath, "How much longer, do ya reckon, master?"

Donovan shrugged and struck a match off his palm and lit his pipe. "It will be dark when we shore up, but who knows with this damnable Mist?"

"I've not seen those mountains again, the ones we spotted from the dock. But then again I can barely spot your face in all this bloody murk," said Earny, sounding nervous but collected.

Donovan nodded, glancing at Ruti, who crouched now on the raft beside Earny's thigh, peering into the blackness of the water below. Occasionally he would undulate in a sudden jerking motion, his head telescoping back and forth like a bird ejecting food from its crop. As the movement, which was involuntary from the look, moved through him, the scales on his body appeared to flex and ripple in a show of color that began at the top of his head and spread out in a wave along his body, terminating at the tip of his tail; if it wasn't magical, then Donovan could find no explanation for it.

As if sensing his gaze, Ruti broke from his trance and looked the Swordsman directly in the eyes. The Root Dragon stared at him blankly for a moment, and Donovan wondered if it was a frown he perceived on the creature's small mouth. "*Suuwahordz-muhn,*" he said; in the hard silence, Donovan wondered if the Dweller might hear. If it did, it did not seem to care that there was a fourth charge in its quarry.

"*Lo uil yoi so'mah,*" replied Donovan, reaching out to stroke the Root Dragon's chin. Ruti drew back from his touch and hissed, eyes turning black for a blink before returning to their normal reptilian appearance a moment later. Donovan withdrew. "My mistake," he said with a frown.

"He'll warm up to you two. Just give him time," said Earny. "What did you say to him just now?" He tried to share his wonder with Jana with a look in her direction, but she did not seem to hear their exchange as she stared empty-eyed at her toes, hands hugged around her knees.

"I told him it is good to have his fortune with us." The Swordsman puffed on his pipe and exhaled. The Dweller reacted to this, and Earny heard the faintest hint of the dark rumbling the folk of Vale knew well and feared, but it died quickly and the creature turned away again. "I've heard it said a Root Dragon can save a single flux of a man's breath and return it later, for a price, should he lose it."

"You mean it'll heal the dead?"

Donovan shook his head. "I doubt that, but the stories must come from somewhere."

"Maybe they heal the wounded. With some of that pearly business we saw near the cave," said Earny.

"The Rootstone is created where the creature lives as part of their adolescence. At least say the old books," Donovan offered. His eyes were distant, a hopeless homesickness spreading within him.

"Do you think it means to kill us when we get there?" Earny asked, nodding towards the Dweller.

"It can hear you even at a whisper, though if it speaks the language I know not" ," Donovan said, then returned to Jana's six-gun, reassembling it with his pipe sticking out his mouth. Earny looked at the Dweller sharply and kept quiet for a while afterwards. "This is the last of the Boon. I may have to take your terms after all. I'm aching for more already," the Swordsman told Jana.

Something registered in her face, far away at first. Then she met his sardonic look and grinned a heartless grin and nodded. "Have your story ready, then. Even Earny's shared his. You're the odd one out."

"A place I'm used to, pray it true," said the Swordsman. There was no humor in his deep voice.

* * * *

The trip wore endlessly, and Jana watched the water and the Dweller and sometimes Donovan in between, wondering if there did exist a place where stuffy know-everything Donovan would be right at home with his proper talk and endless proverbs. That place might have been Kolendhar from all told, and for the first time, she realized his story was not so different from hers and Earny's. They were all three of them orphans, death behind them, seeking retribution or salvation or something in the bleak cast of the Wastes and whatever lay within—for ill or fortune they'd not know until they arrived.

The Swordsman was smiling at her now, and for another fleeting moment she saw him as just a man, thinking how handsome he might be when he wasn't irritating her to the brink of madness. In a world where Donovan the Swordsman was a sweet gentleman and not a self-centered murdering vagabond, he'd be quite a catch for the right lady. Yes, quite a catch indeed, probably snared by a princess built of angel parts more beautiful than Jana could ever pretend to match.

Donovan's words echoed in her mind then: *I swear on the blood of my dearest, it will be so.*

At the time she'd been so heated that his words had slipped past unnoticed, but now with her greatest fear ten paces away and a desperate need to distract herself, they rang with strange power. *My dearest.* Was it a woman he spoke of? A child? She suddenly burned with the need to know.

"Will you tell me why you call me *lue?*" she asked as her thoughts broke.

The Swordsman looked at her, wearing that smug half-grin that boiled her blood. She already wondered how she could ever have thought him attractive. "That is my secret, Hunter'lue."

"Tell me or don't say it again, if it frightens you." Her arms were folded now in classic Mule position.

Donovan laughed, strange and full of throaty wetness.

"I mean it. And if you want your Boon, you'll add your name-calling to the story."

"Are you extorting me now, Lady Jana of Vale?"

She growled softly and clenched her fists. "I'm telling you my terms. Take them or be silent."

"Your terms were given already. I might accept them, or I might not, but it's too late to add an addendum," he said while drumming his sword against his thigh, his grin persisting.

"You two argue like kin, pray it," said Earny, itching at his eyepatch.

"How did you lose your eye, Earnald?" asked Donovan, sitting back, his exchange with Jana already forgotten. She looked at him open-mouthed, surprised by his directness. She'd wondered herself but thought it rude to ask. Apparently, the Swordsman was possessed of no such scruples.

"Now that, ye brother and sister spirits, is a long tale full o' the sordid stuff you'd wanna burn your ears off 'fore listenin' to."

"I'd hear it," said Donovan, "for my life has been free of the sordid sort for some time now."

"Donovan the monk," said Jana with more edge than she meant. He looked at her sharply and there was something strange in his eyes for a moment. Perhaps hurt? She could not imagine her small-minded princessy words causing the slightest pinch to Mr. Kolendhar's hard brain. No sir. She ignored his look and waited for Earny's story.

She was disappointed when the ex-bandit boiled it down to: "Let's just say it was one part salacious housewife, too fond of various pleasures of the fleshy sort more prudent townsfolk frown upon, a crazed mackerel of a husband with a temper, and a hot fire poker. Don't ask the details, blessit all, for I think I may just've blocked 'em clear out."

Donovan nodded, his grin fading. "I've heard it said a man's scars are the record of what's made his life unique."

"If that be the case," said Earnald Avers as he held his small friend Ruti on his thigh, "then half the men I've met in my time should be walkin' around with one eye missing."

Jana, who had been trying to stay grumpy for the Swordsman's sake, could not help but smile.

The Dweller pushed on during all of this, long oar strokes barely splashing.

Jana wondered if it understood their mundane banter. She hoped it did not.

Then the Mist began to part, and shore was visible once more.

3

They drew up minutes later. The Dweller exited first, throwing its long oar to the ground and tying the raft down with a rope as thick as Miss Jana's thigh. Then it stepped aside, quiet as gossamer, and stared at them from the waterside.

Donovan went next. He stood before the Dweller and waited expectantly; Earny suspected that the Swordsman hoped to retrieve his coin, mayhap for the return voyage. When he gave up and beckoned for them to follow, Earny felt his hopes sink. Perhaps there would be no returning, not in this life, pray it. He felt a sick rush in his stomach, but stepped off the raft onto the spongy strand anyway and breathed a hard sigh. The air here smelled of sulfur and something else more putrid.

Fine fix ya got yerself in here, Earny. Fine indeed.

Jana would not follow them at first. Her face was a limpid cream, her pupils distended black balls sunk into the sullen veneer of her skin. The Swordsman called again, and then a third time, yet still she stood, one hand on the pistol hanging by rawhide from her small shoulder, the other flittering nervously against her dirk pommel while she stared at the nothing before her face.

"Girl, Jana. Forward now, for yourself and your fallen. Come!" Donovan's dark voice caromed into the diaphanous terrain, lost then as a rising breeze enveloped them.

Jana's first sudden steps forward seemed to coincide loosely with the Swordsman's final command, but there was no other indication she had heard him. She kept her gaze downward as she drifted past the Dweller, whose tattered cowl regarded their leaving impassively.

The Mist here was so thick they could see nothing beyond a fifty-foot stretch of pebbly ground and virescent scrub before everything vanished into the gloom. For a moment Earny thought he espied the towering natural ramparts of the Ven, but they were lost before he could be sure. "Which way do we go? I can't see a thing," he said to Donovan.

The Swordsman did not answer, and they stood studying the blank, sheer face of Mist towering above them, surrounding them, daring them to choose a direction by the low voice alone and tempt the fates. Donovan pursed his lips, and Earny knew better than to interrupt while the Swordsman was so deep in thought. Finally he said, "Come. Follow closely and keep a hand on the person in front of you. If I say hold, then do so without hesitation. Let's go."

Jana nodded without contesting the Swordsman's instructions, but Earny struggled to choke down a terrible trembling fear in his chest, one that carried on its back visions of crumbling ground and dark pits ready to consume them at the first misstep.

Before they were gone, the Swordmaster stopped and turned back to the Dweller, who was watching them intently, and raised his sword in salute. "Good will and fortune. Many thanks for your guidance."

If the Dweller gave a bloody damn, Earny could not tell.

But as they vanished from view, he may have read something into the slow way the Dweller's hidden eyes turned downward from their backs to the cold lap of water at its boots.

* * * *

Jana held Earny's wrist with white knuckles, following his tangled mop of hair and the rawhide strap of his eyepatch through a stretch of land she could only imagine. The Mist went on far and long, longer than she'd ever seen it stretch. As she moved her scar began to throb again, the first time in days, so sudden and acute it made her groan and stumble.

"You all right, Miss Jana?" Earny asked her.

She caught her breath and nodded and told him to go on.

Somewhere up ahead she could hear the sudden beat of Ruti's wings, and she caught sight of the Root Dragon flashing past as he took off from Earny's shoulder with a shrill cry and flapped away into the wall of the Mist. Earny lurched after him as he went. "Wait!" His step towards the vanishing dragon pulled him off balance and, as a single unit, all three of them tilted and struggled to keep their feet.

When they had steadied themselves, Donovan turned to Earny. "One wrong step in this place and we will all find the Black together. Control yourself."

"But Ruti, sir, he—"

The look in Donovan's eyes silenced Earny mid-thought. Without further comment, he turned and led the way once more. Jana followed and prayed Donovan was possessed of some hard-learned skill or innate magic born of his demonic alter ego that guided his path through this accursed place. Trust in the Swordsman and his deteriorating mind was hard to conjure now, and handing her fate over to his remaining ability did not come easily. That they could all be marching happily towards some bottomless pit was something she would just have to accept, for what other choice did she have? At least that would solve all their problems nice and efficient-like.

With nothing but a tight oval of visible ground for reference, she had no notion if minutes had passed or hours. When the Mist finally did break, the sudden clarity was disorienting. She heard Earny gasp, blinked her eyes clear, and took in the sight before her.

They stood now before a deep trench in the center of the Ven, a narrow pass which carved through the mountains and into the Wastes like the mighty gash of a titan's axe hewn into the fathoms of its granite flesh. It was twilight she saw now, and everything lay soaked in deep violets and blues as if marinating the land for a hungry nightfall. The sulphur smell was more poignant here, burning in her nose, but where it arose from she could not tell. At their feet, hard to spot in the waning light, lay a bed of small stones that shifted precariously beneath their steps. "I've never seen rocks shaped like these before," she said to no one in particular.

"Bone flinders," answered Donovan without inflection.

"Animals, most likely, right?" asked Earny, nudging them with his foot.

The Swordsman did not answer, and Jana took that to mean Earny was not right.

The trench ahead was much larger than Jana had first appraised, and they approached it for a time without seeming to gain much ground. When they stopped again Donovan took a moment to look on it and marvel. "The Mother's Mouth," he said, reverent. "It's said a great battle was fought here long ago, and the soldiers of Pal Myrrah fended off a mighty army in this very pass. Many died, more than you or I could likely imagine." The sparkle in his eyes faded and his strange frown returned.

"What is it?" asked Jana, unsettled by the Swordsman's sudden quiet.

"*Him,*" was Donovan's response.

"The Cleric is close, pray it?" asked Earny. Jana could tell the former highwayman was one scare short of soiling himself. To his credit, never during their journey had he let his fear, which he did not hide well, nudge him from his course or dampen his resolve. In his comical way, she found her one-eyed companion inspiring, far more so than the Swordsman and his arrogant lordly attitude.

Donovan nodded, still watching the great turrets of rock vanish into the clouds overhead. "So close it's like he's siwashed in my very nose."

Jana looked back the way they had come, saw that the Mist was receding, perhaps following their boatman back across the Gestalt. As her gaze followed the receding Mist, she gasped and pointed, drawing her companions' gazes. All three of them could see now the deep crevasse spanning the width of the Mother's Mouth behind them, gaping like a predator's jaws in the farthest pale reach of day. A land bridge, not twenty paces across, bore their tracks, splitting the crevasse down the middle; had they strayed a few paces in any direction, they would have plummeted to their doom and splattered on the rocks like melons.

"I reckon fate spared us quite a tumble, master," said Earny with a bright smile.

Donovan nodded with an odd smile of his own. "I reckon you're right, Earny Avers. True and true."

"Do you think Ruti is all right?" Earny asked, fingering his pocket as if hoping to find the wayward dragon there.

The Swordsman removed his hat and matted at the sweat on his brow with his sleeve. "I think anything that has survived in this world for a thousand years can take care of itself. Let us go." He pulled his hat down over his troubled brow and started forth towards the Mother's Mouth.

Earny followed without comment, but his eye scanned the horizon constantly for sign of their missing friend.

* * * *

Night fell upon them before they reached the mouth of the pass. Donovan discovered a half-circle of boulders as tall as a man where they could camp. Nothing grew most places in the plain at the basin of the Mother's Mouth, but here lay a copse of pine trees sprouted somehow from the craggy flat with branches suitable for burning, so they made camp as the merciless cold fought to penetrate their clothes. The boulders kept the wind off them but not the chill, so a fire would be welcome, Jana thought. Donovan smoldered the tinder and blew it to life, then set the old pine alight also and smiled as it caught immediately. He sat back in the butter-yellow glow with his arms crossed and watched it burn.

Jana saw his hands shaking at his elbows. "Cold?" she asked him.

He looked at her. "If only you knew…"

"What?"

He shook his head. "Nothing. No, I'm not cold."

"Then what?"

"Wishing for a smoke, Keeper save us," Donovan answered. The Swordsman sounded more frustrated than he seemed to want to reveal.

"I've some tobacco for ya, if you'd like," offered Earny.

Donovan shook his head. Jana watched him clasp his hands with a worried frown. She had seen that gesture once too often during this voyage.

"I've no taste for it," he said to them. "Now, Boon, on the other hand..." He smiled at her boyishly. The look was so unlike him that it threw her off her guard.

Then she heard something from the dark outside the reach of their fire.

"What was that?"

Another sound erupted, this one pained and high-pitched, an animal's cry. Jana tensed and her hand fell to her dirk, drawing it halfway from its sheath. She saw Donovan straighten and peer into the night, though he did not reach for his sword. A moment later another noise echoed from the lightless stretch around them, a strangled howl that faded to an unnerving rattle.

Death, she realized. *That's the sound of death.*

She nearly ran screaming into the Wastes when something swooped into the cast of the firelight: it was Ruti. The Root Dragon landed on a tree near Earny, black claws and tacky feet latching onto the smooth bark easily. He crawled forward a few steps and looked his companions over with catlike indifference.

"Bless everything sacred, yer back! I was worried sick about ya," said Earny. He ran a finger along the dragon's neck. The Root Dragon didn't seem to mind.

"You made it. That's great," said Jana. "Would've been a shame if something ate you out there."

Ruti's eyes flashed black again, longer this time than on the Dweller's raft, and he flicked his tongue at her with an aggressive flap of his wings.

"Yeah, yeah. To the Maw with you, too."

"Do you think that sound was..." Earny trailed off as though he couldn't bring himself to finish the thought.

"Better whatever creature slithering in the dark out there than one of us," said Donovan as though the thought was not terrifying. Jana frowned at him.

They sat in silence for a time, and Jana turned her thoughts to her scar, which still throbbed incessantly. She ran her finger along its rippled and coarse length.

"Is it aching you?" Donovan asked.

She nodded.

"Me, too," he said.

"How we planning to get back across the lake, ya figure?" asked Earny.

"The Ferry will be there if all goes according to plan." The Swordsman's too-sure-of-himself tone was back.

"How in the Black do you figure that?" Jana asked, piqued for no particular reason beyond the Swordsman's habit of resting their fate on assumption. She thought of a saying Grampy had about assumptions. Something about asses, sure.

"Because if it is not, then we will surely die here, Hunter'lue."

The weight of that statement, in all its dry glory, hit hard. Hoping to distract herself, she said, "Tell me what this *lue* business is, for the love of it."

He shook his head. "Boon first, Lady."

"Would ya give him some o' yer stash, Miss Jana? Keeper knows you'll never use it 'cept for a snack now and then."

"You sound like you want to quiet me up, Earny," said Donovan with his tight, strange smile.

Earny reddened and stood up at that. "Beggin' yer pardon, sir. No, I mean. That's not my gist, not a bit. I just... Well, I—"

"I'd like to be quieted up in this matter, as well. Be at peace, Earnald Avers," said the Swordsman. In the firelight he looked warm, but Jana had the feeling he'd be pale as an egg in daylight. "So, Lady. Will you take your guardian's request?"

She kneeled and produced Grampy's tin and held it before Donovan, who looked like he might start salivating. "Tell us your story," she said to him.

"No. Now's not the time."

"Then when is? For all I know we're gonna die tomorrow or the day after. I'd hear a good tale or two before I find the Black. And at least then you'll go happy with smoke in your chest," she said, still dangling the leaf tin.

Like a carrot before a donkey.

He stared into her dark eyes with his glimmering green ones for a tense moment, then exhaled a breath she didn't notice him holding and leaned away.

* * * *

After Jana and the Swordsman's standoff, Earny began turning circles like a dog chasing its tail, unsure of what to do with himself and burning with embarrassment. He decided he needed to step away from their circle for an easier breath; he may have overstepped himself with the Swordsman, or he may not have, but either way made no difference, for if he was ever to be taken seriously by this man, which right now was truly the most important thing in the world to one Earnald Avers, pray it true, he'd best keep a tougher watch on that spry mouth of his. Yes indeed.

Deep down, beneath his fretting, he knew he should be minding the darkness around them, keeping an eye on the depthless distance, or listening for the approach of anything sinister, much the way he would have for the Raef Clan in his old, long-gone life. But so flustered was he that his mind wandered anyway, slippery as ever, his attention turned inward. Jana and the Swordsman were still arguing without speaking, eyes sparring, neither of them paying any closer attention to the grounds of their camp than Earny.

And so, in the storied tradition of life, a perfect storm of conditions and oversights welcomed the cold stare of death to their door.

* * * *

Jana and Donovan, lost in their byplay, paid the ex-bandit no mind as he moved for the mouth of the rocky half-circle. Donovan, most days sharp enough to track a fox on a moonless night by sound alone, was weary from his endless battle with the Cold, overwhelmed by the Cleric's sense so dark and heavy in his heart, and suffering from a growing case of Boon withdrawal.

When the long, thin black snake inched from its tiny sinkhole, Donovan heard only the *snap-snap* of the campfire when he should have heard the smooth black scales displacing pebbles and dry scrub. Where he on most days would have turned his head out of habit and caught the movement of something not much thicker than his pinky creeping near, he today turned his eyes to the hidden stars and let his thoughts return to home for the second time.

At that moment, Earny Avers, clumsy on a good day and missing an eye, too, along with all its associated perceptions, caught his foot on a stone and nearly fell face-first into the fire. Donovan, worn as he was, was still faster than most men and rose to a knee to catch the lanky one-eyed man at the last instant. Earny grunted and eased himself upright and straightened his shirt. "For the love in it all! Pardon, again, sir! I'm showin' myself as the nuisance ya always thought, aren't I?"

"We've all had a hard push. A borecat could sneak up on my rear and bite me this moment and I'd never hear it coming," said Donovan, leaning back onto his hands. What he said was a lie, of course; if a man wasn't worn enough to die, then he wasn't too worn to stay sharp. For what end the Swordsman lied, he did not know.

He was thinking this when the small black snake (not a borecat as told, which he would have asked for instead and thanked the Keeper for, had he the chance) sunk its fangs deep into the back of his hand and pumped a tiny squirt of venom, enough to kill a strong horse, into the fleshy mound below his pinky.

4

Jana watched the Swordsman's eyes snap wide, then she blinked and he was already on his feet. His sword rang out of its sheath and looked like it nipped the ground on a broad and rising arc, and then she saw it: a thin black snake, now beheaded, its body writhing for a few seconds before laying still forever. Donovan sheathed his sword, plucked the severed snakehead from the ground, and looked at it with a deep frown.

Earny looked like he'd seen the Reaper himself. "That an Aspy, blessit?"

Donovan nodded and tossed the head away.

The light in Earny's face, ever-present even in their darkest moments up until this point, was extinguished by the Swordsman's nod. He sunk to his knees.

"What's an Aspy?" asked Jana.

Donovan had no response. He looked at Jana, and what she saw in his eyes shook her with fear.

"What is it?"

He examined the wound on his hand without answering, twin holes so small you might not notice if you weren't looking for them. He placed the tip of his sword in the fire, then took his hand between his lips and sucked hard, turning every so often to spit. Then, when the blade was searing hot, he took its bright red tip and dipped it into first one, then the other fang mark. Never once did he gasp in pain as he burned his flesh black, and Jana watched him with wonder.

Then he sat back with a grim look and studied the fire again.

"What's going to happen?" she asked him.

"I'll die. Two or three days at the most," was his answer.

"What?" was all she could muster at first. Once her shock had eased, it was replaced by a passionate desperation, and then she was on all fours before him like an animal. "What the fuck do you mean? What can we do? There has to be something we can do."

"Out here, with no supplies, no roots to pick from… No. There's not." The Swordsman's eyes never left the dancing flame.

"What about that paste? Tha-that nasty paste shit of yours? Maybe that would…" Jana's mind raced. Surely that foul concoction could cure anything; her injured foot hadn't crossed her mind since the day he applied it until now, so quickly had it mended.

"That is for drawing together flesh, not laming poison. Be still, Lady Hunter." Stubborn as she was, his tone left no room for discussion and she withdrew. "I'll go as far as I can, and then you must leave me. Have your pistols ready, as well. The weaker my body becomes, the more the madness may gain ground against me."

Tears, those unwelcome guests she had tried so hard to rid herself of forever, returned to Jana's eyes. "I don't believe it. There's nothing we can do?"

"Aspy's are the most poisonous beast you'll find in the natural world, so you must believe. I never would have thought myself foolish enough to sit so unaware as just now, yet it happened, and for a reason, no doubt. The Ever Circle cares not for us and our quest."

And about that he was right, she knew.

That night Donovan did not sleep. Jana woke as the moon broke through a crack in the endless cloud cover and gilded the world in washes of silver. She did not move, for fear Donovan might hear her, but stayed in place and watched his tall silhouette stand against the moonglow and the peaks it illuminated, his sword propped on the ground beside him like a cane, his rough hand resting on its grip, his hat tilted back as he regarded the newly uncovered heavens, as if contemplating a destination fast approaching.

* * * *

Donovan knew the girl was awake as soon as her eyes opened, but gave no sign. She was quiet, that one, possessed of an instinct most took years of training to match. But he knew if she saw his face now she would want to do something, hold him or coo at him or formulate a plan together, and he wanted none of that. He was content with Rosaline, who no doubt was peering at him through that eye in the clouds yonder, and with his thoughts.

His hand throbbed hard where the snake had bitten him. He had drawn some of the poison out but not all, and cauterizing the bites hadn't killed the venom either. Already the deep tremors were beginning to quake in his calves and at the base of his spine. Soon he would not be able to walk, or feed himself, or wield his sword. Orin, the last of his home, destined to be left on this barren stretch like a child's old toy, the line of his fathers cut short by a thing with a brain no larger than his thumbnail. *Oh destiny, how thee looks on the world with a jester's eye, with mortals as thy fodder.*

Ruti fluttered up from the shadows then and landed on Donovan's shoulder. The Root Dragon hunkered down with its wings back, sensing perhaps the Swordsman's mood. "Decided I'm not so bad now, did you?" he asked in a whisper so the others might not hear him talking frankly with a dragon.

"*Iy kui oen moehet'chi,*" said Ruti.

The Swordsman thought long and hard. When he answered, it was not Donovan of Kolendhar speaking up but his low voice, talking from the deepest pit of his gut: "No, I'd not have you draw it out of me, my friend. My feelings tell me you're meant for something more than saving my hide this night. I'd not have the blood of a thousand years of wonder dead by my accord."

Ruti nodded after a moment, his blue reptilian eyes an uncanny mix of human-like understanding and the unknowable wildness of an ancient animal, and kept quiet after that. The Swordsman noted bitterly that, unlike humans, Ruti held no pretense, nor emotion feigned for political motives. That the small fellow was truly sad he could not trade his life for Donovan's moved him deeply, deeper than a dragon the size of his palm should have been able to.

Donovan the Swordsman of Kolendhar, scion of a thousand years of warriors, and Ruti the Root Dragon, a creature who himself had lived of all of those thousand years in a nook deep within the

Thresh, watched the faint glimmer of the stars as the eye in the clouds closed once more, hiding them from view and leaving the land in utter darkness.

* * * *

They walked in silence the next day, threading Mother's Mouth like a funeral procession, stopping only briefly when they emerged on the other side of the Ven to regard the long stretch known as the Wastes.

"Keeper save! Does it go on forever?" said Earny, his one good eye wide.

The Ven watched over their shoulders, sheer and unnatural, looking out with jagged eyes at a broad stretch of salt flat that would have been blinding under direct sunlight, but beneath the glow of the clouds appeared lifeless and evil. Yet there *was* life here and there: hardy scrub, as well as small lizards and the occasional Aspy, which Donovan veered well out of his way to behead whenever he could.

By sunset, the Swordsman's hands were shaking hard and he had spiked a fever. He lay by the fire with his duster draped over him like a blanket, sweat-soaked and misty-eyed. Jana tried to feed him bites of the gozenberry sandwiches they had made, but he would not eat.

By nightfall, Donovan, who when she first saw him had looked tired but full of fierce vitality, appeared to be on his deathbed. And he was, she reckoned. The dusty flats of the Wastes were the last bed he'd ever sleep upon.

She began to cry again and turned from the fire to hide it.

The dim light of the night sky looked odd to her for a moment, that same distressful swimming sensation she had felt on the Drudge and elsewhere, the feeling that something was growing in her mind, vying for control of her faculties. But, in her despair, she ignored it and breathed deep as fresh tears stung her eyes.

"May I have my Boon now, Hunter'lue?" came the Swordsman's voice, weak and raspy now but still full of that abominable condescension.

She wiped her eyes as inconspicuously as she could and turned to him. "I don't think that'd be good for you in your condition," she said.

"I'm not quite thinking long term anymore, Jana," he said with a dark smile that made a sob twist hard in her chest.

"Will you tell us your story at last?" she asked him, not sure why she even cared anymore. *Jana*. He had never called her that before; it sounded odd hearing her name spoken in his voice. As for the Boon, why not let the dying man have his wish? Grampy would have given it to him if he had been here. She produced the tin and held it before her.

"Your terms still hold, do they?" He chuckled and it came out as a horrible hacking cough. A violent rush of tremors seized him and he convulsed. Jana came to his side and held his head up so he might not bang it on the rock he rested against.

When his fit subsided, he took a deep breath and said, "Very well."

She almost dropped the tin in surprise.

"You want to know of the Cleric and my story, say you."

She nodded.

"Are you sure?"

She was.

* * * *

In his illness, which had grown severe faster than he had anticipated, the Swordsman wondered if this was a good idea, if his companions were not better off with an incomplete picture. But he was dying now, and he had been alone a long time, his thoughts and feelings immured for years without liberation, and once the words came flowing off his tongue they came fast and fluent and he had no hope of stopping them.

5

Donovan told them of a Kolendhar that was, the place as he remembered it from boyhood, and in his memory it was resplendent.

The white-walled city lay wedged between two converging mountain ranges called the Tip of the Sword. Its gates faced the rising sun with defiance—defiance of the dead earth, of the disarray of man, of even the Mist Dwellers, who were not there when the first stones of Kolendhar were mortared but now frequented the hills a stone's throw from its walls. One of Donovan's clearest memories of the city was from his sixteenth year during his return from Sojourn with his master. He remembered the sharp scent of the deep pine as they gained the highest slope of the mountains Cren, and he glimpsed the city from afar with the bloody sunset crowning its edifices, its narrow towers pointed up at the Keeper as if in salute.

"See it well, Donovan," his master had said to him there. "See well the jewel in man's bitter crown, for we'll naught see its like in our lifetimes."

"Why do you say so, Master?" he had asked, still just a young man whose voice had not yet settled into the full deepness of manhood.

"Because the Ever Circle lies not, and men who have undone themselves before will do so again."

And, as is often the way with teachers and students, Donovan knew deep in his core, despite outward appearances to the contrary, that his teacher was right.

Next Donovan told them in his fading, restless voice of the early days of his training. Studies they called them, though they were not the sort of lowborn schooling Jana had attended as a child which bore that same name. Perhaps appropriating the moniker for the Swordsmen's training was an attempt by the common folk to share some part of their lore, to partake in something glorious in defiance of the glumness of their daily lives. No doubt it was that.

Donovan was the son of a man called William, whose trade was bow craft as much as swordsmanship. When Donovan was six— the first training milestone for Study youths—William took him on a cold night away from the city and built a bonfire while the boy practiced with his *shein*, his wooden practice blade. When the fire was roaring, William Maltrese sat with his boy and drew his sword and proffered it. Donovan remembered the first time his fingers touched Orin's drakkenbone hilt as clearly as if it had happened that very day, and he told his companions so. His father pointed to each of the engravings, which began the tale of their lineage near the handguard and worked outward along the hilt, and spoke to him the tales of his ancestors, the great line of Maltrese, men who rose from the ashes of a world none remembered and began the Order of the Sword. To pull mankind kicking and moaning from the depths of barbarism was the goal then, and look what had become! Civilization, oh so grand indeed, beyond the dreams of any who first walked that burnt and ruined world with their calfskin boots and buck hide clothes. Gorin Maltrese was the name of the first, and he had slain the great drakken of Coral's Head with a stone spear, and with his own hands skinned the beast and took the bones from its dead leg, and with those same hands carved the hilt and crafted the blade with help from the Forge Masters and their Cold Flame, and to this day that blade was kept sharp and had never broken.

Then came the part of the hilt which was still smooth and bare, and this, William Maltrese told his small son, was where his story would go. That night, just as father had done with son for a millennia, so did Donovan's father cut a neat line through the soft pad of his progeny's palm, drawing blood. He heated the knife in the fire and mingled the tip in the small red line inching from the wound, and told his son to watch as he made Orin's first new carving in ten years, a small wolf head. Blackened from the heat and the blood, the engraving glowed in the warm fire glow, its eldritch appearance unsettling to Donovan. "You'll have two more of these before your training is done, and after that three more to tell the story of your lifetime. You'll decide what parts are worthy, what aspects are fit for the rest of your line to know."

"But how will I know what parts they are, father?"

Donovan recalled the warm gleam in his father's eyes, uncharacteristic, for his father was an ill-tempered man, and the yet more uncharacteristic softness in his smile as he rumpled his only son's hair. "A man's life is only long enough to do two or three things to set himself apart. Your low voice'll guide you when it's time."

And that was good enough for Donovan, who already knew how to take men's lives yet had lived not a blink of his own.

Then his father dressed his hand and they stood on the Plains of Din, not a spit away from where thirty years later he would receive his scar and his curse from his unlikely nemesis, and together they watched the great flame William had stoked burn out into a crawl of black tendrils marching back towards the sky, as if all of his ancestors had mounted that flame to watch this baptism and now returned, weary, to their resting places in the stars.

Two decades later, his father was called by the king to settle an invasion of barbarians far to the south. William Maltrese bid his son goodbye with three simple words: "Fail me not." Those words and the hard look in his eyes would remain at the front of Donovan's mind until his father was brought back the following spring in a box with a slash through his heart.

And then Orin was his, presented by the king himself while his daughter Rosaline looked on with a smile.

That perfect, supernal smile.

And he had smiled back.

That night he and Rosaline made fierce love under the sterling gaze of the moon, writhing in the rhythmic, heated passion that consumes all, even pain. During those hours there was no duty, no barbarian horde or Dwellers of the Mist or slain father; there was only the dig of her nails into his back and the wild, mindless thrusts as something primal swept him into its throes and used his body to ravage hers.

"Do you love me, Donovan?" she asked him in the sweaty afterglow.

"More than life itself."

"How do you know?" she asked, her chin propped on her slender hand, his hand cupping her breast as she faced him. Even now his fingers recalled her smooth softness, the way her eyes shone blue even in the grim look of the moonlight which robbed all else of its shade.

"Because if it were my life to lay down to save yours, I'd feel nothing but fullness in my heart to do so," he had told her with the complete lack of self-consciousness, the utter conviction, free of irony, that she found so magnetic. She kissed him hard afterwards, and while their tongues danced he felt her tears hot across his cheeks.

They made love again, and then again at first light.

The next day his master came to him, and now was the time to describe the man. He was taller than any of the Swordsmen, even Goesef, and so thin one might fear a strong wind might blow him over. His hair had gone silver so far back none remembered its natural hue, and while some might mock his long and bony build, they'd be surprised to learn those thin arms and thinner fingers had slain ninety-seven men at the Battle of the Fords, or that they had, without reinforcement, routed five assassins who had killed six Swordsmen moments before on their way to the king's chambers. But most of all they'd be surprised to hear that those hands, leathery and as lined with scars as Donovan's would be one day, had taken the life of his wife and son when the great bout of the hert had spread everywhere, killing unknowable numbers of men, women, and children in every corner of the world, even Caer Kolendhar.

But it might not be the hands, nor the build, nor the deeds one might remember him for.

It might be the eyes, for they were harsh and penetrating and of limitless depth.

Cold, killer's eyes, the shade of violets in deep spring.

6

"What are you saying?" asked Jana. She'd gone the color of whey.

"You know what I say, Hunter'lue," said the dying Swordsman. "And you know what I say is true."

"But how? And how have you never spoken of this?" Even when he had found Jana soaked in the blood of her family, wild-eyed and dazed under the shadow of a Dweller, he had never seen her reeling so, or seen so deep a disturbance in those dark pools that were her eyes.

The Swordsman's body clenched and spasmed again, and he gripped Orin until his knuckles lost their blood. Jana did not come to him, still lost in her shock, staring at the tips of his boots blankly while they kicked and stamped. Earny came instead and let Donovan drink from his waterskin. The Swordsman choked and coughed up more than he swallowed, but eventually was able to keep some down. "Many thanks," he said in a lifeless whisper. When he settled again, he said, "It is a long story, but time is something I do not have, so I will keep it brief and tell you how the Swordmaster of Kolendhar became the thing called the Cleric, who we hunt this very night. If you will listen."

And they did listen, and he told them.

7

Donovan and his master, known to some as Morlin Sayre, left that very day.

"There is no time, Donovan. Ready your things now. Go!" Such had been the instructions of the man who had trained him from boyhood, and without question Donovan had performed as bid.

His satchel was ready as the sun capped the sky. He bid Rosaline goodbye, and even as he told this tale to his companions on the long, unforgiving haul of the Wastes, he could remember how warm her body felt pressed close to his, the smell of her perfume rich in his nose as his lips touched her neck. There were no words for how fiercely he missed her, no poetry that could express how the core of him hollowed and ached when they were apart.

She watched from the rampart as he and Master departed, a small white-clad seraph gazing down from the battalion of pennons rippling in the hot breeze behind her. He turned only once to see her there, and he did not wave or salute. To look was enough; if he fell to any other temptation, he'd never pull himself free.

Then Donovan Maltrese turned towards the Cren and followed his master's surefooted march on their last journey together as comrades.

* * * *

They marched for nine days through the Cren and into the Wild-lands beyond. They did not speak; they had spent hour upon hour together for thirty years and possessed the sort of wordless shorthand few attain. At night they'd make camp, and Donovan would find a clearing away from the fire, much like Jana would years later, and there he would move through his forms with the stubborn focus and endless determination that had made him one of the most skillful of their Order. *The muscles must be reacquainted with the forms every day, lest they forget when battle is near and your brain can no longer remind them.* That was one of many lessons Master was fond of repeating.

When he returned to camp, Master sat perched on a small boulder with his pipe in his hands as if waiting for him. He did not look at his student as he sat beside him, but after a moment said, "What do you feel, Donovan?"

A test, more than likely. The Swordsman searched himself. "I feel as if something is weighing on you." It was the best he could come up with.

Master smiled and nodded. "Indeed. Indeed..." He sounded like he might have had more to say, but was silent for a long time. Then he began again: "We go now to find the daughter of a mayor from a town called Eastfield. They do not know exactly how many men hold her, but it is at least two. Last word is that the men are bringing her west. The only thing west of Eastfield is forest and the village of Wolvine. Which means they'll likely follow the Bend all the way across the Wildlands, unless they're the thinking sort, which my low voice says they're not."

"So we pick up their trail by the Old Bridge and track them. And then what?"

Master shrugged and drew smoke from his pipe, which he loosed in thin skeins into the warm summer air. "The Keeper will sort it out for us, as always He does."

Another silence, and this was not uncommon; Master had a way of speaking only when his thoughts were gathered, and his students had a way of speaking only when spoken to, which he nourished.

"What do you think the world was like before all of this?" he asked finally.

Donovan, whose obsessiveness involved his training and his woman but little else, shrugged. "I've not thought about it."

Master grinned and laughed with his eyes but not his throat; in all his years, Donovan had never heard the man laugh. "You should, young Maltrese. In the past lies answers to the present. Mind the

Ever Circle." He finished his pipe and returned it to the small pouch he wore at his belt. He no longer wore armor as other Swordsmen did; most thought this was because he had no need, for even while sparring the most adept of his students, no blow ever landed on his scarecrow body. Later Donovan would realize it was not confidence but disdain which led him to cast those things aside. If only present eyes were as astute as those gazing behind.

"I think it was as it is now and will be forever. A playground for man's single-mindedness."

"About what, Master?" Donovan remembered asking, not attempting to rout his Master's thoughts or foresee his answers.

"Himself. Ever himself."

"There was great civilization as well. We've seen the remains of it."

Master nodded, hands on his hips. Still he did not look at his student; Donovan believed now that Morlin Sayre might have had the same conversation alone. "Yes, if you deign civilization by how tall your buildings stand or what machines you craft from strange alloys. But I do not call it that, Donovan. I surely do not. And look what it has wrought. A breeding ground for demons that man must share. Fate is unforgiving. Not cruel or whimsical, Donovan, but unforgiving. Remember that."

When Donovan nodded, Master added: "I dream sometimes of washing myself, naked in a hot spring. Only I cannot remove the stench, no matter how hard I bear down with my brush." His voice was lifeless, the voice of a man hanging by a thread. "And so I scrub until my flesh peels off," he finished at last. "And it is good, Donovan. Very good."

* * * *

Two weeks into their journey, they came across the trail of the men they hunted and the woman they held captive. Unlike when Donovan would track his master across the bogs of southern Vale, these men seemed to make no attempt to disguise their passing. Donovan's well-trained eyes told him their signs were left in folly and were not subterfuge to throw them off the scent. They would be upon them soon.

As Master predicted, the tracks headed towards the Bend, where they came across the remains of a camp. The Swordmaster dipped his fingers in the ash of the spit and smelled it. "They ate well here. Venison and onions. Maybe a side of toeleaf."

The men of Kolendhar did not eat as well as their quarry that night. They filled themselves with gozenberry sandwiches washed down with water, and every such meal Donovan ate with Jana and Earny years later would remind him of this last mission. Afterwards, they moved westward along the trail until midnight to gain ground, then slept under makeshift shelters while a light mist of rain drizzled until dawn. Donovan remembered watching Master lay beneath his shelter, built of branches and his old, battle-torn duster, staring up at the black clouds without blinking, thinking he must be hypnotized. The Swordmaster clutched his blade to his chest in the fashion kings were oft buried, and Donovan thought maybe he should say something to pull him from his thoughts. But he didn't. The Swordsman's mind was occupied with Rosaline; it was as if his body suffered a physical illness while away from her embrace. He'd wonder for years after if he might have conjured words then to alter where fate would take them, but the answer was likely no; Master's thinking had veered too far by then, too deep into the devilry which would one day claim his soul. A word from young Donovan, soon to be appointed head of the Order, would have done little to change that.

By noon the next day, the trail of the kidnappers was fresh. Donovan found a patch of wet leaves where one had relieved himself still dripping, and the two Swordsmen did not speak again afterwards.

It was Donovan who spotted them first through a break in the tight weave of cottonwoods: two men and a bound girl. The men were the rough sort, country folk from the look. One was taller than Donovan, a burly man with an odd gait which the Swordsman recognized from his tracks. A bowl-shaped crown of oily hair lay draped across his brow and obscured his eyes, which sat too close together and were disorienting to look into. The other kidnapper stood a head and shoulders shorter than Donovan, with a pouch of a stomach spilling over his trousers and a wide bow to his legs. The girl was a crumpled and battered thing that had once been a golden-haired princess, no older than fifteen or sixteen. The men wore flintlock pistols holstered low on the thigh like gunslingers and short swords sheathed across their backs. Hard to get to, those, should sudden battle break out; blades of that length were better suited to hang at the belt. Donovan knew with one glance they'd be lucky to hit anything at all with those guns, but there was a randomness to men's fortune, no matter how ill-prepared—this he had learned the hard way—and so they would be cautious.

On the south side they discovered a rock-spangled hill that rose high enough for a clear vantage. The girl was now seated, her wrists bound behind her, the short man with the bowed legs nearby. His laugh was rodent-like and grating and, as men with annoying laughs tended to, he bellowed it often.

"There were three of them, judging by the trail," said Master. His long features reminded Donovan of a hawk. "Their bags look light. I'll wager the third is out hunting. Far from these fools if he's smart, which he's not." He looked at his apprentice. "What bet you we find him less than a heft away and still hugged to the Bend?"

Donovan nodded. "I'll distract the one in front. Let's ta—"

"No," said Master, swinging his old sword from his back and re-strapping it around his waist. "Wait here. I'll call if I need you."

Donovan began to protest, but the man who had taught him the art of the blade needed not a look or gesture to silence him; the training and years of hard discipline took care of that. So instead he watched as the Swordmaster vanished down the hill and into the woods, silver hair bouncing like a foxtail.

Once he was gone, Donovan listened closer to the kidnappers' chatter. Their accents betrayed them as Northerners, and while they looked as different as a moose and a mushroom, he thought they were of relation, perhaps cousins.

"Leave her alone. I'll not be a one gettin' mah head chopped off fer yer lack of scruples, mind," said the tall one, who Donovan thought of as Bowl.

"If ah have one'a more time crammed down tha shit rung on accord o' yer goodsy tootsies I'll have yer head myself, pray it," grumbled the short one, who Donovan knew as Bow. Their accents were thick and nearly impossible to understand.

Bow and Bowl exchanged disapproving looks. "Nah, nah, don' thinkovit ya heathen," said Bowl.

"What? I didn't think a speck ovit, not tha like ya fancy, anyways."

"Well I know ya, and I tell it true now, this i'n't the sorta job ya let yer blood go to yer sausage by, blessit. Now stay it and leave her be." Beady eyes and strange walk aside, Bowl was an intimidating man.

Donovan watched as Bow shrugged as if to say, *Fine, I can't lie. I was thinking with me blood sausage*, and then sat down and kept quiet.

The Swordsman spied Master and his hostage before the kidnappers did. This third man looked a stout and filthy beggar, a stringy beard strapping his jaw, a red bandanna half concealing a severe bald patch at the crest of his head. He inched forward with Master's sword to his spine, hands up, a wet patch across his crotch.

Donovan tensed, his blood rising, but forced himself to stay put.

At last, the men saw what approached. "Whoa, stranger. Wait just a fine—"

"These men," said Master, stamping out Bow's words. "Are they your friends, Giln?"

The man with the wet crotch nodded, sweat crawling into his eyes.

"Would they feel grieved to witness your death?" asked the Swordmaster of Kolendhar. Donovan could tell Bow and Bowl were unable to hear this exchange, but the Swordsman's keen ears carved their words easily from the wind.

"I don—Yes, for the love in it. Yes, yes. Please!" said Giln, and this part the other kidnappers did hear.

"Let him go. Or I'll 'ave words with ya," said Bowl, who was adept at winning barroom brawls, Donovan had no doubt, but understood not the man he faced this hot midyear day.

"I'm not sure I agree with you, Giln," said Master. "Let us find out."

And then he herded the man named Giln forward at a rapid pace, head low, hand planted on his lower back. Bow and Bowl watched them approach. These men were the sort, Donovan knew, without regard for strategy or subterfuge or anything beyond instinct, which said now to draw their poorly-kept pistols.

"Do it and your friend dies," called Master from behind cover of Giln's body.

Bowl and Bow shared a look which said that when this was done their pay would split only two ways rather than three and, with visions of wenches and feasts and gold no doubt blinding them, they took aim. The man called Giln died with a wet crotch as Bow and Bowl spent their lone lucky shots, better saved for an attacker, which tore open his chest and extracted a bloody mist.

What happened next was finished before Donovan exhaled his next breath.

Master held Giln's limp body upright as Bow and Bowl adjusted their aim. With a fluid turn, Master produced a small knife and hurled it underhand from behind his dead cover with much the same technique Donovan would later use against a man named Carver's head. The knife completed a single rotation, and then its tip slipped into the soft flesh on the inside of Bowl's wrist. Bowl screamed and his aim swept wide as his finger spasmed back, his expended cartridge punching a hole in his cousin's forehead and peppering the leafy undergrowth with his brains.

Before his scream was done, Master was before him, Giln dropped now like a sack of grain, and with one strong kick to the chest Bowl flew onto his back clutching the ruin of his arm. He was crying, Donovan saw, no doubt considering death for the very first time as it loomed near now. This was not a surprise to the traveled Swordsman; such men took on these missions with their mortality forgotten and only bravado to shield them.

"Who paid you to kidnap this girl?" Master asked in a tone that told Donovan this would not end well for his captive. Yet still he could not make himself descend the hill. Not unless called for. Rosaline would have overridden his sense of duty perhaps, and her only just, but not this wretched man.

"Th-the… The Lord of Northend."

"Do you know who she is?" asked Master, gesturing to the girl.

"Suh-suh-some daughter of a lord. From Eastfield."

"What is the Lord of Northend's name?"

"Ah-Antony. Suh-said soh-something about uniting clans. With her father. Please, spare me."

Master leaned away, his blade relaxing to his side. "Good enough, I suppose."

He gathered his thoughts, and Bowl was right not to speak during that time.

Presently the Swordmaster said, "Do you regret what you have done?"

"What?"

"Do you regret kidnapping this girl from her home and her family?"

The man stared at Master through a film of panic. At last, he managed: "Yes, yes. Forgive me! I beggit!"

And then with swift anger Master pinned the tall, beady-eyed man Donovan called Bowl to the ground by his mutilated wrist. Bowl howled agony into the air and beat at the fine leatherwork of the boot crushing his wound.

"A long time ago the greatness of man was desecrated by the same greed and lust that drove your employer to hire you. And even after mankind has lost everything… Even now as we live on this earth the way rats live on a ship, still we cannot cleanse ourselves of it."

Bowl's idiot gaze showed no comprehension.

"Do you wish me to heal your conscience?" asked Master. "To relieve your guilt for taking this girl?" His tone was genuine, and for the first time Donovan of Kolendhar glimpsed the man he would one day call the Cleric.

With Bowl's final breath, he likely thought he was buying salvation. "Yes! Please! I'm so, so sorry, Mister. I'll do anyth—"

And *anything* was Bowl's last word as Master's ancient blade swept forth and severed his head, which rolled towards the girl and halted face up, peering at her with eyes caped in twitching lids. She screamed against her gag.

Master swept his sword downward to shake clean the blood, and then returned it to its sheath. Then he cut the girl's wrists free and removed her gag. "We were sent by your father. Fear me not, girl."

When she had regained her calm, Master led her into the forest where they rejoined Donovan, and so they made their way back to Kolendhar together for the last time.

* * * *

They spoke little for three days. Without discussion, they had decided to take the girl to Kolendhar first rather than to her home, for the great white keep lay closer and her wounds needed tending, particularly a broken arm which Donovan had set with a field dressing but which required further care.

On the third night, while the girl lay sleeping, Donovan and his master lay beneath the open stars in an orb of firelight, the smell of tea trees and the high melody of cricketsong thick in the air, the feel of death still cold on their shoulders.

"Did you have to kill them?" Donovan asked his Master after long consideration. It was the first time he had questioned the man who had taught him the nature of death.

"I needed to kill one of them. The others were happenstance." His reply, as it often did, came smooth and simple and without emotion.

"Nothing you do in battle is happenstance."

A touch of a smile on the corners of Master's thin lips. "What goes on in the back of my mind is my brain's business." That smile lingered while he drank from his waterskin.

"You should have let me come," said Donovan, unsure why he felt like pressing the issue now.

"No. I needed you to watch this, for this will be the last lesson I ever teach you. Man, in all his variations, is a wicked thing. Through and through, to the very dust to which you'll return when you're asleep in the grave. We did not end up the prey in this world by chance. This is our lot, the truth our predication defines. Man's time is over. What we have left here is a vile thing, driven by our selfishness." His eyes were glazed and his gaze distant, his finger tracing mindless patterns across the drakkenbone grip of his family sword. "I am ashamed to be one," he finished at last.

"Then why are you a Swordsman?" asked Donovan, something stirring inside him now. Something like defensiveness.

"That *is* why Donovan. To strive for something greater than man, to be closer to god or devil than to flesh. That is the end of everything I've taught you since you were a boy."

And Donovan did see, as much as he wanted to pretend he did not. He saw clear as morning light from a deep nightfall.

"When we arrive at Kolendhar, I'm going to set out on a journey," Master said after a silence.

"What sort of journey?"

"The kind I must do alone. To the Darklands." The Swordmaster's voice was soft, almost gentle, the voice he might use to settle an infant.

Donovan felt the blood drain from his face. "Why?"

The man who would return years later as the Cleric chose his words carefully. "To see with my own eyes what lies there. To see why no man lives who ventures in, and why demons and creatures of the Maw pour out day by day. When I am gone, all of my teachings, the way of combat—and of living, mind you—that have survived for thousands of years before the world fell and has lasted a thousand years since, will be entrusted to you. My greatest student."

Donovan thought, just for an instant, that he could see a moistness in his master's eyes.

"You are the only thing I've done in my life that makes me glad to be a man. You are my son, as much as the one who feeds the trees from the ground as we speak," Master said softly.

And then, just as fast as it had appeared, the emotion receded. Master rose, tying his hair back from his face, violet eyes fighting the orange gleam of the fire with their own strange glow. "Make me proud, then. I beg it," he said with a grin that chilled Donovan's blood.

And with that, he stepped away from the camp and into the forest and did not return until morning.

8

Donovan's tale was once more interrupted by a hard tremor that shook his core. He gasped for breath and writhed against the dustcaked flatland with his hands gnarled in the air. Jana came to him this time, easing his head down onto her lap. When the tremors subsided, she kept his head in her lap and dabbed at his head with a moist cloth. *He's not going to be able to walk again*, she realized. *He's going to die in this very place. And he knows it.*

The Swordsman's rough fingers probed the ground blindly, finding only dirt and rock. "Orin… Where's Orin?"

Earny paused as if thinking, then seemed to come to an understanding as he nodded and handed Donovan his sword. "Here, Master." Donovan took it from him and his face was at once serene.

Jana found herself thinking of the men they had passed on the road, the way their eyes and faces had lit up at the sight of this man whose sword alone seemed able to will folk together and give them purpose. She thought of this, and of the way the Swordsman's eyes had stayed downturned, ignoring their pleas, and she thought she might have caught a glimpse of what had turned his heart so cold. She stroked his hair and sighed a curl of misty breath into the frigid night air.

"I've not much time, I'm afraid," said the Swordsman. "So I'll be short with the rest of my tale, for the details matter not so much as the whole, and telling it eases the quake in my mind and my heart. Would you hear it?"

Earny Avers and Jana Hunter nodded.

9

When the girl's wounds were mended, she was sent back with two Swordsmen—Goeseff and Vine, no less—and a host of soldiers. She bid Donovan goodbye with a kiss that had warmed his face, as well as that of Rosaline, who watched with her arms crossed at her bosom and her dark eyes narrow. When the lady from East-field's carriage was well on the road, Donovan came to his love and embraced her.

"You didn't enjoy that too much I hope, savior Donovan," she said with a knowing look and a soft smile that melted him.

"And what if I did?" he said, rubbing his nose against hers.

"Then you would do best to turn that carriage around so I might fight for your honor, my lord."

"That would be a sight, you in your princess gown tumbling with another noblewoman upon the road. I'll have an artisan nearby to draw the scene."

She laughed and struck him on the shoulder with her delicate hand. He clasped it close and kissed her deep and breathed in through that kiss her life essence which bloomed bright and warm inside him.

* * * *

That night Master called a meeting of the Swordsmen. Many of their ranks had fallen in recent years, some by the hands of men, others by beasts and Mist Dwellers. Others were away on mission or leave, but all told there were forty-seven ready to hear the announcement of their great instructor. What he said was simple: he was proud to have taught them what he could, but duty drew him away and he would likely not return. In his stead, Donovan would head the Order.

At this, Shadow, who had served as leader of the Black Guard— the king's personal soldiers—gave Donovan a dark look, and the Swordsman knew they'd have words soon; taking the title of Shadow, named after the first Swordmaster of their Order, spoke of high ambitions, ones that did not halt at the second step from the top.

Master Morlin Sayre left Kolendhar at dawn of the next day to the bright call of trumpets and a crowd of thousands, for Swordsman and peasant alike knew his face and his standard and they'd all see him gone, if only to return home and tell those closest they had glimpsed the legendary man as he set out on his final journey. Donovan had not spoken to him in private since they arrived at Kolendhar, and still the chilling coldness in his teacher's voice bit into his mind from the past.

I am ashamed to be one.

And then Master was away, an ant-sized speck on the reach of the Din, the great plain stretching to the Cren and the Wildlands and then beyond, to the dark place at the mouth of the Maw called the Darklands.

He'd not be seen again for four years.

* * * *

It was Harvest Eve in that fourth year when Donovan sat with Rosaline in a birchbark canoe, easing across the small pond called the Maiden's Tear, which lay in the shadow of the castle. Those four years had worn Donovan to a shape closer to which Jana and Earny would know; a year after Master's dust settled onto the Din, the Mist Dwellers had begun to appear more frequently, attacking settlers foolish enough to live on their own away from towns, but also striking into well-fortified places on occasion where no measure of defense had been successful. But that was not the worst of it. Whispers on the backs of peddlers and Swordsmen alike spoke of something new, creatures which were once men, spotted both in droves and alone, wielding claws hard as steel and stricken with an insatiable hunger for flesh.

Blood Demons, folk called them. But where they came from, none could say.

But for Donovan Maltrese, these things mattered little during the moments he spent with Rosaline, which had become precious few the last months. He relaxed as the birchbark swayed on the Tear, and he saw her then the way he'd remember her always: caught by a shard of late-day sun sidling through the long towers of her father's keep, her deep chestnut hair carried by a warm, sweet gust of air still clinging to summer's passion, her ultramarine eyes smoldering with intelligence and wit and empathy. It was that last he remembered most fondly, for he'd never again meet a woman who would know him so well or accept his faults so completely.

"What are you staring at?" she asked him with a sly smile.

"I was wondering the same thing myself," he answered with his own, which felt worn and lackluster, but these days his woman was glad to see it at all.

"One of these days, Donovan, your mouth is going to get you into a situation you won't easily get out of."

"It already has, lady. And that situation sits before me, looking mighty fine indeed."

She blushed and shook her head at him the way women do with men they fancy, something not far removed from the dismissal of a child. Her color faded quickly as she spotted something in the distance. "Shadow..." she told him.

Donovan followed her look and saw him. The man was tall and long—long of arm and leg and face. Donovan saw a skeleton when he looked into his calculating eyes. He and Donovan were of the same age and had begun their training together, but Master had favored Donovan time and again and a deep competitiveness grew now between Shadow and the most recent head of the Order. That Master's opposition towards Shadow grew from the very arrogance driving him to envy Donovan likely never crossed his mind. Such, as Goeseff once put it, was the way of men deeply in love with themselves.

But today Shadow wore a broad smile. Donovan might have sworn he saw fangs in it.

"Lord Donovan! Exactly who I've come to find. And Miss Roslaine! Stand true, for you are a sight this day."

"Can it wait?" Donovan called, afraid he knew what Shadow had in store.

"No, my lord, it certainly cannot."

"It's all right," Rosaline told him. She touched his hand and he took hers in his.

"I'll make it up to you later. I swear it," Donovan said to her.

"I know you will," she replied, her voice full of that edge that set his blood afire.

He smiled and paddled them towards shore, never to make good on that promise.

* * * *

The Hall of Blades was old, built by the first generation of settlers, when there had only been the keep and no city to surround it. The rest would be constructed during the hundreds of years after, but to Donovan this place was the true heart of Kolendhar, and within its gray stone walls beat the heart of the Order itself. But that heartbeat was faint now, and slowing still. If it could be revived to its elder verve he swore he would see it happen, or else die in the process—or so he had thought in those days. The dry smell of that stone mixed with the faint aroma of the royal kitchen (where Sorphin Vaags was busy fixing the hall a fine roast stew which would stand unmatched until Donovan sampled one Mary of Pleasantry's equivalent years later) made Donovan feel comfortable. He was more at ease here than in his bed-chamber, in the wild, or anywhere, for that matter, and now he took a moment to enjoy that ease because he knew it would not last.

He looked at the old blades, those from men who had fallen childless in the service of the Order. They shone in the candlelight from their wall mounts, and Donovan felt a deep sadness. He had known many of the men whose arms lay closest to the cold floor. Two walls now were near full, and soon they would need use of a third. Dire days indeed. Though he'd never admit it to the men he now led, they were holding on by the tips of their fingers and the strength of their wills and nothing else, with a thousand Shade jaws chomping just below their toes.

Shadow entered the room then, attempting to be silent, but Donovan heard him from where he sat at the banquet table and said, "You've come far with your stealthcraft, friend. Master would be proud."

Shadow stopped mid-step, chagrined. "I do love it when you talk to me as a child, Donovan. Please continue."

"What would you speak of?"

"You sound as if you think you know already."

"I pray I am wrong," said Donovan, and he meant it. He had no taste for Shadow's games today.

Shadow stepped to the table and took a seat, placing his blade—Orin's twin—on the table and hoisting his boots onto the chair beside him. "I've just returned from the Wildlands, you know."

Donovan nodded.

"I have some intelligence you must hear."

"Tell it. Without frills, please," said Donovan, arms crossed, hard green eyes impatient.

"I've seen an army, Donovan. Of Blood Demons."

Donovan's breath caught in his chest. "An army you say? How many?"

"Thousands upon thousands. Not a hundred hefts from Kolendhar."

Donovan looked at him with the kind of deep disbelief only grave shock can induce. "That isn't possible."

"Possible. Impossible. It's truth, my friend. They can march on us at whim."

Donovan clenched his fists, mind racing. He rose and marched the length of the hall. At last he said, "We could hold them."

"Do you truly think so? They outnumber us, and that alone can undo us. They will watch us slay their brethren until the bodies pile high enough to top our walls, and then they will use their corpses as a stairway to spill into the city. There is no defense against that sort of madness."

He was right. Men with nothing to lose fought in a way sane soldiers were hard-pressed to match. Give those same men unnatural bloodlust and strength, and then what?

"What do the others say?" he asked Shadow, afraid of the answer.

"The others... You think I've run about the country sharing this news with every peasant I've come across?"

"So you've shared this with no one." If he agreed to this then he was a liar; Shadow was many things, but tightlipped was not one of them.

"I have, but not with many. And those who have heard have all said the same: that it is time to run. This is happening more quickly than we ever could have imagined. We've had trouble enough with Dwellers overrunning farms and testing how far their toes can dip into more civilized country. We are in no place to withhold a siege."

Donovan held silent for a long time. In that moment, he would swear his lifetime's experience entire galloped through his thoughts like a herd of wild horses, with him caught in the middle grasping for wisdom. When he found none, he simply said, "I've always thought our purpose was *not* to run."

Now it was Shadow who rose. "Yes, when the time is right. That time is not now, Donovan. To stand true in battle is righteous and honorable, but not when a greater victory stands on the other side of a wise retreat."

"So you'd run with them? You and how many?"

Shadow shrugged. There was something else behind his eyes, something he was not saying. "Many, Donovan. Let's keep it at that."

"We'll ready our defenses and do as best we can."

Shadow's face turned red. He slammed his fists into the old oak table. "You pigheaded son of a whore. Do not do this to your people."

"It is what Master would have done," said Donovan plainly.

At this Shadow suddenly relaxed, his smile returning, and took a seat once more. "It's odd you should say that, for I have a second chapter to my news."

"I asked you for no frills. Dramatic pauses included." Donovan had long known that he did not like this man, but in that moment he might have killed him just for the pleasure.

"I met someone while I walked the Wildlands. He knows of the Blood Demons. Intimately."

"Meaning?"

"He can control them, Donovan."

Donovan's jaw hung loose. "How?"

"By some magic, I do not understand. He says if we do not interfere and leave Kolendhar without raising the alarm, he will spare those who show loyalty. He plans to sweep across the western villages and then head here."

"Who is this man? I would much like to speak with him."

Shadow leaned in, his voice a whisper, as though afraid even here someone might overhear. "He calls himself the Cleric."

"Is he a holy man?"

Shadow had the look of a boy with a secret he could barely wait to share. "Not quite. And, best of all, he is once from Kolendhar."

"Do I know him? Come, now. Enough with the games!"

"It is *Master*, Donovan. Come back from the Darklands."

Donovan reeled as though he had just been struck. "That's impossible."

"He entered, and a year and some later returned a changed man. That is all I've gathered of his story so far. But if it was to be anyone at all in the world at the head of these creatures, who more fortuitous for us to find?"

"The man who trained us would never let innocents be slaughtered for his own gain."

But what gain, Donovan wondered, would that be? Simple misanthropy?

I am ashamed to be one.

It was as if Shadow knew his thoughts. "The man who trained us thought we should all die for our sins, as well as those of our fathers. This only makes sense. Think of it Donovan! Would you trade the lives of a hundred peasants for that of your woman?"

And Donovan knew without hesitation that, come down to it, he would. A thousand if need be. He'd slay them himself if it was the only way. He wanted to agree, to take Rosaline and lead her to wherever it was Shadow had in mind and bide while the wash of evil broke on the dead rocks of the land and then receded into the dark sea from where it came. But something else spoke in his secret parts; his low voice held a sense of honor that would not be easily overturned. "Now I know why you were not chosen to lead us," he said, quiet but firm.

"And I know why you were. Because you and I are the same, but you are afraid to speak what lies in your heart." He cocked his head, a gleam in his eye. "Will you do as I say? For love?"

If he had known then what would come to pass, Donovan might have answered differently. But in that moment his low voice, which was strong of principle but not always best for survival, overrode all else. "We will hold the keep. I'd ask you to stand with us. We have had our differences, but your skill with a sword is true and men will follow you."

Shadow's smile faded. He retrieved his sword and strapped it across his narrow shoulders. "If you change your mind, you have ten days to let me know. Then I will be gone and you will burn beneath the rubble of this place." He stopped at the door but did not turn back. "Good will and fortune."

And then he was gone.

10

The great city of Kolendhar, the jewel in the crown of man's faded but hardy civilization, the core of all surviving culture and last bastion of the people, fell in a single day to the Cleric's army.

Donovan made provisions and deployed men with skill, but not all of the Swordsmen had returned from their ventures afar and many soldiers had already fled on news of the coming attack. Wise, Donovan would call them later. It would not have mattered if they stayed; nothing could ready them for the onslaught unleashed upon the city that day.

The great gate of Kolendhar, twin doors sixty feet tall, crafted to withstand a heavy siege from an army of persistent attackers, blew open like paper on the might of a gesture from the Cleric, which was infused with some magic the likes of which Donovan had never seen. The Blood Demons poured in without command, as though the Cleric only need think his orders for them to execute in perfect, insane harmony.

Ranks of archers drew and loosed a storm cloud of arrows into the milky sky, most finding throats and hearts and bloody eyes to pierce. While the Swordsmen shouted orders and kept the men in file, soldiers rained hot oil onto the rows of hellish creatures charging into the courtyard and towards the great stair that led into the streets of the city. Swords flashed, cutting claws from disfigured hands, severing long misshapen heads from their terrible bodies. Calvary charged forward, slaying creatures by the dozens. In any other battle, Kolendhar's show of precision and skill would have won the day. But there came moments, Donovan told his listeners, when a man senses an undercurrent beneath all he does, a force so untamable that he might doubt forever forward his ability to influence the mind of fate. That force, call it the Keeper or the Reaper or a three-headed donkey, swept across the Din and into the ruined gates of the city like a dark wind, and beneath it, every last soldier and Swordsman within the walls of Kolendhar fell.

Donovan would include himself in that tally, were he asked.

The Cleric's creatures brought with them great catapults, which they looked foolish manning but wielded to great effect. Before midday the sky rained fire on the white stones of Caer Kolendhar, exploding on impact, undoing stone and raining debris on the screaming women and children fleeing below. At one point three Swordsmen rallied the soldiers fighting for their homes before the great balustrades of the king's balcony, and as one united blade they charged into the maelstrom of claws flooding through the gates. There the Swordsmen cut through the creature's numbers, their blades singing songs of death as they split the air, their eyes infused with the dark glow of battle blood. For a moment, the impossible seemed to happen: the Blood Demons were falling back.

Donovan watched this from atop the city wall, and with the cry of his forefathers he hastened down to the gate, drawing Orin and adding his attacks to the deluge of blood and airborne flesh. As he and the remaining Swordsmen and soldiers heaved their last great push into their attackers, who seemed to stretch endlessly into the Din, a new glimmer lit in those mindless, bloody demons' eyes. Donovan dared not call it fear, but perhaps wariness, and if a thing could be wary, then it had a sense of self, and that meant its will could be broken.

Most of the cavalry had perished now, but some still rode and Donovan whirled Orin overhead and called them down. The soldiers and Swordsmen broke apart and made way for the heavy charge. Blood Demon claws scraped and sparked against the hard steel of the horse armor, and pikes and maces destroyed faces and bodies and cracked the head of the Cleric's army in two.

Donovan fell back from the group to where the archers could see him. On his signal, they loosed again into the clump of mottled faces and dripping fangs and long serrated claws beneath their feet. Blood

Demon corpses began to amass, piling onto each other and, just as Shadow predicted, providing elevated positions from which to attack. Donovan watched this as he hurried back to the wall, where men with more cauldrons of hot oil poured load after load into the unblinking crimson eyes below.

For a moment, so small it would later feel like a dream, Donovan felt hope blossom in his heart.

Then, on the Cleric's command, a new wave of creatures flew forward with abandon through the shattered gates, filling the world with inhuman snarls, eyes aglow with a new sort of frenzy. They tore into the last of the Kolendhar soldiers, ripping calvary men from their mounts and tearing them to pieces. The Swordsmen slew fifty creatures every one of them, yet in the end, it was not enough; they drowned in those waves of maligned bodies whose bones seemed half inside, half out, screamed their loved ones' names into the blackened air, and then never screamed again.

As sunset approached, Donovan stood in the center of the main courtyard, watching the chaos with dead eyes. He blinked not at all, his mind gone numb, Orin clutched loosely at his side, and stared at the throngs screaming and dying before him without seeing any of it. Sometime during the siege, he had lost track of Rosaline, but he believed she was with the king now and they likely were retreating through the secret exit at the back of the city. From there they could easily enter the Tip of the Sword and flee into the country beyond.

Yes, at least she was safe. Things could be all right still with her alive.

Then something struck him down, sending the world into a spiral of red and then black.

When he woke again, his once-home had been reduced to rubble.

Somehow he was outside the walls now, which were rent in many places and billowing great plumes of smoke. He could see bodies of soldiers, dead by the dozens, hanging like dolls between the battlements and piled at the foot of the gate, which had been smashed to splinters. All dead at his command. On his conscience.

And her?

Rosaline. Please let you have escaped. Pray the Keeper.

"She did not, Donovan. I am sorry."

Donovan whirled, and there stood the man he had once trusted and loved. He looked taller now, if that was possible. His already thin face now appeared sunken and gaunt; his body, which had been wiry and athletic before, now seemed malnourished, like a prisoner just recently freed from some horrible captivity. Beneath his eyes hung deep rings like twin blue-black hemorrhages. His Swordmaster's duster was gone, as was his family blade. In its place, he wore a white robe, spun into unnatural smoothness, marred by nary a wrinkle or stain or speck of soil. In his hands, he gripped a spear-like weapon, set with a curved blade long enough to sever a man at the waist. He looked on Donovan with the same smile he had flashed by the light of their campfire years gone. "But she *has* survived. You'll find her within the walls, over there, once we are finished."

The depths of Donovan's rage could not find expression, and in the end it paralyzed him but for one word: "Why?"

"I sent our friend Shadow ahead to speak to you. I had hoped my final lesson would have made a difference, but I see that it did not. But I have not lost hope for you, Donovan. Quite the contrary. I'll need your help when the time comes. But that time is not now."

Before the Cleric was finished speaking, Donovan was already drawing Orin from its sheath with a bloody hand, the ashes of the dead and the destroyed beneath his fingernails, the blood and sweat of battle thick on his face and neck and body, his every inch in agony. Even in the heavy gloom of the black veil blanketing the sky, his blade glowed true.

"Put it aside, son. Let us talk."

But Donovan Maltrese was done talking. In the blind sort of fury Jana Hunter would understand well, the Swordsman, head of a destroyed Order, lover of a woman who now lay somewhere in the ruins of his home, charged and threw every fruit of his training, every nuance of warrior's instinct he possessed into one perfect, killing cut.

The Cleric sidestepped him with almost absentminded casualness. When Donovan's blade speared the charred, broken earth of the Din, the Cleric brought his staff to bear, and in that slow and crystalline lucidity the mind discovers a split-second before disaster, Donovan thought he would be beheaded. But instead the Cleric, with inhuman control, merely touched the end of his staff to the nape of Donovan's neck as gently as a parent might pat their child upon the head.

At once the pain began, birthing as a hot ball of liquid metal in the brain stem and then exploding outwards, boiling his veins, oozing through his pores, a fierce agony that drove him towards madness. He felt his skin blacken and peel back, felt his eyes pop in their sockets and pour a sour, viscous fluid down his face and into his mouth, felt his brain crinkle and shrivel and then burst in his skull. It was more agony than any man should be able to take, yet what choice did he have? He had vengeance to find, and its fire kept him alive.

And then, his energy drained utterly, he collapsed onto his back, staring up at the crisscrosses of smoke and the blank sky beyond.

For a moment he saw the Cleric's face as he bent over his fallen student with interest. "I've said you are special, Donovan, and I meant it. You will hate me at first, but in time you will grow to love me as I have loved you. Now you truly are my son. Together we will build something pure. At long last, something pure. When the time is right, you will find me. Good will and fortune."

And then the bleary scarecrow shape glided noiselessly away. The Blood Demons who had laid waste to the brave soldiers of Kolendhar were gone as well, even their dead, and the long spread of the Din was grieved only by circling birds calling a lonesome elegy; that was all for these men who had lost their lives this hot summer day.

But for Donovan, there would be no such end.

He passed out, already feeling the dark throb where his scar had begun to grow.

When he woke, he would wander into the city, the dead walking amongst the dead, and discover what had become of his woman.

11

"Ifound her then," said Donovan. His teeth were chattering and his voice was nearly gone. His skin was the color of clay and was cold to the touch. "He had made her one of them." He choked on his breath and broke out in a spasming cough. "And I killed her. I killed her…" He trailed off, and then Jana heard a sound she had not thought the Swordsman capable of: he sobbed; one hard, wrenching groan of grief that twisted her heart until she feared it might rip apart. Then he was quiet for a long time.

"I'm sorry, Donovan," she said. "I'm so sorry."

He swallowed and looked up at her through his tears. "It wasn't your doing, girl." He tried to wipe the tears but his hands did not respond. She did it for him. "The only apology I'll accept is for withholding your Boon for so long." The tears were replaced with a glimmer now, and she could not help but smile.

She helped him smoke his pipe—what would no doubt be his last—and when he was done he thanked her and said he needed to rest, and then he closed his eyes and seemed to dream restfully for once.

Earny and Jana watched him sleep under the dying watch of the fire. "What do we do, your ladyship?"

She shook her head. She truly did not know. "We'll see where we're at by morning and decide then."

Earny nodded, Ruti perched on his hand, and then laid down and stared at the featureless sky until sleep took hold. For Jana rest did not come so easily, and she thought of the moments outside her home when Donovan had watched her kill her once-father. She thought of her disdain towards him, even hate, if she was honest with herself.

And all that time he had known just what she was going through—not the empty *I'm so sorry* dunny talk of folk who tried to say the right thing, but *true* empathy, the kind only a kindred spirit could offer. She knew now they all shared those links, even Ruti, who had lost his family an age ago. This gave her some comfort; coincidences like that were the work of a higher hand and not simple happenstance. At least that's what she chose to believe.

She tried to stay awake in case Donovan stirred in the night and needed her, but the way had been hard and she could not resist the heavy pull of sleep for long.

* * * *

"Wake, girl."

An unfamiliar voice pulled at Jana from the dark. At first, it sounded as if it must be a thousand miles away. Then it came again, and the black dreamlessness of her sleep dissipated. She opened her eyes to see a long, thin face staring down at her. The face was handsome, fiercely so, and even as she shrieked and backed away she felt her body responding to it.

"It's all right," said the handsome man, who she saw was dressed in charcoal armor and a long duster much like Donovan's. Earny was missing, but their fire had been rekindled and burned brightly, and for a moment the calm tone of the newcomer's voice did relax her.

Then she saw the Dwellers.

At first she had mistaken them for boulders or perhaps far off mountains, but now her waking eyes saw them clearly, tall heaps of evil muscle all clad in thick black robes. There were twelve of them at least, waiting in a semi-circle around her. She screamed and flew back against the rock wall and drew her dirk, as if that would do a damn bit of good. "Who are you?" she asked, then immediately wished she had sounded stronger.

"An old friend of Donovan's," said the handsome man, his hands up. He bore a sword much like Orin and wore it strapped loosely across his shoulders.

She kept the dirk aimed towards him. "Where are my friends?"

The man gestured with his head, and now she saw them: Earny was on horseback amidst a platoon of soldiers; it looked as though his hands were bound. Another man, this one clad in plate armor, had Donovan's limp body drawn across the saddle before him. The Swordsman was slumped over, unmoving, held in place only by the soldier's persistent grip.

"Is he alive?" asked Jana.

The handsome man nodded. "Yes, for now. But he needs medicine. If we hurry, we might treat him before he dies. Will you come with us?"

"How did you find us?"

The handsome man smiled. "That is what I do, fair lady. Now, will you come? Or shall we stay here and wait for the Reaper to claim our friend?"

Jana wanted to fight, felt the hot rush of blood to her face that every seasoned soldier knew well from battle. But there was no hope of victory here, not even a fool's hope, so she sheathed her blade and nodded.

"Good. I have a horse for you," said the handsome, long-faced man. "Call me Shadow."

They mounted up and galloped away across the moonlit stretch of the Wastes, the ground beneath the hooves of their Clydesdales the color of old bones. The Dwellers raced alongside them, fast as their horses—faster maybe, for she felt like they were setting the pace rather than keeping it—and utterly noiseless.

Jana held tight to the reins, more afraid than she had ever been.

She met gazes with Earny once and saw that he shared her fear.

And so the man called Shadow brought Donovan's circle forth to Pal Myrrah.

12

"**D**o ya think they'll kill us?" asked Earny as they slowed their horses for a stretch. The ex-bandit looked pale and scared, his one eye wide and darting. His face was bathed in sweat that he licked away each time a drop perched on his lip.

Man's most like to trip just 'fore tha home stretch, Keeper knows, so that's when ya hafta buckle down most, girl.

He buckled down hard when life called for it, Jana's father did, harder than anyone else she knew. Harvest was the Hunter Clan's opportunity to head into Pleasantry while folks were primed and eager for trade, feeble and cheap-minded may it be, and Jana and her father would return home carrying back foodstuffs the likes of which they could never afford otherwise, or sometimes a piece of furniture or one of Dad's trinkets. On Harvest Moon, she and Cory would wait by the front window and conjure stories to pass the time using whatever they could spot in the backyard. Jana's stories featured dashing men who bled romance. Cory's—the Keeper's irony knew no bounds—starred giant man-eating monsters and the folk who took the job of slaying them. When she had just about had her fill of his yarns scaring her witless, Dad would appear with a sack flung across his shoulder, or sometimes a wheelbarrow if his prize required it. It shook her that on one of those very days, if she had marked the time right, Donovan had been killing the woman he loved and watching the Cleric level his home to the ground. *Oh yes, a new chair! Even better, a rocking chair! Can't wait to wrestle you for it, Stink. Worst thing in the world would be if I had to eat dinner before I got a turn to relax in it!* She looked at the Swordsman, whose breathing was so shallow he might be dead, and wanted to cry.

"Lady?"

Earny was staring at her. "No," she said. "I don't think so. They would have done it in our sleep. They want us for something else."

"Even me?" he asked.

She wanted to say yes, but what could these men and the creatures with them possibly want with good old Earnald Avers? To keep him as a court jester, maybe? Donovan and she had the odd benefit of being protected by the Cleric's investment in them (an investment that had just squirmed again beneath her skin, as if it sensed the crossing light of her thoughts). But what leverage would Earny have? *Whatever happens*, she promised herself, *you'll find a way to keep him safe. It's your fault he's here.*

"I don't think they're going to do anything to us. At least not soon," she said to him.

Ruti poked his head out from Earny's breast pocket, his small front feet propped up, and looked around. He spotted the Dwellers, who were clustered together off to the side, their massive swords clamped to their hunched backs. They were facing inward in a circle like children huddling to share secrets; no doubt those secrets involved debating the best marinade for man-flesh. Ruti flicked his tongue and ducked back down into Earny's pocket.

The handsome man, the one called Shadow, whom Donovan had referred in his stories, quickened his pace and commanded the rest of the men to do the same. He trotted up beside Donovan and checked him, and then fell back in line with Jana and Earny. "Is he alive?" she asked him, afraid of the answer, more afraid of the way his thin features hypnotized her. She had caught herself staring twice during this short ride before willing herself to stop, to look at the back of her horse's head instead. Now, though, she watched his eyes with a flutter in her chest. *You're worse than a man, girl. Keep your head on straight.*

Shadow nodded, adjusted his sword to the other shoulder. His duster trailed behind him, wafting like a tail. "Barely, but he's a strong one. I just hope we have time to cure him when we arrive."

"But you *can* cure him, pray it?" asked Earny.

"All things are possible, friend. All things."

Jana meant to ask Shadow more, but he dug his boots into his horse then and took off, rejoining the head of the group. She felt a twinge of disappointment the moment he was gone. *What is wrong with you? Are you out of your damned mind?* She would be soon, she knew, her mind as lost to the whims of the Maw as the red-eyed demon version of Donovan and then some. But not yet. Damn the Black and Keeper hold them on high, she would not be mad yet.

"You know what Raef used to say?" asked Earny. He had to speak loudly for her to hear over the forced march of their horses, but she did not think the other men listened or cared what they had to say. She shook her head. "Prisoners are only currency. If no one's buyin', no one's keeping." She looked at him through the thick cloak of the Mist as it followed them along the Wastes like their own personal storm cloud. "Whaddya suppose they're going to be trading us for?"

She thought, but there was only one answer: "Leverage."

"With who?"

"Maybe us, each other," she said. Her six-gun was missing, but her fingers found her dirk, still sheathed at her side. Shadow had made no move to take it from her. *Because it would do you no good, you fool.* Perhaps also because leaving it with her might make her trust him more. For what? Certainly not for any personal reason; the man hadn't looked at her twice since holding her horse steady while she mounted it. And he knew as well as she did that the Dwellers would be fighting over her arms and legs before she could sink her blade into any of the soldiers. She caught herself peering ahead at him again while she contemplated this, only this time he turned and caught her looking. She averted her eyes and cursed herself and didn't look at him again.

Earny watched the exchange with a frown and shook his head.

One of Shadow's men—the one holding Donovan—called out in a strange language and Shadow looked at him sharply, then barked a command to the rest of the soldiers, and as one they beat their horses to a gallop. Jana's horse responded on its own, and she grabbed the reins to keep level. She glimpsed Ruti, his head once again out of Earny's pocket, letting the rush of moving air wash over his small face. Jana imagined the little dunny head was enjoying himself; maybe they'd leap a sudden rise and the dragon would tumble out of Earny's pocket and then she would enjoy herself, too. Even as she envisioned it, she knew it wasn't true, that the sight of what she perceived to be joy on Ruti's strange face had just softened her towards him against her will. She sighed and allowed herself a slight smile and watched the Root Dragon through that new lens. *This reminds him of flying maybe. Or how fast he'd like to fly. Yes, that might just be it.*

Their horses spurned the powder-fine swathe of the Wastes, never more than a hundred feet visible ahead of them through the veil of the Mist, never appearing lost or adjusting their path. These men knew just where they were headed; this place, a hard trek for her and her companions, full of danger, was their homeland. The idea of anyone feeling at ease in this hellish place unnerved her so completely that she had to force herself not to think of it, or that the man from the shed, the one who had ravaged her body and infected her with this evil disease from beyond the Black, waited ahead, his invading hands and piercing eyes anxious to look on her body again. *What if he wants me again? Pray the Keeper, what if he takes me like he did before?* She could not bear it. Never again. If he tried, he'd find a much different Jana Hunter beneath his skeleton body, one that bites and has claws— and her father's dirk, should she find an opportunity to use it. That the person at the center of her misery was the very same man who had trained Donovan from boyhood did not sit well with her; the two disparate aspects would not square in her mind, not only by her measure but by Donovan's, for the Cleric had done as much and more to him as to her, even it was not the same. Still, her bond with the Swordsman had changed during his feverish story, which seemed like another distant night a long time ago; surely not this night, the one that found her escorted by not one but a dozen walking horrors and the Mist they rode. When she looked at Donovan's sagging face, clenched into a twist of concentration or pain, she could not help but think of the Cleric. Sometimes, if she wasn't careful, she saw the Cleric *instead* of Donovan. That did not bode well at all.

The Mist thinned while Jana was lost in thought, and now she could see the stark reach of a new set of mountains, much smaller than the Ven but still imposing; they rose to razor points like a jagged tear in the fabric of the world. Their silhouette drew near quickly as the company forged ahead, so Jana surmised that they must not be very large at all and were perhaps three or four hefts away.

They pressed on without stopping, though they had slowed to a trot now. As the mountains crept closer Shadow fell back in line with them. He stared at her for a while and she forced herself not to look into those dark eyes. "Is there a problem?" she asked him.

"I should ask you. You look afraid."

"Your company is questionable." Jana meant her reply to be biting.

Shadow laughed. "Questionable bedfellows are often found near that which you seek the most." She nodded, still not looking at him, afraid of what she might see. "You are from somewhere in the Thresh, are you not? Perhaps Eastfield, or Pleasantry."

She nodded again and wondered what difference her birthplace made now that she was this man's prisoner.

"Well, which is it, lady? I know much but I do not read minds yet." His voice was smooth and calming. She wanted to wrap herself in it.

He'll kill you as soon as look at you, you fool of a child.

"Eastfield," she said. She thought her voice might have trembled a little.

"I should have known. From the accent. Eastfielders have it thick and it sounds different than other parts of Vale."

"I don't have an accent." She knew her response had sounded defensive. This was not going well at all. She saw Shadow watching her out of the corner of her eye and realized he was amused by her. The thought made her blood boil.

"You hide it well, but it is there, I promise. I have an ear for such things."

"And for finding people lost in the Wastes."

He nodded. "And that, lady, and that. And other things. But I'll not sound my own trumpet."

"Oh good, I get the pleasure of finding out for myself." Just the personality she'd expect in a man that looked such as he, so full of himself that if you broke him in half you'd still have two whole men.

"Indeed. My very thoughts."

They were headed for another pass, she saw, this one much wider than the Mother's Mouth. Hopefully, it was not full of bottomless chasms, too. A break in the Mist, as well as the clouds, allowed a sharp spotlight of moonglow to graze the tips of the mountains, and they gleamed as though topped with snowcaps before vanishing again into the haze.

"What will you do with us, come Pal Myrrah, sir?" asked Earny.

Shadow looked at the ex-bandit's inquisitive eye as if he had forgotten he was present. "My job, as you no doubt have observed, is to collect and return. What my Master's plan holds for you afterward, I know not. But I do know he'd see Donovan alive, so take solace in that. Were you in lesser company, we would have slain you where you snored, highwayman."

"Your old Master as well as your new is what I hear," said Jana.

"So Donovan told you, did he?" said Shadow. His smile did not waver. "Good. Then you have some idea of the importance of the man you are to meet. But I see he has met you already." He nodded towards Jana, who followed his gaze. Her tunic flap lay open, her scar exposed, a purple rope of ruin burrowing through her. She covered up, a throb of embarrassment in her throat. "No need to be shamed, lady. That mark is a great honor. Your disgust is natural and expected, of course. I'd call anyone mad who claimed to understand its true meaning all at once."

"Which is what I will be soon enough." *There it is. That's the tone you were looking for.*

"Consider that not all of what your friend Donovan has told you must be true. He is a man of skill, with a blade but also with his words."

"What are you sayin', sir?" asked Earny, suddenly indignant. "That he lied to us? A Swordsman doesn't lie. That's a sight beyond the dunny river, I reckon."

Shadow threw his head back and laughed loudly. "We have always been diplomats as much as soldiers, my friend. A sword does you no good in the hold of an unruly mayor or a jealous nobleman."

"You're a Swordsman, too, pray it?"

Shadow laughed again and performed the best swirling-hand-bow he could manage on a trotting horse. "Once. That Order has died like so much in this world. A fine flame it was, but never meant to last."

Earny opened his mouth and immediately Jana turned, her eyes as sharp as knives, sensing what the overeager former bandit was about to say. *But there are still Swordsmen! We saw them, true as chickens, walking around the forest tracking Donovan. Said they have a host of men and were starting over. I swear it!* Earny saw her look and remained silent. Jana looked at Shadow to see if he had noticed this exchange, but he seemed swept up in nostalgia.

"The new order is being built as we speak. Something much purer, you'll agree."

"What are you babbling about?" Jana asked him. Her fingers trailed to her dirk and she left them there just to see what he'd do.

The answer was nothing; he hardly spared her a glance. "I'm not the one who could tell you, Jana Hunter of Eastfield. I might sound a wordsmith but it's all a well-conceived hoax. I swear it."

Ahead Donovan moaned and thrashed in his saddle. The soldier bearing him turned to Shadow. There was fear, unmistakable, in his eyes. But of what? Then she realized: it was fear for his own life. If they did not deliver the Swordsman alive to their Master, there would be grave cost.

Shadow nodded. "We must hurry. We don't have much time."

"How far are we from—" began Earny.

But Shadow was away already, galloping his horse to the front of the company. The Dwellers at the head parted for him like a black jaw opening, and he pulled ahead as though racing out from some creature's gullet. "Move you daft bastards! For your lives, fly!"

Jana's horse neighed as the men behind her came too close and pushed into a hard gallop. Earny's mount did the same. The mountains grew and grew and then swallowed them; they rose straight up from the ground, nearly vertical. It was as though this land blanketed a bed of spikes which had slowly over the ages pushed through and now awaited the giant foot of a sturdy Titan to step across them, proving its unnatural tolerance of pain.

You really are the most foolish thing in existence, girl. Pray it true and save us all.

Littered along the bed of the pass were clusters of rocks covered with spidergrass and the occasional skeleton of some long-dead animal. Dusty blank sockets of what might have been a wolf watched Jana gallop past.

At the front of the line, Shadow was still shouting, calling orders she could understand and some she could not, but she wagered that the gist was the same: hurry your sad behinds up or the Reaper was gonna get you. Or worse, the Cleric, the man with the violet eyes.

She tried to figure how much time had passed since Shadow had woken her, or how long it had been since Donovan went to sleep. The dark sky here made it difficult to tell; with the Mist it was impossible. She figured it must have been some hours. She had expected Donovan to die at any moment when his eyes had rolled back and his breathing failed to a wheeze, yet there he was with still the strength to moan and complain. A strong one, him. She found herself suddenly so overwhelmed with sadness at the thought of never seeing those condescending green eyes again that she had to blink back tears.

Let him be safe. Let him survive. Please.

Somehow, through this forsaken journey, she had come to care about the cold, stoic Swordsman and his difficult ways. If he did survive, however, she'd never tell him that. She'd never hear the end of it.

"Lady! Look!" called Earny as he stood on his stirrups and gazed ahead.

And then she saw it.

The Mist cleared so suddenly it was as though it never was; it did not dissipate or fade away; rather it simply vanished, as though dismissed. As it did, they exited the pass, and here the moon was free from its cloak and cast long black shadows across the land.

And there, in the distance, was Pal Myrrah.

The ancient fortress, which Donovan called a staging point for untold wars spanning unrecorded history, stretched from the flat plane of the Wastes like a hulking creature frozen halfway risen from the earth, built of black and grey stones split by white veins, perhaps marble. Some of the balconies were the color of sand from what she could discern in the moonlight. They jutted from harsh towers rising in threes from the body of the keep like trident points. Some of the windows exuded a deep red eldritch glow that pulsed and breathed. *It is the twin,* Jana realized, though she had only heard the Swordsmen's vanquished home described by Donovan. *Kolendhar's dark twin.* And she knew if Donovan were awake he would have thought the same.

"I've never seen a thing the like of it!" called Earny, his hair blown back from the deep lines of his face. He looked like a boy despite his complexion, excited just to be alive here and now, without thought of the future, which for Jana was all too near.

Shadow turned back to his men as they raced across this final stretch. "Faster! If we lose him you will all be responsible. Every last one!"

Jana saw now the Dwellers had dispersed entirely, perhaps back when the Mist had vanished; there was no way to tell, for they made as much sound gone as present. She looked over her shoulder to see if she could spot them, but could only find the half dozen soldiers still behind her, their armor clanking and their big steeds pushing hard, lines of sweat crawling their faces.

"This is it, Miss Jana!" Earny called into the air. Ruti had his small nails hooked through the ex-bandit's tunic, she saw, and was holding on for dear life. *No, he's enjoying the ride just as much as Earny is.*

"Come Black or Maw, come ice or thaw, dance us drunk or thrash us raw, call it true in the darkest blight, here march we from the dark of night!" the ex-bandit roared.

At this Shadow spared a backward glance that Jana thought looked full of worry.

Then he bent forward and dug in his heels as they charged ahead.

As the towers of Pal Myrrah leered, Jana thought she could see a pair of dark eyes watching her from the highest balcony.

13

Earnald Avers was a humble man at heart. Back in his distant boyhood, he had fancied himself little more than a future blacksmith, or mayhap a shopkeep, with the occasional distraction of fine archery or—if he might be so bold—a touch of the written word. He recalled telling his dear departed Mum with enthusiasm his grand plan to be buried twenty feet from where he had been born, worse for wear but with a wide grin across his old face as they tossed him into the black earth. He wondered sometimes whether life dragged men along by the hand, call it fate or the Keeper's will, or whether it was all a big box of totem sticks like the old Soothsayers back home employed to tell fortunes, built from a trillion random coincidences only to be arranged into imaginary patterns by the mind's need for order. He liked to think the former, that his was a life of fortune blessed by some great unseen caretaker. Keeper knew, he could die now and be all right, for in these past weeks he had seen more than ten generations of his family before him. But it was at times like this, watching the hulking shape of Pal Myrrah soaring before and then above him, when he felt like it was all happenstance, that all else was the dream of youth and the desperate hope of the old too fearful to accept the truth, for surely a man like he had no business in a place such as this, no matter how elaborate or incomprehensible the Keeper's plans might be. Surely not. But Earny forgot all about such musings, or that he likely was riding to meet his death or worse, as the great gates of the ancient fortress swung open ahead, its mighty hinges groaning into the night like the call of a dying beast.

Shadow pulled ahead, his sword drawn now, its blade and hilt black and connate with Orin. He twirled it overhead with a cry: "Faster, damn you!"

Earny peered through the thin light to make out detail in the fortress wall. It was high, fifty or sixty feet at least, with slotted battlements stationed with archers. The gate itself was black, difficult to make out in the night, but the gleam of torchlight across the face of the twin doors revealed fine detailing and large gargoyles captured mid-leap from their iron and granite prisons. He tried to spot more Dwellers, but instead found a host of armored troops awaiting them in the courtyard.

They did not slow as they entered the gate. To either side, Earny saw a blur of buildings that could have been living quarters, some with thick smokestacks rising from lead chimneys. The sharp smell of sulphur and hay and horse droppings bit into his nose. Mixed with those was the stink of the long-traveled and under-bathed, the odor of fighting men grimed with dirt and blood and sweat, the kind of men whose underpants stood up straight if you balanced them right. It reminded him of the Raef Clan that was. Was and gone.

He felt Ruti bounce and bop to the rhythm of his horse, which steered itself and ignored all guidance. The little dragon hissed and ducked back down again. *Attaboy. Stay out of sight.* He wondered if his small friend could hear his thoughts; just as he fancied the existence of fate, Earny decided that the Root Dragon probably could.

The keep itself towered ahead, big as a mountain. Earny stared at it with as much awe as he had the Ven; greater even, for this was the work of men: breathing, eating, dying men. For a moment, an odd feeling flourished inside Earny's chest, admiration that the hands of many could turn to a single task and accomplish something so far beyond imagination. It might have moved him to tears had not his horse pulled a harsh right behind the rest of Shadow's host, galloping so hard he feared they'd run their mounts into the ground before they reached their destination.

Earny saw Jana standing on her stirrups, hair blown out behind her like silk. He averted his eye right away; as much as the girl was beautiful, a shameful feeling stung him staring at her like that, and what a foreign notion that was! Earny had professed to many a barmaid that they reminded him of a sister despite his lascivious plans for them, yet in this case, it was true; something in Jana Hunter made Earny warm up from the inside and filled him with a sigh of unsullied contentment. Yet there was a sadness there, too, the sort one experienced when emotions lower than words or smiles formed with another person. *That* was the foundation of his feelings, the sensation he struggled to put into words: Jana knew his pain as well as he knew hers. Or so he imagined.

A second gate ahead already lay open. This one was smaller than the first, but was still greater than any Earny had ever seen in all his travels. Men in heavy plate mail and with high plumes of violet feathers jutting from their helms stood in even rank, their swords held ceremoniously before them as Shadow and company charged ahead, sparing them no acknowledgement.

They reached the doors to the keep and reined in abruptly. The entryway stood tall enough to enter on horseback, black like the front gates and so finely detailed Earny thought he would need a spyglass to savor all the nuance. The stone here rose to cascading arches that made Earny think of overlapping, sandy waterfalls. Here and there great effigies stood carved into niches or perched on jutting corners, some of armed men but others of great creatures. One resembled Ruti, only much larger. He thought he felt the Root Dragon spot it and quiver.

At once Shadow dismounted—he might have just leapt with the momentum of his horse, if Earny saw right—and motioned for the men to hurry. The keep doors opened, revealing a long black hallway filled with torchlight.

"What about them?" asked one of the soldiers. He gestured to Jana and Earny.

"Bring them both," said Shadow, his voice impatient.

Shadow and the two largest soldiers carried Donovan's body into the keep. As the rest of the company hurried inside, the big black doors swung closed behind them with a thunderous sound, though by what hand Earny could not say. The finality of that sound put shivers in him.

The hallway stretched as far as he could see. Between the torches hung great red tapestries of exquisite detail. It all felt so ancient; it made Earny feel inconsequential, like nothing he had done or would ever do could amount to a damn thing, not in a place where mortals could craft such marvels as this. Even the sconces, gilded and laced with scrollwork, seemed otherworldly.

"It's amazing," said Jana breathlessly.

Earny slowly nodded. "That's a word for it, sure."

The hall led to a tall stair. At the top were more large double doors, these of bronze work molded into the likeness of wolves and lions. They opened, on their own or by some hidden mechanism, and there in the center of a great chamber lay Donovan the Swordsman.

Jana and Earny spilled in with the rest. Shadow stood by, hands on his hips, eyes intense. The chamber was torchlit and fashioned from black stone, perfectly round, with great columns at intervals about its circumference. The ceiling was domed and painted, a portrait of a man slaying a great beast—again, said beast looked to be a dragon, only this one stood ten times the size of the man it fought. Earny swallowed hard.

Two men in brown robes knelt now beside the prostrate Swordsman. They were albino white save for their lips, which were a pale violet. Above the bridge of their noses only shadows were visible, and their eyelessness filled Earny with an unnatural cold that ran its fingers along the length of his spine. One of them drew with a dagger a bloody line through Donovan's palm, and through that wound mixed a black powder into his blood that smelled wretched even from a distance. The other held a vial of green fluid and a dropper, and with great care he worked three drops into each of Donovan's eyes, then his mouth.

"What are they doing to hi—" Earny began.

"Silence yourself or I'll do it for you," said Shadow.

One of the robed men brought forth a decanter and poured next a thick, viscous potion across a red cloth and wrung it with a twist. He then laid the cloth across Donovan's eyes. After this, he leaned until his mouth was near to the Swordsman's and inhaled deeply—unnaturally deep it seemed to Earny—and then straightened and tilted his head until he faced the ceiling and exhaled. While he did so, the other robed man leaned down the same way and breathed of the Swordsman's breath, and then he, too, straightened and looked skyward and exhaled. Back and forth this went, some to-fro game like the village children played on their teeters built from scrap found in the woods. At length, Earny thought he could make out a fine mist, black as bat eyes, glutting from those pale lips in wisps. Against that dark mist, Earny noticed something odd about the robed men's teeth as they gleamed in the firelight. He squinted to see them better, and during their next exhale he saw that they were shaped like small yellowed spikes, much like a borecat's teeth. Whether that shape was natural or filed, he did not wish to know.

Then, suddenly, they stopped and rose, hands slipping into their sleeves, chalky heads bowed.

"Will he live?" asked Shadow.

The robed one closest to him said nothing, raised a hand palm-up as if to say, *Who knows?* Then the two albinos turned and exited, and a long quiet filled the room while they studied Donovan's shallow breaths.

At last Shadow said, "Take him to his bedchamber and keep four guards posted always. Tie him down, as well."

"You're still afraid of him even now, aren't you," said Jana. She held Shadow's gaze this time and did not look away.

"Lady," said Shadow, stepping towards her. "You amuse me, it is true, but keep your tongue in your mouth when it carries acid, lest you burn your eyes out."

"I'd take one of yours with me, pray it true."

Shadow's thin smile returned.

"What are you going to do with us, sir?" asked Earny. He wished his voice did not waver so.

"You are our guests for now. You'll be shown to your quarters."

A master of the roundabout, that one was. Earny could spot it a mile away.

"We stay together," said Jana firmly.

"That, I'm afraid, would be against my orders, sweet lady." Shadow bowed apologetically.

Jana, still looking riled from Shadow's show of anger, frowned. "What does he want with me?"

"Who?"

"*Him*." Her tone made Earny squirm.

"Ah. That will be for *him* to tell you. I see much and do even more, but the Master's plans are beyond even my ears and eyes, such as they are."

"How long have you been in this place?" asked Jana.

Earny expected no answer, or at best another show of pigheadedness, so he was surprised when Shadow said, "At Pal Myrrah? A year and some gone now, if I count right. There are stretches where time grows hard to hold onto, especially when the Shades are near."

"Why do you call 'em Shades?" asked Earny, then immediately wished he hadn't. *Stupid, stupid fool of a dunny roller!*

"Why do you call them Misties?" asked Shadow, dropping his voice into a perfect born-and-bred townsfolk accent.

"You take pleasure in mockery. Mum always said that was for the weak and petty," Jana said, folding her arms.

"You overcompensate for your powerless feel by forcing bravado down the throats of those you perceive as stronger. Particularly men," answered the once-Swordsman evenly. Jana's lips parted with a stillborn response. Shadow nodded to the remaining men from his entourage. "Show them to their quarters. I'll inform you about your friend Donovan when I hear word."

"Do you think he'll live, Swordsman, sir?" asked Earny. He felt Ruti squirm inside his pocket and prayed Shadow did not see.

"If I could tell you that, I'd be a magician, One-eye. And that I'm not, nor am I a Swordsman, so call me one again and you'll be one-armed as well."

Earny frowned and clasped his hands at his waist.

* * * *

During much of this, Jana had been contending with the flutter in her belly born in response to Shadow's anger, which seemed simultaneously cultured and sophisticated and barbaric and untamed. She almost did not notice the men moving towards Earny.

They approached, weapons drawn, and gestured for the ex-high-wayman to move. When he was near to the door, Earny turned and said, "Promise me you won't hurt her."

Jana wanted to smile at her one-eyed friend, but fear kept it down. For only the second time since her family still drew breath, a wash of comfort swept over her. She silently thanked the Keeper for Grampy and kindhearted Earnald Avers.

Shadow frowned. "You're a brave one, One-eye. At least braver than your kind are known for. That's merit enough where I come from, even if it's not sufficient to keep a man alive." He paused as if considering his next words. "No harm will befall her by my hand. That I can promise."

Whether that was good enough for Earny, Jana could not tell. Those burly, armored men dragged him the way the albinos had exited. As their footsteps faded, Jana thought she could hear Earny saying, "Ya know, for the life in me I'd never have thought men could find so much black rock in one place!"

Shadow drew near to her then. "Are you truly from Eastfield?"

"I told you I was. Am I going to have to say everything twice to you, yer lordship?"

Shadow laughed hard. "I am no lord. Not yet. Keep your brazenness to yourself."

"What is going to happen to us?" Jana kept her hand on her dirk as she spoke. Still, he paid it no mind. Just like Donovan. *He knows if I make one damned move he'll have my head off before the blade's clear of the sheath.*

"Do you think I lied for the sake of your slow-minded friend?"

"I think there's a reason he's gone and I'm still here. Maybe so you can keep staring at me like that," she said. The bite in her voice made her feel good, like she was chewing away at Shadow's arrogance piece by scrumptious piece.

"If ever I thought I might find a woman as full of herself as I am, I'd have called it a dream," he said, pacing the room. The sound of his boots clicking echoed into the elaborate rotunda above. "It is true, you are here so I can tell you one more thing that I'd not have your friend the bandit hear. Would you allow me to speak?"

"If I'm standing here with my mouth shut it's because I'm waiting for you to say something worth hearing."

Shadow stepped close to her, so close she could feel the heat of his breath, could smell the deep masculine musk of his body, could see every glimmer in the verglas of his eyes. "The Master," he said, forming his breath into words without voice, "He may tell you things. He may whisper that your fate is sealed, that all is for naught, that fighting him holds no chance or virtue. What I'd tell you is this: listen to him, but do not heed all. Some things he will tell you are true, but others are for his design. I cannot say how you might know one from the other, but your heart can guide you better than my wisdom. Stand true. Do not let him sway you. There may be hope yet, Jana. I'd not see a specimen such as yourself lost to madness or wicked plots."

If there was any posturing or roundabout in his voice, Jana could not hear it. Shadow brushed aside a twist of hair from her forehead, his fingertips glancing her skin ever so lightly, and her breath caught in her chest, frozen solid.

Then he turned on his heel and left without a look back.

Jana stared after him even as two of the soldiers led her away.

Then, deep in the heart of Pal Myrrah, she thought she heard a scream.

14

Donovan stood alone at the center of a wide circle of trees. The night sky above had chased the residuum of day to the brink of the sky and replaced it with an ebony crawl sparkling with starlight as if from the dancing dark of a moonlit sea. The trees here were leafless, great redwoods tall as mountains standing endless watch, titans of their time, older than the shambles of mankind. Here the wind rose and fell like breath, scentless and full of winter frost. Donovan felt it burn in his nose and down into his lungs. What was it he was doing here? When had he arrived? He could not remember.

He did not notice at once that Orin was missing from his back, much the way a man missing an arm could still sometimes feel his invisible fingers. When he reached for the comfort of his family scrawl and found nothing, panic set in. Where was it? He began to circle the clearing, squinting in the starlight at the tall wildgrass, searching. He almost called for it, mad as that would be. If ever he had and lost a son, he thought it might feel something like this. The gaze of the dead trees on his back, sprung from the ground like old fence palings, did not help the hard beat of his heart or the shake in his hands. He returned to the center of the clearing, spinning round. His family heirloom was gone. His low voice said it was gone forever.

Forever.

"You look like you've seen the dead," came a voice from behind.

Donovan spun and saw the man standing at the edge of the trees, a dark blotch without form or feature. "Who are you?" the Swordsman asked.

"Did you know," the man continued as if Donovan hadn't spoke, "When the first Maltreses came to the Tip of the Sword, they found a small village. Barbarians, you might call them; savages at the least. A clump of huts plotted right at the nexus. Hunters, they were. Lots of beasts roaming the Din then, buffalo and wildercats and even deer in the spring when the grass was thick."

Donovan took a step towards the man as he spoke, trying to make out his face. His voice was a whisper but rang familiar.

"The place was perfect for what they planned. Your ancestors. A mountain at their back, impossible to attack from, a river winding through. Just right for building a stronghold, for keeping the men fed from the fields. Central to all the places villages were springing up. A fine staging point, yessir. Another lay far to the north, at what would one day be Pal Myrrah, but the Maltreses and their fellows cared not of that. So they went to the villagers and told them their plans and asked them—with no great measure of tact—to leave. But, as you know, the last news a man wishes to hear is that his home is forfeit and that it is time to move on. So the barbarians declined, said their lives and their lines and their future lay on this plain, that there could be no bargaining." The man at the edge of the clearing stopped, tilting his head in a way Donovan found intensely familiar. "Do you know this story?"

Donovan shook his head.

"Your father never told you how the Swordsmen came to plant the first stones of Kolendhar?"

"He did indeed, but there were no barbarians in that tale," answered Donovan. His fingers still twitched, craving Orin's grip.

The man in the shadows sounded like he was smiling. "Men tend to leave out the unfortunate bits while spinning a tale, especially when it involves their own people."

"What became of this village?" asked Donovan. He thought of his father, scarred and tired, sitting by the fire on the Din, tracing their lineage across Orin's grip.

Lost. Forever.

(You won't need it where we're going.)

"What would you have done, Donovan, if you were your ancestor and came across the ultimate canvas on which to paint the future of humanity, and all that stood in your way were some hide-clad cousin-fuckers and their stone spears?"

Donovan knew at once, but could not think it.

"The Maltreses and their men swept into the Din on a moonless night and slew the barbarians, every one, man, woman, and child. And infant, too. Better to not leave future enemies sown and growing before their one-day-city could even find a foothold."

Donovan frowned, did not want to believe it, but knew it was true all the same. The notion that his principles were as thin as cornhusk, ripe to fall away the moment they became inconvenient, had dwelled in his belly like cold metal for his entire life. If he were his forefathers, he would have done the same, Keeper save him. He knew it in his marrow. "Why are you telling me this?" he asked.

"Aren't you missing something? You are, aren't you? What is it, now? I can't quite put my finger on it," said the featureless man.

"You've taken Orin," said Donovan, voice soft and cold.

The shadow of a man threw back his head and bellowed a laugh into the winter sky. "I have no need of such things, my good and faithful friend, and neither do you. Not anymore. And some of you knows it..."

(The Cold.)

No.

"How did I get here?" asked Donovan. "Did you bring me? Where is Jana?"

"You brought yourself here. Impudence is as it does, through and through, heartless are the ones who spoil valor with vanity. Spineless, too, if you ask me, yes and indeedy."

"Triptalk," said the Swordsman.

"True, and tripped you have. Not forever, mind. Not forever. I offer you this branch, a thing to hold onto, yes, but also to wield. Hold it tight and wield it true. And with thanks! The worst is about to come, dear dead Donovan Maltrese of the clan of Maltrese, Order of the wishy-washy sword that was but is no more. But after the worst comes the best! Always it is so. Tell me I speak round-the-bout! See, you cannot! Maybe it's the worst that makes even the good feel like the best, but in the end, what does it matter? People are people and people are feelings, not sense or logic but the push-pull of illusions and egos. Tell it true and pray it high and low, you know it in your heart."

"I am done with games. Too many have been played on my account as of late." Donovan clasped his hands together to stop the shake. He felt the Cold approaching, yet it was different this time; it felt as though it was already here. But still, his mind held, at least for now.

"Me as well, Donovan. Dear Donovan, my love and my lost."

"Tell me what you have to say plainly or get out of my way," said the Swordsman, anger flaring, fueled by the unscratchable itch of the Cold.

"Tell it true! I can do that, for you've done so with me, even if you cannot remember. Something approaches, my dear, something from the East, cold and with many fingers, many legs, many eyes to stare at you with, too many to put out, at least before the many mouths can close down on you. Eyes and mouths, eyes and mouths. Too many! Your sword, if you ever hold it again, might find some of them, even many of them, but never all. You and I will be together before that. Yes, yes, well before. Will you still try?"

Donovan strode forward then, overcome now by his anger. "Who are you? I call upon you by king and stock, tell me your name!"

He fell back as a flash of red eyes flared from the depthless black of the man's head, hands before him, naked without his weapon.

"Eyes and mouths, fingers and toes. It's coming for you, Donovan Maltrese, last of the Maltreses, last of the barbarian slayers. Coming very soon. Choices are hard, choices and choices, you know this is true. Rosaline lays beneath the dirt under the grisly weight of your choices, doesn't she? Well?"

Donovan could not answer. The dark voice, familiar before but now simply insane, spoke true.

"And what choice did you make? Your ideals over your love, no? The many over your few? The hot weight of the right thing, wouldn't you say? And where has this found you? What hath your precious seeds wrought?"

Death. The madman is right.

"Yes. Death indeed," said the dark man.

"You can read my thoughts?"

Another deep laughed that echoed into the cloudless sky. "Read thoughts? Share them? Know them? Care for them? In the deepest dark, what difference does it make? But think of your honor when the choice comes, when the creature comes, the thing you care for yet do not know why, and see the hard choice as the easy out. The easy out is sometimes worst but never always. Never, ever always. Remember this."

"Enough with your riddles! Enough!" screamed Donovan. "Tell me your name or I will cut you down where you stand!"

"With what? Your fingernails? I could do it if you'd care to see. But no, I will not. Not mutually beneficial, that. Not at all, pray nothing, save everything, down and down and round and round." Donovan realized the shadowy man was backing away now.

"Where are you going?" asked the Swordsman, summoning a commanding tone but failing.

"Back from whence, as they say. Back the Cold way. Back to the dark in the heart of the heart where nothing flames. Farewell."

"Stay where you are. Stay whe—"

But then he was gone, faded into the black trees as though he never was.

Donovan chased after him, but before he reached the edge of the trees he heard the footsteps: cold, hard crunches in the frosted grass. First a few, then dozens, then hundreds. He smelled them before he saw them, the stench of maggoty meat or sour fruit or moldy bread, or maybe all of them. Then the first eyes appeared in the gloom beneath the old, dead redwoods, floating towards him like disembodied things swimming in the night. Then the bodies they belonged to stepped into the cast of the moon. They were people, or at least he thought they might be, but as they came closer he saw their flesh was ruined and rotting, festering on the bone, dark purple and green veins bloodless and bare within sinewy gaps in their faces and chests, their eyes milky and unseeing, staring into him anyway. Through him, maybe.

Donovan stumbled back into the clearing. He was a sharp man, his mind and instincts well-honed, and most days (like in the Hunter barn, when the Blood Demon had descended on him) he'd sense danger and react in spite of fear or drug or madness. But tonight he was dull, dull as a rusty spade forgotten in the earth of a dead farm. He never heard or saw or sensed the ones behind him, the creatures with the flesh falling from their bones, their accusing cataracts and jaundiced nails creeping closer. And then they were upon him, seizing him, and his failing senses did not matter anymore. He felt those nails cut into his flesh and hold him fast, felt their crumbling teeth gnaw into his arms and torso and face and neck and deeper, into the muscles and tendons and to the bone.

Donovan screamed as the creatures began to tear him apart.

14

Daybreak threw its savage glare across the Wastes and the sheer walls of Pal Myrrah. From a distance, keen eyes might be able to spot the constant crawl of armored men and other things, some hooded and dark, others misshapen and unworldly. Up and down they crawled, back and forth, in tireless pursuit of their Master's validation. The day grew bright and full around them, then began to die again, giving way to a deepening night thick with shadows. Every now and then a scream would boil up from the stony heart of the old keep, sometimes loud enough to echo into the mountains. Then the sun would rise again and it would begin all over.

Jana listened to the cries of Donovan the Swordsman from her bedchamber, which remained locked day and night. The room was empty save for a bed and an oak dresser that could have come straight from Pleasantry courtesy of Troy Spence or his father, a fancy indoor outhouse, and a bathtub which she had not yet used as no one had had the courtesy to bring her hot water. A single, barred oriel high up on the sandstone wall watched her with a cat's eye moon in the black night beyond, its silver throw mingling with the sickly green lamplight flooding the room. Twice a day the latch would snap back on her door and a slot near the floor would slap open and in would come a pair of albino hands bearing food. To be fair, it tasted better than she would have expected. For breakfast there were eggs and a bowl of fruit and for dinner most nights hot stew with a side of applemud pie. Was it as good as Mum's? Not a chance, but it was better than what they fed prisoners in the Hutch.

For the first two days, she awaited Shadow's visit; anxiously, to tell the truth. Sometimes when footsteps approached her body would tense with anticipation, and then they would fade, down the hall and the stairs beyond, and her heart would sink. A case of the megrims, Mum would have called it. Jana hated Shadow for how he made her feel, wanted to gouge out his eyes or pluck off his nose and feed it to the rats, spite his face, send that blooming ego sputtering back to where it belonged. But why then was she craving the glint in his eyes?

On the fifth day, pacing the room and jumping about and screaming at the door lost its appeal. The whole forsaken place had lost its appeal, whatever it had been. Now she hated it, hated the musty smell, hated the endless come and go of the phantoms outside her door. And most of all she hated Shadow for not coming to her, for not telling her how Donovan was doing.

That's not the only reason you want him to come. Admit it.

She didn't. The Mule could admit no such thing.

The screams came again and pulled bumps from her arms. *He's dying,* she realized. *Donovan's dying. I'm never going to see him again.* Sadness welled up in her and, since there was no one around to see, she wept. When the sobs ran dry, she huddled in the corner with her legs hugged to her chest. Even in her grief, the princess still pulled weight: Donovan should have died days ago, yet she heard him still, and that meant he had outlived his call. Whether certain death had been prolonged or there was reason to find hope, she could not know.

At night she lay on the bed atop the covers with her hands behind her head and stared at the cavernous arches above where two chandeliers hung like ornate stalactites, always lit, as were the lamps to either side of her. Nearly a week had gone now by her count, and still, they had never been refilled. More of the Cleric's magic, no doubt. She could feel him out there, somewhere, in one of the halls or perhaps in his private chamber where his minions brought him helpless young girls to rape and curse. Her fingers wrapped about her father's dirk and she pictured the moment she'd finally feel it twist in his flesh and watch the evil light in those eyes fade and die. Would it come? If it did, the time might be close; she was quite literally at his door.

The next day came and passed. No screams this time, and the silence was more terrifying. *What if he's dead? What if he and Earny are gone? Then what will you do, idiot girl? Stab the door to death with your little knife? Become the Cleric's play toy to use on a whim for the rest of forever?*

Movement from the corner of her eye drew her gaze. Nothing there. She stared after it to make sure, then exhaled a lump of anxiety in the form of a labored sigh. More and more she had been plagued by such phantasms, spotting spiders or snakes or worse skulking where there were only shadows. A constant case of the creeps, as Cory would've called it, had come over her, making her slap and scratch at her legs and neck and arms, sure she had discovered a bug creeping her skin, only each time she did so she found nothing at all. Was it the madness washing over her at last? Perhaps that was how it began. If so, she would have to hurry if she was to have her revenge.

But hurry where?

Her anxiety returned, and the only release for it this time was honesty with herself. Call a hog a hog: she was trapped. Never had she felt so damned helpless.

She found herself waiting more for the screams to return than for Shadow, but a sleepless night came and still nothing. When the first tired glow of dawn grew in the Wastes, the door to her chamber opened and she nearly toppled from bed in surprise. There was Shadow at last. He watched her with that infuriating smile as she struggled upright and wiped the sleep from her eyes. "Should I return later?" he asked.

"What's going on? Where's Donovan?"

Shadow closed the door behind him, leaned against it with his arms and legs crossed. The pose embodied what she could not stand about him: his every movement said the world was his, herself included. If only he had been closer so she might have slapped the grin off his face. "Donovan. Yes, that is what I am here about."

His tone made her heart sink. "What is it?" she asked. She knew her voice betrayed her feelings.

"He may yet survive. The night terrors have stopped, and that is a good sign. It means the venom is no longer within his brain. I expected him dead the morning after we arrived, yet still he fights."

"Why didn't you come sooner?" She hoped he did not take that the wrong way. *Or the right way, pray it.*

"I have been busy, so I beg your pardon. I know your room is not exactly fit to pass time. Is there anything you need?"

"A bath would be nice, for starters."

"I'll have water brought up. Anything else?"

"Why are you doing this?"

Shadow's eyes glimmered; Jana had to make herself blink so she wouldn't stare. "Do what, lady?"

"I'm a prisoner. Why give me anything for comfort?"

"A prisoner? Locked in for your safety, perhaps, but surely no prisoner. You're too important for that."

"Important for what?" she asked, as tired of his games as she was aroused by his voice and his eyes, which seemed to look all the way into her rather than just at her like most men.

"Many things, lady. Many things." He turned to leave.

"Wait," she said before she could think better. "When will I be let out of here?"

"Like I said, you're here for your safety. When your safety expands beyond this door, you will be let free. I should expect we'll know of your friend Donovan's fate soon enough, and I shall report back to you then."

"Report. Am I your commander?" she asked him, willing into her voice even a drop of Donovan's boundless condescension.

"I'm not above suggestion. Perhaps *visit* is the word. I will visit you again when the time comes, if you might find that agreeable."

"Do what you want, but make sure someone tells me what's going on. And I want out of here soon." The thought of her standing in her jail cell making demands nearly made her laugh. *Princess Jana is a queen now, isn't she?*

"I'll send some books up for you as well. Help you pass the time." He narrowed his eyes. "You do read, don't you?"

She felt hot annoyance on her cheeks. "I'm a speck and a heel past the inbreed you take me for, Keeper save your soul."

"Your talk throws me off at times, Eastfielder. Many apologies," said Shadow in his unapologetic way.

As he vanished through the door, Jana found herself considering one thing she had said in particular: *Do whatever you want.* Pray it all, that was the truth. He could have done whatever he wanted to her just now and she would have let him. It made her so angry she could break something, but Keeper knew, she would have let him.

Once his footsteps faded, she waited for the promised books and hot water, only half expecting them to appear. When three of the albinos materialized at her door, two with books and one rolling a wheelbarrow loaded with hot water, she was surprised as much as she was repulsed by their mirthless stares and marionette movements. They drew her bath and left without a word. She disrobed, saw now that the albinos had left rose petals, some pink and deep red and a smoky lavender, drizzled across the water. This seemed pleasant until she imagined their crusted nails plucking those petals one by one. She stepped in regardless, gasping as the water swallowed her legs to below the knee and then the rest of her.

I suppose it pays to be a woman when your jailor is the horny sort.

Her fingertips traced the line of the Cleric's scar and she felt sick. Any hope she'd held that this deformation might be excised had died when they arrived here. She might take the Cleric to the Black with her, but she'd go with his wound fully intact. That she was sure of. She considered what a man's response might be when first glimpsing the nightmare festering across her heart. Utter horror, she imagined. She knew men found her beautiful at times, more so than she believed herself to be, and the expectation her face and shape drew would make the Cleric's mark even more shocking.

But not to Shadow.

That mark is a great honor, he had told her. Bunch of bullycrag, yes, but at least he knew of the damned thing and accepted it. *What a thing to be fussing over, Jana. You're like as not to get killed in this place and you're worried about finding a man who'll love you as ya are.* Silly, maybe, but she fussed over it nevertheless, and each time she drifted elsewhere with her thoughts, Shadow brought her back. She thought of his thin face, his dark eyes, the way they glimmered with confidence, his wiry build, no doubt well-honed like Donovan's. And his voice! Her hands wandered over her scar to her breasts and her stomach as she allowed herself to picture his caress, the way he had touched her face when they first arrived here, only everywhere.

The room was still but for the soft splashes of the bathwater lapping.

Then a soft gasp escaped her lips as she opened her eyes and saw the *thing* dangling from the ceiling above her.

She screamed and leaped from the tub, slipping, barely catching herself. She fumbled forward, scattering wet rose petals across the floor, and found her dirk, but now the creature was gone. She stood staring at the place where that multi-limbed monstrosity had perched, ready to descend on a web as thick as rope, but only the chandeliers swayed above her, too small to hide something so huge.

This is it. You're losing your mind, girl.

But was she? It had all seemed so real.

She frowned. Yes, the creature had seemed real enough to touch, just as she was sure it had seemed real to Donovan Maltrese when he had nearly killed her outside of Pleasantry under the darkest watch of the night.

15

Donovan opened his eyes for the first time in eight days and saw a whirling pool of bulbous, iridescent shapes and writhing lights weaving in and out of the blackness of his mind. He heard something, voices maybe, but they congealed only into a throbbing, shapeless whir. Pain flared in his legs, then his arms, the faint kind that told of severe injury dulled by shock, though he suspected that might not be the case now. He saw that he was bound leg and arm to the bed. He struggled—more for show than anything else—but had no strength and floundered back after a moment.

When he opened his eyes again there was a face six inches from his, a flesh-colored paint daub. Then it came into focus, and Shadow's dark eyes glimmered at him in the torchlight. Donovan realized the ex-Swordsman was speaking. "Can you hear me?" he said. "Donovan? Are you back from the dead, old friend?"

"Back to send you there in my stead," answered Donovan, meaning it to be a growl, succeeding only in a hoarse whisper.

Shadow laughed and drew back. "Keeper bless us, I thought for sure you were lost. And then what to do? I'd have stayed clear of the Master that day."

"The Master," said Donovan. "Call him Morlin, see what he says."

"Two minutes returned from the Black and Donovan Maltrese has jest on the tongue. You truly are a thing to behold. Perhaps I was wrong in envying you when Master left. You might just be the better man, as much as it pains to say."

"Where am I?" asked Donovan, testing his strength again against his bonds, discovering it was utterly depleted.

294

"At Pal Myrrah. We brought you in more than a week gone. You owe me your life, you know."

"I'll thank you properly later," Donovan said, meaning it. "Where is Jana? And Earnald?"

"Your friends are safe."

"Where?"

Annoyance crept across Shadow's face. "Safe is the only answer you're going to get for now, so save your strength. You have much healing to do yet if you're going to be of use to us."

Donovan felt an unfamiliar desperation take hold of him at the sight of his old comrade's expression, overpowering his resolve, indomitable most days but worn raw by illness and long days trekking the hellish hefts of this world. He pulled against his bindings, hoping he might overpower them, but found he could barely lift his arms let alone rip himself free. He looked at Shadow, who was studying him with an even, measuring gaze, the way a scholar might observe an animal in a cage, and the former Swordsman's demeanor in that moment released an abrupt and insane rage within Donovan, magmatic in his gut, seeking violence. It pressed him to an edge he did not know was there, begging for a vent through which to erupt.

You have to free yourself. You must.

(I can help you.)

The notion caught his breath in his throat. He knew he could not give in to that voice, the one burrowed beneath the low voice. Better for his body to die right here than his soul. But even as that thought evaporated, he found himself calling to the Cold, the first time he had ever done so, and begged its help to free him, to give him the strength to tear loose and rip Shadow apart. For that one moment, as brief as a single beat of a fly's wings, the sacrifice seemed worth it. *Anything* seemed worth it to exact revenge on his once-brother. But there was no answer to his call now; if the Cold was eager to finish its conquest of his mind, it was taking a respite for the time being.

"You look perturbed, Donovan. It is all right, I promise you. Everything is going as it should."

"How did you end up here? Where have you been since Kolendhar?"

"I was there, friend. At the end. I saw how you and the others fought. I envied it. Never did I think it was possible to fight to the finish with such fervor."

"You were there?" asked Donovan, some strength budding in his voice. "How?"

Shadow slipped his sword from his back and drew it halfway to study himself in the blade. "With Master. At his side."

"Why? Why have you done this?" asked Donovan. The weight of the dead rested on him even now, the weight of fallen Rosaline and her father, his brothers. Of everyone.

"Perhaps I'm not the one to tell you. Ours is history too clouded to allow your mind to be open. Gather your strength, and you'll learn more soon enough." He turned to leave.

"Gaelin," said Donovan, his tone free of their usual pretense, and Shadow stopped. "Whatever game you think you're playing with Master, you're behind when you believe yourself in front. You won't get out of this alive."

Shadow turned, his sword held before him as if ready to draw. "Never use that name again, old friend, or I'll see my end at Master's hand for the pleasure of watching your head roll."

"You are what you are," said Donovan, so weak, his face numb but for tingles, rope burns at his wrists and ankles a mercifully dull discomfort through his haze.

"No, friend. You are what you make yourself. Or what you fool others into believing you are. How else could you have risen so far within the Order?" Shadow's tone was deep and bitter, the sound of a child affronted by his peers in the schoolyard.

"Would you make yourself the undoing of the world?" asked Donovan, his eyes drifting closed.

"I'd do that and more if it meant putting things as they are meant to be. And so would you, once you see the light."

Donovan felt consciousness slipping away. "What does that mean? You speak in riddles." As he spoke the words, he thought of the dark figure in the forest, the one with the glowing eyes who must, he now knew, be a phantom of his mind. Perhaps an embodiment of the Cold? But what of the men and women and children with the rotting faces?

Shadow smiled and lowered his sword and Donovan thought of Orin. "You'll learn soon. Master will call when you are ready. Be still until then."

And without a sound Gaelin of Kolendhar, called Shadow then and now, was gone.

Donovan hardly noticed; still he thought of the demon in his dreams and the riddles he had spoken until he slipped into the dark of his mind and timeless emptiness greeted him.

When he woke again a day had passed. Four brown-robed albinos hovered over him, hands tucked into their sleeves, their white ghoul eyes glaring. One of them motioned with a scaly hand for him to rise, and he saw now that his bonds were cut. The rope burns did pain him this time, and he touched them tenderly as he grunted upright. For a moment the room spun and he bent forward until it settled. He had been dressed in cotton pants and a tunic which lay open to at the chest, revealing his hellish scar. Of his armor and Orin, there was no sign.

Behind the albinos stood six armored men, whitehawk feathers dyed violet jutting tall from their helms. "Come with us," said the one in front. A harsh baritone. He gestured for the door and Donovan complied.

They marched in silence. Other hallways intersected here and there, long stone boreholes stretching into the cold shadows beyond. Creatures hewn from granite watched them pass with uninterested reptile eyes; Donovan would not have been surprised to catch them peering at him afterwards. His legs burned and the room whirled and tried to pitch him over. The burning cressets braced near the walls cast a faint green light across everything. Nauseating, Donovan named it. This place was Kolendhar's twin. Twisted, yes, bent until it was unrecognizable, but sheared from the same cloth. What had happened to the men who built this great fortress, no stories told. Donovan was sure it was an ill end. These things always had such.

But drowning out all was the *itch*, that awful, mystical halfbreed of instinct and feeling that had salvaged his quest in the bog outside the Drudge, the one that bored its hooks into his core and trawled him from the single flower planted in the mound of Rosaline's grave through a sea of madness and across the ruins of the world. His weakness forgotten, he almost dashed ahead of his host. It took every last bit of his will to hold back.

The hall dipped into a long set of stairs. Donovan had the sense that they were lower than the ground now, descending into the hot gates of the earth where demons bred and slept. At the foot of the great black steps lay a wrought iron double door twice as tall as a man. As they approached the doors, the soldiers took up post to either side and the albinos took in both hands the mammoth holds. Without a sound—Donovan wondered if their tongues had been cut out—they heaved the doors open, those ancient hinges squealing into the dark, and stood aside. Within was a banquet hall, as grandiloquent as the king's had been at Kolendhar. A long blackwood table of fine ring and grain stretched a hundred paces across a pale stone floor. Black tapestries woven with purple runes billowed on a sourceless wind, glazed with drumming firelight. The shadows here were stark and fathomless; it was as if he gazed into the Black itself.

"Enter," said the man with the baritone voice, indicating the doorway with a gauntleted hand.

Donovan barely heard him. The *itch*, which had dragged him to this place tooth and nail, across wilderness and marsh, across mountains and the Wastes, across more pain and suffering than a man should be able to withstand, throbbed in his every inch, burned behind his eyes, clawed outward from his guts and screamed in his skull.

It was here.

He was here.

His jaw set, his mind torn in a hundred directions, all of which terminated in this same place, Donovan Maltrese stepped into the dark grasp of the banquet chamber to meet his destiny at last.

IV

DWELLERS
OF THE MIST

1

Something had just clicked within Earnald Avers's mind. Such moments of clarity happened every now and then, the most prominent example being the moment he stared into the foggy distance on the last day of Raef and his former companions' lives and discerned the Swordsman. Recently, however, the miracle seemed a daily occurrence. Mayhap a man, even a slow-witted one born of a simple mother and a drunken father, could grow given the right circumstances and effort, grab onto the old reins so to speak, and turn the horse towards smarter lands, even if he knew it could never get there.

He watched the rain-soaked ceiling cross boards twenty feet above as they flicked the occasional raindrop his way, which he had time to dodge, the aching hardness of the stone floor beneath him preferable to the splintery cot to his right. His cell itself was half again as big as an outhouse; he had to keep his knees bent to lay out, which was probably the point. Comfort was not a concern here when it came to prisoners, he took a wager. The place stunk of death and sickness; every breath brought memories of the hert with bright, numbing clarity. Some of that smell came pouring out of what he had deemed The Pit, where he emptied himself each morning with his shirt tugged up over his nose, not that it helped. The rest came from everywhere, from within the grain of the stone itself and whatever nightmares lay below, deeper in the tower, where he heard screams that seemed to echo for hours before fading into the ether along with the soul of whoever had made them. He wondered if Jana fared any better than he. He hoped she did. Earny Avers could take a beating, yessir and pray it, and had no fear of closed spaces, but this was no place for a fine young lady such as Jana Hunter.

He turned his good eye from the ceiling to the torchlit hall outside his cell as the lone tower guard strolled past, jingling his keyring to an uneven beat, humming some tuneless folksong to himself. The odd jasper-green light that was ever-present in this place danced a jig across the worn edges of his cuirass and the bronze weave of his kidney belt. Peligro. That was the only word Earny had heard the man say. Otherwise, he never spoke, but merely rapped on the old iron bars of his cell when Earny made any sort of noise at all. Peligro the Wide and Crafty, that was what Earny had fallen into the habit of calling him. Crafty at what, he did not know. Perhaps making sandwiches, given the plump knob of his gut.

Then there was the man's pet borecat, an animal that crawled straight from Earny's nightmares. Borecats were known as cunning and untamable hunters, prowling the deep forests with their hellish black teeth and eyes that could see a full heft on a moonless night. Earny would have thought keeping one as a pet impossible given the tales he had heard, yet here was proof otherwise. One of the other guards had named the beast Algenor while attempting to stop it from eating his rations, for the borecat was ill-trained by his master. That altercation had not worked out well for the guard, and it was by sheer luck that Peligro had happened by and pulled his pet away before too much blood was spilled. That had been Earny's second night in this forsaken place. The borecat still prowled the halls on its own now and then, but Earny had not seen it for days now.

Earny listened after Peligro was out of sight, heard him uncork a flask and drink deep as soon as he thought no one could see. There was no hiding the sway in his step or the stink of stout, so he wasn't sure why great Peligro the Sandwich Engineer bothered being stealthy about his vice. *Drink up, good sir! It's only you and Earnald and the rats here. Let's make a fest of it all!* Keeper knew, they needed it after a week of quiet and bar-rapping and gloomy water to wash down stale handfuls of bread.

As Peligro's smell weakened (of his fat body as well as his stout) and his off-key humming faded, Earny made a small *chk-chk* sound with his tongue and Ruti climbed up from his pocket and perched on his chest, stretching his wings and yawning. "Have a good sleep?" Earny asked him. Ruti seemed to nod, his tail swaying in a way Earny decided was sleepy, his slitted pupils expressionless and unknowable. Earny was worried about his tiny friend. He had offered him some bread and water, but the little Root Dragon always declined, content to crawl up onto his shoulder and fall asleep instead. How long could such a small thing go without sustenance? He hoped, given the fella was over a thousand years old, that a week or so amounted to a long foodless morning and nothing more as far as dragon time was concerned.

Earny sat forward as easy as he could, careful to keep his boots from scuffing on the floor, and held the bars gently, peering into the hall after Peligro, straining to make out the big man's lumbering silhouette. He could not, and his senses assured him the ogre was gone for now. He turned the other way, where the faint curve of the hall showed him the bars of other cells but little else. He waited for other pairs of hands to appear, for scurvy fingernails and bloodshot eyes to drift in from the darkness and offer some pale cousin to company, or maybe even comfort. *Ah, poor baby Earny's in needov sum titmilk and a blanky! Let's oblige 'im, fellas!* Raef said to him from the dead, his half-fleshed skeleton grinning his wide sheeny grin. Earny kicked him in the mouth and sent his bony head rolling into the Black. *Good riddance to ya.*

"Psst..." Earny called towards the row of cells as loud as he dared, then listened for the drunken stagger of Peligro's heavy boots. When no sound came, Peligro or otherwise, he tried again. Since the evening he had been thrown in here by his nape like a misbehaving child, Earny had attempted this routine daily until the sun went down, when like clockwork Peligro would return and take a seat at the center of the tower cellblock, his feet up on his knotty alder wood table, and drift into fitful sleep full of drunken perverse mutterings which Earny had learned to block out. But as the week appeared and went and the next followed, Earny had begun to give up hope that anyone lay huddled in those dark cells too afraid to return his whisper. And what if they were? It wasn't as if they could help him escape, all hedges in the barrel; too long in this place would break a man's spirit. And too long in this shithole was not long at all.

So Earny lay back on his hard bed and returned his thoughts—free-flowing and slippery as always—to what had clicked moments before. Two things, really, each of which might have been readily apparent to a more endowed man, but to Earny seemed a revelation: first that he was only alive because they were not yet sure what they'd need for leverage when it came time to put Jana and Donovan to whatever plans the Cleric had in store, and second that he would be executed soon after or left here to rot either way. Donovan had warned him of this long before, but it took the damn bloody stink of the place for the truth to settle in. Things might have been long and hard for Earny for much of life (and by much, he meant every bit he could remember), but the last thing he was going to do was allow a bunch of demon-breeding man-haters to drive him to find the Black in this forsaken tower in the middle of the Keeper-forsaken Wastes.

How to get out, though, was a different story altogether.

From what he recalled—he admittedly had been too busy staring at the carvings and tapestries on the way here to form any mental map of the keep interior—there had been several sets of stairs and long stretches of hallway frequented by guards and worse. Far too dangerous to traverse with fighting on the brain, but too bare to sneak through either. What then was his plan, even if he could escape his cell? And what effect might his escape have on the treatment of Jana and Donovan? Little, he suspected, but such reactions were hard to predict when dealing with folk of the insane and malicious sort, so it was best to be over-wary rather than over-sorry.

Ruti scampered down his arm and stood on the back of his hand, head cocked up, tongue flitting restlessly. "*Niya moei simpo lagda naya,*" he said in his small voice. The Root Dragon's tone was impossible to mistake: *We've got to get out of here, and soon.*

"You said it, my friend," answered Earny. He glanced at his diminutive companion, who had stowed away inside his pant leg while he was searched upon arrival at the tower. What a botch that had been! Ticklish was old Mr. Avers, and his giggles had nearly earned him a beating from Peligro. Apparently a good chuckle was frowned upon in Pal Myrrah.

As if on cue, Peligro returned, the bast soles of his decrepit boots scraping the cool stone in a stumble farther down the hall before he trudged past Earny's cell. Ruti was already in his hiding spot atop the thick beam that crested the cell door, hunkered onto his white scaly haunches, looking alert. Earny sat up as the big man appeared between the bars, bulbous cheeks red with inebriation, thickly whiskered chin squished downward into hard creases and pale rolls, one hand on his hip and the other on the haft of his whip. He stopped before Earny's cell and glared in his taciturn way, his dry, runnelled lips working hard but saying nothing.

Earny resisted the urge to initiate conversation; the last attempt had ended in a whipping that layered his old wounds from Raef's cat-o-nine-tails with a fresh burn. Instead, he looked up blankly with a curious eye and watched the Pal Myrrah jailer the way one might watch a big dumb bear in the forest, praying it did not become agitated. But Peligro the Sandwicher took no agitating today. He rapped against the bars with the haft of his whip and watched Earny's non-reaction with a deep frown that bunched the pasty expanse of his forehead into channels of displeasure. He looked like he might just go away for a moment, but there was something different in great Peligro's mien today. Earny spotted the source seconds before his fat sausage fingers produced the cell key with a fumble and clicked it into the lock: a deep brown and purple bruise on his temple with a deeper gash at the center. Someone had spoken to Peligro today, and spoken hard, and now the Sandwich Engineer had no choice but to pass the love along to someone else. And in this tower, far as Earny could tell, there was only one someone else.

Before he could react, Peligro had the door open and was upon him. Knobby and sandwich-laden he may be, the man could move when he wanted to. He grasped Earny by the tunic and hoisted him to his feet without effort. Earny brandished his hands, the crisp vision of what would come next flashing into his mind like a lightning strike. "No, sir. I beg ya, please. I only—"

But Peligro was not interested in pleas or questions or answers in the hot red bath of his rage.

What he was interested in was blood.

So he drew it from Earny, first with his fist, crushing it into the ex-bandit's moppy, thinning hair with a meaty *smack*, again and again, then the hard heel of his boot, seeding bruises and drawing the muted crack of a snapping rib, and then with his whip. Earny lay belly-down, lost in the white light of his pain and the swelling burn behind it, forcing himself to thoughts of cool lakebreeze and crisp spring air, to the gentle scent of pine and the feel of cold, dewy grass beneath bare feet. And in those thoughts he stayed until Peligro hunched over him wheezing, thick beads of sweat rolling off his obese face onto the bloody ruin of Earny's back, his hands propped on his knees. Then, without question or statement, Peligro the Tired left Earny's cell and locked the door behind him.

Earny held onto consciousness afterwards. For a while, he waded in a deep pool of pale colors, always just a stroke ahead of the blackness threatening to swallow him up. It was tempting to sink into that dark pit; there at least he knew there would be no pain, at least not until he woke with his skin stiff with dry blood. But he held on anyway, for no reason beyond pride; no pain of any measure had ever knocked Earny cold, not even when he lost his eye to that angry heathen on the dusty floor of a farm cottage all those years back. No, there would be no knocking Earny Avers senseless with hurt, not this or any other cold dark evening.

He sat up with a grunt, then immediately clamped a hand over his mouth and peered outside his cell. Peligro was gone again, hopefully not to cross someone else who might stoke his anger and leave him wanting for more blood. One of those whippings Earny could stand, but not two.

Ruti fluttered down from his perch and landed on Earny's knee. The bright blue pupils of the Root Dragon's eyes, at once humanlike and alien, glittered nervously in the dim torchlight, the soft scales along his back retracting in an expression Earny interpreted as sad. "It's all right. I'll live, pray it," he said. Ruti did not seem so sure.

As if to prove the Root Dragon right, Earny hunkered forward, gasping in pain as his ribs caught fire, and hugged his arms around his belly. The rib was broken, and every breath he took birthed from an ache and spiked into a stab. Ribs or back alone he could deal with, but the agony in both brought its own questions, the most dire being whether it would hurt more to sleep belly-down or on his back. He suspected the rib would hurt less and that made him frown. The last thing he wanted to do in this dank place was sleep face down with his nose buried in Keeper-knew-what all night.

He sat quietly for a while, rocking, breaths shallow so as not to agitate the fruits of Peligro's whip. To distract himself, he willed his fogging mind to focus on the real task at hand: he had to escape this place—*had* to, or else he was going to end up dead. But more than that, Earny sensed in the pit of his pits that Donovan needed him to escape as well. For what and where to? Well, that he couldn't know yet. But the Swordsmen was keen on heeding the low voice and the wisdom it whispered, and Earny had told Donovan he wanted to learn. Right now, Earnald Avers's low voice said to get a'movin. But first, there was the girl to see to. He wanted to know, bleak as it sounded, that even should he be caught and killed, it would cause no consequence to her. And there was only one way to do that.

He looked at Ruti. "Come up here, would ya?" he said, patting his knee. Ruti, who had returned to the floor, complied and scampered back up Earny's shredded pant leg. "Now, you do understand what I'm sayin', don't ya? Far as my blitherin' can be understood, I mean."

Ruti stared at him with his tiny eyes darting. "*Ueli.*"

"I don't know what that means. That mean yes? Nod if it does."

Ruti nodded his small head. And was that a touch of a sardonic smile? *Miss Jana might be right. Bit condescending for a little thing, isn't he?* thought Earny. He decided he liked that about the Root Dragon; a man who was above giving a bit of shit now and then usually lacked somehow. Or a dragon.

"Good. Well, I wish I could understand you as well, but me, I'm lucky I know a fart from a whistle, with all the brains I got." He swallowed down a gasp of pain. When it died he said, "I need ya to do somethin' fer me."

Ruti nodded again. In the firelight, his white skin looked half green and half orange, and his scales rippled with other colors with each twist of his body.

"You remember Jana?"

Ruti nodded. He hissed and his eyes blinked full black before returning to their normal blue.

"Come on now. She's a nice one, her."

Ruti did not seem convinced. He extended his wings and shook them like a bird drying itself after a bath.

"Well, puttin' your differences aside, I need you to find her. Make sure she's all right. I don't quite know how yer gonna tell me if she is or isn't, though. Guess I'm gonna hafta ask you a bunch of questions and you just shake yes or no. Think you can do that?"

Ruti seemed to consider it, then nodded again.

"Good. Oh, and one other thing. I need you to listen in on whatever talk's going on. See if you can figure out what they plan to do with her and with Master Donovan." At the Swordsman's name, something seemed to pass across the Root Dragon's eyes. Sorrow, maybe? Regret? Earny shared some of the sadness. "You think he's still alive?"

Ruti nodded without hesitation, and that was good enough for him.

"Listen for any talk of me, too. Keeper knows, I wish Donovan told me more about goings ons. I'm last on the pole, far as importance goes, but I can't leave without knowin' the girl's in one piece."

"*Pouy siei kaena dey.*"

"If you're asking how I plan to get clear o' this place, well… Couldn't tell ya if my guts depended on it. But I'll think of somethin'. Meantime, you get going. Ya can't let anyone spot ya. Ya know that, right?"

Ruti nodded and fluttered his wings.

"Please don't let anyone see ya. Please, fella. I'd hate to be the one who brought ya out of the woods just to get you stepped on by one of those albinos or the Sandwicher there." He nodded towards the way Peligro had stormed off. "Promise you'll be careful?"

Ruti once again nodded, then turned to leave. He stopped halfway and, so fast it made Earny jerk backwards, crawled up his sleeve, and licked him softly across the cheek. It felt dry and weird, and Earny loved it. "Why thankya. I'd return tha favor but I don't think you'd enjoy it," he said with a chuckle. "Now get, and watch fer tha guy with the keys. He never goes far."

"*Ueli.*"

And with that Ruti of the deep forest fluttered up through the bars and out into the hall.

Earny held himself and bit his lip against the pain, listening until the tiny wing flaps were inaudible.

Somewhere deep down (he hoped not his low voice), he had the awful feeling he'd never see the little dragon again.

2

The Swordsman entered the vast circular banquet hall with his fingers twitching and drumming. The battle dance, some of his brothers once called that heightened unconscious expenditure of energy. They flicked and swayed and opened and closed, yearning for the hard drakkenbone hilt they knew so well, for nothing else would sate or still them now. That he could not grasp his family sword for the foreseeable future did not diminish the dance; if anything his fingers became more restless, his shoulders and arms overrun with coiled energy that yearned to be unleashed upon an enemy. *The time closest to our true self, the moments we feel as our natural minds did during the first days of man, are the ones just before battle. That which is primal is pure, Donovan. Remember that.* And Donovan *did* remember; during every waking moment it was as if his master from Kolendhar walked with him, a ghost encamped in his mind, where too many bedfellows dwelled already.

He paced the room, his bare footsteps echoing into the chamber. Three large chandeliers pointed down at him like jeweled fingers. Black, those ancient adornments were, fashioned from polished stones that overlapped like scales. They diffracted the dim candlelight as they swayed, perturbed by a draft, curved arms outspread like demonic octopuses. The endlessly burning candles throughout the room threw a hard, orange-green light that flickered and shifted across the arabesque walls, giving the chamber a fluid aspect that was disorienting. Great sandstone pillars chiseled into robed women bent at the knee rose from the floor at intervals, their delicate hands supporting the rotunda above. The table was set, Donovan saw, with an assortment of fruits and meats and wines that made his stomach grumble. He didn't know how long it had been since he last ate.

He paused near a marble bust crafted into a face so burned into his mind's eye he gasped when he saw it. It was as though his old master stood before him, peering up with pupil-less stone eyes. Unnerved, the Swordsman continued along the perimeter of the hall, his rough fingers tracing the smooth filagree with an artisan's care, the *itch* pounding hard at the inside of his skull. He tried to ignore the sensation the way a man living on a mountain might try to ignore an avalanche rumbling towards his hut, but it did no good; with every passing second, the constant thrum within his head grew more and more overwhelming. Beneath his fervor, Donovan felt the ache of his legs and the searing remains of what the Aspy's poison had done to his body. His hand was still swollen and purple, the holes where the animal's fangs had injected the venom burned black and blistered from Orin's heated tip. He regarded the wounds impassively and then did not look at them again.

"I had the bust brought in from the remains of Kolendhar. Virgil crafted it. You remember him," said a voice from behind that raised bumps on the back of Donovan's neck. The Swordsman turned on his heel, eyes narrowing, and there was the Cleric. He was tall, taller than Donovan remembered, rawboned beneath his immaculate white cloak, which glowed with unnatural light. The harsh glister of his violet eyes pierced the distance between them like an arrow loosed from full draw. He leaned against one of the caryatids, beside the bust, his skeleton fingers folded, a toothy smile caged by anemic lips. His staff was nowhere to be seen. "I care very much for the likeness. What do you think?"

Donovan had to plant himself with his hands at his sides. In his mind he was across the room already, the Cleric's rangy neck crushed in his hands.

"I wonder sometimes, in places like this, what part of man drives him to create. For is not art something to separate us from the beasts we feed upon? Lost now in the fires of what was, I think. For shame."

Donovan could stand still no longer. He paced, eyes fixed on the Cleric, unable to bring himself to speak.

The Cleric did not seem concerned with Donovan's mood. "The ones who say we differ from beasts because of creation are right, but not the way they think. We strive to create because of the very thing that makes us selfish, impure, prone to folly, prone to destroying ourselves. Art is a measure of man's self-importance." He smiled his thin smile and then lashed out. Donovan's eyes, keen as they were, could barely follow his old master's movement; he was leaning against the caryatid one moment, and next, he was holding Orin in his delicate grasp. From where he had drawn the aged blade, the Swordsman could not say. A moment later the upper half of the bust's head slid free and struck the floor with a thunderous *clunk* that echoed into the room. The Cleric held Orin at his side, his smile fading.

"Give it to me," said Donovan, the tremble of rage in his voice.

"Don't worry, I will. But to what end? *My* end, do you think? Perhaps you'd hear me out first."

"We've had this talk before."

"And it did not end well for you did it, dear Donovan?" said the Cleric in his silken, bass voice that reminded Donovan of the deep flow of distant water or the long grumble of a far off storm. "Or perhaps it did and you do not yet know it."

"I have nothing to sa—"

"Please," interrupted the Cleric. "I've given ear to your iron will and honorable assertions. Repetition bores me and no doubt strains your patience." He gestured towards the table. "Will you eat? You've been unconscious for days and you are looking…worse for wear."

Donovan *was* hungry. What that food was laced with, he did not want to know. But what could the worst be? They had just spent time curing him. Why kill him just as he was regaining his strength? "You were never one to play games before."

"No games, Donovan. Not here. Here all is truth and your ever-feared triptalk is a relic. The thoughts that consume most men are useless once you strip the mind of pretense. Come, drink." He poured Donovan a chalice of rice wine and offered it. The Swordsman inched forward and accepted, studying the Cleric's violet eyes. As he stepped away he caught a deep whiff of spiced meats and creamed corn and went insane with hunger. Donovan was seated before he could stop himself, his hands buried in the porcelain bowls, scooping clumps into his mouth like a savage, wiping his chin with his forearm before reaching for the next. The Cleric watched with a smile. "Good. Get your strength back. I need the fabled Donovan of the Maltreses feeling clean and fed for the path ahead."

Donovan shot him a hard look. Glaring with a mouthful of venison (which was just as savory as he had imagined) must have looked absurd, but he held his former instructor's gaze anyway before returning to his meal. He followed the meat with rice wine, which burned on his tongue and all the way down, and licked his fingers when he was finished. "You say the roundabout is done and yet still you speak in riddles." The Swordsman stood again, resisting the urge to snatch another hunk of meat from the serving plate, and returned to pacing. "Why did you sack Kolendhar?"

The Cleric seated himself, sliding Orin into its sheath. The sound filled Donovan with warm comfort. "Good Donovan, always to the point. As a boy, they said you'd be slow and without coordination. Do you recall? Even then it was whispered you'd not slay three foes before you sliced off your own arm. And now look at you!" His thin face beamed with pride Donovan could only call fatherly. That look faded quickly and his eyes became distant as he said, "The Order's purpose was one of salvage."

"Is that what you call it?"

"That is what it was, no matter the name you give it. Everything we've seen as we've walked these forsaken forests and mountains, it is debris, blown towards the nether on a wind made of time, and the Swordsmen laid in the eye of the storm grasping for every scrap they could hold onto."

Donovan began a rebuttal, but choked on it before it could find voice. What the Cleric, his old master, said was true. What he had known in his heart but never spoken, the thing that held his gaze roadward when women and children called for his aid, that kept his sword sheathed while men died at the hands of foes he might have stopped, hung in the air now like a cloud. It was all for nothing. All of it.

You should because you can.

Perhaps Jana Hunter was right. Perhaps he should help the weak simply because he was able. But what if he did not *want* to help? What did that make him? He thought of Rosaline, wondering what she might think of these thoughts. But again, what did it matter? She was lost, body and soul, lost in a sea of blood at his heels.

"You killed her."

"I set her free," replied the Cleric simply.

"By making her into one of those things?"

"You could have come with Gaelin. He gave you word before the attack."

"I thought..." said Donovan, trailing off. He could not finish. What had he thought? As he remembered the last stand of Kolendhar now, it seemed so foolish, so rank with naivety and stubborn boyish fancy he felt sick to remember it.

The Cleric cocked his head, waiting intently for the end of Donovan's thought. When he saw it would not come he leaned back into his chair, a great walnut throne upholstered in fine petite point designs, and sighed, grasping Orin's hilt. "I've dreamed of this time, Donovan. Of this very moment. In my mind, it would come with peace and agreement, after a nice long talk and a settlement between two men. But you would not listen to me, so great was your rage."

Donovan leaned in, aware of the fierce glow in his eyes. The Cold, thankfully, was still recessed in his mind; still not gone, but asleep. "You say this is *my* fault?"

The Cleric shrugged. "Faults, wrongdoing, honor, fate... All threads of the same cloth."

"That's not what you taught us."

"I am not above folly, Donovan. Even now. Things have not gone as I foresaw and I am forced to deal with the aftermath of my miscalculations." He rose again, walking the room like a man perusing a house of wonders. Donovan stared at the empty plate where the Cleric had sat and frowned. "Tell me what happened in the Darklands."

The Cleric stopped short, his narrow shoulders hunched. "How have your nights been? Filled with dreams, I suspect." His tone threw Donovan off-balance; this was not what he imagined at the end of his hunt. "Tell me of them."

"I dreamed of Kolendhar. And of Rosaline," said Donovan, a hard lump growing in his throat. "And other things…"

"Of murder."

Donovan nodded.

"Did you come here to kill me?"

"I came to be rid of the madness."

"Madness!" said the Cleric. He chuckled, a raspy, sick sound that turned Donovan's stomach. "Is scavenging the land, living off the scraps of a dead society any less mad?" He faced his old apprentice now, eyes alight. "You are not the same man I left at Kolendhar. These years have changed you."

"Not so much as you, Master." It felt odd to call this man his master. But Morlin Sayre *was* there, deep beneath that sickly face and the dark energy it exuded.

"Oh, I don't know. I've not changed so much as you might think," said the Cleric with a smile that might have been wistful.

"Was it you in my dreams these past nights?" asked Donovan. He did not think it was, but he watched the Cleric's face closely for sign otherwise.

"No," was the simple response. "Dreams I cannot touch directly. Only through this madness you speak of that I call release."

"Release from what?" said Donovan, anger rising. "You killed that girl's father. Did you free him from love of his children and his wife?"

"As I once taught you, Donovan, man is at his core bestial. We are feral things, you and I, strung along a trail of subterfuge that fails us at every turn."

"You killed her father," Donovan said again, quietly this time.

"And many other fathers, my son. And fathers to be, as well. It pains me to do such." His eyes narrowed. "You look surprised. Yes, it does pain me. But strength is facing pain and performing one's duty regardless."

"Strength is in right action. That was the first thing you ever taught me," said Donovan, his eyes on Orin again, dangling from the Cleric's fingers.

"Folly, like I said. If I could do things again, they would go differently. All but you and the girl. You are my greatest achievements and the point of all of this. It's taken me many attempts to find truth in the lies of man. Not all were successful. Some could not sustain their own lives. Others do well as servants." He gestured with his head and Donovan followed his gaze. There, near the door, stood a Blood Demon. Just as Jana's father, this one looked once-human, deformed now into something macabre, it's long jaw and serrated teeth dripping white threads of saliva. Its ichor eyes regarded the room, unblinking, the rolls of its doughy skin rippled and veiny, the dead yellow of an etiolated plant.

Donovan's heart leapt. How did he not see it enter? Or hear it, Keeper save them! He thought then of Jana's father and the way he had stalked through the house as silent as a butterfly before striking.

"Do not fear. You are in no danger," said the Cleric. He gestured and the Blood Demon lurched forward. Its claws dangled like half torn branches, each bayonet nail long enough to pierce a man's heart clear to the other side; Donovan stared at them as the Cleric touched the thing's slick forehead with a smile.

"You created them," said Donovan.

"You might say I found them. Like a sculptor finds his art within the stone."

"For his self-importance."

The Cleric nodded. "Indeed. The only act of creation to escape that snare is one of true sacrifice." He gestured and the creature turned and trudged away. A small bronze door drifted open as it approached. It vanished into the black hallway beyond without a sound.

"Cure me," said Donovan. When he had been an eager student stricken by an insatiable appetite for his master's gospel, these sort of talks had been ineluctable. Now, with the endless disdain behind the Cleric's voice brooding like a battlemad battalion set to charge with or without reason, he felt sick. "Now. And then we will talk more."

The Cleric threw back his head and laughed again. "I'd as soon cure you of being human."

At that, Donovan's warrior instincts prickled to attention, spurring the hairs on his neck upright, dousing his mind in blue-hot hyper-awareness. His body lunged for the Cleric with his mind still one step behind, hands thrust forward, madness separate from the Cold beaming in his eyes. The Cleric slipped into a duck, so delicate it might have been a dance. The Swordsman had time to think his foe was laughing—*laughing*—and then Orin's hilt, carved by a thousand years of his ancestors, cracked into the back of his skull and his vision exploded into stars. He felt his palms and knees slap the cold stone of the banquet floor as he fought to stay conscious.

"Now," said the Cleric with the tone of a vexed parent. "We will talk straight at last, since you hunger so to escape pleasantries with an old friend. I have need of you, Donovan, just like old times. But first, get yourself keen and ready." He considered his next words. "I need you to ignore your low voice, for it has no place here." His hard knee-high foldover boots clacked past Donovan; the sound reminded the Swordsman of teeth. He shook his head to clear it, saw the floor materialize from the red-black coating his eyes, still spinning. "Stand up," said the Cleric. He planted his boot on the fallen Swordsman's shoulder and kicked him to his back. Donovan rolled over with a gasp, then fought to his feet.

The Cleric spoke again after a moment. "Do you know what lies beyond this great ossuary we call home, Donovan? I've been there, yet even still I cannot grasp it. The Maw itself, perhaps. I've seen things, things that would rot your eyes in your head, heard sounds that would peel your skin to the bone." He snapped from his trance, turning to his old ally. "When I returned to this land, I came before the leader of the Dwellers and formed a pact. Their kind would swear allegiance to me, to be at my beck for whatever purpose I saw fit."

"As oarmen and escorts, I've seen so far," said Donovan. *Bitter man*, Rosaline called him. Even in his imagination, her voice made him crave her touch. "I want you to undo this."

"In time."

"Now, and then we'll talk."

"I'll watch you chase this until you collapse, my son."

And he would, no doubt. Donovan wanted to fight on and squelch this man's bluster with pure will; the old Donovan would have. This Donovan, however, was weary and still close with death, his mind weak from battling the Cold and the demons that plagued his unconscious. His feet were swollen from a thousand hefts of marsh, sand, and mountain, and his arms hung sore from a hundred death swings and the corpses he littered the world with them.

No. There would be no more fighting today.

"What would you have me do?" he asked.

"The Dwellers possess holy ground near Pleasantry. The Mist has kept men away, but it will not keep you."

"Holy ground? I've heard stories but I thought them myths."

"Whatever gods they worship, I know not. It does not matter. What I task you with is the death of the Dweller King. He is there now, awaiting my orders. Bring me his heart, for I'll need it to fashion your cure. This is the first of two matters."

"What could this gain you? They've already sworn themselves loyal."

"Worry not, my friend. What must concern you now is completing what I bid in time to salvage your mind, and that of the girl."

"What can you do with its heart that you could not do with your magic alone?"

At this, the Cleric laughed, a hissing and sick sound. "Nothing I've done is wrought of air, Donovan. A mason needs brick to fashion a house. And for the house of your sanity, not just any Dweller heart will do. I need it cloven from the King itself. The sooner you return with it, the sooner I will provide the cure to you."

"Why would you offer this when you're so proud of what you've created in me?" asked Donovan, unbelieving of every nuance he heard.

"My creation does not end with you, Donovan. I'd understand the very things too minuscule for any eye to see so I might press onward. You and the girl have taught me much, but there are other things, things only creatures such as the Dwellers can show, and I'd have their teachings in my mind." He looked Donovan from toe to head. "I'd see you happy again, now that your terrible role in all of this is coming to an end."

"Happy?"

The Cleric nodded, an odd light in his stark eyes.

Donovan's eyes darted to random points along the floor as if answers might lay there. "How can a man kill such a thing?"

"You're no longer just a man. Be ever mindful of that." That twisted sound of pride had returned to the old master of Kolendhar's voice.

Something frozen and hollow ensconced itself across Donovan's heart: resignation. "What else?"

"Once the Dweller leader has been slain, I want you to return to Pleasantry." For the briefest flash, Donovan thought he saw his old master's eyes glow brighter than the torchlight. The *snap-crack* of the endless flames fought the overbearing silence in vain. "There you will slay them all, man, woman, and child. Then and only then will I undo your curse."

Whatever Donovan had expected when he stepped into this place, this was not it. "Why? What could the folk of Pleasantry possibly bode for you?"

The Cleric brandished a ghoulish finger, a soft *tsk-tsk* slinking through the razor line of his lips. "You are a soldier, the fist of those wiser and more informed. You should be familiar with this arrangement. Do as I say, and you'll have your life and your mind to finish out as you wish, free from all this, and free from the Order, too."

Donovan opened his mouth to argue but could find no reason. What was left for him now? The Cold would take hold within weeks, and then what? A life spent prowling the deep timberland, or maybe the boreal gullies far beyond the Din, where fewer travelers might hap upon him, as much a creature of the Maw as the Blood Demons themselves. And what better future favored Pleasantry? Soon the Cleric's demon army would sweep them over as it did Kolendhar, and they would man, woman, and child, fall to a maelstrom of claws and fangs. Or worse, be turned.

You cannot. You were to protect them.

(They'd kill you for a hot meal and warm bed. Even for one night.)

No! I cannot.

But he could. Keeper save him, he could. What was worth fighting for had burned with Kolendhar. His love, his people, his life, were all inhumed in the charred craters beneath those mountains of rubble. "What about the girl?" he asked, so softly he worried the Cleric did not hear him.

"She will be cured as well."

"What can you show me that will prove my trust wise?"

The Cleric smiled his narrow, devil's smile, then hurled Orin towards Donovan. The Swordsman caught his family blade and drew it in the same motion; the ring of the thousand-fold steel and the cool touch of the drakkenbone hilt nearly made him cry out with joy. "Take it and wield it well."

Donovan looked at the sick and weathered man in the reflection of Orin's blade with a frown.

"Are we settled?"

One last shred of Donovan's mind, kin to boyhood ideals, begged to say no, yearned to charge the Cleric and end this, even if it meant his own death. But the bitter pull of the past, the voices of a thousand starving faces screaming obscenities as he fought for their honor, the toothless grins and milky gazes of men who owed him their lives and in repayment sought murder and the ultimate prize of a Swordmaster's sword, chided him. He realized then that it might be the Cleric who was right; maybe it was Donovan of Kolendhar who had changed.

"I see you are conflicted. Take time to heal and to think. When you are ready, tell Shadow and he will see you off."

Donovan nodded, his mind whirling like a dancer trapped in an endless pirouette.

"The heart of the Dweller King. Bring it to me," said the Cleric. His words were a whisper, but somehow they thundered even in their quiet rasp.

The Cleric gestured and the armed host outside opened the huge double doors, motioning for Donovan to follow. He did as bade, Orin tapping his back with sweet familiarity, the endless throng of dead from his dream awaiting his call in the unknown before him.

3

Three nights after she saw the creature scaling the sheer wall of her bedchamber, Jana lay across her patchwork organdy bed-cover with one of Shadow's dusty books open before her, the old pages faded and brittled by untold years and dry beneath her fingertips, but still legible. As reading went, her skills were lacking—Tomson and Grampy were the only older Pleasantry folk who knew how, and Grampy had taught her along with other children on his porch beneath lavender twilit skies in between steep tokes of boon, which affected his...clarity, one might say. The lessons were sporadic and had spanned only a few years, yet were enough to open her mind more than most in Pleasantry. This book was beyond anything Grampy had taught her, but it did have pictures, drawn with a fine-tipped quill or brush with minimal strokes, enlivening the text, which helped. From what she gathered, it chronicled the plight of a minstrel stricken with a case of hertweed that had slowed shy of deadly but never healed. A living, breathing weapon, cast out by his town, he withdrew into the forest and lived off the land for years.

One day the minstrel stumbled across a young woman unconscious and wounded in the road. Reluctant to expose her to his illness but sure she would die if abandoned, he carried her to his hut and nursed her to health. Once she woke, he discovered the woman was blind, a condition she had suffered since childhood. Ignorant of the visible signs of his disease, she stayed on with him, confiding that she had no life left to return to. The minstrel knew his case of hert was still contagious, that every moment the young woman stayed with him allowed its invisible claws to carve further into her frail body, but the warmth of companionship after so many years of solitude overrode his conscience and so he kept her on anyway. Her approaching ruin settled heavily on his shoulders, however, for over time she had reawakened his humanity, and soon his selfish resolve began to erode. For two months she resisted infection, gregarious and imbued with wanderlust during the day, cooking with his assistance in the evening, then laying with him at night. During that time the minstrel knew peace like he never had.

When sign of the hert showed its baleful grin at last, first as subtle blemishes on the woman's skin that spread into scurvy-yellows muddled by a spreading rash, then as a red crawl of veins overgrowing the cataract clouds of her eyes, he was overwhelmed with remorse. A hard case of Mum's megrims set in, to make light of it. One night, while they lay together in the colorless night and he could watch her suffer no longer, he pressed his pillow to her face until her breath gave out, weeping the entire time—Jana had difficulty picturing the same man murdering his blind and sick woman and then shedding tears about it after, but who knew to what depths such madness ran?

After her body was burned, the minstrel took to the forest again, forever forward devoid of companionship, alone with his songs. It was an illustration of this moment which Jana stared at now, a sketch of a despondent shadow plodding the endless, solitary gloaming.

She put the book aside.

These last days had passed more easily thanks to her new distractions, but being cooped up in a pen like this—a large and extravagant one, yes, but still a pen—had driven the fidgets into her like her Mum would not have believed. If only Stink were here. With his imagination on their side, this room could become an endless road or a magic cave or a long, blood-soaked battlefield or the stomach of a flesh-eating giant. Beating the snot out of imaginary monsters with her bare fists would do wonders for her spirits right now, and if monsters were in short order she could always pretend Shadow was there, fantasize about breaking his pretty face into a hundred welted pieces.

As the day trundled on she paced the room, watching the light grow and then fade through the oriel, wishing desperately for the wild breeze and open vista she knew lay just beyond. It was so close she could smell it, Keeper damn every last demon in this place. She spent some time crouched by the door, peering into the keyhole, which twinkled with faint light but provided no sightline to the hall outside. She scoured the room, searching for would-be lockpicks, finding none. Then she examined her furniture and wondered what battering ram could be fashioned if only she could rip the wood from its bolts. All of these things sounded rousing and hopeful, yet she knew it was the false kind of hope, the sort that did more harm than good. In the end, she sat cross-legged on the floor staring up at the twin chandeliers, hoping the creature who lived in her mind might show itself again. At least that would be some kind of company.

When the door opened she was too numb to be surprised. There again was Shadow in his cocky resplendence. He closed the door behind him and adjusted his sword. Jana found herself thanking the Keeper for his sudden appearance, for it was simpler to imagine clocking the endless grin off his face when he was standing right there. That she felt heat growing in her belly already made the vision all the more enjoyable. "Good evening," he said with a flourish and a bow.

"What is it?" Her voice rang dry and angry in her ears. *Why hide how you feel?*

"Am I disturbing you? If you are busy I can certainly return later." She cocked her head and her eyebrow and he laughed. "Jana, Jana… I feel like you'd stab me in the heart with that dirk should you find the chance."

"Would it get me out of this damn room?"

"Lady, if you managed to sink a blade into my flesh my men would let you stroll free out of pure terror."

She stood, straightening her tunic—and concealing her scar. *Why bother? He knows of it already. Plus, who are you impressing, stupid girl?* She adjusted it again, leaving the very tip of that ropy purple flesh vine visible, watching Shadow's dark eyes to see if he would look. He did not; to him it was as though the scar didn't exist, or better still that it was just another part of her body he considered beautiful, if he considered her at all. "If you're selling me on not killing you, you're doing a poor job."

Shadow stood there looking amused.

"How is Donovan?"

The ex-Swordsman sighed and looked at his toes, and for a terrible moment Jana held her breath, a cold clutch of fear in her gut. *He's dead. You're all alone here. Surely they've killed Earny off already, too.*

"He is alive. Weak still, but his strength is returning. The healers here are skilled, that is certain."

Jana did not realize how much tension her body was holding until she released it with a gasp. She looked at the ceiling and thanked the Keeper.

"You look relieved. You care for him, don't you?"

Jana's relief gave way to annoyance. "Will you let me out of here now?"

"Master has not yet given me instructions for you."

"You're a good dog aren't you." She felt afraid as soon as the words left her mouth. This was a dangerous man, a murderer. If only she could remember that. All it would take was one poke too many and that would be the end of Jana Hunter and the Hunter Clan entire.

To her surprise, Shadow did not flinch. "You test me time and again, Miss Hunter, and never find a chink. How long until you give up?"

"When you break." She reached for her dirk as the quip left her lips.

"You won't need that. I'm here to protect you."

"And who exactly is protecting me from you and this…routine of yours?"

Shadow stepped towards her and she shrunk back. That she reacted at all made her angry enough to see red. She wasn't afraid of this man, regardless of who he was or what skill hid within that thin wildercat frame of his. After all, bound within her flesh lay some demonic madness growing like a hellish tree root, wrought of power brought back to the world of men from the bowels of the Darklands by the Cleric himself. What fear could a simple soldier put in her? He stopped so close she could feel the heat of his body, see every fleck of color peppered in the dark bowls of his eyes. Damn everything to the Black, she wanted him to take one more step and press against her, felt comfort in the idea of his hands on her body.

"Kill me if you would. I won't defend myself. You have this once," he said.

The dirk trembled in her fingers. She clenched them tighter. She imagined free air and open ground beneath her feet so vividly her mouth watered. But—the Cleric aside, hopefully—perhaps she was not a killer after all. The dirk slipped from her grasp and clattered on the floor. To her surprise, Shadow did not smile triumphantly or laugh or gloat. He touched her chin as he had that first night and tilted her head. If her heart kept rigorous pace before, now it felt like a runaway carriage crashing into her chest. Her breath locked in her throat as Shadow's rough fingers traced her cheek and along her neck, leaving a trail of fire behind. She became fiercely aware of her body, the heave of her breasts, the heat in her stomach raging uncontrolled now, the tremble in her thighs. He leaned closer, considering her lips, eyes narrowed as if solving a frustrating puzzle. She closed her eyes and forced her breath still and anticipated the touch of his mouth.

When she opened them again he had turned away, her dirk in hand. "I've been known as a master of the roundabout, Jana, but I'd tell you... I come to deliver my news in person not because I lack messengers to send in my stead."

To Jana his words echoed in an incomprehensible jumble inside her head, drowned by the drumbeat of her heart.

"When Donovan leaves I do not think he will take you with him."

"Why do you say that?"

"He hinted at as much. He thinks you'll weigh him down. He's probably just worried for you."

"Ha! Donovan worried about me. He dragged me along till he found what he was looking for and now he's done with me." The Mule dug in. That *was* what the Swordsman was thinking. Bet your stock on it. She wondered if she should be so quick to accept Shadow's word, then recalled Donovan's oath the morning after madness nearly consumed him: *I will fight this war until I find the end, whatever form it takes. I swear on the blood of my dearest...* On closer examination, that statement left no earmark for her. Maybe he thought of her as leverage or something from which to mine a cure if need be. *That's just the anger talking, girl. Calm your head and then think it over further.*

"You look upset," said Shadow. "I understand. Travels breed companionship. If only you had known Donovan as I had, you might have been more prepared."

"Is Earny still alive?"

"The highwayman? Yes, and in good health. He is being kept in another tower."

"Will you let him go? He's got nothing to do with any of this."

"He was your companion, no? Did you force him to this path?" asked Shadow. His voice bore that same ambiguity, convincingly genuine and gratingly condescending.

"He's just a sweet, stupid man who wanted to help. That shouldn't earn him a hanging." The thought of poor, dear Earnald stretching at the end of a rope made her stomach spin.

"If I can arrange for him to leave with Donovan," said Shadow in a tone that set her on careful watch, "will you grant me more of your trust?"

She considered it. Strange, unnatural attraction aside, she felt drawn to Shadow for practical reasons. To have someone partial to her, ready to give favors and let slip news could be useful. Would she ever trust Shadow the no-longer-Swordsman who barked at the Cleric's command and had betrayed the home Donovan loved? Never truly, no. But the Reaper wouldn't drag her down for faking it a little.

When she nodded Shadow returned to her side. Again that merciless heart pounding; his steps seemed to close around her throat and squeeze out her breath. "I know you've been alone for these past days and that it is not easy." He looked at the book open on the bed. "Are you enjoying it?"

She nodded.

"Good. That one, in particular, holds a special place for me."

"Because it's about a vain man who puts his petty needs above others?"

"Because it says two people can savor a lifetime's worth of pleasure and happiness in no time at all if you let your feelings burn bright and embrace them with abandon."

"I'm not sure that's what whoever wrote it was aiming for."

Shadow shrugged. "If an author's goal was the only thing to glean from his work, he might not be much worth reading."

"I guess not."

Shadow smiled, then broke into a laugh. "Good Jana Hunter, the only woman to coerce me into arguing literature. A thing to behold, you are." He headed for the door then. Jana had to stop herself from chasing him down and grabbing his hand and begging him to stay. *You're just raw for companionship. That's all.* Yes, and glue feathers to a horse and it'll fly.

Shadow might have read this all in her eyes. He went to leave.

"My dirk," she said.

"I think it might be for your own good if I hold onto it for now."

"Give it back," she demanded, feeling her face flush. "Now."

His eyes laughed at her. "I'll come to check on you again and to let you know what goes on with matters of your friend Earnald. It will not be as long between visits from now on. I swear it."

She did not speak, afraid that her voice would give away her regret.

He left with a smile that drew flutters inside her.

As she lay back on the bed, she recalled his touch, the sharp tingle of it, and lost herself to fantasy until day was replaced with a cold, inky night.

4

lumoethongomanetuharuti, called Ruti by OneEye and his *kai'nae*—
the other TwoLegs who traveled with him—beat his wings
against the fusty air of the great stone Cave, rising to the cross of
felled and carved trees supporting the walls above. As soon as his
nails found purchase, Ruti folded back his wings and stayed moveless, reaching out with every aspect of his *kai*, what his kind (when
there had been a kind to have) would have called *senses* in the TwoLeg
tongue. His scales flexing, his *kai* opening to the world, he allowed the
details of the environment to wash over him.

*The whistle of a breeze beneath the door at the end of the hall. The smell
of food, putrefying, digested, regurgitated, boiling in water elsewhere, charred in
a firepit outside, half-eaten in hand several levels below. The displacement of air
as things moved to, fro, clusters of thronging TwoLegs in metal scales marching in
time, strange PaleFaces scuttling in encrusted robes, the crawl of heavy containers
rolled on ranks of smooth, felled trees within the depths of the Cave. The shift of
energy, signal fires all, coalescing, disintegrating, something vivid, something faint,
energy transferred from one TwoLeg to another, lost between them, drained from
one, given to another, unleashed, immured, kept in balance by the flow of* Naar,
*the Ever Circle, present everywhere, made of everything, cognizant of nothing,
formative of all. Rats navigating the crawlspaces meant for heated pipes embedded
in the walls. Water squirming, crawling between tiles, pooling, drumming the floor
in rhythm. The echo of footsteps, patting, tapping, scratching, scuffing, shattering
the bones of a prisoner, displacing dirt in the courtyard, stamping to stay warm
on the Cave wall beneath the moonglow. Voices sputtering the guttural mouth-
sounds TwoLegs named language, signaling nothing, communicating instead by
tone and inflection, the content of the sounds themselves useless even to them.
Red glowing figures, immaterial, radiation of the very machinery of their flesh*

made perceivable, phantasms glimpsed through the thick, squared rock, congealing impressions of TwoLegs milling about, fading to the faint blue of a twilight sky, others bright crimson with exertion, their strength a blossoming cloud, their exhaustion a cool dying ember receding into blackness. The overflow of thoughts, not readable within the minds of the observed but echoing into the reflective stuff of the world, reverberating through the lo'ai, the barrier that coordinates the comings and goings of everything that lives, that dictates the creation and destruction of all, the chaos that is governed by whim yet is operated within an unyielding order initiated by the birth of the universe itself.

His *kai* brought the deluge of details to Ruti without end. He made no effort to dwell on any single aspect, but rather allowed the sensations to course through him. Tracking what was most useful from the river of information took little effort, for this Cave housed far fewer things than the forests and plains and mountains to which he was accustomed. For that, he felt *na'lai, thankfulness.*

He took flight again.

The hall below weaved and flitted under the restless torchlight. To a man, it would have seemed almost silent, but Ruti could hear the large TwoLeg, HarmBringer, the one called *Peligro,* as if he paced just below. Down the hall and the spiral descending path a ways he prowled, his lumbering gait clacking uneven rhythms to an audience of stone. His essence shifted and plied, bulbous like his build, the fragments of his thoughts ricocheting and glimpsed in pieces by Ruti's *kai,* incoherent, every word the color of rage. Was he the goal of this quest, or the enemy of it? Both or neither, maybe. Like the one that TwoLegs might call Ruti's father might have counseled (though for *Ji T'ai'lo* there was no such thing, at least not the way TwoLegs understood), this moment whispered for patience.

Ruti swooped down, the rush of old air interred in this space for time immemorial soaking his *kai* with its memory, the echo of hundreds of years of death still reverberating, colorless, among the stones. He flew through the bow-shaped cell chamber, his attention drawn briefly to the stain of colors, called a *painting,* said the *ai'alothae,* the Memories, above Peligro's wooden platform, hung within a large *lunette.* A drakken battled a man till the end of time in those colored gobs. That Ruti recognized those TwoLeg creations, let alone a drakken on sight was a gift of the Memories as well. The Memories materialized from time to time, approaching fireflies on a moonless field, a part of his maturation. In time he would know all that his forefathers did—if he was meant to last that long. For now, they came piecemeal, a word here, an experience there, leaving him to interpret and apply them, another instinct to guide him during his journey.

He peered with his stark blue-ringed eyes into the darkness separating the cells from the stairs, distinguishing form and texture where a TwoLeg would see only black. For an instant he was distracted by the presence of the thing in the cell farthest from his *kai'nae*, OneEye; the thing, whatever it was, shifted, and Ruti caught sight of deep yellow scleras and the silver, lifeless irises they encompassed. Then nothing but the colored radiation of the thing's crouched form, the noise of its wordless thoughts, the movement of energy inwards from its surroundings, as though it was draining the space around it, returning nothing.

He spread his wings and glided silently to the cold stone floor, his small feet disturbing twin puffs of dust. *The scent of charred TwoLeg food. The sweep of sand blasting against the outside of the Cave on the desert wind. The sudden expansion of energy exploding outward in a space not far from here, signaling the death of something, a TwoLeg probably, one whose color was now fading, the heat of their body's motion cooling, soon to vanish.* A piece of a thought expelled into the ether by that dying soul reached Ruti's consciousness, but he let it wash through him without consideration.

Holding his breath, Ruti inched along the hall until he reached the swirl of descending stone platforms—*stairs*. He could no longer hear Peligro now, could not locate him with his *kai*; the man must either be very still or gone. Stillness was not enough to mask creatures from his awareness most times, though *kai* did not tell all.

He landed next on Peligro's raised wooden platform where the TwoLeg often sat in the evening.

Debris, remnants of food, dried dollops of once-edible viscous fluids, splatters of liquid laced with alcohol, a meatless bone, a small stack of pages bound in the cured and tanned skin of an animal. Fading warmth on the wooden surface, the shape of a TwoLeg's hand. Peligro. The barest hint of intent, a ghost of a thought, barely that, an inclination to take up the feather nearby and dab it into the black substance encased in glass and streak it across the paper bound by that once-animal, making the contents of the mind tangible. The wordless desire to do so echoed into the lo'ai, *weak to begin with, almost faded now.*

Ruti sensed Peligro had never made good on those thoughts.

He sniffed the dry bone and recoiled.

An image grew in his mind, the picture of a thin object, one of many, dangling from a circle of metal. The clanging of those objects echoed in the vault of his *kai*, followed by the *click* of the barrier opening, the one holding OneEye, *Earny*, captive as Peligro did violence to him, unwarranted. A roaring wave of red and orange, OneEye's pain, was still tangible to Ruti in the room. He ignored it; the echo of the circular ring that opened the barrier was hidden here as well, not a sound but an imprint left on the fabric of the world. It was somewhere just below him. Or at least it *had* been. *Kai* did not always account for time.

He eased to the topmost sliding wooden box within the platform, taking the old metal bar bolted to its outside between his teeth. At first, it would not budge. On the fourth tug, it opened a short way. He perched on the edge and peered inside. Crumpled paper, rawhide threaded through old hard material, small squares—*tesserae* said the Memories, metal things rusted and forgotten, taken by force from their owners. Ruti reversed direction and eased the box shut. When each box had been checked and no circular ring found, he set off down the stairs.

His *kai* warned him of TwoLegs in their metal scales, the expenditure of their bodies through movement an arc of visible waves, not seen but received and interpreted by Ruti's body without conscious direction. They were not at the foot of the stairs where he expected them, but he knew they had just passed here moments ago. OneEye's cell lay on the second level, just above where he stood now. Ruti sensed three floors in total above him, but his feelings told him Peligro did not venture that way often. The effort the large TwoLeg expended to ascend just one floor, to OneEye's level, left barely enough left to do violence. He must lay somewhere up ahead.

The hall at the end of the stairs was long and without swinging barriers. Ruti had the sense of navigating the veins of a massive creature that was ready to yawn and stretch and kill them all at any moment, and so he avoided touching the piled stones that comprised the area lest he awaken it. His *kai* opened further as he moved, combing for useful details from among the crash of perceptions that enclosed him. *Sickening TwoLeg food scent stronger now, its weightless skeins invisible to the eyes but oppressive to his* kai, *gathering in a cloud in the stagnant air above him. The thunder of an insect's antennae scraping the stone, smelling, feeling, searching for sustenance. The stab and riposte of emotions between the TwoLegs ahead, the movement of pressure not worldly but rather of emotion, the dynamics of interactions and the energies borne of them perceivable to Ruti as sunlight was to others.* He flew on.

As he approached the swinging barrier, a *door*, along this stretch, he could hear more clearly the grumbles and guffaws of at-ease Two-Legs, their scales cast aside, their metal instruments of violence resting against wooden platforms and piled stones nearby. He landed beside the door, which he saw now was made from oak, and hunkered to gaze into the firelight beneath. He spied the heavy waffle weave of fabric enclosing the feet of TwoLegs staggering this way and that, sometimes alone and sometimes in clusters like a multi-legged fluid-gulping monstrosity. Ruti's ears were sharp enough to make any TwoLeg seem deaf, even the one from OneEye's *kai'nae*, the one who had nearly died, called Swordsman or Donovan, and he picked the multitude of voices within the smaller cave apart and sorted them. No Peligro.

"Keep clear of me, dun-nubs, for the love in it!"

"Call me that again and we'll see who's called nubs from now on."

"You fellas crank it about like jam rag whores, pray ya gone."

"What's a jam rag?"

Ruti filtered away their jabbering, searching for the circular ring and the freedom-giving objects it kept. *The run of sweat down a Two-Leg's neck, soaking his shirt, the fabric expanding. The movement of metal against the wooden platforms where they sat, holders of fluid fitted with rings meant for hands with five fingers to grasp, alcohol-laced fluid foaming, spilling, swallowed in sustained imbibements. Mucus in their skulls, snorted, cleared, ejected through the mouth. Heartbeats thrumming, each contraction mingling energy and heat into the similar expulsions of the other TwoLegs. Memories in this room of violence, laughter, conspiracy.* No sense of the metal ring.

Holding his breath, Ruti backed away.

He stole further into the great Cave, mapping its intricate cross-section in his mind, at times keeping to the stone creatures carved and fastened high above, their details worn bare by the passing ages, or to the shadows of half-circular spaces behind similar stone fashionings of TwoLeg figures, their granite eyes keeping watch over barren halls. One time he thought he heard the large TwoLeg's distinctive grunts and followed the trail, reaching out with his *kai*, but when he found a cluster of other TwoLegs wearing only half their scales and lounging in the hall, Peligro was not among them.

When at last he came across a conversation that rose above his ever-vigilant filter, Ruti held his breath and chanced touching down near the base of the door. This one was ajar, and he perceived the ambiguous, colored glows and the flow of intent and feelings and the numberless conjunctions of thought and action and time within the room well before he spied the five men there holding council. A more detailed wooden platform than elsewhere in the Cave split the space, furnished with containers of fluid and slaughtered and roasted animals and freshly harvested fruits. The TwoLegs picked at them as they spoke.

"The pass is too narrow for that. We've need of supply lines north of the Barren as well, if we're to go that far," said a TwoLeg with a thin stripe of a beard sketched along his jutting jawline.

"Agreed. But that's for next spring or later, mind it," answered an older TwoLeg swathed in brown wool, a crescent-moon-shaped medallion dangling from his neck and blinking in the hearthglow.

"Whether the girl has spoken of the Order is what I want to know," said a TwoLeg Ruti could not see, though the nature of what his *kai* received from that one made him recoil.

"Why would she know anything about that?" asked another unseen TwoLeg.

"Because," said BrownWool, "men's tongues loosen in the company of desirable women, and she walked many hefts with this man Donovan that Master is so fond of."

"She knows nothing," said a third unseen voice. This one Ruti knew was called *Shadow*.

"You sound sure of yourself," said ThinBeard.

"Didn't you know? That's him bottled and corked, that man right there."

"Don't forget Ruun, my boy Shadow," said BrownWool.

Ruti saw Shadow step forward, a thin, imposing silhouette against the fire. "Do not forget who you speak to, Fren of Coaltown that was. Ever," he said, the veins on the backs of his hands rippling as he gripped the back of an empty seat. Around him, the invisible caustics of his energy, made from emotion or intent or action or a combination of them all, slow to move and ever-shifting in most TwoLegs, solidified and expanded in a thrust of promised violence that made Ruti flinch.

The other TwoLegs Ruti could see recoiled from Shadow's tone and said no more.

"What will Master do with this Swordsman?"

"Set him loose, I suspect," answered Shadow.

"Is that wise?"

"Would you argue with Master over it?"

"Not I. But you might succeed with it."

"Where would he go?" asked BrownWool. "You and he are the last of the Order. Why do we speak of them like they are a threat?"

"Because," said Shadow, stepping suddenly towards the door, eyes narrowed and lips pursed, "Master would tell you it's best to consider everyone a threat until they're dust beneath your heels."

Ruti shrank away as Shadow's animal-skin-enclosed feet approached, and he inched aside as the thin TwoLeg peered into the hall. The Root Dragon could see the bottom of the TwoLeg's sharp chin, the point of his nose, the tips of his fingers wrapped around the door. All it would take was a wayward glance and the Root Dragon would be found out. Some creatures, TwoLegs included, betrayed their actions before they committed them, signaling their plans in ways those with strong *kai* might foresee and so avoid them. This TwoLeg did not; it was as though he was a void from which no energy or sign could escape.

After a final look, Shadow stepped back the way he had come without glancing down and closed the door. "Remember that always, friends, and we'll find life easier, don't you agree?"

Ruti did agree, and he had learned what he needed to: Swordsman Donovan and AngryMouth Jana were alive.

Pleased with his progress, he inched back from the door, his focus turned to Peligro and his circular ring of freedom, his *kai* diminished in a rare moment of distraction.

For as long as he could remember, Ruti had enjoyed the benefits of the Memories and the expanded consciousness of his *kai*, as well as hardwon knowledge gained from a thousand years in the wilds. He had faced wolves and bears and worse during that endless stretch and always escaped with his life, at times by fighting (in his own way), other times by stealth. But old as men might think him, he was still a child, prone to miscalculation, and his attention lay focused on Shadow's withdrawing feet and his next course of action when something huge and feral crept forward from the darkness, spittle draped in webs from its black teeth, and lunged at the little dragon with a hungry growl.

5

Donovan knelt in his room with Orin at his feet and did something he had not done since he was a boy: he prayed. He reached with his mind into the world, to the Keeper, tried to feel Him, to divorce himself from his body and the very air around him and touch the ethereal. How did one contact the unseen? He did not know, but it felt akin to the little magic he had ever invoked and so attempted it with brittle faith.

What do I do? Damn me all the way to the Black, what do I do?

If the Keeper had any answers, he kept them to himself.

His scar tightened its grip on his torso, his own personal boa snake to crush the breath out of him at its whim. It felt scaly and hot there within his flesh, as if excavating his muscles and guts with small, spiny tendrils. The better to control him with no doubt, a puppeteer threading the joints of its marionette. The next time the Cold invaded his mind would be the last, or perhaps the time after that; no matter what trials he endured, he was near the end with no hope of deliverance. What sounded preferable? Diving into the fire or throwing himself onto the spikes? Rosaline would have known. Perhaps it was her whispering from the Black now to stay true and hold to his crumbling ideals, the same ideals which had burned Kolendhar to the ground, that had changed her. The bier built of those ideals supported his pride still. Was it worth the pain?

You should because you can.

What man in this world set his ideals above his own survival? Would Tomson? Would anyone? Even his fellow Swordsmen Goesef and Vine had left their convictions to the wayside, hiding in Rend, building an army for their own good and protection. And wasn't that the way of the world? Even tales of what existed before the Shift, when society thrived and commerce crossed the lines of nations and the sea itself, told of a place where every man's selfishness fed a greater good. Was there never a higher justice in those days to be summoned and recited while doing murder in the name of survival? Donovan had an idea his tale was not so unique as he might think.

He nearly flicked his sword to his hand with his boot as Shadow had once taught him, but instead he bent over and picked it up. It was good to feel his family blade again, comforting. He pressed it to his chest and tried to envision murdering innocents, women, and children, rather than succumb to death or madness himself.

The fire or the spikes.

The heart of the Dweller King…

Sickened, Donovan envisioned falling on his sword right here, watching the lifeblood drain from his stomach, finding the Black in this ancient tomb built from the bowels of a mountain. Would that be any more favorable? What if the Cleric's magic kept him alive even while his body was dead? What would he be then, with nothing to withstand the Cold and its tireless onslaught? It might end the same either way, with the spikes *and* the fire.

He lay on the floor, staring at the ceiling of his bedchamber with Orin across his chest. He recalled the villages he had visited while the Order still lived, the villagers whose strife he had come to assuage, the townsfolk he had liberated from bandits or disease or even from themselves. He thought of rescued daughters and avenged deaths, settled quarrels, and returned property. And what had it gained him? Hateful glares, yes plenty of those, wanting looks and covetous eyes. He thought of Raef, Earny's old master, on the road to Pleasantry. *We'll let you pass with no trouble for that bright shiny piece you've got strapped to you there.* And that is what he had become. A lifetime of training, generations of amassed wisdom and lore and history, and the Order was reduced to men carrying bright shiny swords that the very people they protected sought and would kill to possess. Maybe all people were that, the children future highwaymen and whores, the women assassins who would bed you and slit your throat in your sleep—gotta get that sword, that shiny sword—the shy or withdrawn the ones who would poison your drink and lift your satchel while you wheezed at the Reaper's feet.

But not Mary. Or Jana, or Tomson, Earny, not even poor Shag or that old fella, the one Jana called Grampy.

Exceptions, all of them. What did that prove?

His thoughts whirling tirelessly, Donovan waited for answers he knew did not exist.

Then he thought he heard a growl and a loud crash somewhere deep in the fortress.

6

Ruti's *kai*, a font of awareness that would have rendered a Two-Leg numb with its unbridled volume, was as unpredictable as the comings and goings of the wind. At times it gave the Root Dragon a false sense of prescience, the sensation that he was joined with *Naar* itself, providing firsthand as though through his very veins knowledge of his environment and his enemies, facilitating survival. Other times his *kai* was strangely silent, blinding him to dangers and leaving only his Memories and his senses common to other beasts to keep him safe.

Now he lay fixated on the men before him, the wash of their expended energy and intent visible to whatever receptors in his body facilitated *kai*, spectral reds and blues and shades of purple intermingling, muddying individual forms while shaping a clearer combined whole. He focused on the shape of Peligro, visible through the stacks of stone as a splotch of erratic wavelike light for a fleeting moment, joined by the sudden appearance of his metallic ring, which sounded now in the stone halls like a bell. And, uncharacteristically for him, the Root Dragon also focused on OneEye, Earny, the Root Dragon's first *kai'nae* for as long as he could remember. He sensed that his new TwoLeg companion would be pleased with the news of his own *kai'nae*, his *companions*. Very pleased.

Then the sensations burned into him.

A violent storm surge of hunger, all-encompassing, burning into the air like torchlight. The exhalation of a breath, held rumbling in a prolonged effort of stealth and then unleashed. The stabbing intensity of energy drawn from the stillness of the room around them, thrust forth then, a give and take essential to every moment and every actor within those moments across all of creation. The

339

sensation of displaced air, not seen or felt but witnessed all the same, read by Ruti's kai, vivid as dawn. The groan of joints, a rumbling landslide resounding in a canyon. Something cavernous levering open revealing a spiculum forest, wet with hunger. Thick, viscous fluid splashing on the dusty floor, every drop the sound of a storm. The memory of a hundred animals hunted, slain, eaten, the taste of their flesh rebounding from the lo'ai *as though Ruti himself had consumed them and not the creature that stalked him.* And then there was something lower than those feelings, lower than *kai,* a voice that was not born of memory or the Memories, that was not instinct or reflex. Ruti knew not what to call it, but it appeared at times by its own whim, an apparition from his depths, its purpose to pluck a singular reaction from the stream of his *kai* when the space of even one more breath would mean his ruin. It was that voice, low down within the Root Dragon, that warned him to leap now before his conscious mind could comprehend what it was receiving.

Instantly Ruti was in the air, first with a leap six times his body length, then with the furious beating of his wings as he rose higher and watched a coalblack animal crash headlong into the door, slamming it closed. Dazed, a guttural mew spilled from BlackDeath's chest as it shook its head clear. The creature was huge, taller than a TwoLeg if it stood on its hinds, sable fur matte and thick as horsebrush. It writhed on the floor, its expenditures perceivable to Ruti's *kai* not in the ordered and restrained way of most TwoLegs, but boundless and chaotic. The ripple of the creature's hunger spasmed and expanded and contracted, warping any intermingling sensations from the surrounding area. The hall flashed with the bright colored shockwave of effort from the creature's failed attack, fading as it regrouped to a cool center, then warming again as it rebuilt to a second attempt.

Already Ruti was away, propelling himself forward with hard, long flaps. His *kai* whispered to him, interpreting for him. *The pads of BlackDeath's feet scraping against stone as it gave chase, their sound the roar of a dragging boulder grinding along a mountaintop. The creature's intent collapsing inward and then thrusting outward, cone-shaped yet immaterial, disrupting the push-pull of everything in its vicinity, whipping one way and then the other in search of its quarry. The gasps and mutterings of TwoLegs in this room and that, reacting to the movement and sound without their chambers. A growing sense of a void, enormous and with its own invisible arms to grasp and pull, giving chase, a pit drawing its desired prey closer. All around a notion of threads, not earthly but something celestial, each of them a potential future, his future, all leading to one point as though by a winding spindle in the center of that void.*

Ruti drew as much strength as he could muster and flew as hard as he could to escape.

Twice BlackDeath gained enough ground to spring and snap, and each time Ruti yanked his tail a hair's breadth away as those black spikes clacked shut in a burst of thick fluid just behind him.

Guided by instinct and that lower, unnamable voice, the Root Dragon banked into an intersecting hall, and now he could hear the shouts of the TwoLegs left behind whose meeting had been interrupted by BlackDeath's barrage, as well as more TwoLegs calling out ahead. Through the old piled stone halls he could detect their outlines, pulsing with an influx of energy and awareness, rising and moving with aggressive intent. The threads he had witnessed just before split suddenly, some still leading behind to the void, others ahead to where reflections of the TwoLegs' plans also promised his death—or worse, *ai'tau*, what the Memories called *imprisonment*. Ruti had no innate fear of finding the Black, not like OneEye and his *kai'nae*, but there were things to do still: his mission first; second and more distant, the burning cavity within his breast and what it housed. With those tasks in mind, he pushed his wings against the old Cave air, allowing a thousand years of Memories and their inborn instincts to waft from the unlit past and guide him.

BlackDeath took the corner close enough for Ruti to feel the disbanding breeze of its oversized paws. Thrumming within his *kai*, the creature's intensity palpitated, made substantial by the Root Dragon's understanding, not built of anger but rather a loosed primal motive that drove it forward without need for reason. Ruti's Memories told him those pads and fur and the long spikes they sheathed were better suited for miry tracts or the pitted mountains its species hailed from, and moments later those paws lost traction from the momentum of its turn against the smooth stone floor. BlackDeath skidded to the far side of the hall, crashing into the wall and displacing a large, heavy woven fabric hung there by TwoLegs as decorum, an intricate handmade thing of multicolored threads. It folded over BlackDeath's head, turning its world dark, and the large beast scrambled to free itself.

Ruti pressed the advantage, banking hard through an adjacent archway and over a flight of wide stairs. The hall widened into a musty chamber, the roughhewn stone overlaid with grander paintings than the one of the drakken. A great battle waged within those colored strokes; vicious longfaced hooved creatures, encased in metal scales much like the TwoLegs that rode them, snorted in a frozen rear while enemy TwoLegs readied long pointed weapons for impaling thrusts. Ruti noted the details in an instant and then continued.

The chamber itself was large, perhaps a hundred TwoLeg paces across, and every ten paces a boulder chipped away into the shape of a TwoLeg's face and shoulders stood atop a thin platform. Ahead, from the far hall, shouts of alarmed TwoLegs and thumping footsteps echoed, their every move telegraphed to Ruti's *kai*, their colors converging, their intents honing on where the Root Dragon hovered. Behind, BlackDeath had escaped and was gaining ground.

Cornered, Ruti ducked away, the soft chant of his forefathers light in his mind, and hid as best he could.

* * * *

Peligro's day was growing worse by the minute.

With the first birdcalls of the early morning had come a reprimand, replete with the humiliation of prying onlookers bearing witness to the division officer denigrating Peligro like a toddler. An extra portion of stuffed eggs soothed him afterwards, but Hedge, the cook in this wing, was as bad with a pot as he was with a bow, and his sludge tortured Peligro with the lower abdomen pains of the tumdrums for the rest of the morning, followed by more unpleasantness in the late afternoon. Hours later, for no worthy reason by Peligro's estimation, he had suffered another scolding at the hands of the sadistic son of a whore who called himself Shadow, again to the bemusement of idle guards whispering to each other in the shadows and laughing. Pelgiro wondered what sort of grown man called himself *Shadow*. It reminded him of the sort of bullycrag a child might declare while beating his Studymates with a branch in the courtyard. If ever that pretty one lost the Master's favor, Peligro would be the first to lay a whip to his scrawny back.

Now, as the day drew from a bleak morning into a cold evening long with shadows from a beclouded sun, things had grown somehow worse: Algenor was into some sort of mess, judging by the noise. As soon as the shouting had begun, Peligro had known his pet, if you could call the forsaken animal he had rescued from the Barrens as a cub a pet, was behind the commotion. Training a borecat was more something one boasted about than achieved, laudable if true and the stuff of reverent whispers when proven, yet despite his best efforts to seed them, rumors of his success had done little for his standing in the war machine of Pal Myrrah. As of late, the creature had proven itself more trouble than he was worth, driven mad no doubt by the confinement of this damnable fortress. Peligro knew one day the fucking thing was going to be the end of him, and not just in a manner of speaking; Shadow would certainly remove his least favorite guard's head from his shoulders for any reason at this point. Even if one of the north wing guards, drunks, and inbreds all of them, went out of their way to attack the borecat in a stupor and destroyed half the stronghold in the process, guess who would pay for the aftermath? Peligro, last totem on the pole of fuckall.

He fast-walked behind other men now towards the sound, which at first they expected to be a disturbance by the recently rearmed Swordsman until a familiar roar and the drum of a three hundred and fifty pound animal barreling after something resounded through the halls. Whatever that something was, it had better be of unfathomable value to all involved, else that goosenecked motherhumper of a cat would be hutched up and reft of food and daylight for a week.

They maneuvered the halls towards the west war room, the one closest to Peligro's tower, called the Eagle's Breach; the name sounded like a grand to-do, but in truth, it was little more than an empty cone of brick given him to pace while his two prisoners died of boredom. Certainly, it was nowhere near the precious assignment promised when Shadow had drifted through the town of Ordell months ago recruiting ex-soldiers weary of barroom fights and eager for a cause or even violence, but it was not poor enough to warrant desertion either. Would good Peligro the Whipping Boy ever risk fleeing a man such as the Master anyway? The very thought of the Cleric's attention on him for *any* reason, let alone with retribution on the mind, made Peligro's blood turn to cold jelly.

When he reached the west chamber he was huffing. Ahead, the six men he trailed drew their broadswords, all of them Northern steel and ringing that peculiar note they seemed tuned to produce, and again came a vexed growl from Algenor who stood on his hinds with his front paws propped on the bust of one ancient king or another.

"Algenor!" Peligro said between wheezes. "Down!"

Algenor looked at him—he swore sometimes that borecat's eyes were human—ears pinned back, long whiskers drawn into what looked like a frown, green tongue flapping anxiously.

"Down I said, fer the love of yer mother!"

Algenor, chagrined, lowered himself with a mew, toppling the bust and its pedestal. It shattered with a crisp thunder-crack, sending king one-or-another's nose tumbling to Pelgiro's boot.

Shadow and his officers arrived in time to see stone shatter and the pieces settle, and the tall, thin Cleric's Second looked from the borecat, who lay now in the center of the chamber with folded paws, to its owner. "Is there a problem?" he asked.

Peligro stared at his toes and shook his head, his cheeks jiggling for an instant afterward. "No, your lordship."

"If that animal disturbs me again, I'll run it through."

"Yes, your lordship."

As he and the others headed away, Shadow added, "Clean up the mess."

"Yes, your lordship."

When everyone was gone but the borecat, Peligro looked the creature in the eye. "You motherless…" He started forward with one stout hand cocked and Algenor hunkered lower, supplicant eyes rolled upward. Two things stayed Peligro's strike: first that this fool animal was the only other living thing he loved; second that it might maul him should he push too far beyond his favor. Instead, he stroked that thick mane and then knelt and plucked up the shattered bust piece by piece. When he was finished, he gave the borecat a sidelong glare. "Do that again and someone's gonna have yer head."

And, with that, he left, back to his tower, his accursed tower.

* * * *

Ruti's consciousness lay still within the swarm of motion around him, invisible to the others in the room but all-encompassing to himself. *Converging thoughtlines weaving into a fabric threaded for this moment alone, plied from the very undercurrent of their existence. The uncoiling of muscles bound for violence, releasing their tension, the moving sinew groaning like twisting leather. Steel DeathBringers lowered, the TwoLegs' stern faces unfurrowing in time. The churn of* ra'no'thet, *the* battle blood, *leaving their bodies in a rush, replaced by an overabundance of nonchalance. A unifying disdain for the one called Peligro, HarmBringer.*

The exchange between the TwoLeg called Shadow and Peligro afterward was clear even though Ruti did not comprehend all of their sounds. The inflection of their tones, the posture of their strange upright bodies, the dance of their eyes; those details and more told Ruti the story where their unknown words did not. Then the fabric was unraveled, undone as quickly it had been formed, diverging clusters of thought and motion trailing the TwoLegs in their metal scales like ghosts as they marched away. BlackDeath's feral and disordered energies, a mix of honed instinct and aimless stimulation, stalked off in one direction, while large TwoLeg Peligro went the other.

Ruti listened for a while, tracking both by ear as well as by *kai*. When the creature was gone and Peligro HarmBringer not yet to the tower, he crept along the wall from his hiding spot on the painting— in plain sight beside a spatter of colors meant to portray a flying drakken. No doubt the drakken pictured was enormous judging by the painted figures below it, but by perspective, it matched Ruti perfectly. Ruti flexed his scales, feeling his body reattune to its surroundings, something he had learned was necessary to ensure his instincts and *kai* did not mislead him. There was Peligro's faint, rounded aura, piercing through the stone corner separating them, the ring of metal and the long thin treasures it bore jangling at his belt with every step. He focused his attention on the large TwoLeg as he took off and flew hurriedly after him.

Other sensations broke through the wall of his attention as he navigated the hall. *Men returning to their imbibements and their slain and roasted animals, excited by the prospect of action moments ago, diffused now and eager again to do nothing. A flash of TwoLeg teeth, their jaws rocking open and loud, pained sounds ejected from their throats, their colors communicating mirth despite the noises they made. The scrape of a stone somewhere against a steel weapon, indistinct but threatening, violence promised with its every movement, accompanied by wits dulled by alcohol.*

Ruti paid them no mind.

He glided the unmoving air into the hall, wary of every door he passed, expecting each to open despite his *kai* promising they would not. Even without reading the interplay of pressure and desire and action that comprised the TwoLegs' essences within those doors, Ruti could hear them moving back and forth, drinking, writing, working.

A loud crash startled him, as did the bursting cloud of color and feeling that his *kai* associated with whatever caused the sound. Without thought, he veered to another nearby hanging fabric, this one woven to form a crest of some sort. He glommed onto it, extending his claws, and listened. The silhouettes of the men within the next room flickered, all shadows and light, their movements exposing his *kai* to distorting shimmers that were felt but unseen. The shapes stumbled to upright a fallen table along with the metal objects that had gone tumbling from it, and then returned to their revelry.

When he felt all was clear, Ruti opened his wings to lift off and, as he did, the creature, BlackDeath, sprung its second attack, shredding at the fabric the Root Dragon clung to like paper, moonyellow eyes unblinking and full of ravenous intensity. Ruti squealed, the Memories screaming to him from the dark of the ages, his *kai* disoriented and useless, and fell beneath the ruined fabric with BlackDeath sprawled atop it. Thrashing, pushing ahead with all of his strength, he could not move. The creature growled and snapped above him, its long teeth slimy with hunger, separated from him only by a fold of fabric. It would have him in moments.

Panicked, Ruti summoned the *nai'voe*, the power that allowed him to take from the essence of others and generate his sustenance, the same force he had used on the FireTail in the forest while OneEye and his *kai'nae* looked on. But the voice low down told him it would not work, that there were no angles from which to attack, that the creature's thick fur would allow no direct connection with its skin. The threads around him, sparkling supernal things to his *kai*, evaporated, leaving a single path forward. That path, his impending death, while not the most desirable thread of fate, did not faze him; finding the Black was a natural stone within the cave of life. But by failing now Ruti had let OneEye, his *kai'nae* Earny, down, and that thought pained him. He hoped OneEye possessed *kai* enough to know that he had tried. He had most certainly tried.

Perhaps too intent on the designs of the fabric where it had spotted the Root Dragon, BlackDeath lunged again, missing its mark, and now Ruti was suddenly free to slug ahead towards the white funnel of light on the far end of the fold that enclosed him. His *kai* refocusing, the threadlines of his fate revealing new possibilities, Ruti surged ahead. The hunger and ferocity of the creature beat down on him in waves like hot breath, yet the sensation was indicative of the creature's inner turmoil and represented nothing physical. Ruti ignored it, and as he emerged from the tube of fabric he began to take off once more.

Realization lurching over him, onto him, a sudden stormfront of attention manipulating the perceived weight of the room as it projected its full strength onto his back. The snap of a paw larger than a TwoLeg's hand crushing downwards. The smack of bestial eyes blinking, as loud as snapping twigs to Ruti's kai, burning into him as its black form closed in.

The creature had him at last.

Then the creature's paw crushed down onto the fallen fabric before Ruti was able to free himself, pinching his tail as he struggled to lift off. The Root Dragon pitched forward, jaw thumping the floor, and then beat his small wings, fighting to heave free. BlackDeath raised its muzzle, a tongue the color of algae swiping at its jowls, dripping thick hunger fluid everywhere. With savage light behind its eyes, it lunged, claws droning through the air. To make its attack, the creature was forced to adjust its mass again, and this loosened the fabric pinning Ruti enough for him to pull free. He fluttered into the air and made one last effort to escape.

Had Ruti's *kai* been prescient in truth and not just in semblance, had the creature wound farther back, had the Root Dragon been a century younger and smaller, he might have cleared the approaching strike. But, as it was, BlackDeath's long first claw reached just far enough, etching a jagged line into Ruti's side. The Root Dragon yelped, pain flaming through his torso. His flight adjourned prematurely, he corkscrewed in midair and fumbled to the floor in a heap.

The color of the room draining, energy and focus oscillating in the nether, stolen from the environment and ravaged by the tornado of the creature's hunger. The raising of the creature's hind legs, tail undulating, its claws scratching into the stone floor, each tile there a whetstone. The push off of the creature's feet, lunging forward, overwhelming kai *with a maelstrom of hues and raw energy. Whispers from the Black, the stories of the line of* Alumoethongomanetuharuti *dissipating into the wind of this moment, preparing to be lost forever.*

The creature drew back and pounced one last time.

But somehow Ruti sprung upwards with some hidden reserve of strength then, and the creature's teeth gnashed the floor where he had laid moments before, hewing loose the tip of its left canine. Howling in agony, blinded by it, its rage transforming all else in Ruti's *kai* to the unrecognizable refractions of a windswept lake surface, BlackDeath galloped forward.

A trickle of black blood inched from the wound on Ruti's belly; it dripped from his toes as he flew with abandon. No longer could he distinguish anything with his *kai*; there were only his primary senses and his instincts left to guide him. Close behind he heard the *pat-pat, pat-pat* of BlackDeath's strides, heard those hunger-drenched growls growing louder. When the big animal leapt at last, Ruti knew it was close enough for a kill, that it had waited an extra moment to be sure.

He added seconds to his life then by dropping into a nosedive. The creature barreled ahead and the Root Dragon blurred past and plunged his claws into BlackDeath's soft underskin, summoning the *nai'voe*.

But it would not come. He did not have the strength.

.Then came a frantic TwoLeg's voice from down the hall: "Algenor! Algenor stop it! I said stop!"

BlackDeath rolled and crushed its body downward and Ruti sprung free, landing between those brutish paws, and it was there, he was certain, that this contest would end. He was too weak, the agony of his wound too debilitating, the creature too quickened by rage. He stole a brief look at the victory in his hunter's eyes, a look that like him bore generations of instinct bred into the material of its being, called forth unconsciously in untamed surges.

Then its jaws snapped down, encircling Ruti's head.

They never had the chance to close.

With a grotesque *crunch*, the creature's elated gaze widened and then relaxed into a death stare.

Above, the one called Shadow withdrew his sword from the animal's skull.

"Algenor! No!" screamed Peligro. "No!"

Shadow whirled and shook clean his sword, spattering the fat HarmBringer with flecks of blood. Peligro recoiled, wiping at his face, staring at the blood he found on his fingers after, which Ruti knew through *kai* was still warm with the creature's fierce vitality but was cooling rapidly into the air, appearing to the Root Dragon as visible gaseous streaks, as if agnate to a soul fast departing.

"Tidy this, too," said Shadow. There was no inflection in his voice for Ruti to comprehend. Then he vanished through a nearby door and eased it closed behind him.

A long moment of shock passed before Peligro the HarmBringer willed himself to move. His agony stretched beyond the surrounding halls, out onto the windswept walls of the Cave, and maybe even into the sandy plains, too. When the shock had passed, he knelt beside BlackDeath and sobbed, his arms girding the broad spill of his gut. When he could cry no more, he trudged whimpering back towards the innards of the Cave and did not look back.

As his sighs grew distant and his hunched shoulders turned a corner, Ruti, half-suffocated, crawled from beneath Algenor's limp mouth and savored a deep and precious breath.

7

When Donovan reached for the cold iron release to his chamber doors, he found it unlocked. He gathered himself as best he could, then exited into the icy gloom of the corridor with his eyes downturned like a dutiful child approaching his father for an impending punishment. His mind raced in all directions, each firmly cinched and stretched until the pieces came apart end by bloody, sinewy end. Each time he returned to the same decision; it was time to commit fully to it now to see it through.

The worst of today would be the girl Jana. He could not bring her with him. Too cavalier, that one, too full of youthful passion. Donovan frowned. *Too much like yourself. Yourself a long time ago.* When he had marched away across the dust-washed Din with the smell of death on his back and his woman's blood on his hands, he had thought the gates of his humanity locked and rusted shut forever. But somehow Jana had reached through the bars and touched it; he might have otherwise forgotten it existed at all, and maybe he should have—it would make this next leg of his journey far easier.

The guards outside did not react to his appearance, their plumed helms giving them the look of stoic birds as they contemplated the wall before them. Donovan guessed he had been awake for…how long? Days surely, hard to say how many, and already he had had his fill of the stink of this place, the close and heavy quality of the air and the hollow drone of its vast enclosed halls. He longed to be free of it.

The guard with the deep baritone voice stood aside, regarding him with keen eyes possessed of the sort of awareness that caught much but troubled over little. Donovan saw a flicker of wariness in them as they—by accident it seemed—regarded Orin.

"I'd like to see Gaelin," the Swordsman said to him.

The guard straightened. The man's body looked as tense as bowstring even if his eyes seemed only half-awake. "Lord Shadow is in congress at the moment."

Donovan wondered what sort of congress the man implied. "So get him out of congress. I'm not full on time, soldier," he said. He expected the guard to argue, but instead, with down-turned eyes, the guard nodded and gestured to his fellow and then trotted away, his ring mail clanging to an uneven rhythm like a man-sized castanet.

Donovan watched him go and thought it was as though he regarded a herald couriering his soul, wrapped neatly in parchment, to the gathering dark where devils would consume it with delight.

8

After hunting down his breath and licking clean his wound, Ruti slithered from beneath the newly dead creature and alighted, perching again atop one of the monstrous stone carvings above the hall, awaiting HarmBringer's return. His *kai* eased back into his awareness, a gathering swarm of impulses. Peligro's turmoil, before so large it had enveloped much of the Cave, now had retreated to a small, unimportant throbbing that was nearly burned out. Ruti knew this was not due to his lack of care; the TwoLeg was nearly out of fuel for his internal fire, and the vacuum left there would need to be filled soon. He would most likely do so by harming OneEye.

The HarmBringer came and went, first accompanied by a stubby TwoLeg clad in breach cloth undergarments and a metal scale strapped across his chest. The new TwoLeg's enthusiasm waned before he appeared around the corner, the thinness of his loyalty to Peligro a diminishing green aurora soon replaced by a deep blood-colored disdain. They pushed a large open box that rolled on circular tree segments into the hall, and then grunted and moaned and hefted BlackDeath's corpse onto it. As they rolled it away, the creature's yellow eyes stared back at Ruti, unseeing but still full of hungry longing even in death. Ruti regarded the lifeless beast and the lack of anything extrasensory at all around its limp form; no energy or influx of unseen forces showed in the aftermath of its slaying, no disbanding field appeared to his *kai*. He supposed that meant that nothing lay on the other side of death, that all were destined to become as stones once their lifeforce was spent.

When Peligro returned, the space around his large body had become a black void into which all latent emotion in the places he traversed vanished. When he turned the corner in time with *kai's* impression of his actions, his eyes were puffy, his lips quivering and laced with the hunger fluid, though Ruti suspected the TwoLeg was not searching for food. He passed beneath Ruti and the Root Dragon followed at a distance, each wingbeat driving hot coils of agony through his body.

Minutes later Ruti had retraced his route back to the where Earny was imprisoned, and he crouched now beneath Peligro's wooden platform, between his boots, peering up at the sharp inward knock of the TwoLeg's knees and the metal ring dangling just beyond, strung over his stomach. HarmBringer's dark center had grown as time wore on, within it now the sensation of rage and murder, though Ruti could associate no color with it, which was unusual. It made him worry for OneEye.

He stifled a pained sound as he adjusted his body, waiting for the TwoLeg to settle. The torn scales along his ribcage had felt like a blue hot fire at first, but now the pain had dulled to a throbbing ache. The bleeding was slow but constant; he would need to do something soon or blackness would consume him. Worse, his *kai* was fading again as well. In moments he would be without it, forced once again to navigate the Cave half-blind.

Gruff muttering in the TwoLeg tongue erupted from above, those useless sounds formed by odd mouths that only half communicated. They filled the chamber as HarmBringer's dark energy funneled through some sort of invisible netting or filter, nearly imperceptible to Ruti's unraveling *kai*, a division within the large TwoLeg which the Root Dragon understood as fear mixed with complacency. The words he could make out were half unintelligible, half full of curses, most directed towards Shadow. With patience learned and practiced over a thousand years of biding, forced and otherwise, Ruti hunkered, leaking his *che*, his *lifeblood*, onto the stones beneath him. Then, at long last, HarmBringer's mumbling faded to snores. Ruti wriggled ahead one tiny step at a time towards Peligro's feet, found holds for his nails, and began to climb.

As the Root Dragon neared the inward crook of HarmBringer's knee, the big TwoLeg sputtered and fumbled at the air before sinking back into his seat, his fingers folded across his gut. Ruti paused, his *kai* exposed to a sudden flush of details. *The drum of an overstrained heart booming in the silence of this smaller cave within a Cave, thudding against its barrier of bone deep within the fat folds of its owner. The wet sucking sounds of every inhaled breath, each answered by a whistling exhale. The waft of alcohol, of dead animal flesh trapped somewhere in the TwoLeg's mouth, spoiling now. The sick scent of unhealth within, his body absorbing the fuel of its rations with difficulty, spilling forth that smell from his gut and his pores. The reappearing darkness, an infection of intent and twisted emotions and designs of revenge built from every spiteful moment collected over a lifetime of hatred. The unremitting trajectory towards the infliction of those designs on the world, on Shadow in particular. The unlit gap of his center growing outwardly until the room itself became dark, swallowed by rage.*

The sensations shook Ruti to his core.

Recovering, the Root Dragon waited until the HarmBringer's breathing slowed and became even again, then continued upward.

At the peak of the knee, Ruti stopped again. His side felt as if it was being torn open more, and a black rill of his blood now spotted HarmBringer's pant leg all the way down. His sight, not that given by *kai* but of his eyes, swam in a vat of deep, spongy red. He felt weak, so weak. The threadlines ahead said he might fly again, perhaps only once more, but uncertainty was a necessary part of *kai* and so he accepted that it might not be so. He hoped that at the very least he would be able to drag the metal ring back to Earny. The end of his strength was approaching fast now.

When the red receded to the corners of his vision and his breathing was merely painful and not agonizing, he studied the ring hanging before him, within reach at last, looped around the HarmBringer's belt. The loop opened at a moving segment that swung past a small levering clasp. Ruti's *kai* told him the ring and its contents weighed more than his entire body, and this gave him pause; whether he still had the strength to move it, he did not know

He inched nearer, small blue eyes flicking from the swelling hills of HarmBringer's face to the clasp, his wings drawn tight against his back. His awareness opened one last time, filling his mind. *A thousand hairs along the TwoLeg's arms rustling and flicking on the breeze from the end of the hall. The growing cloud, unworldly in substance but bearing towards dark deeds, roiling within the barely contained outline of HarmBringer's feelings. The coming outburst of violence and angry cries, promised by the exchange of his most inner core with the world around him, unconscious but purposeful, signaled also by the minute twitching of his thick fingers. The unfettered disgust emanating from him in all directions, aimed at nothing in particular.*

Watching and sensing all of this, Ruti closed his teeth around the clasp and paused to observe Peligro's breathing. His *kai* studied the dark outline of the TwoLeg's presence, its borders even and measured while in the throes of sleep, containing all that rage. Then the Root Dragon eased the clasp open. It resisted at first, then snapped wide with a soft *shlink*. HarmBringer shifted and scratched himself, but his eyes did not open.

Ruti eased the ring onto his mouth, braced himself for the coming pain, and then began to rotate it with all his strength. Bright white agony blazed in his belly. The slick surface of the metal slid easily through his teeth, and three times he had to bite down harder for purchase. One last rotation and it would fall loose.

Some flash of warning sparked, not of *kai* but maybe from the buried voice, causing Ruti to clamp down onto the TwoLeg's belt as a fierce *hiss* pierced the air from the cell across the way. HarmBringer's eyes snapped wide and he lurched upright drunkenly, swinging his arm towards his mouth. Ruti swung from his waist, teeth clenched, pain like he had never experienced carving into him with every movement. The thing he had sensed earlier within the cell across from Earny, the unreadable entity outside of *kai* that sucked inward the energy around it while emitting nothing of its own, had stirred. As he swung, he glimpsed something pale and skeletal slapping shriveled black fingers onto the bars there and cold silver eyes staring out from the lightlessness. Then Peligro stumbled three awkward steps forward and lunged with his whip, striking the barrier. The momentum of his belly swung Ruti loose and he strained to flap his wings, to will his body to stay aloft, but he was too weak. The ground hurtled up at him and the world exploded into bright flashes of pain.

Behind him, Peligro continued hammering the bars, grunting wordless sounds.

Ruti waited for the throb in his head to ebb, then peered through the growing redness of his vision towards the TwoLeg's seat. The metal ring had fallen loose and lay on the stone floor there, its flower of thin metal dangling objects swirled around it. He inched ahead, small muscles driving. The darkness he had felt within HarmBringer had been unleashed, its barely contained aggression channeled to a pinpoint towards the silver-eyed being's cell. Ruti was thankful for its depths now as the TwoLeg threw his every frustration at the cold indifference of those metal bars.

The Root Dragon reached the fallen ring, mustered up whatever strength he could salvage, and heaved. The ring was heavier than he expected; even were he not wounded it would have been difficult to lift. But Ruti's devotion to *kai'nae* OneEye's wishes filled him with resolve and, with the last of his effort, he hoisted the metal ring into the torchlit air and towed it across the chamber, feeling as though his flesh was being stripped from the bone, leaving his guts to fall through.

Peligro the HarmBringer finished his assault by ejecting a thick wad of mucus and hunger fluid into the blackness of the silver-eyed thing's cell. He stood there afterwards, chest heaving, covered in a thick film of sweat, his shoulders hunched over in exhaustion and defeat. Once he regained his breath, he stumbled back across the room and retook his seat, unawares, just as Ruti entered Earny's cell behind him and slipped from sight.

9

The last meeting between Jana Hunter and Donovan Maltrese rushed by and left her in its wake before she could make heads or tails of anything.

Staring at the deep crow's feet and smile lines of one of Shadow's books, her mind wandered to her father. His memory felt like a good friend she had lost touch with, and it comforted her to reacquaint. In the deep grain of the half-calf book cover, she saw sudden familiar shapes, a kind smile inset with kinder eyes, the thick bristle of a mustache craning upwards lazily at the corners in a look of pure warmth. *Get yer rear to the Shodan, girl, pick yer mom a fistful of dry-hedge 'fore she gets in a tizzy and messes the applemud. Go!* he said to her, then patted her backside with a meaty, callused hand and roared a thunder roll of laughter. And she went, the wild underbed of the Shodan crisp beneath her moccasins. The bittersweet blend of apples and dewdrop stew cloyed the whole way. *Yes, Dad. Sure I will. And don't give me that scowl! I won't mix berries with the hedge this time, Keeper save! It was Stink last time anyhow. Stink and his redbark twig-sword and brown gossamer crown.*

Jana looked up from the book and felt true, heavy sadness sitting on her shoulders. She did not know what to say to it. But there were no tears, not this time. She had spent enough nights crying herself into a rocky sleep, enough hours staring at the back of Donovan's head through a glaze of misery as they marched along the Drudge. Jana Hunter was all out of tears now; whether that was to be celebrated or mourned was still a chase without bounty in her mind.

The door to her chamber opened, and for one long breath she waited for Shadow to reappear, to push her against the wall and ravage her without a word until she was a sore and sweaty mess. Instead, an older man with a harsh, knotted face and an eternal grimace entered. A fine white scar traced aged pain through his brow and across his eye, which was milky and sightless. He looked her over the way a merchant might his overturned wagon on a muddy roadside, then said simply: "Come."

Easy as that, I get summoned to my execution. Could that be it? Was that why Shadow was nowhere to be found? Was he too smitten with her to face her death stare like a man? A hot run of emotion she named foolishness flushed through her; if she knew men, Shadow was no more smitten with her than the last ten pretty young girls who had crossed his path—and no doubt fallen, legs unfolded, to his wiles.

"What is it?" she asked the one-eyed guard.

"Come."

"I'm not a dog, much as I smelled like one before. Where am I going?"

The man frowned deeper. "Come. Now."

"You know *two* words, do you? Keen and shiny, you," said Jana, unmoving.

The man with the scar stared at her for a long time, then took the longest breath she had ever heard. "Your friend the Swordsman awaits."

Jana bolted upright. "Donovan?"

She was on her feet before she could think, flying past her escort, who could only watch with a look of disapproval.

Halfway down the hall, she realized she had no idea where she was headed and waited for her burly companion to take the lead. He did again (taking a great while to do so, as if to reassert his dominance—oh how she hated men sometimes) and beckoned to her once his point was clear.

She followed her guide through the warm torchlight, watching the long webby tangles of his gray-dappled hair with a small smile. Earlier, when Shadow had spoken of him, all she wanted to do to Donovan was pull his head and his smug grin clear off, perhaps toss it out a window for good measure. Now she planned to leap into his arms and hug him. How he had managed to survive from so close to the edge of death puzzled her, yet she could not bring herself to worry. Be thankful for what's in the hand, long as no one's hurt the worse for it—that's what they taught at Studies. *Donovan's alive and maybe we'll get out of here. Sure, and maybe I'll get my hands on the Cleric, too, and banish this scar away while I'm at it.*

Yes, yes, all that will happen, easy as that.

After an endless ravel of intersections, her companion halted and opened a door to his left. "Enter."

"Okay. Good talking with you," she said as she slipped through the door and heard him close it quietly behind her.

And there, in his stoic glory, was Donovan of the Swordsmen watching her with a frown. "You look like you just fell off a mountain of dunny and rolled all the way down," he said grimly.

"Then you look like you were buried alive under it," she said, glaring but with an inward smile. How she thought this man could betray her seemed beyond even the Princess's capacity.

"Good to see you too, highness." He took a seat near the fire, which burned the same sickly green as every flame in this place. But even so, Jana saw now that Donovan was unwell, his hard green eyes sunken into deep rings, the rest of his skin waxen somehow even beneath his deep tan, as if you could see through him if you held him up to the sun.

He nearly died, didn't he? He went right to the edge.

"This place is Kolendhar to the heart, only blacker," he told her. "If I didn't know better I'd say the same men built it, or at least it birthed from the same plan."

"Bout as cozy as a snakepit full of rotting game. I've taken two baths a day since they brought the tub up at last and I still can't get this slick feeling off me."

Donovan's thick eyebrows arched. "Baths, you say? Fair treatment for a prisoner. You must have met Shadow, then."

Against her every effort, Jana felt her cheeks redden.

"Mind that one, pray it true. If ever a man was rotten to the pit, it's him. Even as a boy I remember him taking a fancy to severing cattails and using them as whips to chase their owners round until they fell dead from blood loss. It takes a mind born wounded for that sort of business."

Jana, who could not in her deepest imagine Shadow as anything devoid of sexuality as a boy, let alone one who tortured animals, nodded and shrugged. "He's been kind to me."

"The ends, Jana. Always the ends. Staring at anything else is akin to fixing on the bow and missing the arrow flying forth."

"Why don't you teach me to wipe myself while yer at it."

"Small steps, Hunter'lue. Don't want to overwhelm you."

She couldn't help but laugh and she hated him for it. "You're lucky you're so hateable that you come back around on the likable side sometimes."

"I've been called many things, highness, but lucky is not one of them."

"Well you're alive, aren't you?" she said, arms crossed, sensing the approach, distant yet, of words she was not going to like.

Donovan nodded as if this news was dubious proof of her point, then leaned back with his boots up on the table. Jana noticed now the room in which they stood. The left wall, above the fireplace, was papered with a massive map, meticulous in detail, depicting lands from the Wastes all the way to Pleasantry and beyond. In the far corner, a suit of plate mail watched from a series of rods holding it mounted in place. Bright blue jewels in the pauldron shot icicles of reflected firelight into her eyes. Donovan looked right at home in a place like this; she fancied the thought of him staring down a long table such as this, attended by grizzled war veterans waiting solemnly for his next decree. Donovan the general. Anywhere else left this dark man out of place.

"I'd give my arm for some of your Boon," he said. "Sometimes the thought of it gives me shivers."

"They took it, along with the six-gun," she said with a frown. She had never gotten the chance to become proficient with it. Maybe she could coax Shadow into finding a place for her to practice her marksmanship. *Sure. Right after he bakes you an applemud pie.*

"Of course. Bathe her and whisper sweet nevers down her ear, but don't give her the Boon, oh no," Donovan spoke through a frown so deep it seemed to spill onto his neck.

"How did they cure you? We thought you were halfway to the Black for sure."

He looked at her, his frown fading a bit. "That is something I'd know as well. As far as I've heard, an Aspy bite means death come miracle or the Keeper's hand itself. Yet here I am, aren't I?"

"Yes," said Jana, another smile creeping across her lips, one that she grudgingly accepted. "There you certainly are, grumpiness and dogma and all."

"I dreamed while I was under the poison," he said after a long, thoughtful pause. "They were so real I'd swear they were visions."

Jana blinked; the notion of Donovan sharing any piece of himself without goading seemed as likely as falling into the sky. "What were they of?"

"A man who spoke in riddles. He was familiar, so familiar..." He trailed off, then seemed to remember himself and replaced his vulnerable look with his usual general expression of disapproval.

"What did he tell you?" Now her curiosity was piqued. And that, of course, would be when he said—

"Nothing of consequence. The sort of inanity only fever can drum out of the mind." He stood then, pacing the room.

She noticed him reach around his waist to hold his scabbard with the tips of his fingers and wondered if he even knew he was doing it. "Have you seen Earny?"

Donovan nodded without looking at her. "He's just outside."

"Why isn't he in here? If anyone's gonna need a good hug after all this it's him," she said.

Donovan squared off with her, hands on the high back of the chair where he had been sitting. "I'm headed back to Pleasantry, Jana. I leave tonight."

Excitement fountained into her chest. "Well, it's about bloody time!"

The dark look in his eyes stilled her. After a moment of consideration, he said, "Earny and I are going. You'll need to stay here for now."

And suddenly Lana Preole flashed before Jana's eyes and the world turned red.

"What in the forsaken fuck are you talking about?"

If her rage shook Donovan, he didn't look it. "There is no explanation I can give you now. Only that you must trust me. I'll not forget you."

"Not forget me. *Not forget me?* The only reason I'm here is because of you, you piece of dunny sucking—"

"Quiet your highwayman mouth. You've spent too much time around Earny."

And she did quiet for a moment, because she could either halt herself from attacking the Swordsman or speak intelligibly but not both. Shadow was right, as was her gut. Donovan was going to abandon her now when she needed him the most. She'd be alone here, with her scar, with the coming madness, with *him*.

"There is danger in Pleasantry, and there is no use to you being there. And the Cleric wishes you to stay here…"

"So he can have his way with me…" The words exited her clenched teeth as a hiss.

"So he can be sure I'll return. Much as you think me a traitor in this moment Jana Hunter, I will return for you. I'll not let the madness take us while I still draw breath."

"How do I know? Tell me how I can know that I'll be cured, too, and not just you? Why should he cure me anyhow? You're the great mighty Swordsman, his buddy from the good old days. I'm just a girl he fucked halfway to death against her will. Against my *will*, Donovan. Do you know what that's like? Do you have any fucking idea what that feels like? To know that *thing* was *inside* me? I scrub myself sometimes till blood comes out my pores trying to get rid of the feeling. Only I can't. And now you want to lock me up with him for…how long? Till whenever you manage to mosey back this way?"

"If you call holding off this madness with every shred of my being while I do the dirty work of a madman moseying, then yes."

Something in his tone bit through her rage. "What dirty work?"

"The kind my sort are built for. We're good for little else, history says." He turned from her, facing the map on the wall with feigned interest.

"I saw things while you were unconscious. Creatures. So real I thought they could bite me," she said, barely a whisper.

When he looked at her she saw his eyes filled with worry. "It's the Cold setting in."

"The Cold?"

"The Cleric's madness. At first, I saw things where I knew there was nothing. That was better in a way, better than seeing your friends as ravenous beasts and having no chance of telling the difference."

"It will take me before you get back with whatever it is you're planning to leverage our cure with, won't it?"

Donovan sighed a sigh that bore the weight of the world and shook his head. "Not if I can help it, Jana. And right now, for better or worse, I'm the only one who can ."

She nodded, feeling more helpless than she ever had, even more than when she and Stink had crouched in the ravine with their parents freshly murdered and blood-frenzied Dwellers on their tail. At least then she could act, wrong as her choices might have been.

The door creaked open and Earny entered, and for a brief moment the world seemed a shade brighter. Good old Earnald Avers, looking worn and tired but alive. His eye was red and puffy, as though he had been weeping. "Hello, Miss Jana." She ran to him and hugged him hard, but as soon as she embraced him he grunted in pain and withdrew. She looked at him, not understanding. "Back and ribs're a bit sore, don't mind me," he said, eye shifting downward. "I was worried fer ya, girl."

"I can't believe you're alive, save us all," she said through her first full smile in weeks. The look on Earny's face wiped the smile away. "What's wrong?"

Fresh tears welled in Earny's lone eye. He reached into his trouser pocket and produced a small sculpture of Ruti, intricately detailed, carved of the same incandescent rock that Donovan named *ai'che*. He held it up and Jana reached for it, then pulled away. Donovan looked on with a frown. "Keeper pray... Is it?" she asked, a hard ball in her throat.

"It's my fault," Earny said. "Damn everything, it was me. I sent 'im out to look fer ya and he came back with a slash 'cross the gut bleeding his last, hardly able to keep 'his head up or his eyes open. I tried to hold tha wound but I fell asleep, and when I woke he was like this, turned to stone, back tha way he came." He wiped at his nose and his tears and a sharp pain filled Jana's heart. "He was my friend," said Earny. "I'll keep him with me, fer tha now anyway. He'd wanna see things through, I'm thinkin'." He nodded as if to convince himself of this fact.

Donovan looked on with a hint of sadness which Jana measured as real. "Meet me outside Earny." He stepped to Jana awkwardly, hands on his hips. "Please try to trust me. I'll be back as soon as I can. I swear it." He looked like he might say more, but when she stared at him, conflicted and wordless, he left, still noiseless as a shadow.

Even though it must have pained him, Earny grabbed her and hugged her so hard she had to pull away to take a breath. "You take care of yerself, girl. If I had any say in it, I'd bring you along or stay here and keep ya safe. But ol' Earny's not the biggest pea in this pod, no sir. But I'll come back." He leaned forward as if sharing a great secret. "Even if you doubt the Swordsman, you can count on ol' Earny."

Jana could not help but smile and embrace the reformed bandit again.

When he pulled away at last, he seemed to ponder something long and hard, as though making a decision of great importance. At length, he reached into his trouser pocket again and produced a large iron keyring full of keys and presented it to her. "They didn't search me on the way out. Makes sense, it does, seein' as how I'm free to go now so what's the point? Ruti brought it to me. Last thing he ever did. I don't know if any of those opens any doors you'll be behind, but it might be worth a try. Just be careful and try and wait. Better we come get ya than you start runnin' round the Wastes with Blood Demons on your scent. But if you need to…" He nodded at the keys again, then patted her hand with his wrinkled, rough one. "Keeper save us all."

She nodded and found now that she did have tears, and they were running freely.

Earny Avers gave her one last hard hug, then trudged away.

Her milky-eyed escort entered soon after, and never saw where she hid Earny's keys.

10

She stood alone at the sandswept balcony, hair mussed, chestnut eyes blinking black between night's fading starlit censure of the new and fiery dawn. Behind her, the trident spirals of Pal Myrrah towered, a colossal eagle with granite talons, bathing the dead stretch of the Wastes with an inky profile. She felt it there like intent eyes, a tingling of the back, an erection of small hairs. Rough stone met her fingertips, ancient as the alp it mounted. She was gripping the railing tight, her fingers stiff and sore, as though it was the only thing keeping her from slipping into an abyss. Maybe it was.

She turned her gaze skyward. Like they had one cold night along the Drudge, the stars made her think of her father. If only he were here now. What would he think of her? What demons would she suffer for one last hard warm embrace, strong as ironwood and just as earthy? She'd suffer the Cleric again, perhaps. It might just be worth it.

A piercing violet stare flared across her vision and a cold breath dove into her chest and solidified there. She was in his thoughts now, in the rear and of little consequence, but present nonetheless. Soon he would descend upon her and she would be plucked up as easily as a field mouse, and then the terrors would begin again; endless, numbing terrors. But no, not numbing. Numbness would be a blessing. If only such bright things might grow in this place.

Beneath the terror, acidic betrayal. Indignation even. That her trust should be given, not in brashness but in long and fierce consideration, then left to the wayside along one man's road to self-fulfillment, melted the cold inside her and brought it to a boil. She did not feel the hatred towards the Swordsman that she bore his once-master, but it was something akin to it even if it was lesser. She was certain she would never see him return to these gates; Ruti would come back to life first, a souvenir from the Black tight between his small canines. Donovan was gone for good now, and damn him to the Maw for it. She would have pounded her fist into the wall and pretended it was the Swordsman's face if only she could rip her hands free of the railing. But she couldn't. Not until she was done watching.

The groan of Pal Myrrah's gates echoed deep and primordial into the withering land beyond. A spill of torchlight swept forth from the opening only to die in the dust a hundred paces out. Then two shadows materialized, man-shaped at first. They elongated into thin black serpents as they moved further from the light, away from the fortress. And then she saw them: one man shorter, hair depilated by a long hard life, an eye removed by a jilted husband some years gone; the other man tall and broad, his age-old family keepsake strapped to his back, his wide-brimmed hat pulled low. Together her companions marched forth from the keep as though leaving a relative's hospitality after a savory supper.

They stopped just within the throw of the torchlight, and then she heard the clop of horse hooves and saw two albinos dressed in drab robes scurry forth pulling a big black stallion and a smaller white and brown mare. They handed the reigns over, heads bowed, and retreated into the dark like bleached jackrabbits fleeing a predator. Nothing worthy of note there; everyone's afraid of the Swordsman, even her.

They mounted, the Swordsman more deftly than his fellow. Without word or look they turned and pressed their horses into the gathering cold, small as flies from her vantage. She held her breath until it burned, then let it slip free in a slow hiss.

Then, at last, the Swordsman reigned up and turned.

From here she could not see him, at least not his eyes. Nor did she want to. The tears might come back, for now she knew that deep swells of emotion still tided within her, repressed for weeks but still waiting just beneath the surface, and she did not wish them to reemerge.

Without salute or gesture, the Swordsman turned away again and followed the dissipating wake of his smaller companion towards the palisades beyond.

Minutes later she saw something else: a group of riders, eight or ten in all, cloaked in black. They sped out through the gates but curved wide to the west, and somehow she knew at once that Shadow was with them. He had left her here, too. She was utterly alone. The men in the black hoods were staying wide of Donovan so he might not spot them, so that they could track him and Earny to whatever dark place and deeds they were headed to, and then...

Then what?

She did not know.

But she felt hollow like she hadn't in a long time.

11

On horseback, the trek through the Wastes seemed shorter than Earny recalled save for the mad last lap to Pal Myrrah while the Swordsman had clung to life by a thread. This time they moved during the day only, keeping watch at night for Aspys and worse. Most nights Donovan stayed apart from him, his hat dangling from his nicked and callused fingers and dancing on the salty breeze while he stared at the endless deck of clouds and lost himself to thought. *What did a Swordsman spend all that time pondering?* Matters of intrigue and the roundabout, kings and countries, and the grand old rusty war machine if Earny had to guess. But maybe there was the off-chance it was something small and personal, something even a simpleton such as Earnald Avers could relate to, though he doubted that; he suspected even the mundane aspects of a Swordsman were grander than him. The only way to know would be to ask. Dragging a bit of it out the man's lips would be the hardship in it, if it was even possible at all. Would it be of use? Maybe, maybe not.

They pushed hard the next day, through Mist, through a large patch of Waste skirted with scrub and spidergrass; it looked to Earny like the mammoth tonsured head of a monk. Around them, drifts of sand swept across the land in rippling tethers diving under and over each other in a dance. Every day the piercing eye of the sun birthed low and bloody on the horizon and yawed deliberately upwards before driving hard for the dark waiting arms of twilight.

On the bright break of a new day, Earny saw in the distance a great ragged structure on the horizon and another shorter one, more damaged, poked through with holes showing a white sky beyond. They looked to Earny like dual hourglass-shaped cups waiting for a titan to happen by and drink deep from them. Time had worn them to skeletons for most of their height. What the old folks might have used them for, he could not guess.

And so they rode, ate their rations, slept, and then moved on, day after day, a sullen air hanging over them. No words were exchanged. Each night they took their meals from their panniers and cooked them over a small fire. As he ate, Earny would watch Donovan's expression turn inward, chasing whatever dark thoughts were tormenting him, and the ex-highwayman would venture no conversation. It made Earny miss Jana terribly. As much as he sought guidance and instruction from the Swordsman, their travels were not the same without her. Especially now with this new, darker Donovan who seemed as if he was about to be crushed by some final weight that had been dropped upon his shoulders.

Soon the days ran into each other, and Earny was no longer sure how long they had been traveling, how long it had been since Pal Myrrah. They crossed tracks sometimes, human and not, and Earny wondered if they were made by the Cleric's men or someone else. No telling why anyone might travel these forsaken lands. They trotted past droppings that must have come from large beasts, though they saw no other signs of such things. Days later they happened across half-eaten human corpses and three packhorses dead in a cluster, killed by some disease or maybe dehydration or both. The men were covered in sores and their flesh had a green tint that Earny had never seen before, and so they kept their distance and did not disturb the bodies.

They traveled on, and by the next day the Mother's Mouth was fast approaching, ready to swallow them and their mounts whole. Earny knew that at the end of this trek lay Pleasantry, a place to which he never expected to return. It was a fine enough town, he supposed, but the prospect of stepping foot there again filled him with dread. He wished he knew where that feeling came from, foul-mood Swordsman aside. Miss Jana would have known, he was sure of it, and he wished more than almost anything that she was here to tell him. But she wasn't. He was on his own, Keeper pray for them all. Even with the Swordsman alongside him, he was on his own.

That night Earny lay on his bedroll, his sassy brown mare (he named her Cora, after a serving girl he had fond memories of from his two-eyed days) tied off nearby to a piece of petrified deadwood whose origin he could not fathom. His six-gun, returned now, rested just beneath his fingers, and its cold touch felt comforting. Ruti lay on Earny's chest, or the stone thing that was once Ruti, staring at him with expressionless iridescent lumps for eyes. Gone because of Earnald Avers and his foul luck, like many a character in the junk play of his life. *All well and good by yer tree, happy as a hog in dunny, till foolish old one-eye here plucked ya out and sat ya in harm's way. Damn me to the Maw and anywhere else I can burn.*

And who next in line but Miss Jana to fall off the stage and out of the story forever?

Whether the Swordsman had any intention of returning here in time to save the girl, or at least give it a fair shake, Earny did not know, but he had given his word, and the word of the new, reformed Earny was strong as oak. He'd be back one way or the other, even if he had to ride a Dweller all the way across the Gestalt. Pray it very true.

Much had changed since he last stood watch for his old and now dead clan, not least of all the flesh on his back which bore Peligro's fresh stripes of ruin mingled with his old ones from Raef. One thing had not, however: he would stick by the Swordsman for as long as he could and be of whatever aid he might until this matter was finished. Whatever *finished* meant. Something deep inside him said finished involved deeds darker than any he had witnessed so far.

He ran a finger along the smooth carve of the late Root Dragon's back, took a deep, wavering breath, then forced himself to sleep.

12

Grampy squatted on his haunches and squinted at the long thin furrows of his garden, frowning. In a day long since lost on a wind long since blown, anything planted by these old and strong hands, younger then but still old, would flourish and sprout and fill with flavor beyond what could be easily replicated. But right now the earth was dead, dead and dusty, full of angst and bad manners. The minds of men seeping down into the sod, no doubt. What better metaphor for people's ceaseless quibbling and shortsighted nonsense than a patch of dirt too corrupt and free of useful stuff to amount to anything but a stinky dunny-colored lump.

The process of straightening ached more than usual. Time stretched alongside pain, so they said, and none believed it more than he. Somewhere halfway up he thought of Jana, wondered where she might have gone with that surly Swordsman. Away to the north it seemed, but who could know past there? Towards that man, the Cleric, as far as Tomson told. And what then? The sort of devilry that put a curse in a pleasant woman the like of Jana Hunter never worked in reverse. Destruction and creation charge headlong towards collision, never in concert. Months gone she was now. Damn him to the Maw with his tail between his legs, he missed her good-natured grin and her fire-spitting tongue. He'd never see her again, like as not. Such was the way of this life, this self-imploding remnant of a used-up world that had already tried to destroy itself but never quite finished the job. Who needed Misties and Blood Demons to whittle away at humanity's numbers when humanity itself was more than fit for the job? Save all the evil folk the trouble, beg a man for speaking the truth and blessitall.

Long, painful minutes later he was inside.

The hut smelled of deep earth and long year, a musty sweetness that warmed his bones from the center. It made him think of his wife, too, her soft chocolate eyes flecked with the tiniest bit of garnet red, almost like stars. So far gone he couldn't picture her young, back when they first laid together beneath a lucid sky as the waves of the world aimed mankind's boat toward the rocks, but they were oh so much farther out, and who needs to worry about such things for they'll never head in this lifetime? But they would in Grampy's time, though not his wife's pray it true and Keeper bless her good and wholesome soul. And reckoning lay just beyond the next ridge past those rocks, if his years and pains and trials had taught him a thing worth remembering.

He wiped away scant tears from his leathery face with an even more leathery hand, his inner wound stanched like often it was but never healed, never stitched quite tightly enough. Gone's gone and here's here, his father used to say. Or maybe it was his uncle. Point was someone said something that seemed pertinent to his present situation and he was going to run with it.

Another night in an endless stretch of nights, each an augury of the next, unending with this lone sane man (he felt as much anyhow) whipping round through the cold and murky days waiting for the wall to appear out of the mist so he might slam face-first into it and find the Black at last, and perhaps even his lost loves, too.

Out of habit he peeled back the heavy wool blanket on his cot and fluffed the down pillow that one of his more abiding neighbors had gifted him ten years gone, removed his moccasins, and eased his tired rump onto the pallet which was little more than some blankets folded over and over again and stuffed with hay. And there he reached a crossroads.

To smoke Boon, or not.

He reached for his pipe and his elbow and shoulder cracked like dry twigs. His leaves were dry and half drained of flavor by age, but they'd do for now. He'd given the best picks of his stash to Jana, for which he wanted to feel bitter but couldn't. The sting of generosity, that was.

Grampy struck a match and puffed his pipe and felt his old lungs fill with smoke, his tongue enveloped in that tangy, wonderful flavor, and as he exhaled a deep phlegmy cough wracked him. For the first time in—how long? A decade?—he put down a half-finished pipe and bothered it no further. *Too old for Boon? Too old for livin', then.* And wasn't that the blasted truth of it?

He eased onto his back, his mind afloat in a haze, one of mind and body and maybe spirit, too. He wanted to sleep but sleep would not come. *What is the name of it are you 'sessin' bout ya old dunny-sniffler?* Whatever it was, it was rolling a neat ball of dread right in the center of his chest and it would not let sleep take him or even approach.

He looked down over his toes (which were sticking up from the bottom of the blanket) at the door to his house, once made of metal with science lost a thousand years ago, now of some oak Grampy had sawed into even cuts back when he could still see two feet in front of his face. He looked at the window, which had glass mounted in it when they first found this old abandoned plot but now was open to the air, saw the feather and stone talisman dangling from the lintel outside, visible from his vantage and outlined by a steelblue stroke of moonglow. To help in the Warding, that piece was. To aid him and his family, Pleasantry, keep them safe from disease, from Misties and Demons, and most of all from the feller in white and whatever evil pumped blackness through his withered veins.

Grampy sniffled and wiped at his eyes and swallowed down a grunt of anger.

Fine good all his superstitious tokey-bokey shit-fer-all Warding had done. His wife and kids were in the ground, families left and right at the skirts of town eaten or worse, and then this man, the Cleric, wandering through the place like he owned it, right smack through the center of years of Grampy's pathetic attempt at putting up... what? A magic curtain? Spectral armor visible only to the initiated perhaps? If so, then Grampy was not one of them. Faith then. Yes, that was what it was about. Cold and unrequited faith.

Then again, wasn't it only in the moments of deepest despair that faith even counted for anything?

This last thought nearly brought Grampy out of his bed and back to his knees, ready to sink deep into himself and drag forth whatever remnants of strength he might have and project them skyward like a fisherman's net, only this net was as big as a mountaintop and fashioned from light itself, and when it enclosed Pleasantry the openings in the threading would slip shut with plates made of the Keeper's flesh itself and nothing, no Mist Dwellers, no demons could hurt this backassed town. Not on Grampy's watch.

Time wears a man thin though, no matter how thick his resolve when he starts.

As these thoughts clambered about Grampy's skull, sleep crept from his periphery.

He had just about decided to cast the Warding once more out of habit when his snores began.

13

Earny and the Swordsman walked the Drudge with their heads bowed, their shoulders forward and weary, appearing as they navigated the fog like a pair of refugees seeking asylum from some besieged city far away. Their horse's hooves slogged through mud as deep as a man's finger, throwing brown muck in clumps with each step. All around them, trees, dead and leafless, sheared outcroppings of rock, and nothing else living, no fellow travelers, no flutter of birds overhead. Only a sense of emptiness, stark and profound. Something was amiss in the world, Earnald Avers decided, more so than even before. Things had been happening during their time at Pal Myrrah. What exactly, he could not imagine.

Behind them, the Ven, the Gestalt, the Dweller boatman (who had seemed far more eager to cross them back, despite not collecting his toll this time), and endless weeks of marching their horses from sun up till sundown, resting only in spurts, watering their mounts where they could, themselves only as often.

Somehow, despite his fears, Donovan's madness had not returned in all this time. There were moments when Earny spotted him off in the distance, and to his lone working eye it seemed the Swordsman was shivering, arms hugged around his body, teeth gritted tight. But he never spoke during those moments, and when he turned back towards camp his eyes were the vibrant green of Donovan and never the glowing red of that other one.

As they traversed yet another day, the sun ever blanketed in incandescent clouds, the relentless drear overwhelming, Earnald tried again to make conversation with the Swordsman, who still had said hardly a word during all this time. "Do you think we're almost on Pleasantry, sir?" he asked.

Donovan rode with his reins grasped by loose fingers. His sword watched Earny stoically.

"Forgive me, yer lordship, but…" began Earny.

"If it's Pleasantry you seek, Earnald Avers, then look forth," said the Swordsman suddenly.

And there it was, rising from the fog in the distance like a clump of warts on the backside of a gargantuan golem. The adobe huts of Pleasantry and the fewer, sturdier buildings from before the Shift huddled together like a pack of small, frightened animals. Thin streamers of smoke wafted lazily upwards from chimneys worn from rain and wind and untold years. Tired men covered in a long day's worth of filth trudged here and there. The dull lick of firelight flickered from the one called Grampy's window, the house closest to the road. The bell tower rose from the center of it all, a shoddy black finger gesturing to the sky.

As they approached, Earny could hear the calls of women and children like birdsong. People began to gather and gape as they clopped their horses past the threshold of the town, the folk around them halting their work and sharing furtive, distrustful glances.

"Get outta here, demon-lover!" screamed a man somewhere in the distance.

"We told you to get gone, you and your demon whore!"

"Who'll pay for Creel and his boys, pray it?"

"Leave now or we'll string your guts for the crows, demon-lover."

Donovan never looked up, didn't seem to even hear them. Earny recalled the look of Pleasantry when the Swordsman first arrived, distant as he had been to witness it. The people then had looked on with wonder, even the oldest face (perhaps not that man Grampy's) lightening and infused with new life. And he remembered the cheers, alien in this wet plot, bright peals of joy and wonder as the Swordsman drove the Misty back to the hellhole from which it spawned.

Now those same voices screamed curses and worse.

Earny looked at the bright burn of hate in a woman's eyes, a woman he had never seen before, but who hated him now for the simple fact that he traveled with Donovan and therefore must be an embracer of the dark. Those eyes shone from the sunken barrow of her face with a ferine aspect so severe that Earny found it hypnotic. His mouth opened to say something, to greet her or to profess his innocence or even to acknowledge her fear and attempt to soothe it.

That was when the stone was thrown.

It came from his left side, which of course was blind—from the right, he may have had a chance of dodging it—a rock about the size of a fist, gray and encrusted in mud, spinning towards him from a dozen feet away. A fine throw indeed were he asked under better circumstances. Then a sharp, jagged edge stabbed into his temple and everything went shades of red and black as his head snapped backwards.

"Get the fuck out of here you demon-loving sonsovbitches!" cried a man from the direction of the stone.

More screams, then another rock. This one Earny saw, for it came from his right side, and he threw his hands up in defense. But Donovan Maltrese, once head of the Order of Swordsmen and near-mute for the last month, seemed to have had enough now.

As Earny was ducking, Donovan lurched backwards and rolled across his horse's backside, sword somehow already in hand. It gleamed and reflected the cold dead sky and a piercing *cling* split the air as the rock spun off to Earny's right, where it struck one of the old swirling corbels of Shag's Inn with a *thud*.

At the sight of the Swordsman with his blade drawn, the crowd hushed. *It's as if they don't think of the blade till he's got it out.* But then, that might just be the truth in it; the folk of Pleasantry, all things considered, were not the keenest.

Look who's talking there.

Earny dabbed at his head and found blood and grimaced. That one would ache for days.

Donovan stood ten paces from the bell tower, his black stallion waiting patiently nearby, a rooster pecking meal at his feet and indifferent to the Swordsman's imposing air. He turned in a circle, taking time to look every person he could in the eye, saying nothing. Then, without word, he sheathed his sword again and headed for

Tomson's house. Earny struggled to dismount, nearly fell, then scampered up the hill as well, risking a glance over his shoulder in case other would-be stickball players sought to practice on his head. But no more stones came, and when Tomson's door open they were greeted with a smile, the first in weeks. "Donovan. Never thought I'd see your smug again, pray it true," said Tomson in his deep, thick voice. He offered a hand and Donovan embraced it distantly. "Come, come. Fore the rabble can stir themselves up any more."

Earny did not need to be asked twice. He and Donovan entered the house, and with a growing frown and a look outside, Tomson closed the door.

* * * *

Donovan studied Tomson's face later with scrutiny. A bowl of Mary's stew warmed his stomach from the inside, and Earny sat beside him gulping down stout with vigor, which was just as well; the ex-highwayman could use a dulling of the senses after the wound had suffered, which was bound now in bloody muslin.

Tomson leaned back and folded his arms, lost in thought. "They have holy ground you say?" He laughed and shook his head. "If you were any other man on the road I'd kick you out on your ass and throw rocks with the rest of them. But if you tell me Misties get on bended knee somewhere and talk to some sort of god or devil or the Keeper himself, then I'll say I believe ya for now."

Donovan nodded. "Thank you for your trust." Even as he spoke the words, a sharp pain grew outward from his gut. The voice from his dreams called out from the nether: *Choices are hard, choices and choices, you know this is true. Rosaline lays beneath the dirt under the weight of your choices, doesn't she? Well?*

How many more to lay beneath the dirt?

Demon lover...

"Where is this place?" asked Tomson.

"Somewhere northwest from here. I'll scout ahead."

"Begging the pardon, lordship," said Earny, who looked instantly unsure if he should have opened his mouth at all, "but what do we plan to do once we're there?"

Donovan shot him a look of annoyance that made him recoil.

"I'd like to know this also," said Tomson, who was stroking his chin with his forefinger and thumb and furrowing his big brow.

"Truth told, I'm not sure yet," said Donovan.

"The last thing any of us needs is to stir up the Misties and get them warring on our town," said Tomson flatly.

"Whatever happens..." began Donovan, "I'll make sure the Dwellers are led away from here."

Never the good liar, were you?

(Eyes and mouths, fingers and toes. It's coming for you, Donovan Maltrese...)

Tomson nodded, only half-believing, judging by the look in his eyes. "You said before you weren't interested in helping us. Now you're bent on hunting Misties on our borders."

"My interests are still my own," said Donovan.

"Well, tell me what you need and I'll see what I can oblige."

"I need men," said Donovan. "Two or three to help. Good fighting men, if you know any, and not the like of Creel."

"The like of highwaymen are more your taste?" asked Tomson, glancing at Earny. "I don't know your face but I know your dress. You and your like frequented the Thresh just south of here, didn't ya?"

Earnald nodded. "We did, sir. Not tha finest way of livin' mind ya. If it means a thing, I never partook in tha action of it all, but standin' by is a hair short of that and I know it. All I care to do now though is repent and find reckoning, should the folk I come across see fit to humor it."

Tomson sized Earny up with a long hard stare. "You mean that, do ya?"

Earny nodded. "From my deepest pits."

A long moment of thought, then Tomson said, "Who in this forsaken place hasn't sinned or gone the dark road for a few nights' peace of mind and food in their belly? Only thing we can do short of stretching necks with rope is try an' better ourselves I suppose. I know men, Earnald, and I see a shine in your eye tells me you mean exactly what you say. I should have you hung or stoned for what you've done, but I won't. Don't make me sorry for it."

Earny bowed; his mop of hair swung down and back again with the motion. "I won't sir. Pray and blessit, I won't."

"You're lucky in your company, that's all I'll say."

"Not luck," said Donovan, surfacing from his thoughts. "Earny here is a more capable tracker than you'd believe."

Earny smiled, teeth snaggled and stained, and adjusted his eyepatch. "Thank ya, sir."

"What happened to the girl Jana?" asked Tomson. "I thought you meant to protect her, else I'd never have let you go with her on your arm."

Donovan sighed deep. He wondered what had become of her in these last weeks, left behind in the dark walls of Pal Myrrah at the Cleric's mercy. But what other course instead? To let her bear witness to what he was to do? To include her in it? The truth was he would never be able to face her gaze under the weight of the Cleric's charge. If he ever saw Jana Hunter again, it would be on their way to the Black. "She is safe enough for now."

"Safe's a broad word, friend," said Tomson, and he was right, Donovan knew. "If any harm's come to her by way of your leaving her alone…"

"I'd fall on my sword before you'd have to lift a finger," replied Donovan. Another lie. *You're getting better at this. You had plenty of chances to fall on it before, if you had an ounce of nerve.*

Tomson seemed to think things over, then shrugged. "I know a couple o' boys can keep the right end of a blade or axe pointed towards the enemy. One of them even fancies archery, makes bows and arrows. Can hit a thing or two with 'em, too, if you believe it. I can talk to 'em, see if I can convince they'll be safe near a Misty with a Swordsman watching their backs. Not sure what good they'll do you fighting the likes of that. Akin to stopping a tornado by passing wind into it, I'd warrant."

Donovan's frown deepened. *They won't be safe. They'll likely be the first to die. The first of hundreds.* "That would be useful," he said, more evenly than he thought possible.

Tomson rose and put his hands on his hips. "I'll fetch them for you, and try to quiet down the crowd while I'm at it. You stay here and wash up. I'll have Mary heat a bath for you. You boys look like you could use it." He took Donovan's hand, then Earny's. From the door, he turned and said, "Keeper bless us all, it's good to have you back, Swordsman."

And then he was gone, leaving Donovan to his thoughts.

Earny had taken Ruti's petrified body from his satchel and placed him on the table. Now he studied the small remains of his friend with his one good eye fogged over by deep thought. "Do you think Dragons find the Black same as we do?"

Donovan was not sure the ex-bandit had spoken until he saw him staring expectantly. For a fierce moment, a strong heave of anger swelled from the pit of the Swordsman's stomach and he considered cracking Earny's dullard smile open with a quick strike. The sensation was squelched as quickly as it had flared. *The Cold is still there. It's joining with you now. It may no longer need to engulf you; why bother if it is you?*

If Earny read the conflict in the Swordsman's eyes, his face did not reveal it. "I think all manner of creatures find the same death. It's part of what binds us together," said Donovan, though his mind was still elsewhere, trying to imagine his two hands doing what his mind could barely picture, and soon. The hard push back south to Pleasantry took longer than he had wished even with the horses, and the ever-present, ever-growing glare of the Cold was becoming hard to resist.

"Are you all right, Swordsman sir?" asked Earny. The earnest concern in his voice snapped Donovan back from his thoughts.

"As fine as you'd expect, everything considered," said Donovan. The Swordsman leaned back and adjusted Orin across his lap. "You should leave me soon, Earnald. My path ahead will not be a safe one. And it's not one I'd have you risk your life for. My aims are selfish. Selfish."

Earny's face became a portrait of sadness. "Are you commanding me to go, sir? And shy of gettin' Jana back and cured?"

Donovan shook his head. "I'll not give up on that. If all smiles on us, she and I will be cured together and then fate will take us where it pleases. But I think your part in our struggle is at an end these next days."

Earny sunk into his chair, his fingers absently stroking Ruti's remains. With a loud clearing of his throat, he straightened again and said, "Beggin' yer pardon though, lordship, but I would like to politely disagree with you. I've got somethin' I can offer to ya, and to Miss Jana, pray it. What exactly that is, well, we'll just have to wait and find out. But I can feel it in my guts. Last thing I'm gonna do is heave off leaving you with whatever business the Cleric's got ya buried in and not see my part to the end. Besides, I'm sicka folks tryin' to get ridda me." At the last, he smiled thinly.

Donovan wanted to argue but could not. "I'd tell you you're a good man again, but I wouldn't want it to go to your head."

"Oh don't worry, sir. My head can't hold all that much at once to begin with," said Earny, grinning now. The Swordsman could not help but smile back.

A sudden crumbling sound snapped the Swordsman from his brief reverie. He leapt away, frightening Mary, who had entered bearing a jug of stout. She screeched and shrank back as Orin rang free from its sheath, and Donovan stood there beneath the old beams of Tomson's house, ready for battle.

Earny paid the Swordsman no mind. His attention was fixed on the table. He leaned down until he was eye-level with the Ruti statue, lips drawn tight. "What in the name of it—"

Then the bright particolored rock that was once Ruti split asunder, cracking in one jagged fault from nose to tail. The plates of the body split into their own fissures, shapeless multi-sided chunks of *ai'che* that shifted and writhed and separated like air-cooled rock on a bed of lava.

Then a small black tongue, forked at the end, flitted through the snout of the rock and Earny started in surprise. "Keeper save us all…"

A blue-ringed eye appeared, the crust of the iridescent rock falling loose, revealing a small face. Leathery wings drew back and shook free their enclosure and spread as wide as they could, and now the Root Dragon, born a thousand years ago and alive this day still stood atop Tomson of Pleasantry's table and stretched his legs and then his back and swished his tail back and forth. He stared up at Earnald Avers as if nothing had happened at all.

"Ruti? Is it really you?" said Earny, his voice quivering.

Donovan watched as the Root Dragon climbed forward onto Earny's waiting palm, then to the collar of his tunic, then to his shoulder.

"Keeper bless this day and this day again! For the love in it. Ruti! How… how can this be?" Earny ran his shaking finger over the Root Dragon's back.

Donovan sheathed his sword. How could he not have seen it before?

"How is he back from the dead, master Swordsman sir?"

"*Aila koeth numoni tol,*" said Ruti in his small, tinny voice.

"He was injured badly, so he secreted his store of *ai'che* to heal. That's one part of the legend I'd not heard," said Donovan, who was filled with a sudden warmth he both treasured and rejected.

Earny had Ruti back in his cupped palms again. "Yer lucky I kept you on a whim and didn't bury you yet. Couldn't bring myself to part with yer stony eyes just quite. Oh, bless every single one of everything in the bloody fucking world. Ruti!"

Ruti regarded Earny with his strange distant-yet-present stare from the ex-bandit's outstretched hands, then scampered up his shoulder.

Now Donovan saw Mary, who was watching this all open-mouthed from the kitchen entryway. "What in creation is that?" she asked in a breathless whisper, her hand planted across her heart.

"This," said Earnald Avers with pride any father would identify at once, "is Ruti. And he's pleased to make yer acquaintance."

Ruti flapped towards Mary and hovered there, looking her in the eye. "*A'ni koe ta.*"

Mary of Pleasantry smiled and nodded to the miniature dragon flapping its wings before her.

Then she turned on her heel and fled the room as if afraid for her life.

14

Donovan watched through the window as Tomson stood at the last big flagstone outside his front door with his thumbs under his belt and his head cocked as if listening to the wind, waiting for a telling sound. If it came, he gave no sign of it.

Once Mary was calm again—and a second introduction made to Ruti the Root Dragon—she drew a bath, which Donovan accepted but Earny did not. The ex-bandit was on his knees in the common room flicking a pebble across the old wooden floor, which Ruti would pluck up and then alight with a soft *fwap* and return, forked tongue flicking, blue-ringed eyes shining. Donovan watched this for a moment with his odd crooked smile, then drew closed the curtain separating the bath area and eased his scarred and tired body into a tub of steaming water with a gasp and then a long sigh.

The tub itself was old, probably older than the house, made of some glass-like material Donovan knew no name for but had come across during his travels, more often in pieces than not. This one remained surprisingly whole save for a fist-sized hole or two broken from the rim. A drain near the bottom told him there was once an automatic system for the disposal of used water, which might have accounted for stretches of underground tunnels he and others had discovered here and there where things with long claws and fangs now lived and no exploration could be attempted.

As Donovan's thoughts wandered, he touched first one pale scar on his chest, then another and another still, then, at last, the black vine from the Cleric's curse which had spread and forked in these last weeks and now encompassed half of his torso like some mutated multi-headed worm. Every once in a while, when his attention wandered, he could feel it slink and sidle beneath his skin, and one time he *saw* it happen and his mouth ran dry. Beneath all of his thoughts, the Cold bided, crouched in the dark like a ghoul, claws ready to submerge into the soft tissue of his brain.

When he was dry he found his clothes missing and a new set folded neatly on a chair. In the next room, Mary was washing his clothes in a small gray basin. Annoyance touched off inside him. "What are you doing?"

"You've been long on the road and ya smell of it. You kin borrow those clothes from Tom till these are dry. And don't be lookin' at me that way, fine sir. If any needed a woman's touch high and far in this place, it's you, pray it." She looked him up and down. "A tad big on ya, but that's better than smellin' like a dog's ass. I kept your little knife-things aside. Figured you wouldn't want 'em rustin' up 'fore you got a chance to kill some more with 'em."

Donovan pursed his lips.

"Yer welcome," called Mary after him.

Donovan nodded to himself and tried not to think that sweet Mary's end would be coming soon, along with all the rest of them.

* * * *

By midday, his clothes still were not dry and he and Earny stood in the center of town. A wagon rolled by, its felloes black with tar and mud, its bed full of grain. The driver looked sidelong at them, his drawn face old and tallow. He was missing his left arm just above the elbow. A limp fleshy sack sealed by a half-healed scar flapped with every jostle of the cart. Donovan nodded at him, but the man only scowled and turned back to the road and whipped his horse harder.

Ruti had taken refuge inside Earny's pocket, and he poked his head out now with his feet propped forward and watched with interest as four men approached, two large of hand and broad of chest, the hard and weathered sort Donovan needed. The other two were thin and one of them even lanky. Dressed in ragged skins and ripped wool all of them, they looked like the rejects of some pathetic army long since annihilated.

Tomson nodded. "More than I expected."

"The more the better, I'm guessing," said Earny.

The two big men nodded to Donovan. "This is Brig and Corly," Tomson informed him.

"Pleased and blessed," said Brig, a smooth alto, and Donovan saw now his forehead bore a neat slit across it, like a permanent extra brow crease. His forearms were scrawled in wineink tattoos, and from his belt hung a row of long fangs tied with a black run of leather.

"Fine to meet ya, Swordsman," said Corly, who was a head taller than Brig and was missing half of his right ear, which appeared to have been removed by something not wholly sharp in a jagged line.

Behind him was a man familiar to Donovan. He stood before the Swordsman with his head down and his eyes pointed at Donovan's boots, which were his only clothes escaped from Mary's industriousness. "You're the one called Mullville aren't you?" said Donovan with a frown.

Mullville nodded and looked up at last and Donovan saw now a waif-like pain that weeks or maybe months ago he had seen from a distance, only then it had been zealous rage instead, stamped out in a hurry by one hard blow from Tomson's arm.

"Last you saw of him, he was being hauled off to the Hutch with his nose gushing," said Tomson.

Mullville teetered on his heels and shrugged. "After Tom here knocked a fit of sense into me, I regretted what I done. I fought before, way back whenever when Pleasantry had a mind to hold a militia. That fell apart quick as a scarecrow, but I've had brigands in my way once or twice. I'll stand true by ya."

Donovan looked at him hard as if he was a difficult puzzle. "I'll trust you now if Tomson vouches for you. I've seen a man's ability to change in the deep ways." He looked at Earny at the last and the highwayman adjusted his eyepatch nervously and stamped his feet. Ruti shifted beneath the fold of his pocket, but none of the other men saw.

The last man was Earny's size but a third lighter. He wore a bow cut from yew wood as long as he was, finely crafted by Donovan's measure. At full draw, it could no doubt run through a buck's neck from a hundred paces. But against a Dweller of the Mist, who could know?

"This here is Two-Shock," said Tomson.

"Greetings to ya," said the man with the bow.

"Two-Shock?" asked Earny.

"We call him that," said Brig with a grin. "Got hit by lightning twice in the same spot a year apart just about to the day, didn't ya, Two?"

Two nodded sheepishly. "Ya. Got me a scar bigger 'an a drab's baby chute."

"Mind your tongue for the life in it!" said Tomson, shaking his head.

Donovan was grinning. "You men are of fine stock. I can see it in your eyes, even if you don't believe it." He let his gaze linger on Mullville, who could not hold it. "Stand true, friends, and with thanks." He paced then, his fingers reaching around his waist on their own to hold loosely the tip of Orin's sheathed blade. In his mind, he saw each of these men, afraid now but holding fast, dead on the leafy floor with their guts exhumed and their lifeblood staining the trees about them.

(Not just these, but all of them. Every one...)

Donovan planted his feet and looked the men over. "I'll be going into the forest alone today. If what I've been told is true, I should be back before dusk. I ask you to wait for me and stay rested and fed. Tomorrow, if all goes well, we'll set forth with a plan and we, all of us, will be put to the test. I cannot tell you more now. Just that I value your faith and commitment."

"I'll be coming with you, too," said Tomson, folding his tree-trunk arms.

"I had guessed as much," said Donovan. He wanted to reach for the man's shoulder in a gesture of camaraderie, but stopped himself. Closeness would only make the inevitable even more difficult.

Is this worth it? What is your life valued if you lose your soul?

(Your convictions are empty, your principles made from dust.)

Silence!

His eyes refocused and he saw the men staring at him oddly and he wondered how long he had disappeared inward. He shook his head to clear it and scanned the distant hem of trees to the north.

"Beggin pardon, but are you looking to kill Misties, save us?" asked Two-Shock, his fingers interlaced and resting on the end of his bow now like a walking stick. The other newcomers nodded and grunted similar curiosity.

Donovan mulled over his response. Many a man had marched forth to war in this sunless world filled with hard resolution only to find revealed what they once called courage to be ignorance, and on first proof of folly whirled on their heels and were away before their puff of dust had settled. But then again, if his plan hoped to work, if he was to have any chance of felling a Dweller, he could not do it alone. Little more than pawns for his placement on the board these men were, meat puppet distractions at best, but necessary all the same. And meat puppets who ran were not useful. Better to feel them out now than discover his true allies the hard way.

"Yes," said Donovan. "I aim to rid the northwest woods of a Mist Dweller."

Gasps and white-eyed disbelief among all.

"How in the name of it do you kill somethin' like a Misty?" Two asked.

"When Tomson sent Dumprey to fetch us, he'd not said hair or thumb bout no Misties," said Corly, fingers wrapped around his belt till the knuckles turned white.

"I figured there were brigands about needin' a good boxin', or a flesh-mad bear at the worst, wager a thumb," said Brig.

Tomson waved at them with his hands open wide like a shaman blessing the newly married. "Peace, people. Donovan here thinks it can be done, but he's gonna need all of you I figure. Isn't that right, Swordsman?"

Donovan nodded. He had planned on three, but four was perfect. Just perfect. He watched the men with their shifty stares and fidgeting hands and read them clearly as ink on parchment. Not many fought for something as ethereal as an ideal anymore; if anyone knew this best, it was Donovan Maltrese. That these folk had put forward their fighting foot for the sake of the whole spoke of a particular breed the Swordsman had not expected to find here. And if there were these many, then why not more?

What would you do with more, Keeper save? Build a rabble army and storm Pal Myrrah?

(They'd crush apart on the claws of Master's Blood Demons like wheat on a grindstone.)

"Swordsman?" said Brig, his voice turned downward and raspy. When Donovan looked at him again he said, "I'm brave as the next man, maybe more so, dependin'. But stupid I'm not, least not come matters of my ass staying in a single piece. So I'd love to hear it tell how we're going to stick it to a Misty."

Two-Shock nodded eagerly. Tomson frowned and looked at Donovan as if he too hoped to divine this knowledge from the Swordsman's cold green eyes. Behind them, Earny folded his arms against a rising wind full of chill and looked at Donovan much the same.

"I'll do the killing. But I'll need help," Donovan told them at last.

"Can a Misty *be* killed? Tell us honest, or is this some fool mission you've cooked up with grease left over from yer pride?" asked Brig.

"You left us scratchin' our behinds before, an' I know Tom here asked the question. We've been lucky these years with the Misties keepin' clear of town, but anyone dumb enough to live on the outskirts been killt now, last of all your little friend's family. And you turned Tom down at the time. So why now you so keen on stickin' yer sword in somethin' as unnatural as one o' these things?"

"How'd you find out about Miss Hunter's family?" asked Earny.

Two-Shock answered. "Couple of us saw smoke risin' up from yonder and followed against the better know of it. Found the Hunter place in a pile of char and blood everywhere, tiny pieces, too. Which Hunter they came from I couldn't tell ya." He looked suddenly pale and sick.

Donovan heard this as though from a great distance, echoed forward in drips but reluctant to coalesce into words. "I said you'll have to trust me."

"Why should we, all bullycrag aside?" asked Brig. "What've you or yer folk ever done fer us?"

He immediately regretted his words.

Anger flared from Donovan's stomach into his skull and beat there like a drum. The man had asked the finest question of all, one that laid all in its truest light. The Swordsman stepped forward into Brig's space and the big man with the wineinked arms retreated a step in response. "Since beyond the memory of your eldest imagined forefather I and mine have kept more death and madness from your doors than you'll ever know." He began to pace so that he would not lash out. "You think times dark now? Have you crossed things unnatural that hunt you and feed on you and your neighbors without discrimination? Yes, I know this. Now think of what might be if the rest of it, men and things you could never conceive of, were let run through this land and every other land and put you and your children and your wives under the sword or the nail. What if nothing protected you at all anymore? Would this world still be bearable with fivefold the danger?"

The men had frozen where they stood. None offered an answer.

"These things bleed, they live, and they die. And I can kill them. That's all you need to know," said Donovan, barely above a whisper.

The men shared glances that said much without words.

"All right," said Brig. "I beg your pardon again, good sir. I'll trust ya. Keeper save us all if yer wrong."

"I'm not," said Donovan plainly. Somewhere, he thought, Jana Hunter might have just shivered with annoyance.

"I'll follow ya, Swordsman. What else am I gonna do wit' myself, come Misties calling but stand in the thick of it all?" said Mullville, his sad and droopy eyes glittering with something new.

Corly looked at his fellow townsmen like they were mad, then shrugged in a way that said he might share in that madness. "I'm in."

Donovan nodded. "I'll be back by dusk as said. Tomson, mayhap Mary could find enough stew to keep these boys' bellies warm and full until I return."

Tomson nodded with a smile. "I think she just might, Swordsman."

Donovan nodded, gestured to Earny that he should wait as well, then without closing marched towards the Shodan with something black eating him away from the inside, the men staring after him like abandoned children left at an orphanage. He could feel their gaze upon him, and somehow knew that each bore a look of longing in their eyes that would have stung him had he paused to look back.

15

Jana took her half-eaten meal and swept the leftovers into her pouch where it piled into a mess of pork and now-mushy vegetables. She had stowed five days' worth if she rationed right, provided they didn't spoil. She stared at that goopy pile in the old leather sack and imagined scooping finger-fulls by moonlight while wandering the dusty span of the Wastes, stretching out the hunger, keeping it just shy of overtaking her. Well and good, all that, but what of the Mother's Mouth? What if Mist still brewed thick there? And even if it did not, how would she cross the Gestalt? A firm handshake with the Dweller and an exchange of niceties to pay the way back?

Back to where?

She pushed those thoughts away. All that was worth bothering over now was this moment, right here. Dad and Grampy would often say that: now's the now. She used to ignore them. From as early as she was able to think in words, Jana Hunter had been a worrier, a planner, an obsessor, one that Donovan might have appreciated in her severity. How to get by in this world without marrying whatever foolish man was brave or stubborn enough to saunter by the Hunter Estate had once been her life's plot entire. Now her plot was even simpler: leave Pal Myrrah, armed if possible, and get as far away as as she could. Maybe then the dreams would stop.

They had begun soon after the Swordsman abandoned her, at first only on occasion, then more frequently. Now they arrived almost every night. She began to ache for the time in between, when sweet blackness would take her through the night into the gray wash of a new morning without interruption. Twice now she had forced herself to stay awake, to push her body to whatever its limits and beyond, but

391

each attempt found her first nodding, eyelids heavy, as though iron bars dangled from them, shoulders slumping forward slowly, slowly, until she found herself against the wall or across the bed and the impending dark swallowed her.

Then *he* would come.

This was her longest stretch yet, five days now without rest. Her legs felt as though they were made of straw, and all around her the world swam disembodied, dreamlike (but not nightmare-like, not like *those* nightmares, Keeper save her), though sometimes possessed of an alien clarity. She felt sleep tugging at her even now, and she slapped her face to chase it back. In another place keeping lucid would not have been so hard, but here, with four fine walls and a massive bed piled with boring books and nothing but circling madness to keep her company, it was nearly impossible.

It won't be long now. Just a few more days. You can do it.

But could she? She had told herself so during both prior attempts. Then there was the alternative, the searching fingers and wandering lips of *him*, skin cold like a corpse and enveloping her, hungry, so hungry, for her body, her sex, her soul, to mingle with the foulness growing inside her, to bathe in it. In Jana's dreams, she could feel her ropy scar respond to his touch, dancing just beneath the skin. Then he would plunge himself into her and the scar, too, would burrow deeper and stretch its forked legs and arms. Then she would wake, as sore and violated as she had felt that morning in the shed, the one that she had burned to the ground, yet another pile of charred remains littering this bleak and ruined world.

Jana drew up the string around her sack and placed it beneath the bed in the corner where the legs of the night table there would obscure it. Then she took the saved half of her water and poured it into the vase, which once had stored dead flowers but now was emptied and wiped clean as best as she could manage. How she might seal the vase once she was on the road, she had not quite figured out yet.

The oil lamp on the table flickered as she stood near it, and she stared into the writhing flame and lost herself for a moment. He had left her. They both had left her, but it was more the Swordsman that made her angry enough to burn.

She had seen his betrayal coming all along but willed herself to ignore it, and now here it was to greet her with a broad smile and a swift slap to the face, truth bedight with pain. Every moment of kinship shared, every look or argument dressed in goodwill, every harrowing moment survived—it was all a bucket of steaming shit. All of it. From the very beginning he had planned this, to take her along and study her, perhaps use her as a bargaining chip come time to deal with the Cleric. Maybe all that fuckery about giving her a pistol so she might shoot him in the head if the need arose was the truth—Keeper bless them, she'd do it now and gladly. But that was where truth ended with the Swordsman. She had never before let a man manipulate her so utterly, moving her this way and that like a pawn. At the time it had been hard to see the truth past the pile of dead family, she supposed, the thought curling into a hard lump in her throat. She wondered now if any of his story about Kolendhar and Rosaline and the rest of it was true, or if it was piled to the sky with lies like the rest of what he had told her.

She allowed her emotions to run unchecked then, loosed like a wild animal, the anger sharpening her, keeping her awake and keen. She turned her thoughts to Shadow, the man who had seduced her in every way the Cleric did not, who somehow had made Mean Mule Jana Hunter a doll to pose, to toy with, to use however he so wished. That he did not make good on his temptations, that she would never know the feel of his body pressed to hers, his delicate but strong hands in her hair, on her back, her hips, made her relieved but so very angry.

What doesn't make you angry anymore, girl? You're a regular firebrand, you are.

Shadow was the sort any girl worth her stones knew the measure of. Whether they had consummated their thoughts or not, he was gone now. Like Donovan, his ideals came before all else; surely before the silly village girl who had caught his eye. And yet nothing he did could compare to the pain the Swordsman had inflicted. If someone had asked her before if stuffy Donovan Maltrese and his penchant for Boon and condescension could ever affect her more deeply than a man like Shadow, she might have laughed or slapped them or both, but the Swordsman had hurt her in a way only a true friend could.

The Swordsman. A friend.

A silly village girl.

You are from somewhere in the Thresh, I gather. Maybe Eastfield, or Pleasantry.

In perhaps the slowest response in the history of responses, Jana suddenly wondered at Shadow's seemingly inane question while on horseback as they traversed the Wastes. What matter was it to him whether she hailed from Pleasantry or Eastfield or under the third rock from the left somewhere in the Shodan? At the time she had thought it a simple flirtation, or perhaps—Keeper clock her on her silly noggin—sincere interest despite her cautionary answer. Now, knowing his mind better, gauging him further, she recognized the subtle inflection behind his voice. Whatever interest Shadow, and by default his master the Cleric, might have in the people of Pleasantry, it could not be benign.

Something hulking and dark moved in the corner of her vision then, and she snapped her head around towards it. Only cold empty stone and the flick of torchlight met her gaze. Outside, a blue ridge of moonlight crept across the bars of her window. The moon might have been alive, the prying eye of a sky-bound creature peering in at her, but inside the room there was nothing. She knew this as any rational person would, yet her every fiber said that what she had glimpsed was real. If this was just the beginning, she could not bring herself to imagine what came next. What future was there in a life of madness? Who would be the one to put a bullet through *her* corrupt brain when the time came?

Now I understand, Donovan. Now I know where that haunted look came from. At least part of it.

Apathy overtook Jana. She had planned to make her escape in three or perhaps four days depending on what rations she could steal away, but those plans were overshadowed now by a growing vision in her mind. She saw herself alone in the Wastes, clambering slovenly over the scoria of the Ven, eyes glowing with madness, feasting on beast and man and woman and child alike; no years lay ahead spent farming or hunting or loving a man or enjoying what meager pleasures life afforded. Instead, she would amble about an endless nightmare world, a creature of darkness like the Blood Demons, until she was slain. If that was her fate, then what was there to escape to out there? Why run from *him* here when there was only that horror waiting on the outside?

For not the first time, she looked at the vase full of her future drinking water and pictured it smashed, wondering if the potsherds might be sharp enough to open her wrists and drain all of this misery onto the floor in a neat red pool.

Not your wrists. Your throat. That's what you'll cut if you're serious. Might as well commit to it.

She shook her head as if to forcibly remove the thoughts. What in the name of it was she thinking? If only her father could see her now. She could picture the shame in those big eyes, usually so full of mirth, and the image nearly made her cry again. What would Father Hunter do were he in her place? Likely cross his arms and say something akin to, *Guess I'll just hafta buckle down and take it day by shitty day, won't I?*

And so she would, too.

Again something slithered through her peripheral. She shrieked and fell away, and this time when she looked the shape did not disappear but hunkered low, a fifteen-foot serpent as thick as a man's leg. Its unblinking eyes, as large as limes, regarded her from across the room. Then its head divided into six fleshy segments, opening like a malformed hand as it blared a screech-howl into the bedchamber that made her skull vibrate. Black slobber oozed down its exposed pink, warty flesh and gathered on the floor.

Jana pressed to the wall and screamed.

The creature was halfway to her when the door burst open and in came Leto, the grizzled, scarred man entrusted with guarding her, supposedly anointed by Shadow. He looked from Jana to the floor where she stared, but she was only partially aware of him. She felt her heart ricochet inside her chest, felt her fingernails, long since worn down, digging at the cold floor for some reprieve it could not provide. "Snap from it, girl. All right, come on now," said Leto as he tromped towards her and took her by the shoulders. Jana felt herself lifted, felt her bare feet dangle, limp, against the sandstone. She had to force herself to focus on the old soldier. "That's it," he said to her, gruff even in his gentleness. She craned her neck to look behind him, but the thing was gone, whatever it was. She knew it was never there, that it was her mind and the Cleric's magic, but it did not matter. It was as if she was fractured, and when she was in that other Jana Hunter her rational mind was gone and the madness could take her without a struggle.

When her breathing slowed Leto asked, "What is the matter with you?"

She shook her head and could not make words.

When she was able to stand, he released her shoulders and stepped away. "Too much time cooped in a room like this…"

She could barely hear him. She nodded like a drunk.

"Have you eaten?"

"Yes," she said weakly.

"You look like a good fright. When's the last time you slept?" She shrugged and his frown deepened. He turned to the door and gathered her empty bowl and cup.

"Leto," she said, still barely a whisper.

He turned to her, looking perturbed until he saw how unsteady she still was, how sunken her eyes had become. "What is it?"

"I want to go outside," she said. "Even into the halls. Anything to get away from here."

"You know that's not gonna happen, girl. Best not to spend whatever time you've got left wishin' for the impossible."

"Shadow would have let me. I know he would."

"Lord Shadow isn't here," said Leto. He narrowed his eyes, which to Jana said he worried that he had just said too much.

"Then who would you ask permission from? Aren't you in charge?" she asked him, finding his eyes at last. "Please. Please let me out of here. Just for a few minutes. You can follow me around if you like. I just have to be free of this room. Please."

He stared at her for a time, then made to go. Halfway out he said without looking back: "I'll see what I can do, girl. No promises."

Then he left.

Jana sank back down the wall. She decided then and there that she would remain awake until Leto returned, perhaps then to be free of the endlessly closing walls of this room. Then her eyelids sagged closed, leaving her submerged in a churning dark where the only light was born of two violet eyes watching her, coming for her, enveloping her.

16

Donovan returned at dusk as told. Earny spotted him from the window and was reminded of his first glimpse of the Swordsman, the black-hatted shape free of detail, only now behind him lay a band of bluish haze against the blacker trees rather than fog.

Ruti scampered up Earny's sleeve and perched on his shoulder and hunkered low with his tongue flicking. "*Swoeldz-miehn.*"

Earny looked at his little friend with a grin. "Suh-wordz-man."

"*Sowallds munn.*"

Donovan dismounted his black stallion and strode to where Earny sat on a barrel outside Tomson's house. At first he did not speak. Earny was about to ask him how his scouting had gone when the Swordsman said, "How do you, Earny?"

For a moment Earny was taken aback by the Swordsman's casualness. "Doin' fine, seeing as how everything's a sight past insanity, pray it."

Donovan nodded as if this was profound and deserved diligence.

"What'dya find out there, Master sir? What you were lookin' for?"

Donovan made no sign that he heard the question, but when Earny opened his mouth to ask again he said, "I found the Dweller's holy place. They were not there, I do not think. But they'll be back. I found stores of food and other things."

"They store their food, sir?"

"There's much about these folk we don't realize, my friend. I'll not underestimate them come time to scuffle." He put one muddy boot up on the edge of the barrel, once filled with stout by its smell, and touched Ruti's chin with his finger. The Root Dragon hesitated, curling backwards. Earny held his breath, waiting for the small

397

dragon's eyes to turn black, for him to snap at Donovan's finger, to raise his wings in aggression and hiss. Instead, he seemed to come to some sort of decision, carefully considered from the look, before climbing the sleeve of Donovan's duster and licking the tip of his nose, much to the Swordsman's chagrin. Then he took flight and eased back onto Earny's shoulder.

"He's comin' round to ya, Master. Told ya he would."

Donovan ignored him. "Are the others inside?" he asked, gesturing to Tomson's house.

"Yessir. They bitch like a buncha housewives 'round the knitting circle, but they seem able enough. I'll keep a watch on them fer ya."

Donovan's frown dug deeper into his face. "Earny…" He trailed off.

"Yes, your sirship?"

When the Swordsman spoke again, his tone was changed and Earny would not hear its like for a long time. "You've been a good companion. Your heart is warm and your mind is keener than you think. It's been an honor traveling alongside you."

Earny felt shock and then deep sadness. "You'll not be dying here. I've got a good feel 'bout these things," he told the Swordsman.

"Whether I do or not is not what troubles me. I have to ask you for something. You'll not want to do it, but I beg that you do me this one honor."

Earny snapped upright, setting Ruti into the air. The Root Dragon looked at him with his big blue-ringed eyes and then settled back down to his shoulder. "Anything," said the former highwayman with conviction.

Donovan faced him squarely and took him by the shoulders. "I need you to leave Pleasantry tomorrow. When the men and I set off to hunt the Dweller, I need you as far away from this place as you can get and just as fast."

Earny's stomach dropped to his knees. "Wha… Why're ya askin' me this, sir? What've I done wrong? I can fix it. I swear." When Donovan made to answer, Earny couldn't let him out of fear. "Please, sir. Don't throw me by tha way now. I might never be a Swordsman the like of you, but I'm trying. You said you saw it. I'm just on the edge of it all now, I can feel it, bout to make somethin' good o' myself.

Please don't send me away." He considered getting on his knees, but remembered his first meeting with Donovan on the Drudge and held fast instead.

"Whatever you think, never worry that I was displeased with you. It has never been so. You've shown me a side of people I thought did not exist."

Earny felt his body slump over and adjusted his eyepatch. "What side's that, sir? The slow-witted and overbearing one?" He took a long deep breath and sat down again with his hands on his knees. "I'll wait for you to leave in the morn, then I'll go the other way."

"Do you swear you won't follow me? Swear it."

"I swear, sir. I do." He thought things over for a moment. "What about Miss Jana, sir? I promised her I'd come fer her."

"I won't leave her to rot at Pal Myrrah. Don't worry for that. If you hear word I've been killed by the Dweller, then you do as you will. But while I'm alive you'll not trouble yourself over Jana anymore. Do you hear me?"

"I hear ya well, Swordsman. All too well."

Donovan nodded and stood watching the moon, which hid behind a sheet of cloud and glowed faintly in the night. Earny stood beside him for a while and relished the moment and thought they'd never share another one like it again.

* * * *

Inside Tomson's place, the other men were as Earny told: bitchy, itchy, and full. Donovan heard raucous laughter from outside the door, but when Tomson opened it everyone hushed and stared. He waited for Earny to enter behind him and removed his hat and ran his fingers through his oily black hair. *Already time for another bath. Maybe I'll have Mary draw me one. Might as well find the Black smelling like flowers.*

"You find what you were lookin' fer, Swordsman?" asked Brig, who had an old fighting axe propped against the table beside him now, the handle wrapped in leather. The business end looked sharp enough.

"I did," said Donovan, taking a seat with a sigh. His muscles burned, every one of them. Worse was the Cold, which had grown

ten times in strength since he set out. He knew his hands were shaking
and he knew it was half battle blood from anticipation and half the
barely staved madness.

"You gonna share what in the meaty pit of it ya found?" asked
Corly, a short sword sheathed in a patchwork of leather beside him.
Likely made with the craftsmanship one would expect from a Pleasantry
citizen, but sharp enough to cut a thing or two before it broke.

"I'd hear it, too," said Two-Shock. "If there's somethin' shorta
cuttin' men in two yer handy at, it's makin' a man itch on the inside.
S'not fair in the littlest."

Mary entered with a jug of stout and offered it to the men, all of
whom agreed, even Donovan.

"You got a bottomless well o' that stuff out back, Mary?" asked Brig.

"Even if there was, you folk'd drink enough to make it
un-bottomless I warrant," she said with a grin.

"Outta here woman. And that's enough for these men. I won't
be treating headthrobs and the dizzies come tomorrow morning, not
with these types," said Tomson, arms folded, a glimmer in his eye that
made Donovan feel warm.

All of this gone in less than a day.

(You won't have to do it yourself. Praise the Keeper for that at least.)

"So out with it, Swordsman."

Donovan traced the rim of his mug and stared at the pitching
plane of his stout and thought hard. How much to tell them? What
to tell them? For if he lay full light of truth on himself, his plan was
far from complete. Much of it would be in reaction, dependent on the
actions of a wild creature born of the Maw who none on this earth
save perhaps the Cleric understood.

Why not tell them to enjoy their last night in this world?

*(It's a blessing. Who here loves their lot or land? Fingers and toes, fingers
and toes…)*

"I found what I was looking for," began Donovan. He immediately
regretted his vagueness. It would invite unwanted questioning. Master
had taught him always to reveal just enough information to move a
man where you wanted him to go without tempting him with asides.
But then, diplomacy was never Donovan's strong suit.

"Which was…?" asked Brig in the tone of a man approaching his last nerve.

"The Dweller holy place. It is real."

The men exchanged incredulous looks. "Buncha bullycrag I thought that to be," said Corly, elbows propped on his knees and his chin propped on his palms.

"Me, too, pray it. Are you sure that's what it is?"

Donovan nodded. "I've told Earny the tale of Tholpin who once tracked a Dweller back to its den and witnessed more of their culture than any man since. I thought there some truth to the story, but not until recently did I seek it out."

"How'd you find it so quick?" asked Earny, petting Ruti through his pocket. The Root Dragon had not yet made an appearance before anyone except Mary, who still seemed to think she had imagined the incident.

Donovan shot him a narrow look. "I was given information before we took leave to return to Pleasantry. A map, specifically. And what I found was just as promised." He reached into his satchel and unrolled a piece of parchment as long as his forearm onto the table. Across it were fine brush strokes and finer calligraphy. It was map of Pleasantry and the surrounding forest. Earny adjusted his eyepatch and leaned in for a better look. Donovan studied the map as well. There was the Hunter, and the Thresh, and the Drudge, all shown in accurate shape by his recount, and there was Pleasantry, designated by a small sketch of a hovel (again, accurate in spirit), and there, a few hefts to the northwest, was a small rectangle with an odd rune scrawled across its center. Donovan pointed at it with a long fingernail jammed with grit and looked at the faces of the other men and saw a dumbfounded expression on all of them except Tomson. *Of course. None of them can read anyhow. I could tell them this was a drawing of the Keeper's ass and they might just buy it.*

They all leaned closer anyway in a show of understanding.

Donovan retreated and let them look. He thought in that moment that he could not do this, that he would run outside now and take his own life as he had been too cowardly to do before, or maybe tell the men to wait here in the morning and seek out the Dweller by himself and end the line of his ancestors in one great foolish charge.

(It won't be you. It won't be you. Let them defend themselves if they can.)
You should because you can.

He stood and rested his palms flat on the table and looked them all in the eye. "It is about a day's march from here. There's a chance they will not have returned when we arrive, so we'll move to ambush them when they do."

"We're going to ambush a Misty," said Brig, incredulous. "I'm not sure what yer experience's been with this sorta thing, but Misties don't get ambushed by nobody. You don't hear 'em or see 'em or smell 'em, then you see Mist, then yer dead, and ya still never heard them."

The men nodded with agreement and shared looks.

Donovan frowned and shared their nod. "I know that has been the way of it, but we have surprise and foreknowledge on our side. The Dwellers think themselves the top of the order of things. The last thing they'd expect is for us to seek them out, and certainly not in their place of worship."

"What exactly does a Misty worship, Keeper save?" asked Mullville, who had been sitting against the wall silently looking ready to weep until now.

"I still can't wrap my noggin round notion of a Misty worshipping anything," said Two-Shock.

"How do you figure what somethin' like that is anyhow? They could worship the Maw or they could worship runny eggs for all we know," said Corly.

"Maybe they worship stout. In that case, Mary'll be the life in them!" said Brig with a hefty chuckle which they all shared except the Swordsman, who pretended not to hear.

"So tell me," said Tomson, still studying the map. "What's your plan?"

"We'll circle round and approach from the west. There's a ridge there overlooking the site." He pointed at the map. "We'll see if they're somewhere we can spot them. Even if they're away, we'll see the Mist well beforehand."

"What if they spot us first on the way over?" said Tomson.

"You'll see when we arrive. There are remains there, scattered throughout. I scouted the surrounding land and saw sign of their passing, and it radiates east and north…" he pointed at the map again. "In the direction the construction of their site points to. I can't claim to understand it, but by swinging round and coming from the west, I don't think we'll see them before we arrive."

"And what if you're wrong?" asked Corly, whose fingers were shaking visibly.

Donovan looked him in the eye and shrugged. "Then we'll have to make it up as we go." He flipped the map over, and on the back was a rough charcoal sketch he had done himself. "This is the layout of the site. We'll post lookouts here and here." He pointed to the ridge just west of the site, and an arroyo just south. "The arroyo has a shelf near the top with thick scrub that will hide two men well enough."

"Won't hide the smell of a man, though," said Mullville.

"That's where our prayers and surprise will play, Keeper save us," said the Swordsman. The word *prayer* felt odd and foreign on his tongue.

He regarded his map and felt Orin pressing against his back, taking comfort in the sensation. "I'll be here," he said and pointed to a patch to the east. "If anyone sees it coming first, it should be me. When the Dweller arrives it should, if all told be true, begin to pray. And that is when we'll strike." He looked across the room. "Two-Shock, you'll lay down fire from here, on the ridge, and draw the thing's attention. As you do, Brig and Tomson will attack from its rear, aiming for the release on its sword. I've studied its mechanism as closely as I could given the circumstances. There is a catch that gives when the blade is twisted, but it is already strained by the weight of the sword, and it's reinforced only in one direction. Strike it with your axe or your sword a time or two and you could bend it."

"You think a latch of some kind'll stop a Misty from gettin' his sword free once he gets the urge to use it?" said Brig with a deep frown.

"For long enough. With his attention on you and your retreat, I will push in from the rear and cut its throat. If all goes well, it all should be done in minutes."

"Things tend not to go well when it comes to bloodshed," said Tomson grimly.

Donovan nodded at him and knew that it was so.

"What's gonna stop this thing from grabbin' one of us by the ankles and rippin' us in two, pray it true?" asked Corly, who looked about one second away from fleeing out the door and never looking back.

"My sword hilt deep in the back of its head, more than likely," said the Swordsman without irony. "I promise you it will be over more quickly than you expect. I'll not miss my stroke."

The men all leaned back with looks of deep thought and deeper consternation. Earny was the only one not engaged; he stared out the window at the fog-shrouded night with a sad, almost wistful look. He glanced at Donovan and the Swordsman felt a deep pang. How was it that he could move forward with this plan? How could a deep part of him cry out that it was wrong, yet something deeper could still drive him forward like a string puppet, manipulated by invisible hands towards this dark end as if he possessed no will to reject it?

Suddenly Brig nodded to himself. "I think it could work."

"You do?" asked Corly, deadpan.

"It's not exactly the most devious plan. Is this the best you could come up with?" asked Two-Shock.

"Don't mix devious with over-thought," said Tomson, to which Donovan agreed. Still, it gave the Swordsman pause; was this plan well enough to gain him what he needed? What of the other element, the piece he'd not yet shared with the others, the one that they'd learn only when it was too late?

You could just lead them away. Tell them to up and leave Pleasantry and never return.

(The Cleric would know. He can see you now. He watches your every move and knows your mind.)

Maybe he doesn't.

But he did. Donovan could *feel* him now. He knew now the *itch*, the feeling that had dragged him from distant deserts through marshes and forests and across the Gestalt, was not him sensing the Cleric, but the Cleric sensing *him*. The thought chilled him to the marrow. No, no trickery would work here. But why was this his charge? What could the death of these people gain him?

What does it matter? The Cold will have you in weeks.

(Do you think he'll cure you? I'm coming for you now.)
No!

Would the Cleric cure him? Or Jana for that matter? He thought he might. If any knew Donovan to be an asset with his mind intact, it was Master. But the Cleric was no longer Morlin Sayre, no longer the man who had brought the Order to its full glory. He was a man who had walked where none should and seen things the Keeper kept from mortal eyes for a reason. How could anyone trust his word?

Because you have no choice. Because the truth is you value your life and yourself more than anything, more than these inbred thieves and robbers who seek to help themselves and no one else. Why are they allowed to follow their greedy hearts to their own gain and not you?

This he did not know the answer to. All he could think of now was the look of the folk on his return, already turned against him, already renouncing their good will, already set to stone him to death given half the chance, not to mention loot his sword so it might hang on a wall somewhere or be lost down the side of a mountain on a drunken evening.

"Donovan?" asked Tomson. The burly mayor looked concerned. "You all right?"

Earny was watching him nervously.

He knows. He'll be glad to leave tomorrow, Earnald Avers will.

"I'll be well when this is over. Do we see eye to eye?"

Tomson looked grave, but nodded. "I—we—are placing our trust in your hands, Swordsman. Our lives and the lives of our families. I know you've said it before, but I'd have you say it again. Can we do this?"

Everyone stared at him, in each of their eyes the unbridled look of dependence and pitiful hope that children outgrew as they became men save in moments most dire, when matters hung by too few threads. Donovan looked at Tomson, and for the first time in his life lied smoothly. "Yes we can do this, and we'll be drinking together and talking of it in the end. Mark me here and now."

That seemed good enough for Tomson, who raised his mug and offered toast, which the other men partook in hastily, anxious for more drink. "To time without Misties, and mayhap a few months of peace till Blood Demons or worse turn up to shit on us again and ruin it all."

"I'll drink to that!"

"Pray it all true and kick us while we're down."

"Keeper save us, we're fucked but I'll drink."

Donovan drank with them, Mary's fine stout burning into his chest. Tonight he would bathe and he would think and maybe even pray. In the end, it would make no difference. He was a lone man holding back a cracking dam with only his fading will. This would be his last great stand against it, his one final push to hold the Cold at bay, for the next time it swept over his mind like a cloud of locusts, the man he was, who he sought to save, Donovan Maltrese of the line of Maltrese and head of a destroyed Order, would be lost.

He set down his mug without a word and stepped outside and did not see the men again until morning.

16

When Earny said his goodbyes to the Swordsman they were short and awkward and felt inadequate. They stood behind Tomson's house amidst the stubble of yellow grass and the bunches of catclaw and shared a nod and a parting wish of luck, but Earny could find no words to describe the opposing tides of his feelings and he thought Donovan had no means to hear them now anyway. During the conversation, the Swordsman's hands were shaking hard, and at one point he folded his arms to hide it. Earny had become used to watching for these signs, and they troubled him more now that he would no longer be at Donovan's side. Once, as the Swordsman stared out towards the forest where he would soon forge ahead with the other men on horseback, Earny thought he saw the faintest gleam deep in the emerald-ringed recesses of his eyes, a hint of that bloody, unnatural light that preceded the coming of the other Donovan. But then it was gone and probably imagined. Yes, that was all it was. Imagination was a powerful thing, and this old Earny had too much of it to begin with.

Ruti emerged from Earny's pocket, where he spent most of his time, while a pale semblance of daylight still shone. He hovered before Donovan's face, his eyes blinking fast, his small feet dangling in the cold morning air.

"*Suhwoord mun.*"

Donovan bowed to his small companion. "*Poen dai ouy thayimuoh.*"

"*Fey lah.*"

On the way through Tomson's house, they came across Mary, eyes puffy and red from a night of weeping, taking Tomson into her arms and crushing him against her large bosom, whispering words

407

that Earny could not hear but knew the like of too well. How many men in the history of this world had heard such words from the love of their life? And how many had never heard that voice again afterwards? Earny wondered if the cold and indiscriminate nature of the world made any such moment less precious in the Keeper's eyes. He'd like to think it did not.

Outside, their foursome waited on horseback, all with dark and solemn gazes and tight, drawn faces. Brig was first, the swirling tattoos showing on his bare forearms seeming to twist like snakes as he leaned back and gripped hard the cantle with an odd, savage light in his eyes. Mullville now had a bow of his own, the twin of Two-Shock's. The other men were similarly armed, and as Earny looked at them head to toe he knew none of them, not even Tomson, who now bore a thick-bladed knife as long as a man's forearm, would do a lick of good fighting a Misty. This battle, or slaughter more likely, was Donovan's to see to the end or else no one would. The question was, could even a Swordsman stand a chance against those hellish beasts? Earny knew there was pride in him, the deep kind born from a long line of expectation. But pride was only good for tripping a man on the way to his downfall as far as Earnald Avers was concerned.

There were others watching the party gather and depart now. The folk of Pleasantry, most days content to scrape a living off half-wilting crops and sick farm animals and the occasional errant deer, now were drawn out of their hovels by curiosity and not just a little hate. *Why hatred? What better news to a man on this plot than the end of a Dweller of the Mist? Overshadowed by the curse no doubt.* Even if they knew not that the Swordsman bore a curse that was twin to Jana's, they knew he had broken bread with the last of the Hunters, and that was enough to brand him an outcast.

"That can't be it…"

"Whaddya hear tell of this?"

"Where's Tomson headed? Who's gonna settle things come the Brandersons muckin' with my stock?"

"They're out to hunt a Misty."

"No one can hunt a Misty, not even a Swordsman."

Hunt a Misty? Anyone could do that, even a dog. Kill a Misty, that's the point o' contention.

But while the folk of Pleasantry before seemed ready to stick a knife or pitchfork into Donovan and Earny upon their arrival, now they had gone strangely docile. Men with faces black from the earth, hands nicked and filthy from chasing swine through a sty, now stood up on fence palings, eyes bright like children at play, earnest hope in their expressions. A woman with one foot missing hobbled out from her front door, a long oak stob jammed under her shoulder to support her weight. She looked at Donovan and he looked at her, and then he turned away and mounted his black stallion from Pal Myrrah and it was as though he had never seen her.

Donovan wheeled his horse northwest then and it reared as it turned, and for a moment the Swordsman looked like some black creature birthed from the dark, half man and half horse, silhouetted against a brief wink of autumn sunlight that held no warmth. A shiver dug its way through Earny's body. Even now he could see something was different in the Swordsman's eyes. They had always been sad before, the sort of sad Earny knew as well as anyone, but now those eyes filled with some other blackness, something akin to how Raef's company looked when they were bracing for murder or worse. Whatever that look came from, Earny prayed the Keeper that the Swordsman would find his way through it.

As if hearing his thoughts, Donovan's gaze snapped towards him. The Swordsman gave him one last curt nod, a look of longing in his eyes no worldly medicine could salve, and then he whipped his horse and drove it forward and did not look back. The other men followed, their unshod hooves blinking muddily, the folk of Pleasantry one and all staring at them going by in single file. They marched their horses onto the Drudge and through the north entrance to Pleasantry, and then hooked hard northwest and clopped into the thick of the trees. Soon they were gone, with only the scored mud behind to say they had existed at all.

Earny looked at the dispersing townspeople, already slipping back into routine now that the spectacle had ended. He saw the man called Grampy sitting on his porch, a look somewhere between apprehension and quiet acceptance scrawled on his face that only the aged could manage.

Afterwards, Earny stood in the center of town near the bell tower. He stared at the old and rusted thing there and the man atop it, who seemed to be asleep now, and lost himself in thought. He had no depth perception anymore; it had stayed for a month or two after the loss of his eye, but eventually it had faded like a distant memory, leaving only rudimentary estimation in its wake. He guessed the tower to be thirty feet tall, but who could say and what did it matter? To his rear was an old underground shelter with heavy iron doors that latched from the inside. It looked like it hadn't been used in sometime, if ever, but for four parallel scratches which could have come from a wolf or bear.

And it was then that Earny faced the truth in his heart: he could not bring himself to leave.

You promised. Your word is strong as oak, isn't it?

Ruti poked his head out from his pocket and stared up at him and Earny looked back, overtaken by his thoughts. He had promised, yes, but his promise hadn't mentioned a timeline had it? The day of was implied, yes, but the meat of the promise was to leave after the Swordsman. That sounded good and rational to him. Besides, wasn't the point of this to keep Earny away from the business of the Dweller? He'd be well enough away right here. Pray it and Keeper save every cursed one of them.

He made his way back to Tomson's house, and when he knocked on the door Mary opened it and was still weeping. Unsure what to do or say, he took her into his arms and hugged her hard and felt Ruti squirm as she crushed into him. She seemed surprised at first, but after a moment she hugged him back and never minded the tiny thousand-year-old creature between them.

17

Shadow watched Donovan leave with his wretched war party from the plateau on the lee of the mountain, which jutted forth from the forest like a massive tongue thrust outward in an eternal gesture of insult. At the foot of the escarpment below lay Pleasantry, the center of the Cleric's thoughts, the nexus of all of fate's impenetrable threads. Those threads had led them here, to this point, so close to the new world promised them all that he could taste it.

Pleasantry. Master's small obsession.

It was here their bane was seeded, as told by seers and Master alike. And it was here where the first of their last steps would begin, right in that seamy mudflat which would run red before the week was out. It was Donovan's right to do this killing, yet Shadow wondered if he truly would see it through. The Cleric knew Donovan's mind and as his every step so long as the Swordsman took breath, so Shadow dared not challenge the course of that plot. Not until the right moment at least, where new mettle and old might be tested to show Master where the strength here truly lay; certainly not with Donovan Maltrese, augmented by the will of the Maw or not.

The bricks from which this new world would be built could not be weak, *must* not if the tower they dreamed of would stand the test of time. And by ensuring this was so, Shadow would entrench himself in unwritten history until the end of time, the only purpose in this forsaken land to which he would gladly give himself and his life. Master had already told him no; it would be a single clean stroke of Shadow's blade that would change his mind.

Things would be just right soon enough and, as always, the great pleasure would be his.

As he turned back to his horse and mounted, he thought briefly of Jana Hunter. For the barest of moments, a possible future flashed behind his eyes, nights of peace free from war that would find them together, tangled in a sweaty mass beneath the stars, their hearts pounding post-coitus, whatever hope that could be salvaged from this barbaric world spread before them in all its grandeur, theirs for the taking. Then the vision was gone as fast as it had come, cut clean by the same discipline which had allowed Shadow to taint his blood with *alamast*, the same rigidity of ideal.

From horseback he motioned for two of his men, cloaked in black and waiting near the forest, and they fell in behind him. Together they too swept northwest, following the Swordsman, leaving the rest of their company in their wake.

18

Donovan and his companions rode hard through the forest until the undergrowth grew too thick, forcing them to let their horses pick their path. At one point the way swept steeply upwards, all of them leaning forward in their saddles while the horses shambled up through tufts of buckbrush leading to a plateau rife with rimrock. They maneuvered back down from there along a path covered in treacherous gravel that tapped the hardpan below in warning but caused no accident.

The Swordsman looked back over his shoulder at the men who trailed him and wondered, as he did sometimes, at the constellation of events, random or ordained, that had led them to this exact moment in this exact place, to the exact end Orin or the Dwellers would beget. Would their forefathers have worked as hard, loved as fiercely, believed as passionately if they knew the futility of their combined lives? Donovan wondered if his progenitors would have found peace with his present course, even if they disagreed with it. He knew the answer to this already, and he shunned it before the accompanying pain could arrive.

They crested another steep hill as midday drew near. All around them the scrawny elongate pines remained the only green showing, them only some, the rest bare and naked and half-stripped of bark so that there was little sign they lived. In the mouth of a small valley, they stopped and ate a cold meal while the men looked at the featureless sky and spoke little. Donovan ate apart from them, seated on an overturned rock that had been here since the old folk ruled the earth and likely longer than that, maybe when nothing ruled the earth at all. In this light what he planned to do seemed palatable, the way a shaman's medicine could be swallowed despite its sickly taste.

"You think we'll come on it 'fore nightfall?" asked Tomson.

Donovan nodded and scooped stew into his mouth and did not look at his companion.

(The easy out is sometimes worst but never always. Never, ever always. Remember this.)

The madman was right. He was right, whoever he was.

He imagined this world with Rosaline still in it, his love, his all, alive if only he had made a different choice. He wondered what his future now held that would not have been had he charged the Cleric with Orin held high back at Pal Myrrah, if he had possessed the stuff within him to reject out of hand the task he now undertook. That he hadn't rejected it said the man Donovan, who once had headed the Order beneath the High Lord at Kolendhar, truly was dead.

The heart of the Dweller King. Bring it to me.

They set out again soon after. As the horses plodded and picked their way, Corly spoke up from further down the line. "I heard tell o' a village set out to kill a Misty way back."

"Where in the fuckovit did you hear that?" asked Brig, wearing the same scowl since he finished his lunch.

"Aways back. Recall that wagoner came through from Raistlin? The one with the feathers stickin' from his hair?"

"I do," said Mullville in his dry droning monotone.

"I don't," said Two-Shock.

"Anyhows, he came through, told some of us the story. So this isn't a first, guess is my point."

"Well what happened to 'em?" asked Brig, and all of the men save Donovan turned to look at Corly, who shrugged.

"Misty killed near twenty of 'em, never got a scratch on it," he said dismissively.

A dark silence fell over them.

"Wish you'd keep your fool mouth shut, Corly," said Mullville after a while.

"Quiet now," said Tomson. "Folk from Raistlin didn't have a Swordsman at their head, did they?"

Corly agreed that they likely did not.

They did not speak again until they happened upon the ruins of something huge.

From a distance, Donovan thought it was stone, but as they drew closer they saw that it was metal, rusted and blackened by centuries. Most of what remained appeared to be a skeleton, tubular and ribbed, but here and there flat sheets of metal lay pinned by bolts, most twisted and misshapen and caked in orange rust. To one side, a structure jutted straight out like a great fin, which also was rusted and destroyed by the ages, leaving only an outline of whatever it once had been. On the other side was a hole the same width as the fin, no doubt broken off by time or weather or something unimaginable. Hardy vines curtained much of it, dangling and threading the metal, giving it the look of something belonging to the forest more than the world of men.

"What in the name of the bleeding earth is that?" asked Two-Shock.

"Somethin' from 'fore the Shift, I warrant," said Brig.

Corly leaned forward as they all paused to take a look. "A carriage o' sorts, ya think?"

Donovan, who had seen this before and another as a boy shook his head. "It's some sort of flying machine, left from the old folk."

"*Flying* machine?" asked Corly.

Donovan nodded. "We've found things like this on pilgrimages. There's a book that somehow survived from before the Shift, or there used to be, back at Kolendhar. Inside were drawings of things such as this."

"You gonna tell me how somethin' that big built o' metal's gonna fly? A saltbeak can barely stay up on a tired day."

Donovan shrugged. This conversation already felt long ago and distant, a soft echo lost in the storm of his mind. "I didn't say we built them, I said we've found them on pilgrimages."

Tomson stroked his chin. "What a life was like back then, I can't begin to fathom," he said, then looked at the Swordsman. "You think there's a chance of things ever being the like again?"

Donovan shook his head. "Who can say. But would we want them to be? Whatever virtues they had, all that's left is ruins and a world full of death."

"If I had a machine flyin' me all over creation, last thing I'd do is waste time squabblin' with a buncha fools on the road," said Corly.

Donovan dug his heels into his stallion and pressed on. "If I know the nature of man, they spent just as much time squabbling no matter how many flying machines and anything else they had at their disposal."

They moved on, Corly and Two-Shock staring long over their shoulders at the ancient wreckage until it was swallowed again by the forest.

When they were farther along the road Brig asked. "You gonna tell us how you ever managed to find this forsaken thing in all this wood?"

"What about the man you came looking for when first we met. Was this knowledge having to do with him?" asked Tomson, speaking as much to himself as to Donovan.

"I heard and then I looked," said the Swordsman, and he left it at that.

Corly laughed. "Hell, I've been lookin' for a six-foot blonde with a mind for usin' her mouth, but that doesn't mean I'm gonna find it."

"You just aren't lookin' in the right place," said Two-Shock.

"Not like there's a lick of choice in Pleasantry after the Blood Demons finished work with the outer farms. Not since Jana up and left," said Brig, his tone betraying regret.

"Who'd want a piece like that, all fucked up with scars and carrying the Reaper in her anyhow," said Two-Shock.

Donovan did not turn, but his tone carried crisp and easy. "Never speak ill about Jana Hunter again, or we'll have words and they will be short."

If most men had spoken such to them, Donovan thought they'd start a brawl or worse, but they had accepted him as leader now, more for the living symbol he supposedly provided than for his qualities as a man, and they quieted down and did not speak again until the forest parted, revealing a structure hidden within its bowels that was ancient and alien, tucked away where no men had likely trod before.

At last they had arrived at the lair of the Dwellers.

They paused to regard it, all of them speechless.

Then, after gathering their resolve, they pressed forward, following their grim leader towards their fate under the dim glow of the fading day.

19

For the second day straight Leto appeared at Jana's door looking ruffled and downtrodden, and with one scarred hand he gestured that she could exit her bedchamber and walk the halls of the east wing for the better part of an hour. Jana did not know who the milky-eyed soldier had spoken to of this (she assumed he had informed *someone*, else she might be speared by an over-zealous guard while she wandered), but as she stepped out of that nightmarish room and breathed deep the bittersweet scent of torchsmoke hanging in the hall, the word *grateful* was at best a pale avatar of her feelings. Hidden now was the keyring Earny had given her, and as she turned to face Leto she heard the faintest *clink* of the keys shifting, though if the burly fighting man noticed the sound he gave no sign. *With all that armor on him, he's probably used to ignoring that sort of noise.* She prayed the Keeper that was true.

Yesterday he had kept her within sight for most of the hour, waiting at intersections and watching her stroll the long stone passages like an enraptured child. This had proved tiresome to him already it seemed, for this time Leto only nodded to her and then retreated the way he had come, leaving her to her own devices. "I'll be back by the hour to check on ya, so you'd best be in your room by then else you won't get the privilege anymore, ya hear?" he told her. Jana nodded and smiled her best smile at the old soldier. He didn't smile back, but the look in his eyes said her charms had worked. Once he was out of sight she hurried away down the hall, trying to stay silent.

As she left her bedchamber behind, the last of the nightmares returned to the front of her memory. More vivid than before, she only recognized them as nightmares now because afterwards the Cleric's claw marks, so vividly seen and felt as he ravaged her body, were nowhere to be found; only the growing scar. Jana never looked at it anymore, at least not directly. Instead, she'd focus on her stomach or her right breast which was yet untouched and watch the dark infestation from the corner of her eye. Never a direct look, however; she had decided she wouldn't give it—or *him*—the satisfaction.

As for her fate, she had made up her mind about that as well: she would escape Pal Myrrah, and hopefully Donovan and Earny would find her and together they'd be cured. If not, with her last scratches of sanity, she would take her own life.

She moved near-silently, her bare feet patting the old stone floor, the tapestries and doors she passed slathered in that awful green torchlight. Already, after one sojourn, she knew her way around this area, and now with Leto gone off she was anxious to explore further.

Jana turned a corner and discovered two men in armor, both with high plumage jutting from their helms, and felt a rush of fear that she had been found out. But the men merely glanced at her and nodded and one of them said, "My lady." Noticing her hesitation, he added, "Be glad Leto's got an eye for young girls in distress, him being a father and all." And then, with that useful bit of information, they were gone, the quiet *chink* of their armor and rough sound of their leather bootfalls echoing.

Jana passed door after door, pausing to study each, moving on quickly, keeping a mental finger on the pulse of time, a rush of expectancy pounding in her veins. Yesterday, while walking alongside Leto, she had seen something, men entering a room while each bearing a basketful of arms and contraband with the look of things confiscated, and then saw them exit empty-handed. She scanned the area for it now, the room with the crest above it, with the oriole.

She spotted it from an intersection and stole forward, hunkering low, and sidled into the alcove as she produced the keyring. Three dozen keys jangled from it, and she measured the keyhole with her eyes. Then, one by one, she began to try the lock.

As she did, her mind wandered to Donovan. She wondered if she was at all in his thoughts—most likely not, she decided. And poor Earny. A long haul alone with Donovan as company was not a fate she'd wish on her bitterest enemy, let alone sweet and kind Earnald Avers of the Thresh. Without Ruti to distract him, she feared the full brunt of Donovan's considerable personality would lay hard against him, and those were not healthy terms for anyone, Keeper save them.

Behind all of that, always at the back of her mind, lay the Cleric. Whenever his thin scarecrow face appeared in her head, she practiced aiming her six-gun right between his violet eyes and pulling the trigger and watching his brains spew from the back of his ruined skull. As she pushed yet another key into the keyhole, her free hand crept unconsciously to her chest where still she felt the sting of his clawing, a sensation leftover from the nightmares. A shiver grew in her.

Approaching footsteps and voices echoed presently, and she pulled a key free from the door with a *cling* and cursed herself and all the world as she jammed the ring back into its hiding spot. The sound continued as she peered into the hall. No one was visible there. She returned to moseying to and fro along the corridor, doing her best to look a dazed mess. At length, another rank of soldiers came by with the air of men anxious to get to where they were going. They marched by, serried and carrying short lances propped on their shoulders, and barely spared Jana a glance as they disappeared around a corner.

When she could barely hear their footsteps, she returned to the door. *If I was half the daughter of my father I should be, I could pick this lock and be done with it in a breath.* Taking things apart and reassembling them had been Dad's strong suit. In a way he was akin to Mum that way, only with her it was recipes, and Stink had been primed to take up that mantle from his father. Jana recalled arriving home to a dissembled rocking chair, their Mum's pride, and Stink had pieced it together again before their parents returned home from market. The world had seemed just right then, like it would be that way forever.

She was picturing her father's face when one of the keys—the thirty-first, if her count was right—slipped flush and the lock clicked easily open. She grinned triumphantly and slipped inside.

The room was plain, with sandstone walls and floor, a high oriole window, and a dusty ghostwood table. A mess of bowls and plates, empty but for bones and slivers of steak fat and rice grains, said that it was used for a meal not long ago. More of the eerie and sickening light from the magical torches was present here, these not made of wood but old cressets beset by rust. The flames within flared high, never requiring refueling.

In the rear of the room lay a large chest, its lid crafted with fine filigree, the wood lacquered and shining. She knelt beside it and found it unlocked. And then, why not? What madman would wander all this way through the Wastes and worse and storm this fortress just to loot whatever lay within this chest?

How about a mad woman, pray it true?

Within the chest was a store of items, dross mostly: satchels, vases, knives (rusted and useless), trinkets (some her father would have loved), and then a multitude of tools, a tack hammer, gauntlets. Near the bottom she found what she sought: her six-gun, the chamber still loaded. She had expected it to be stolen by now, to be worn like a trophy on the belt of one pompous soldier or another. But then, it had been Shadow himself who confiscated this, and her guess was that he would hold nothing but disdain for such a weapon.

She dug deeper, past a book and fine jewelry, and there at the bottom of the trunk was her father's dirk. A feeling of warmth grew, so sudden the small hairs of her arms stood at attention, and her eyes moistened even if they wouldn't manage tears. She plucked the blade up, holding it aloft like an offering to a strange god of trifle, and then tucked it into the waist of her pants.

The halls were empty for the return trip. In her room, she hid the six-gun and the bullets and the dirk beneath the mattress and tucked and arranged it until it seemed undisturbed, and when Leto returned to check on her she was already laying across the bed with a book open. After a long quiet he said, "Everything to your satisfaction, girl?"

She nodded without looking at him.

A gray eyebrow cocked. "Good. Well. You're looking healthier already." He made to leave, then stopped with a look of deep consideration. Without looking up he said, "We can try this again, long as you mind your behavior. Else I'll be strung up right next to you."

She smiled her finest smile again, the one once reserved for calling men visiting the Hunter Estate with swelling egos.

"I'll send someone up with dinner," he told her, and then closed the door behind him.

Once he was gone, Jana closed her book and stared at the cover. Additional food stores and a well-explored route were all that remained before she attempted her escape. These she would spend the next few days readying, and then it would be time. But the truth was, beneath the obsessive planning, she was afraid. Chances were she'd have a half dozen spears in her or an arrow in the back or a host of Blood Demons tearing her apart before she took one free breath. Or better still, the Cleric would appear from the darkness and sink his claws into her and drag her screaming to the Maw.

Stand true, girl. It's either try or sit here waiting to go mad.

It was settled then.

Any day now she would leave Pal Myrrah, and whatever lay beyond would be up to fate, the Keeper, her six-gun, and Donovan Maltrese.

20

The Day of the Dwellers.

That would be the name whispered in the villages and the highlands, in firelit grottos and hovels built of mudclay and stob.

From the few still with breath to whisper of it, word of these hours would grow, the stuff of self-deputation, instilling the despairing and the irresolute with a newfound passion to walk the dreary world and speak man to man and recount that one day, uniquely terrifying among days of endless terror, so that others might know the advent of a new Shift, a day things unimagined or ignored until now changed at last, as a few ordinary men stormed the lair of the Dweller King.

A day of reckoning.

A day of massacre.

The day a Swordsman changed Pleasantry, and so the world forever.

21

The lair of the Dwellers was a perimeter of gray stone, octagonal in shape and as tall as a man but for the entrance, which sprouted eight flying buttresses like a stone multilegged beast crawling forth from an age-old demonic undercroft. A pathway of flagstones drew up the middle, each wide enough for Donovan to lay with his legs outstretched and still have room to spare. To either side, massive dolmens stood six feet off ground, which had been burned or somehow sterilized and allowed no greenery to grow. The dolmens themselves were five times the size of one suited for a man. They stood endless as death itself, keeping vigil on this place of worship and earth where likely no man had set foot before. At the end of the flagstoned path was a dais which bore some winged and massive effigy of a creature whose characteristics had been long since worn away by wind and sand and the fingers of time. Here and there heavy ropes of vines crawled and forked and crawled farther, the leaves so dark a green they could have been black under the fading late day light.

Of the Dwellers, there was no sign, and Donovan was pleased with this if nothing else.

The Swordsman steered clear of the entranceway and motioned for the men to dismount, and together they led their horses back the way they had come and covered their heads with tarp, tying them near a runoff which they hoped might cover their sounds.

When they returned to the Dweller holy place they scaled the ridge Donovan had described, and from there they could see the structure entire. The Swordsman could see now that it was not quite an octagon, for the southeastern part where the entrance lay was elongated, a great bulging flint tumor, and here they could also see that the dolmens and even the flagstones themselves seemed to indicate the southeast. Rents here and there in the walls might have been hewn by decay, or perhaps battles had taken place here and this destruction and the flinders of stone and other things scattered around the hem were their footprints. Scattered about were the remains of animals and humans, thigh bones and spines and skulls, some thrown aside, others piled neatly in corners. One of the skulls seemed to face Donovan and stare at him blankly, and the Swordsman stared back and wondered who might look at his skull one day and what they might think.

They ate another cold meal, and as they did flashes of lightning sparked on the horizon, sketching the hard jags of the mountains there in lines of blue and white, winking against the lampblack sky and then disappearing again. The thunder cracked and rolled over them and the wind blew hard, and Donovan pulled his hat lower on his head while he watched the other men eating, wondering if this meal might be their last.

It's not done yet. You can still walk away.

(The heart of the Dweller King.)

And what if he can do nothing with it? What if all this death is for naught and in the end it is still the Cold that waits for you?

Donovan considered this as he swallowed a cold scoop of stew. Such thoughts were of no use to him. *Ineffectual and hollow are soothsayers, and you'll not be one of them*, Master said to him from the nether, the lost Morlin Sayre who was now the wicked thing called the Cleric. This was the chance of salvation given to the Swordsman, and its odds of success were greater by no scant margin than spending the last days of his sanity wandering the world in hope of some alternative.

Death is the alternative. No need to search. You carry it with you everywhere.

For the first time in his life, he knew he was afraid. He had felt fear before, of course, but never had he admitted so. Should Tomson ask him now he still would not, but in his own heart, he knew. He was afraid to die, more afraid still of this body living on after his ability to reason had been robbed from him. And yes, he was also afraid of what he would feel when these men and Mary and Grampy and the rest of them lay lifeless and strewn about Pleasantry, disemboweled or worse. He should not look on them once they were slain, but he would do it anyway. No aftermath of such a deed should be turned a blind eye.

"When do you think it'll be back?" asked Two-Shock, whose hands were shaking. He tried folding them first, then quickly sat on them.

"I'm not sure. Perhaps not for some time. We'll need to be patient."

"I know you've not got the lay of the land in your mind as the locals of us do, Swordsman," said Tomson, "and none venture up this way since nine trips out of ten it's soaked in Mist, so most steer clear. But I know roughly where we are, and by my reckoning there's a shortcut to town should we need one."

Donovan was curious about this, and he watched as Tomson scrawled lines in the dirt with a stick, and there he saw they had curved so far west in marching here that a short ride had been stretched to half a day.

"You sayin' we're less than an hour's trot from Pleasantry?" asked Corly. Tomson nodded. "How are you gonna tell me the Dwellers show up that close to town holdin' hands and singin' songs and never a once came callin'?"

"I don't know. Maybe some of our prayers made it through," said Tomson.

Donovan thought of this and frowned. Dwellers appeared and disappeared at will, and at all corners of every land he had visited they beset men like a plague. Entire towns, hardy for two or three generations and armed with fine defenses, would be snuffed out in minutes. What of Pleasantry was different then? Was it this difference the Cleric sought to extinguish with Donovan as his instrument?

I am no instrument.

(You've always been. It is your lot.)

Be silent.

As the voice that Donovan knew as the Cold spoke to him, he felt a sudden great surge blossom inside him that was too sudden to hold back. He pitched forward onto all fours, gasping. The other men flew back with their mouths agape and watched as the Swordsman rolled onto his back and began to bend and twist and contort, teeth gritted, saliva pooling in the corners of his mouth, eyes screwed closed and his hands half-clenched and gnarly.

"What in the name of it?" said Corly, whispering through a gasp.

"Tom what's wrong with him?" asked Brig.

Donovan heard their voices, tinny in the blackness of his mind, and sometimes their words would transform into unearthly snarls and hungry howls. He was slipping, and he knew it with the very last shreds of his humanity.

He was slipping.

No! Not yet! I'm almost there. Please!

If the madness was listening—*could* listen—it was not responding. He felt a hot arrow of pain galvanize his muscles, felt foam bubble at his lips and crawl down his whiskered cheeks, felt his hat roll off and down the ridge, could do nothing but lay there as if trapped and brace himself while his body bucked and convulsed under the roiling storm clouds.

"Keeper save us. What do we do?" asked Mullville, horror in his eyes as he fell back a step.

"Grab him and hold him down. Someone get me somethin' to put in his mouth."

Donovan felt strong hands grip his arms and legs and hold him pinned. Then a callused hand took his face and squeezed open his jaw and in his mouth now was the earthy taste of a stick thrust between his teeth. He bit down hard and growled in his throat.

No. Not here. Don't let it be here. Please.

(It's coming for you. Coming.)

Anything. I'll do anything!

(There's nothing left.)

And then Donovan felt himself fall. From what and into where he had no concept. His stomach dropped and swooped and his flesh broke into tingles and he tried to wave his arms as though he might sprout feathers to glide with down to the bottom of whatever abyss this was.

(Please no.)

It's coming. It's coming.

Fingers and toes…

And, just as he felt himself approaching that point from which no return could be expected, he discovered his innermost reserve, one he knew not consciously but that he drew from at times, the well he had watered from on days when his endless push had steered him closest to starvation or exhaustion. With a howl that became a scream, he climbed back into his body and retook command of his limbs and broke free of the men's grasps. He stood then, still screaming, tendrils of lightning crawling from the sky and seeking the earth in the dark miles behind him.

The men recoiled, watching the featureless figure of the Swordsman.

"His eyes were glowin'. I swear it," Corly said. He could barely get the words out.

Tomson put a hand on his shoulder. "Quiet with that now. Ya saw the lightning and nothin' more."

Then Donovan's shoulders relaxed and he fell to a crouch, catching his breath. He lay his head in his hands.

After a long silence, Tomson approached, still wary. "Are you all right?"

When the Swordsman was sure he had control of his mind, he nodded.

Tomson crouched as well and put a hand on his shoulder. "What was that?"

"A sickness. It comes only occasionally. Better now than in the middle of a battle."

But when the other men came forward they had the look of ghosts. "How do we know it won't come over ya in the middle o' fighting tha Misty?" asked Brig.

"Because it won't. If it came now, it won't be back for weeks. That is the way of it," said the Swordsman. He hoped the forced conviction in his voice was enough to sway the men and be done with this. It seemed to work. After consideration, they nodded and returned to their seated position, and for the next hour they took turns casting worried looks at Donovan.

As the storm drew closer, Donovan showed Corly and Brig their hiding spots, leaving Mullville and Two-Shock on the ridge for cover and to provide support with their bows. Then he took Tomson with him and together they climbed a tall oak to the southeast and found a sturdy set of branches to settled on and wait. The silence there was long and awkward and Donovan felt no urge to break it; once, a long time ago, he might have been given to pleasantries (he'd never think that word again without picturing throngs of blanched, sleepless faces looking on him first with naive hope and then with rage and covetousness), but that time was long dead now. Instead, he watched his plan again and again in his head, as though by exposing himself thus he might escape the pain, come the reality.

When Tomson spoke, the Swordsman started and had nearly forgotten he was not alone. "Whatever just happened back there, that's the work of this Cleric, isn't it?"

"I've said to you, my—"

"Your business is your own. Yes and yes to that bit," said Tomson with a deep frown. After some thought, he added, "I can respect that, Swordsman. I truly can. I won't make any more trouble of it for you." And then he stared at the ground below and stayed quiet.

"You don't have much of the accent this part breeds," said Donovan, not sure why he felt now like pursuing conversation. Maybe for one last chance to speak as Donovan the Swordsman of Kolendhar, for once this strong and principled mayor lay dead along with Mary and the future murderers and rapists of Pleasantry, then that Swordsman would be no more and only his animated corpse would walk the earth.

Tomson nodded and smiled. "Enough of the nonsense folk get themselves into around here comes of ignorance. Can't fix something if you don't know there's somethin' to be fixed. But they've gotta take blame first, and that's a fact. Most people like to think they're entitled to something or other, much like you must find often since you're just what we've all been waiting to come along to save our sorry asses. And I'm no exception to that. But all a man can do in this miserable shithole of a life is strive for good things even if he only reaches some of 'em, or maybe none of 'em. So I'm called leader of this bunch, even though come the nitty, you've seen how much sway I hold over them, which is to say not a hair or lick if I'm honest with myself. So what can I do but show them that just because we live in the mud and shit into buckets and barely keep enough livestock and vegetables growin' to feed ourselves, and half of us are gonna die of disease or get eaten, that doesn't mean we've got to be down low foolish dimwits. So, I've found me a book or two and I've gone to Studies, late though it be in life, and I've tried to find more of the tongue you seem so versed in."

Donovan listened to what the man said in a daze. That such a simple rant could reach his core spoke of how vulnerable he was in this moment. "You're a fine man, Tomson. I've not met your like in a dozen villages."

Tomson laughed. "There's a lot of folk out there, Swordsman. I warrant there were a lot more 'fore things went to shit, but you haven't met a tenth of them to my reckoning. Don't give up just yet."

Donovan looked Tomson in the eye and could not help but consider his words.

* * * *

They took turns sleeping in the tree, and it was Donovan's turn when night broke open into a pale predawn, the distant mountains held in mist-shrouded silhouette against the red rim of the sky, as though some great wildfire burned in the vast firmament beyond. He woke Tomson with a shake and the big man stirred where he lay propped by a tangle of thick branches. He stirred and rubbed the sleep from his eyes and was alert quickly. He looked at Donovan and the Swordsman worried that the other men had not awoken. He peered back towards their positions but could not see them from here.

He and Tomson were both looking towards the ridge, where Mullville and Two-shock lay, when the Mist appeared beneath their feet, silent, impenetrable. Donovan shifted his weight and then froze as the top of a ragged black cowl and the crude iron crown it bore glided, noiseless, three feet beneath him, and under that shrouding cloak, terrible bones and massive tendons twisted and worked and drove forward a body thirty feet tall into the gates of the holy grounds.

Tomson saw it next and his eyes went half white. He stared at this thing and the Mist that trailed it like some spectral entourage, and then he looked at the Swordsman as if to ask what they might do next. Donovan gestured with his hand to hold fast as he watched the thing born of the Maw or somewhere far darker pass the great dolmens with no sound—a field mouse would have been more audible against the loam and gravel and those old cracked flagstones.

Donovan clenched up inside; this was it, the moment he had been dreading for weeks on the road. He suddenly wished Jana was by his side, that he had her defiant chestnut eyes to look at and discover himself within by some odd way he could not name, or maybe to hear her laugh or to see her scowl—anything to bring out that other side in him, that soft side only Rosaline saw full but that the young girl from Pleasantry somehow touched. Now that part was asleep and numb and nothing here would wake it.

Then he saw Mullville peering over the ridge, mouth hanging open, and a moment later Two-shock's head popped up like a gopher from its hole and they looked at each other and then at Donovan. The Swordsman motioned for them to hold as well. He looked for Brig and Corly, but they were hidden by the brush and now were closest to the Dweller King, who approached the great statue of the faceless and featureless winged creature and then seemed to squat, its huge sword scraping the earth behind it.

At last, Brig appeared, creeping forward and looking at Donovan. They sat a hundred paces out from the creature and faced opposite the ridge. Donovan motioned for them to wait, then espied the ridge and found Mullville's eyes and began to count down with his fingers. Now would be the test, and much would depend on these men whose fighting ability he had no measure of beyond Tomson's estimation.

One by one his fingers closed and the men tensed visibly even at this distance.

Five. Four. Three. Two…

And then chaos erupted.

22

By the count of three Mullville and Two-shock had their arrows notched and at full draw. Both men's arms shook with strain, and then Mullville's bow loosed a count early and sliced wide to his left, striking the winged statue with a small discharge of sparks. The Dweller King rose and faced them and roared a terrible bellow that shook the ground, and for an instant Donovan thought of his march through the bog the day he found Pleasantry, of the rumble in the deep fog which had driven him to his first meeting with Jana Hunter.

The creature was still reacting when Donovan motioned for Brig and Corly to move. Mullville and Two-Shock already had their second arrows notched and let them fly, and these found their targets and stuck halfway to the fletching in the beast's flesh. It reeled back and spread wide its razor claws, howling at the sky in pain or rage or both. Brig reached the Dweller King first, his old axe held high overhead, Corly behind him with his shortsword drawn, which next to the massive soma of the creature before them looked ridiculous and ineffectual. The third volley of arrows flew through the thickening Mist, which now cloaked the south wall of the enclosure, and Mullville's shot again flew wide but Two-Shock's struck the Dweller in the shoulder, pushing it back a step, and now the great beast reached with a gray hand for its sword.

Donovan leapt from his place in the tree and landed in a somersault. While he rose, Orin slid free from the sheath his father's father's father had crafted, and he approached the beast as Brig's first blow fell. Brig's aim was true, and when his axe blade ricocheted off the catch holding the lower end of the Dweller's sword, the axe was notched. Brig was a big man, more powerful than his fellow townsmen, and Donovan saw that his blow had bent the catch askew. The Dweller growled again and swung its massive arm in an eight-foot arc and Brig dropped to his knees in response. Behind him, Corly tumbled forward with more dexterity than Donovan would ever have guessed, and when he rose his shortsword flashed in a rising arc and he too struck his mark and now the catch was bent at a deeper angle still.

Had Corly faded to his right or retreated backwards or ducked in place he might have avoided what came next, but instead he swept furiously forward for a second blow. The Dweller brought its great fist around and Corly twisted left, but the thing was as fast as it was huge and it caught him on the shoulder with a *crack* that sounded like a breaking tree branch. Corly spun away, limp, and struck the old stone of the wall behind him with a *thud* and landed facedown and did not move.

Mullville and Two-Shock did not relent in their assault. Two, then four, then six arrows found home in the humped flesh of the Dweller King's back. The seventh and eighth clanged uselessly against the broad side of its sword.

Brig's axe whirled again, but this time the Dweller veered away and the notched weapon sliced through cloth and nothing else. His momentum swung him around as the Dweller reached for its sword again, but Donovan's tactic had worked and the blade did not pull immediately free. Donovan watched Brig gain his balance and make a run for Corly's limp body. He hefted him up to his shoulders and bounded forward towards the entrance. "Donovan!" he screamed as the Dweller slid forward like some killer shadow and swung its fist again, shattering the dolmen beside him like it was made of eggshell.

Tomson circled wide of Donovan and backed to the wall near the closest buttress, soaked in sweat that steamed off his thick neck and bushy hair. He held his knife and crouched but did not move, and Donovan thought this was the wise thing to do. Ahead, the Dweller was giving chase to Brig and was almost upon him.

Then the Swordsman stepped forth out of the selvage of Mist with Orin held low to his side and the Dweller King eased his charge and turned to face him, and there these two black things both with dark magic inside them watched each other in the cold silence.

Donovan thought of his father, his faded memories belonging to a life on a path not parallel or intersecting of this one but on a separate plane altogether, and along this new trajectory they made no sense at all. Then he felt the rush of battle blood and thought of nothing else. Orin rose in his grasp into the swirling Mist overhead, and the Swordsman charged forward as the Dweller moved to meet him. And still, even in this moment, stretched so long it could have been a dream, he could hear the Cold calling to him.

(Use me. You cannot win without me.)

Then he reached the Dweller and feinted left and Orin cut in a wide stroke, its acid-etched edge sharp enough to cleave the very air itself. But the Dweller did not take his bluff and it leaned away, the tip of Donovan's sword swooping past the bulge of its thigh, and then with a roar, which the Swordsman felt in his skull, it lurched forward and the catches on its back snapped, the square and massive blade there sweeping the air towards him. Donovan leaned backwards, sliding on his knees like some drunken dancer, and the waft of the passing blade blew his hat from his head and sent it tumbling into the forest. The blow that would have bisected him struck the wall instead with a thunder crack, shattering the stone there into a million pieces.

Now Tomson appeared, knife low and ready, and as the Dweller recovered from its swing he stabbed forward and sunk the blade through the creature's shredded cloak where its leg might be if its hidden anatomy resembled anything human. The Dweller cried out and cocked its sword back as Tomson tried to yank free his blade. No good. It was stuck fast. He dove away and landed hard on his shoulder, and Donovan heard him groan in pain and saw that he could not rise. The Dweller pulled the knife, as small as a thorn in its giant hand, free from its leg and tossed it aside.

More arrows flew from the ridge; the two men there were alternating now, and the stream was constant. Some missed and flew overhead or clacked on the stone or embedded in the ground, but others found thick rolls of cloth and sometimes flesh. The Dweller reached for a boulder left from the remains of the smashed dolmen, and with a growl it heaved it like a stickball towards the ridge. Mullville and Two-Shock screamed and turned and ran as the stone, six feet across, crashed into their position and blew a cloud of debris into the morning air. They tumbled down the hill and Donovan heard their cries of pain but could not see them anymore.

The Dweller whirled again to face the Swordsman, its sword, longer than the man it targeted, swooping downward like an iron bird of prey. Donovan's mind, a perfectly honed machine of war, went blank, and his deepest instincts, the ones bred into his person by generations of warriors, took hold, and in that glorious time when the world and its troubles mattered not and the only thing corporeal was the intoxication of battle itself, his arms and legs grew a consciousness of their own and moved likewise. The Dweller threw blow after deadly blow his way, and each time the Swordsman writhed, dodging, ducking. Then Orin clashed with the heavy black sword and could not hope to move it but a little and bright blue sparks fountained from the strike, burning on the flagstone at their feet afterwards like eyes of the dead peering up from the Black until the last remnants of their souls were extinguished.

Tomson recovered now; from the corner of his eye Donovan saw him rise to his hands and knees just as the Dweller posed to strike again. Then the big mayor of Pleasantry scrambled forward screaming and, as the Dweller's sword fell towards Donovan, Tomson loosed his knife like a circus tosser and it sunk to the haft into the Dweller's arm. The creature howled and its blade struck the ground where the Swordsman had been moments before, lodging there. Donovan felt his body move forth on its own then, running up the edge of the frozen sword, and with the cry of his forefathers he felt his arms whip Orin around and through the blackness of the Dweller King's cowl, slicing the cloth there and some of the flesh within. The Dweller screamed in agony, black runs of blood drooling from the severed flesh in the cave of teeth that was its mouth. Donovan landed in a crouch behind the great beast and thrust Orin into the flesh of its back until only the hilt showed, leaving the creature to clutch wildly and thrash, attempting to shake loose that buried steel.

When Donovan was a boy, he had come to know an instinct most men possessed but few paid heed to, a voice that was barely a voice, a tickle in the rear of consciousness, cousin to the low voice, maybe. He found it now, and it told him Mullville had regained the ridge and was readying an arrow. The Dweller found its bearings and brought its fist crashing down towards him, and Donovan felt himself (the Cold?) spring from the way and leap to the Dweller's fist, then onto its opposing arm. That same distant part of his mind sensed true the sound of Mullville's bowstring snapping taut, then the high whine of the fired arrow cutting the air. At that moment, the Swordsman planted a mud-caked boot into the folds of the cloak beneath him and launched himself from the Dweller's shoulder. Without thought or look, his hand reached into the cold air and his fingers closed around the wayward arrow. With a hard twist of his body, he flung the arrow downward from midair with much the same technique he had taught Jana months earlier (and also shown the dead men of the Raef clan, now rotting beside the Hunter River). The repurposed arrow flew straight and true and sunk deep into the Dweller's dark cowl in a bouquet of black blood.

The Dweller King arched backwards as Donovan landed, then reversed direction and its closing fist clipped the Swordsman's chest with barely a knuckle, yet struck with enough force to send him flying. His breath exploded in one hot exhale and the world spun in a whirlwind blur, then the ground rushed up at him and sharp and fiery pain exploded. When he tried to rise, he only managed to flounder limply and roll onto his back.

Behind him, Brig returned to hold the Dweller back. Together he and Tomson hacked and stabbed without finesse the maelstrom of shredded black cloth and the demon it housed. The Dweller King roared and pulled its sword free of the earth, and with force enough to cleave the nose off a mountain, it brought that razor edge about. Tomson and Brig both ducked and crawled away, and behind them the winged effigy disintegrated and rained ancient gray pebbles on them. On the far side of the grounds from their scuffle, Donovan rose, dazed, and felt dumbly at his head. When he looked at his fingers they were stained deep red. The color woke something in his bruised body, refocusing the world, and there sticking from the Dweller's back like an ivory mole was Orin. Donovan felt his mind fix on this and nothing else, and when he found Corly's dropped shortsword and took it up as his own, he was almost surprised to find it in his grasp halfway into his charge.

Still reeling, the Dweller turned and its massive grip found the Swordsman's body and enveloped it. Donovan felt the air squeezed out of him, felt pain like he had never experienced. The world went shades of red as the Dweller lifted him high, and if the monster had its full senses, had it not been grievously wounded, it might have crushed the guts out of him and his quest would have ended right there. But instead, the Swordsman was lifted over its head and there in reach was the arrow sticking forth from the Dweller's ruined face. Donovan lashed out with his feet once, twice. On the third, he found purchase and drove the arrow further into the creature's flesh with his boot. The Dweller called out again and dropped the Swordsman, its great black sword slipping from its limp fingers. The blade was heavy and held high, and it fell as if guided by its own accord until it embedded itself halfway through the ancient beast's thigh and stayed there.

Donovan landed in a crouch and circled the creature, who was grasping at the great freshets of blood bursting between its fingers like oil, and then the battle blood took over completely and he was at the Dweller King's back with Orin drawn free from the black, spouting viscera, grasping the protruding arrows there, pulling at them like a morbid ladder, planting his boots into its back for leverage and pulling at its cloak to heave himself upward, tossing another arrow aside when it slipped loose. And as the creature who led the beasts that had terrorized this land and other lands like it for as long as people could remember thrashed and splayed, Donovan stood upon its shoulders like some black herald of a war long lost in the annals of the Maw itself, his ancestor's sword gleaming in the pale light, and with a scream that echoed into the forest he brought it to bear one last time. Whether by his fury or the Cold or with the help of the Keeper Himself, this time his cut fell full and true, and the Dweller King's head was lopped off, the ancient iron crown it bore clanging once, twice on the ground, then rolling to a halt at the foot of the demolished winged statue where it had been bowed in prayer minutes before. Its great body shivered and undulated a moment longer, as though still fighting to stay clear of the Black, and then it sunk forward and Donovan rolled away, landing hard on the flagstone just beyond. The Dweller King crashed prone behind him with a rumble that seemed to shake the ground itself, spasmed, and then did not move ever again.

The silence after was long and deafening.

Tomson rose, bruised, bleeding at the cheek and from a long peel of skin removed from his shoulder. "Keeper save us all."

"I think He did," said Brig, who was crouched over Corly's still body.

"Is it dead?" Tomson asked the Swordsman, who nodded.

"Corly's hurt bad," said Brig, and when Donovan came to the fallen man he saw that his left arm was twisted at an odd angle and hanging limp within the skin, completely dislocated. Blood crawled down his chin and pooled at the base of his neck. "We've got to get him back to town."

"What are they gonna do fer 'im there?" asked Mullville, approaching from the entrance with Two-Shock in tow. Both men were scraped and bruised and covered in dirt and debris but seemed largely unharmed.

"Maybe Grampy kin do somethin' fer 'im," said Brig.

"Fuckovall that. Load of good Grampy's little spells and powders did for the Hunters and all the rest."

Donovan watched the men talk from a distance immeasurable, and may have acted differently thereafter had he been listening. He strode through them without a word and mounted the Dweller King, and as the men's conversation faded and they turned to watch wide-eyed, he thrust Orin into the dead flesh there and did not stop cutting until he was soaked in thick black blood and holding the heart of the beast, which was larger than a watermelon, in his hands.

"What in the name of it…" said Brig. He sounded as if he might be sick.

But the Swordsman offered no word and the other men could summon no answer of their own.

Tomson carried Corly's limp body back to where the horses were tied off. Donovan marched ahead of them, the still-hot sack of demon blood pulsing vaguely in his shaking hands, the harsh rope of the Cleric's scar coiling tighter around him.

(You have to do it. They're going to die anyway.)

Not just yet. I might need them still.

(You never needed them.)

He felt that familiar surge in him and threw all his might, even the lowest parts usually occupied with speech and thought and control of his body, into holding it at bay. When he stumbled drunkenly, Tomson went to his side and asked if he was all right, but Donovan did not answer, did not even think to.

(Kill them. Do it now and be done with it. They'll all be headless before they can draw.)

I'll leave them for last. For last when the rest is done.

(I'll do it. Stand back.)

But he would not. They reached the horses and Donovan slipped the wet dead thing he held into the pannier and stood with his hands on the horse looking at the ground. He could not speak for a while.

"Donovan," said Brig, sounding irritated. "I'm as messed in the noggin as the next o' ya, but Corly's gonna die if we don't get him back now."

"He's gonna die either way," said Mullville, dry as ever, but now desperation lay beneath his usual tone.

"Well then we might as well let 'im die warm and comfortable then, eh?" said Brig, throwing Mullville a hard look that made the smaller man shrink away.

Somewhere in the endless push-pull of Donovan's mind, he considered that, as of now at least, they had killed a Dweller and all survived. *Whatever I might've thought men possible of, this was not it.* And the truth was, he knew that he *did* need their help, that without these men he would be dead in the Dweller holy place and soon eaten.

You owe them your life.

(They would've killed you themselves if you didn't offer something they craved.)

Not Tomson…

Tomson touched his shoulder and the Swordsman started and looked at him with something dark in his eyes; the mayor of Pleasantry flinched away from the look as if struck. "Donovan..." he began, then looked uncertain if he should continue.

"What are we doin' fer the life in it!" said Two-Shock.

The other men nodded and looked at the Swordsman for answers, but instead they found him gazing past them into the deep of the forest. They followed his gaze but did not see what he saw, and Donovan narrowed his eyes and clenched his teeth. "You stay here. No matter what happens. Wait until midday and then head back for town."

"Where are you going?" asked Brig.

"They're not done with us yet," answered the Swordsman grimly. Without request or explanation, he stepped to Mullville and took his bow and quiver, which was still half-full.

"Hey just what do ya think—"

One look from the Swordsman, aglow with a faint redness, shut him up. Donovan mounted his stallion and Tomson came to his side. He pointed at Corly. "He's going to die if we wait that long."

"If you don't do as I say, you're all going to die anyway. Now hide!" said the Swordsman, and then he was off, his big black mount galloping through the forest. As the men disappeared behind him and he steered towards the holy ground once more, he heard the first roar. Soon after, he spotted the first traces of gathering Mist.

He rode down the hill and over the embankment, across the arroyo and up the slanting hill beyond and into the center of the Dweller holy ground. There he reigned in just short of the dead king and spun about. Outside the stone walls, the Mist was growing thick. He watched it all without fear or adrenaline or emotion at all; all of these things were relegated to holding back the barrage of the Cold in the back of his mind.

(This can work to your advantage. Save yourself the effort of it.)

I'd do it myself if that is the path I've chosen.

(Fingers and toes, fingers and toes...)

But for once the damnable voice from the madness brewing inside him spoke a truth he could not ignore. Even in his mind, he could not picture doing what the Cleric had charged him to do, and here was an easier answer. *The road of passivity is ever the road to wickedness, and one you'll not recognize until you've lost your way entire*, said his master, the true Morlin Sayre.

And yet wasn't his way already lost?

Another deep roar shook him from his thoughts, and he brought his stallion around to face the Mist just outside the northwest end of the holy grounds. Then the wall of stone there geysered outward in a throw of heavy debris and clouds of dust, revealing three Dwellers, each tall enough to look down on the roof of Tomson's home. They saw their slain leader and the Swordsman who had killed it, the blackness of their deep cowls revealing no reaction, their hunched and inhuman posture impossible to interpret. Then Donovan watched as they drew their swords as one, as though they were possessed of a single mind, and together the Dwellers flowed forth over the ruined wall and across the flagstone towards him.

The Swordsman dug his heels into his mount and rode hard the other way, his mind half-drowned in madness, the massive creatures of the Maw tight at his heels.

23

The Swordsman spurred his mount through the thick of the forest and the Dwellers followed.

He took the path Tomson had mapped out for him, the short way, from all told. He hoped that was true, for how long could he keep this pace? Behind him, the Mist Dwellers flowed without sound over the dead land, the Mist dragging behind them like an oversized cape, their swords ready in gray and terrible claws. They passed around and over trees, at times without disturbing them, other times by crashing straight through them, raining great splinters of oak or cherrywood down on the Swordsman. Then he looked back over his shoulder and saw one of them was close enough to strike.

The first Dweller lashed out with its blade and Donovan ducked in his saddle and prayed his horse would keep its head. The blade was long but swept just short of the animal's withers, missing rider and mount completely and obliterating a tree beside them instead. Exploded wood filled the forest air, and behind him Donovan heard the tall tree, half as old as Ruti perhaps, come crashing down onto the frosted forest floor. Seconds later the other two Dwellers passed over the fallen trunk, soundless as cloud shadows.

Donovan slid Orin home into its sheath. The familiar feel of its hard corners digging into his back gave him comfort as his stallion's hooves pounded the earth. Looking back over his shoulder, he drew Mullville's bow from across his body and held it ready. Then the forest brush opened into a clearing with a deep and craggy ravine at its foot, and Donovan nearly dropped his weapon as he pulled the stallion's reins hard to the right. The big horse slipped on the gravel of the rimrock but kept its footing, and together horse and rider plunged down the hill into the ravine with the Dwellers just behind.

The black-cloaked demons were clustered now, almost falling over each other in their bloodlust. Donovan twisted in his saddle and notched an arrow and aimed—it had been many years since he had fired one, but more years still had been spent honing and practicing until his fingers and forearms were numb and Master Archer Othos had been a hard teacher—and even in this contorted position his arrow found its mark, taking the lead Dweller in the throat. The big creature lost momentum for a second or less and kept its charge.

(Enough to lead them, not lose them.)

They'll track the horse scent either way.

(You must make sure...)

His hands were shivering and he choked on bile that he swallowed back down with a burn. Around him he saw things begin to move, other creatures fanged and blackeyed and wicked crouching in the shadows or perching on trees or flying high overhead ready to swoop down and pluck his eyes out. Then he shook his head and slapped his face and there were only squirrels and birds fleeing his course while his horse galloped through the undergrowth, agents of the Reaper fast on his trail.

At the far end of the ravine was a narrow defilement, one that might be too narrow for the Dwellers to follow through. He pushed through easily and looked back and saw the great black beasts twist and flow amidst the craggy rocks as easily as smoke and lose no time, their great swords overhead, ready to fall the instant a deathblow came within reach.

Donovan was looking back when the fourth Dweller appeared before his horse, hidden teeth leaking yellow slaver, its sword already swinging as it materialized from a new cloak of Mist to the north.

Donovan's instinct, honed to a point most days but now almost preternatural with the benefits of the Cold (if only were it without the terrible drawbacks), fed him through senses unknown to other men in amounts even Ruti would have struggled to process, and in one smooth motion he leaned back in his saddle as the Dweller's blade hissed through the air above him. Without missing time he raised up and stood, Mullville's bow ready, all four Dwellers pursuing him with their wicked blades whirling, the shreds of their cloaks like ruined tendons dangling from bodies that seemed weightless, almost to float, leaving little trace of their crossing.

The battle blood was high before, but now it flushed into Donovan's mind in a tidal wave and already his hands were moving. An arrow notched, aimed, loosed. A Dweller with a hole in its throat. Another in its shoulder. More demons appearing around him, one spiderlike and massive, clinging to a tree, looking down at him with great bulbous snake eyes and long razor fangs.

A fox. It's not real. It's not—

(They're real. They're all coming for you.)

No!

Behind him, a thick copse of trees gave the horse clearance below, yet at Donovan's level would have dismounted him, but Donovan was fast on his weakest day and the growing heat of the Cleric's scar, which now enveloped half of his body, burned inside him and lit up his mind. The Swordsman turned, still standing on the saddle, and drew Orin, severing the small branches about him in a tornado of steel that left him cut and bleeding but still upright on his tiring horse. Behind him, the Dwellers, in need of no such finesse, shouldered through the trees with a chorus of roars and sent two tall pines toppling into the forest. Still they did not slow or veer and they seemed tireless.

Of course they are. They're agents of the Reaper. And when's the Reaper ever too tired to collect?

The forest cleared then into a broad plain of high grass and wheat, and the Swordsman pushed through it. There, in the not so far distance, he could see the rising chimney smoke of Pleasantry. He pushed for it, thinking his horse might die before they reached it, and then he heard the rise of a foul wind. When he looked back, the lead Dweller had launched itself into the air, silver-edged sword raised over its head in two immense hands. Donovan could not think or plan or do anything then but act on his low voice, the one that told him that if he did not strike now and first and use his smaller size and greater speed, then he and the horse would be cleaved in two and fed upon right here in this spot. And so Orin curved upward faster than the Dweller's blow could fall, and that shining edge hammered and folded a thousand times in a fire burned out before the memory of anything living caught the thick gray trunks of the thing's wrists and severed one of them where it joined the claw. The Dweller's blow swept askew and thudded in the earth and the creature followed. The three behind it were too close, too overcome with zealotry, whether from simple hunger or from lust for revenge, and they plowed into the mountain of dark flesh that was their comrade and fell over each other into heaps that made the earth rumble.

As the Swordsman looked back on their diminishing forms struggling to rise, he smiled darkly to himself, then reseated and quirted his horse.

The stallion's strength seemed limitless, but Donovan knew from the feel of its shoulders that it would collapse soon. He prayed he would make it in time.

He considered what he was about to do as he pressed his mount harder.

The thoughts would not hold.

The world felt hallucinatory, built of disparate aspects of a dream stitched together only by his utter exhaustion. The question of his coming actions came and then drifted away and were gone before he could consider them further, so depleted was he, mind and spirit, by his battle with the Cold.

Then he was through the last of the straggling trees and onto a field, just beyond the limits of the now-condemned town of Pleasantry, population two hundred and fourteen.

24

Earny heard the cries from inside Tomson's house. Mary had taken a break from cooking and was busying herself with a quilt she had been tending to for some time, but when the calls outside began, half excited and half hateful, she dropped what she was doing and looked out through the fretwork window and frowned.

Earny looked at Ruti, who was stationed on the dining room table. The little dragon lifted off and landed on his shoulder, then crawled into his pocket with his head poking out as Earny made his way out the front door. Outside there were more calls, people looking northward towards the plain leading to the forest and the switchback, some folks cursing to one another or to themselves, more still questioning what in the Maw was going on, and underneath it all the lowing of cows and the muttering of chickens. Then the man stationed atop the bell tower woke from a fitful nap, rubbed his eyes and peered into the fog-draped distance.

Earny neared the edge of town, and off to his right he saw the old man Grampy on his porch with his cane across his lap, seated in his rocking chair. He seemed concerned but too tired to rise, though when Earny looked closer he saw a look of sadness in the old man's eyes that he wanted to name guilt, as though whatever was approaching was his fault and his alone.

Then Earny spotted him, the Swordsman's stark black shape—odd to Earny's good eye without his hat—approaching fast on a galloping horse, his long duster trailing out behind him. Of the men who had gone with him, there was no sign. He could see now that Donovan was worse for wear, his face cut and bleeding in places, his clothes shredded, the rest of him caked in a weird black coagulate.

The ex-bandit felt relief and sadness at once; he had nurtured a feeling the Swordsman might survive this sortie, but the other fellows were good men and their loss would be mourned. He meant to tell Donovan so, but the Swordsman did not look at him and did not slow his horse as he raced into the middle of town and beyond, spraying Earny and Ruti with mud.

What in the forsaken name of everything holy is going on?

He looked at Ruti, who shook his head to remove a drip of mud, and the Root Dragon looked back at him. That was counsel enough for Earny. The man who once served under Raef the Big and Old and Ugly jogged after Donovan as fast as he could.

The people of Pleasantry watched this transpire with the same tired and angry eyes, the eyes of people on the edge of desperation, the eyes of men who would trade anything at all for relief from their lives.

On the far end of town, he found the Swordsman unstrapping the panniers from the stallion—one of them looked full to the brim with something gushing a black fluid—and he stood with his hands on his hips, watching the bloodied Swordsman warily. "Master Donovan, sir, I'm so gla—"

Donovan turned and looked at him, and at once Earny knew those eyes, the ones he had feared on the road and waited for but never witnessed himself; the red eyes of the other Donovan were here, their inhuman light tearing right through the center of him, only this time there were no ropes to hold him back from tearing Earny's throat out. Earny fell back and winced and waited for it to come, but instead of attacking Donovan shook his head and doubled over, his fingers in his hair, slapping at his face, and when he looked up he was shaking but his eyes were green again. "I told you to go!"

"I-I know, Master, sir, but I was thinkin', come time fer it, I wa—"

Donovan swung his fist suddenly and his blow caught Earny in the head before he could react, turning his world black for a moment. When the world faded in again he was on his side in the dirt and Donovan was racing away from town, the pannier slung over his shoulder, his sword jostling with each step as if some living thing scaled his back.

Earny sat up, head throbbing (and bleeding again, for the Swordsman had struck him right where the stone had two days before), and looked at the toes of his boots. He wasn't angry—far from it; he had disobeyed an order and this was the other end of it. Better a smack to the head than a whipping, Keeper save him.

He rose to his feet and watched the Swordsman disappear into the fog with a long sigh.

Then a new sound began.

The bell atop the old tower was tolling.

25

Donovan curved hard east, to where a path led up through the Shodan onto the promontory he had spent a night staring at from the pressback in Shag's Inn. Against his shoulder, the Dweller King's heart bounced and splashed grotesquely, its wetness seeping down his back and legs, some drips worming their way into his boots. His breathing burned in his chest, cold and hot alternately. Behind him, the screams of those about to be slain echoed into the faceless sky and vanished there like precursors to the souls of those who voiced them.

The forest on this hill was steep and thick, and Donovan's body was near exhaustion. He was barely aware of this, his mind no more reactive to this death march than it would be to a mild ache on a normal day. The fire of the Cold flowed freely through him now, invading his every thought, painting the world in its madman's palette. He wondered if there was any way he might reach the Cleric with the Dweller King's heart in time to be saved, to escape his curse once and for all.

There's not. You'll never overcome it this time. It nearly has you.

(I've done it before. I can do it again.)

He reached the dying scrub at the lip of the promontory, and there below him was Pleasantry in all its filthy, impoverished splendor. He saw the townsfolk hurrying from their hovels, some with children in their arms, others carrying the sick or wounded. Again and again the bell in the center of town tolled, the watchman ringing it visibly panicked as he faced northward, away from town, and even from this distance Donovan knew the poor soul did not risk a blink.

Not far from the bell tower lay the Hole, the great underground shelter of Pleasantry, built in what time and by who none knew for certain, said to be an underground foundation or storage place or dungeon left from the world before the Shift. Twin iron doors that barred from the inside stood open like arms, and in twos and threes the people of Pleasantry poured in, falling over each other, trampling one another, some men grabbing the ones in front of them by the ankles to trip them or shoving them from the way to reach the shelter first.

It's just as Master said. We're all crabs in this forsaken barrel. Even me.

And what greater proof of that than Morlin Sayre's student doing just as foretold?

At the edge of the field a great curtain of the Mist appeared, drawing like a veil over these dead lands where even the greatest farmers could barely cultivate life, and at its head rode the four Dwellers, one minus a hand but still with its sword. Over and around each other they moved, too deft and light for creatures so massive, and this spoke of magic Donovan did not understand and that the Cleric likely did not either.

Why must I do this? Why?

(Because he'll know if you don't.)

That can't be all. To what end?

But the Cold had no answers for him. He wanted to leave this place, to spare himself from watching the fruits of his dark toil, but if the folk down there were to suffer and die in this place for his deeds, then he owed it to them to watch.

He stood fast upon the promontory and braced himself against the Cold. Below, the Dwellers reached the Hole moments after the last man dove through and slammed shut the doors shut, barring them from the inside.

25

Grampy was almost the last person inside the Hole.

Only the one-eyed man, Earny was his name, and the man charged to keep the tower, Owen, came after. He eased down the rickety steps as fast as his brittle bones would carry him, his cane arm wobbling something horrid. For a moment he thought he might not make it at all; surely he wouldn't have if he had come alongside the mob. One hard spill and that would've been the end of it. But, as in the past, the Keeper saw fit to keep him alive and kicking just a few minutes longer, and in these last minutes he wondered what might have been had he kept vigilant, if his Warding, superstitious tokey-bokey-shit-fer-all may it be, had done some good, and now if in these past days his waning resolve had doomed them all.

A great ball of sadness, woven for decades, rose in Grampy's throat and he began to cry silently.

Inside, the faces of the men he knew, each one with a name even in his hazy brain, backed to the wall or against each other and stared at the doors with their eyes wide and their teeth bared, their knuckles white where they gripped railings or the pipes that once moved water or something else but now were just the rusted remnants of a dead society. To his left was the man with the eyepatch, and he looked scared shitless as the rest.

Maybe we shoulda just ran. Maybe the Hole's nowhere to be come this sorta reckoning.

But the thought held little weight now that the chaos and knee-jerk way of it all had played its ill-advised course; they were here and death was about to drop from above unless some old iron was enough to keep the Reaper's fingers out.

Grampy sat down with a grunt of pain and laid his cane across his lap.

If a hundred and nine years of living taught a man a thing, it was patience.

Then something massive and of unearthly strength reached the doors and began to bash them in.

26

Donovan watched the Dwellers pummel the doors to the Hole with first their swords and then their bare fists. Within minutes the old iron was bent and ruined; it would last only moments more, and then one by one the people of Pleasantry would be fed upon like shoal by a shark and that would be the end of the story of this tired tract. The end of him as well, for even as he stood there watching from afar, Donovan knew that whatever remnants of himself might still live from Kolendhar would die alongside those poor country folk.

"That will do, Donovan," came a familiar voice from behind.

Donovan did not turn towards it. "No one has snuck up on me since I was nine years old." *Except Creel. You're not who you once were.*

"Master taught us well."

And there was Shadow, Gaelin, once captain of the Black Guard. He stood with his sword drawn already, dangling at his side, his posture reeking of false casualness. His black Swordsman's armor seemed to swallow whole the halfhearted daylight, and his delicate, beautiful smile turned his features ugly now; he looked a monster to Donovan, and it did not take the Cold to make him look so.

"So, there is no cure then, if he'd send you to kill me."

"Oh, I'm sure there is. That is not what he sent me for."

"Then what?" asked Donovan, and during this the sound of the Dweller claws assaulting the doors to the Hole echoed from the sky into the dark of his brain until it rattled his teeth.

Shadow took a step closer and studied Donovan's dark and bloodied face, his own newly cleaned and shaven. Donovan saw in his way the strange beauty of this man's build and countenance and the compelling energy that seemed to emit outwards from his eyes, and he knew well that many women had fallen under his spell instantly and entirely as if by some magic. In his darkest parts he wondered if Rosaline had ever found such a draw to him.

No. She was too sharp for that. She knew too well what he was.

And Donovan had, too. But too late, as it was with his Master.

(Rosaline lays beneath the dirt under the weight of your choices…)

"Why these people?" he asked Shadow.

"I'm not one who'd know Master's mechanizations."

"And you see yourself as outside his hate?"

"Not yet."

Something in his tone drew Donovan's attention, and he stared hard at Shadow's unblinking smile. "There's something here he'd destroy."

"Maybe he just liked the idea of seeing if you'd do it. What greater way to see his point proved then to have his student indulge in the same self-serving folly he condemns?"

And to Donovan, who had known Morlin Sayre for his entire life and had spent more time with him than anyone still living, this answer rang true. His heart sank into his gut and drowned itself there. Could that be all? No, there was likely more to it, but even if that were a single brick in the Cleric's wall…

Another thunderous *clang*. The Dwellers hunched over the failing doors of the Hole like hounds fighting over a scrap of meat, swords dropped to the earth now, using their claws to needle through the door cracks and pry the iron apart.

Images and voices in Donovan's mind.

You should because you can…

Fingers and toes, fingers and toes…

(Madness?)

Jana. Earny. Shadow. The Cleric. Raef. Tomson. Villagers with pickaxes, unnamed vileness in their eyes—Mary ladling stew into bowls—men stoning Earny, raising Jana to burn, eyes alight with some deep wickedness, teeth bared like rabid dogs—Earny's rescue of Jana from the highwaymen Donovan had left her to—Donovan himself, the Swordsman of Kolendhar, leader of the Order, standing here watching while these men and women and children, innocent or not, future leaders or future whores and criminals, all bereft of the very thing that makes greatness a prize to be sought, the stuff the Swordsmen and any likeness of them had been built of since time immemorial.

Could it be so simple?

In the end, it was the image of Jana standing before her burning home, set ablaze by her own hand, the eviscerated remains of her parents carried in trembling scoops in her cold fingers to be properly cremated.

Horror. Unknown horror.

And yet strength. Unknowable strength, whose bounds could only be discovered by the searching eye of faith itself. What other thing could men cling to on this great turning rock in which the darkest horrors were only matched by man's unbridled strength, not in hand but in mind and spirit, the sort that could never be dominated, not by terror, not by predators, and certainly not by the Cleric's misanthropic designs?

What if the very thing that drove men to do such wicked things was symbiotic to what drove them to greatness? If so, where lay the crossroads? And if found, where sat the road sign?

Will the people come? Will they fight?

No. I don't think so. World's not ready for that.

The world? Or us?

The road of passivity is ever the road to wickedness, and one you'll not recognize until you've lost your way entire. Master's voice.

And then: *You should because you can.* The simple words of a naive young girl.

Because you can.

And he knew at last that it was so.

For the first time since Rosaline's death, his way, the way of his line and the Order, and the would-be trajectory of mankind itself through the darkness of this world became clear. It was time to end this madness—*his* madness—once and for all, on his terms, in his way.

And so did Donovan of the line of Maltrese, thirty-fourth bearer of the blade called Orin, look on the Dweller attack in the center of Pleasantry and then to Shadow with an old light in his eyes that his friends, in a life that seemed ages ago, would have called his steeliness; others, his obsessiveness. "There's emptiness at the end of this road.

We've been tricked by the greatest roundabout a man or beast has ever played."

"Fighting for your life isn't emptiness, Donovan."

"We swore an oath long ago, words that the men whose bricks built our keep and whose seed built our bodies wrote in their blood when that blood was all that kept the world alive."

"It's too late to undo this," Shadow said, a darkness in his eyes that was not there before.

"If we work together, we can stop them. It's not too late," said Donovan. He took a step forward and Shadow lashed out then and he was so fast. His fist caught Donovan square in the jaw and snapped his head back in a bright burst of blood. He fell to his hands and knees and spat until his lip throbbed.

"Of all the things I've waited for in this life, this I've burned more deeply for than all others," said Shadow, to himself as much as to Donovan.

Then a host of men appeared from the forest, some with swords and two with pistols of a finer condition than those once carried by the Raef Clan, and no doubt more functional. They pressed forward, all scars and scale armor and tense hands thickly veined, eager to grow the death count fast approaching below.

Donovan rose first to one knee and then to his feet where he swayed, and then gained his balance. Ever in the back of his mind throbbed the Cold, watching, waiting. He reached for Orin and drew it, and as it cleared the sheath it did not ring, as if the steel itself mourned the work of its owner. He held it ready at his side and traced a half circle in the dirt and stared bleeding at his old comrade. "Vigilance to the end. Strength till the Black we find," he told Shadow, and there was something in his voice that seemed to give the once-Swordsman pause. For that one moment, faint and indecipherable as it was, Donovan thought Gaelin of Kolendhar might change his mind.

Then Shadow stepped back into the ranks of his men and motioned, wordless.

Some opened fire, and the rest charged with bloodlust in their eyes.

But none were prepared for the whirlwind of death that had come upon them.

27

The first men with swords stayed widely spread so the pistoliers could fire, but between the time when their fingers levered back and the hammers fell and their ammunition discharged, Donovan tumbled forward onto the ground. The bullets scored the earth behind him in tiny mushroom-shaped clouds and already he was up with Orin carving. He engaged the first two soldiers and dispatched them with as many cuts. The second man he caught and held aloft, the low voice or the Cold or all of it together warning him a second volley of bullets was incoming. The shots struck the corpse as he kept it on its feet, the impact driving Donovan back a step while blood exploded outward from its chest onto the understory. He saw the hunting knife sheathed at the dead man's thigh then and, just as his Master had once done for the daughter of the mayor of Eastfield, Donovan drew the blade and threw underhand and the tip of the blade took the gunman in the eye. His head snapped around and his finger palsied and spasmed off a single shot, then he fell dead in the dirt with the dagger still wagging.

More men came and more were cut down, yet Donovan did this with only half-consciousness. Beneath it all, his senses called to him: *Keep Shadow in your mind. He will bide till the right time and then it will be too late.* But already he had lost the ex-Swordsman, silent as Donovan himself or perhaps more so. More men drove into him, and he cut one's arm off and then his head and then sliced the other across the stomach and his bowels spilled between his boots and he sat down in his guts and died there.

A man with throwing knives maneuvered to his flank. He threw one, then the other and Donovan cut them from the air and then charged, slicing the man's head open from temple to jaw. His eyes rolled back in his head and blood leaked from his mouth as he toppled prone and convulsed in the scrub.

(It's coming. It's taking hold. This is the end of you.)

"NO!" cried Donovan, out loud though he did not mean to, and then more men fell to Orin's wrath with fine lines carved through their flesh and bones, their weapons spinning from dead fingers and clattering away into the brush. More men approached afterwards with murder in their eyes and where was Shadow?

His low voice spoke then. Through the battle blood mixed with the Cold in some dark alchemical halfbreed of instinct, he heard a finger pulling back a trigger, heard the very brush of the pad of the index finger against the weathered iron. The second gunman was behind him, with two more soldiers wielding swords attacking from in front. If any of these men survived their encounter with this last leader of the Order, they might have told the tale once or twice in taverns or elsewhere and received looks of bewilderment or disbelief or guffaws and dismissals and then never spoke of it again. None would have the chance. The discharged bullet flew straight and true and would have felled the Swordsman, but Donovan was a man possessed—no longer just a man, as the Cleric had said—and with a cry, Orin sheared the moist air and thin filaments of sparks flew like streamers from its edge and the halves of the bullet, for it had been fully cleaved, flew wide of each other and punched holes in the approaching soldiers. The gunman was gaping and stumbling back, face as blank as an idiot, when Donovan's silver spike, kept clean of rust by a mindful Mary of Pleasantry, flew from his hand and impaled his throat.

The Swordsman spun and none were left, and that was what he had feared.

Shadow's blade, Orin's black twin, fell then from its high stance and sliced open Donovan's duster and the flesh of his back. Donovan arched with a cry, arms flailing. He felt first a numb shock and the pour of boiling acid into his spine, then collapsed to his hands and knees with his old comrade leering above him.

In the distance, the largest of the Dwellers crushed into the iron hold of the Hole with one mighty fist and bent it enough to find a grip around its edge, and even from here Donovan could hear the people of Pleasantry screaming.

28

Earny pressed back against the wall next to Grampy and trembled as he saw first one, then four massive gray fingers with long curved black claws reach through the ruined opening of the door to the Hole. The creature outside peeled back the old iron like it was paper, already cords of wretched spittle raining in, and as it tore loose the door whined like a dying thing and one hinge and then the other shattered and Earny heard it land somewhere when the Dweller tossed it aside. The other door still held somehow and one opening was not large enough for these things of the Maw to get in, but they reached anyway, their claws slicing open arms and legs, men and women falling screaming with blood between their fingers.

Then a great gray hand reached again and this time it was a young girl it closed around.

Earnald adjusted his eyepatch, drew his basilard, and with a battlecry that was not Raef's or Donovan's but his own he moved forward and hacked at the demonic fingers as they hovered above the girl's lame body. The Dweller outside hissed in pain and its claws splayed and knocked Earny onto his back. It swept across the front end of the Hole in what seemed frustration, and then withdrew.

Earny regained his breath and rose, helping the girl to her feet. Ruti, who had been crouched in his pocket, peered out now, and then the Dwellers set their efforts on the second door, the one reinforced by the thick iron rod that reached between the wood and the earth and held it fast, and they threw their force against it until it began to give.

29

Shadow gloated for only a brief moment, then delivered his killing cut, which on any other day would have beheaded his old nemesis. Now, though, even while deprived of its natural strength, Donovan's body was driven by a force beyond just his will or his training. He rose to his feet, Orin swinging outwards, his arm limp and yet somehow strong enough to deflect the strike. He stumbled backwards afterwards, barely able to stand.

Shadow struck again before Donovan could gain his balance, and then again, and only the barest of margins kept each precise strike from removing Donovan's life from his body. Parrying, thrusting, sidestepping, they battled across the sparse scrub to the hem of the trees. Then Donovan made good his first attack, sweeping Orin at an unpredictable angle that would have killed any of a hundred other men. Yet here more than ever he found that he may be more than a man but he was not a god and his attack was ill-timed and imprecise. Shadow avoided it easily, his eyes smiling, whirling his sword into a ready position. Then, with no tell beforehand, the former leader of the Black Guard caught Donovan square in the chest with a mighty kick and sent him reeling back until the aged runnels of a forgotten ironwood crushed into his back. His breath vanished in a single hard push and Orin spun from his fingers.

He watched Shadow approach, legs strengthless.

(IT'S COMING. IT'S HERE.)

NO!

"NO!" he screamed.

"You're done," said Shadow, a thin smile of almost erotic satisfaction splitting his handsome features. "Say hello to the Reaper for me."

If Donovan had any retort, it was not waited for.

While the people of Pleasantry shrieked and screamed and prayed beyond them, the former captain of the Black Guard swung for Donovan's neck with a fierce battlecry, his Swordsman's blade shearing the air with a killing blow that whined with its inhuman call, a perfect cut to end the line of Maltrese for good.

It was perhaps the finest stroke Donovan had ever seen.

And yet, just as their Master had taught them both, the Ever Circle was forever to be minded, bereft of consciousness or concern for the affairs of men, which were petty in the eyes of creation, and wherever a thing opens so it must close.

Donovan's boot, searching blindly for Orin, found it at last, and as the young boy Gaelin had once taught the boy Donovan, a year older, in the fields of Din just outside the gates of the High Lord's stronghold, the last of the Maltreses flicked his sword up to his hand and parried Shadow's blade wide and the ex-Swordsman's steel cut into the old ironwood rather than flesh. Without pause or thought Donovan's other hand drew a silver spike and plunged it into Shadow's thin body, then jammed it home with his palm just below the breastplate, piercing his gut.

Shadow's eyes stayed calm for a moment, blinked weakly, and then opened wide as he stared at the blood pooling in his palm. With an animal growl, he drove his knee forward into Donovan's groin and white pain carved through the Swordsman's torso longways as he keeled over.

"It didn't have to be this way," said Shadow. "You could have spared us all. You could have spared Rosaline." Donovan heard but could not look him in the eye. Shadow did not seem to care. "Eater and eaten, friend. The way of us all."

And with that, he took the blood cupped in his hand and forced it into Donovan's limp mouth, holding his palm clamped there, and crushed his knee into the wounded Swordsman until he swallowed it all.

Donovan leaned back, gagging, blood bubbling on his lips, his vision sliding towards blackness before rekindling into a macabre light that glared bright crimson behind his eyes. It tore asunder the last of his mind's stop gates and filled his body with a new strength that terrified him even as it relieved him of control. He grasped Gaelin by the breastplate with that strength and hammered the hard part of his skull into the soft part of his enemy's, once, twice, feeling the bony plates there crack and give with each strike, signaled by a dry crunching sound. Gaelin, named Shadow after the first and greatest of the Order, stumbled back a step, and then Donovan, holding Orin in one hand and Shadow's sword in the other, swung outwards with both of them and Shadow's beautiful head left his limp body and rolled into the forest.

The screams of Pleasantry's folk echoed into the sky as the Dwellers broke free the other door and reached into the Hole, so ravenous in their need to reclaim lost ground or pride or whatever alien thoughts possessed them that they seemed concerned with little else.

But when Donovan heard these screams, he was no longer a Maltrese or a Swordsman or even a man, but yet another dark creature of the Maw built from the Cleric's design, fueled by a power beyond reckoning. Yet somehow, deep within the recesses of his madness, a part of him, perhaps the strength of will he had just lately lamented, drove him down the hill and towards town.

30

Earny moved without thinking and accepted halfway through that this act of insanity would be the last thing he did on earth. The hinges to the lone door to the Hole ripped out of the wall with a screech and the crossbar, already bent, went next, and then there was a pause and he saw one of the Dweller's reaching for its sword.

Maybe they'll chase me and leave the others.

The thought came and went and left no time for reflection.

Then he darted up the steps and somehow between the Dwellers, who did not react at first through their frenzy, so unexpected was the sight of one of their prey charging towards and past them. Keeping his eye straight ahead, Earny raced into the center of town.

As soon as his boots were pounding the muddy road, busy most days with horse and cart and rarely travelers although more so of late, the Dwellers turned behind him and screeched, a high-pitched sound of rage he had not heard from them before. He chanced a look over his shoulder and saw them all face towards him, three hovering over the Hole and one far beyond searching for other food perhaps (and yes, it was, for there was the rear end of a cow dangling from its hidden jaws and all the lowing had ceased).

Earny was still looking back when his foot caught something hard and he went tumbling forward, his first thought even in midair to protect Ruti. He cupped his pocket and folded his arms and bent his body so that his shoulder would take the brunt of the fall, and he landed hard and scrambled onto his back to watch his death approach.

But now the Dwellers were not looking at him; all of them had turned towards the south entrance of town.

Earny followed their gaze and saw a thing approaching. He might have called it the Swordsman Donovan, who Earny had walked much of this cursed countryside with, but it was not. This was that other, and not in the fleeting way he had seen him before. The man Donovan was gone, and in its shadow came this demonic thing with gray skin much like the Dwellers and fierce red eyes burning in his skull like steel in a blacksmith's forge. The demon that once had been Donovan was sprinting forth, two swords trailing behind him like twin razor tails—given his new nature, Earny would not have been surprised to learn they were truly new appendages and not mere weapons.

As one the Dwellers hovering above the Hole readied their blades.

Donovan charged, screaming, the sound comprised of not one but many voices. The possessed Swordsman reached the Hole and leapt, still bellowing into the cold air and the encroaching Mist and the Dwellers to either side of him swung their massive swords, and then Earny saw a flash of steel impossible to follow and Donovan was tumbling in a tightly tucked ball. He landed on the far side of them, his swords still held out behind him, his shoulders heaving, his call drowned into a gurgle that faded slowly to silence, and he did not turn to look at the creatures again.

Then came a quiet that seemed preternatural, insubstantial as a dream.

Earny saw that the two Dwellers closest to the south entrance, their great blades swung in time at The Swordsman, had both missed their mark, both finding the flesh of their fellow in the process, slicing halfway into each other's dark and hidden bodies. Great spouts of blood flooded from where those massive swords stuck in tethers that dyed the mud black. The Dweller to the north did not move for a moment, and then its head—still hidden by its cowl—fell loose from its shoulders and landed in the mud. Moments later the other two Dwellers' heads rolled free as well, leaving hunched mountains of dead flesh to stand eyeless watch behind.

Behind these corpses, the fourth Dweller watched as Donovan stood swaying on his feet, his breathing loud and fierce, the breathing of a bull tired and injured but still ready to charge.

Ruti alighted from Earny's chest then and fluttered high into the air. The highwayman scrambled after, tryin to reach him, but could not and fell on his face in the muck trying. He watched as the Root Dragon flew to demon-Donovan, who had dropped the black sword and now held only Orin aloft, pointed at the Dweller.

The Dweller of the Mist approached a step, hesitant much the way the first of its kind in Pleasantry had been upon sight of the Swordsman in what seemed all those ages ago. Ruti hovered, then landed gently with his small feet on Orin's blade and stayed there with his wings open and his black tongue flicking like a carnivorous bird.

Earny watched the Dweller recoil from the small dragon visibly.

Then the great gray clawed hand raised its sword in a salute that mirrored the one Earny had seen Donovan give by the Gestalt, and without a sound the Dweller returned its weapon to the massive unseen clasp mounted to its back, wheeled, and flowed back into the Mist as noiseless as it had approached. Seconds later the Mist was gone and the Dweller, who would not have had time to make its escape, was nowhere to be seen.

Earny stared at this and the image of black-cloaked Donovan, his back torn open by a grievous wound, standing still with his sword aloft and Ruti atop it.

Then the people of Pleasantry saw this as well and, just as before, ran from the Hole with their arms in the air and smiles on their faces, even some of the wounded. And while they might have cheered for the Swordsman when first he came to this land poor of faith and hope and then later reneged, now they each held a new hope in their hearts that might never go out, and so did Earnald Avers, formerly of the Raef clan, now of an Order he could never truly join, and yet would dedicate his life to if given even a hint of a chance.

For an instant, Earny feared for the people of Pleasantry as they approached Donovan, feared that his madness might turn on them and that he would massacre them all. But before they could reach him, the Swordsman's legs wobbled and spasmed and he dropped his sword. Ruti took off and hovered over him, and the people saw this and held back while the Swordsman's exhausted body convulsed much the way it had while in the throes of the Aspy's poison.

Then Donovan Maltrese collapsed at the edge of town beside his family sword and lay still and did not move again, his breath gone, his heartbeat stopped, his low voice silenced, his great life snuffed out.

V

THE CLOSING CIRCLE

1

"Wake, child."
 The voice crept from the mass of shadows and fangs that was Jana's dream. Her eyes opened on their own, the trestlework high overhead bathed in the blue drear anterior to dawn as outside the distant corrugated rim of the mountains birthed a new sun as it had when the old folk walked and flew, and as it would still when there was nothing to walk this world at all. The chandeliers watched, swaying almost imperceptibly on a nonexistent wind. For a moment, she heard the creak of the iron fixings and nothing else and wondered if the voice was left from her dreams as it had been many nights before.

"Look at me," said the voice, this time from near the wall across from her bed.

Jana lurched upright and pushed her feet and hands into the bed until she was mashed against the fretted headboard.

The Cleric sat within a pale frame of predawn light, his staff across his lap, the spotless gather of his white robes shifting about him like the surface of a milky pool and not cloth. He was looking towards the window at the lightening sky, thin scarecrow fingers folded, knifelike jaw set, violet eyes swimming with deep thought.

Jana felt her fear and rage rush to the surface. "Stay away from me. Stay away!" She wanted to cry but stopped herself, attempting to find a semblance of calm amidst the chaos of her emotions. She looked away from the source of the voice, her gaze on the folds of her bedcover and her heaving chest above, caging her feelings with refusal to admit his proximity, to see the truth, to look at him; she could not look into those eyes as they turned towards her, the ones her mind saw every night but always denied.

"My child. My dearest child," said the Cleric, running one ghoulish fingertip along the black lacquered length of his bladed staff. "You should not fear me. I am the only friend you have left."

Jana shook her head; she did not want to react to those or any other words this man might say, but just as his curse and the scar it birthed possessed her body and mind no matter how she resisted, so did his voice beg responses against her reason.

The Cleric regarded her, and she felt his eyes on her skin like probing fingers. "I have news for you," he told her in that same velvet tone that never spiked or waned but flowed in an even curve that delighted with its sound. "Would you hear it?"

She jammed her hands over her ears like an infant and stared at the hills of her bedsheets. She could not allow herself to listen. To listen would be to concede, and Jana Hunter of the Hunter Clan would never do such, not for the pleasure of her greatest enemy. She knew she looked like a child sitting there crosslegged with her ears covered, but she did not care.

The Cleric sounded amused when he spoke again. "Your family were Eastfielders, Shadow told me. He had taken a liking to you. More than I would have condoned. Not because of his station but because of yours, you see. Gaelin was never a man to stay within another's shadow for long, pardon the pun, and yours would have been no different. So alas, while my news is sad it is also the word of inevitability. As your family was, though I am sorry for that as well."

Don't listen to him. Every word he says is a lie. He's sorry for this? For the ending of the world he has built with his own two skeleton hands?

As if reading her mind, the Cleric leaned back and his smile faded. "You think me a liar and a manipulator. You think my words mere triptalk and little else. You have that in common with Donovan. All things to him away from the straight and narrow must be roundabout in truth. It was his folly, I think. Else his choices at Kolendhar would have been different and things would not be now as they are…" He trailed off and looked away from her again, as if he would have spoken the same had he been alone. "Donovan is dead. And so is Shadow."

Jana looked at him sharply. "That's not true."

"It is, whether you choose to believe me or not. You are already my guest here and my creation—my greatest, as I told Donovan. A beautiful mistake you might say. Ever since I returned from the dark places, I have sought that which might succeed us when we are all dust in this earth that does not love us or hate us but is indifferent to us. I thought it would be you and he. But to replicate what I've accomplished…" There was sadness in his voice, the sort her father might have shown while reflecting upon a trinket he wished to give Mum as a gift but could not quite locate; it convinced Jana more than any words could, and she put her head in her hands and fought the tears but they came anyway.

"I know you hate me," said the Cleric. "And, as all things, this is expected and will pass into an unknown, as will we all and our deeds with us. But know that more than any woman who has walked this world, you are of a kind unequaled, and so will be your place in what transpires from now until the Maw takes us all."

"How…" said Jana. She did not want to speak, but her body did as it chose, her own personal Mule. "How did they die?"

The Cleric laughed. "How do men ever die? By the sword or fang or worse or better. Shadow thought he might usurp me and mayhap take you for his queen. But you cannot untwine fate, child. We all ride its course, and whether we choose to end it now or let it end later, we have nevertheless done just as fate always intended. Gaelin's fate was to succumb to his arrogance. I taught him of creation, of the folly of man's subservience to his greed. But he never listened. That is another flaw of man. Always his own best counsel he kept, and no one is more ill-equipped to perceive a man's plight than he himself."

Jana's mind raced. She felt a distant sadness at the loss of Shadow, yet this was the sort she had experienced as a child when discovering Mum had cooked a different meal than anticipated and the feeling was fleeting. Then she imagined Donovan, last seen full of vigor and distraught by something beyond her reckoning, now dead and cold somewhere, those fierce green eyes that looked upon her as if a child with smug indifference now staring forever at nothing at all.

Oh, Donovan. Keeper save us all.

She truly was alone. There would be no rescue. There would be no chance meeting in the Wastes that might undo this horror inside her, subjugating her inch by inch. The end was fast approaching, the only truth of it this man or demon sitting before her. She looked him in the eye and this time she felt only the rage and none of the fear. "You sent him for a cure to our...condition. Was it all a lie?"

The Cleric looked long and hard at her—she noticed now that he breathed far less than a man should. His fingers wrapped around his staff. "It is true I sought something that might help you and he both, a piece or building block you might call it that I have yet to manipulate and see what else can be wrought. You might call it a cure, for if I discovered such useful things they would be applied in just such a manner to enrich your gifts further. But in a way, I did send Donovan to his cure just the way he wished it. It was the final piece to understanding my purpose in this world. If the very seed of my thought, the man I had shaped with words and training since his days of swaddling clothes, could still fall to this plague that I see and smell everywhere, not just in this world but left from some other world where buildings towered and machines crawled the earth like living things, then there is some innate cancer at fault with mankind and it must be remedied as such. Donovan escaped this madness by his death. And he taught me much." The Cleric's stark eyes became unfocused and he turned inward again.

Jana could not take her gaze from him. She thought of the shed, where Teddy Fen had once inundated her with inept kisses, where this man the Cleric had impregnated her with his madness and left her mind shattered forever. "What will you do with me now?"

The Cleric smiled and rose, the end of his staff clacking on the sandstone. "Where this takes us, who can say? You'll stay here and perhaps in other quarters come time so you don't...damage yourself. And should I send scouts to recover the thing Donovan might have brought me from that town of the damned, you will be first to know if I discover something of note."

"What town?" Jana asked, her head cocked. "Eastfield?"

"Pleasantry, my child. That place where lies fate's crossroads, and where I was shown much in my time beyond the rim of the world, where my eye and my power and that of the Dwellers, too, was blinded by something of what make I could not tell you. But it was there and there only that fate would be twisted one way or the other, towards my vision of salvation for humanity and its few reasons to be saved, or to my undoing by the hand of some farmer or would-be warrior. Many things real and philosophical have met in Pleasantry these past months, and now we will see what remains."

The Cleric moved towards her and she recoiled, skin crawling, heart spurning in a frenzy against her chest. He reached for her and she could not move, just as she had not been able to in the shed. When his fingers were about to caress her cheek they paused, his thin face frowning.

He left then without another word. She listened to his footfalls vanish down the hall and decided in that moment that tomorrow she would flee, and if she died trying then she, too, would find a cure for this madness as Donovan had.

She lay back down and stared at the ceiling and thought that if Earny Avers had any intention of making good his oath, she hoped he was on his way to doing so.

2

Donovan's body was placed on plankboards tied with leather and propped upon a makeshift bier in the center of town. His wounds had been sewn closed and his face cleaned by Mary and others; it shone there pale and lifeless in the dying light. From a distance, he looked as Earny remembered him, asleep for the next few hours before the next leg of some great journey whose end could be speculated upon by common men but never grasped. His duster remained on, the cut from Shadow's blade mended along the back, the rest shredded by travel and battle. Earny held Orin now, but he felt an impostor for doing so. He would not leave it to be stolen, though, nor would he ever draw it. Maybe he'd find someplace in the mountains where men did not trod and bury it there and let the earth reclaim it.

"We'll leave him for folk to pay their respects till morning, then we'll light it," said Tomson, arms crossed, wearing a deep frown. His forehead was bandaged with linen, as was his shoulder. He looked at Earny and saw the deep sadness in his face and patted his back. "It'll be all right, lad. A man of his sort was never going to last forever in this world. Luckily, he lasted long enough to show us this side of him, so we best not forget, or what was it for?"

Earny nodded, but well-meant words did little for open wounds. He clasped his hands and wept silently from his good eye. When the sobs subsided, he looked for Ruti, but his small dragon friend had disappeared soon after the incident with the Dwellers and was still nowhere to be found. Earny hoped he was all right; two friends in one day was more than this old Earny's heart could take, pray it true.

He turned and studied the ruined doors to the Hole, which men were already at work repairing. Another Mist had come through and sent the people screaming and huddling in their homes, but with this white monstrosity no roars or swords appeared, and once the cold breath of the Maw was gone so were the dead Dwellers and none could say how or where. Earny wished they had had a chance to take a good look at those corpses; knowing the manner of thing you fought eased a man's fear.

He spent the day wandering town, where the air was a potent amalgam of elation and great sadness. He visited Corly's house, where the injured man still lay unconscious. His arm had been splinted and a clot bled out and his wife was waiting to see if he'd ever wake again. Earny prepared her dinner as best he could and helped her lift Corly's limp legs onto a pillow, and when darkness set in he embraced her even though he had never met her before and left dragging his feet through the dimming twilight.

As he watched the mud and horse tracks and the furrows ground out by wagon wheels and the black water pooled within pass beneath him, he thought of what to do next. Jana still awaited him at Pal Myrrah. Could he trek all that way alone and stay alive long enough to rescue her? How might he, all bravado aside, manage his way across the Gestalt? Perhaps word might spread among the Dweller community that he, Earnald Avers, was the same man who had walked the Drudge with one Donovan of Kolendhar, and that man had slain four of their numbers and his comrade was no one to balk at. But no, Earny Avers would be sliced apart and chewed upon and swallowed whole and shat out before he'd get one word out of his bumbling mouth to a Dweller. Maybe he could convince Tomson or Brig to come along, fighting men such as they were, their ambition boosted by their skirmish with the Misty.

Last thing they're gonna do is press their luck. They'll look at ya with hard frowns and shuffle about and stare at their toes and tell ya they've gotta keep busy wit' the wife and a baby on the way and the fields have to be tended, see, and there's just no way though they'd like nothin' better than to help.

Earny shook his head at the lighting stars as though they were the source of his frustration and marched on towards Tomson's house. When he passed Donovan's resting place there were swags of flowers along the base of the bier tied with string, and one man knelt before the dead Swordsman with his hands clasped, asking that he be forgiven for speaking ill, whispering that his anger was misplaced and that he'd do anything to repent. Earny frowned and headed up the hill and thought he'd not spend another night in Pleasantry for as long as he lived.

He sat awake in the orange orb of Tomson's hearth and studied the cutting flame as it danced, poking the black air above it. Tomson came in with Brig and Mullville, and they poured stout and drank and Earny felt it burn all the way down.

"I don't know about you folks, but I got a mind to sleep till Harvest and then take a piss and sleep some more," said Brig, sipping stout and staring blankly at the fire.

"I don't think I'll ever sleep again, truth told," said Mullville. His eyes, most days dark and downtrodden, now looked as dead as the Swordsman's. "Every time I close my eyes I see a big black pit fulla teeth bout to chomp me in half."

"That'll pass," said Tomson, and he sounded like he believed it. "Dreams of that sort are your mind finding a way to work matters out, sometimes the sort it's not built to, so it takes a sight longer than you'd want."

Earny took a quick sip of stout, then spoke. "I always thought dreams were yer brain arguin' with some other part of ya that knows and sees more than we kin hold onto while we're awake. Usually it's sayin' somethin' important, but most folk don't pay a lick of attention to it. Then when it passes it's cuz it's too late or cuz you listened or you didn't." He remembered his mother telling him that; only the words and not the voice.

The other men looked at him and did not speak for a while.

Earny adjusted his eyepatch. "But what in the name of it do I know?"

Tomson downed the rest of his stout and tabled the mug. "You're a good man, Earny. I see now what Donovan saw in you. He was nothing if not a fine judge of character, I warrant. He'll be missed by us almost as much as by you, Keeper pray."

Earny nodded and smiled. The mayor meant well, but did not know of what he spoke.

* * * *

In the grim midnight dark, Earny woke to discover Ruti creeping up his pallet and to his side. He had not seen the Root Dragon all day, and his heart lifted at the sight of those blue-ringed eyes and darting tongue. Ruti crept close to his face and folded back his wings and pressed his side to Earny's cheek, squirming to get comfortable. When Earny ran his finger along Ruti's back, the little dragon arched like a cat and tilted his head and nuzzled his companion.

"I missed ya, fella. Where'd you find yerself all day?"

Ruti looked at him with something in his eyes, too human to be denied, which spoke of deep sadness.

"Somethin' tha matter?"

Ruti seemed to nod.

"I miss him, too. That it?"

The tiny dragon whiffled his wings and beat his tail and pressed hard against Earny's face. In the moonlight, his tiny scales appeared incandescent, and they felt smooth to the touch and almost slick, yet Earny found them also strangely comforting. He thought he could feel the fierce beat of the little thing's heart; it raced five times the speed of his even while at rest.

He stroked under Ruti's chin.

"You think everything will be all right?"

Another nod.

"Somethin's wrong isn't it? Somethin' besides Master Donovan and all."

Without warning, Ruti flicked his tongue lightly across Earny's face, and the ex-highwayman drew back and laughed. "Whaddya doin' that fer?"

The root dragon crawled carefully onto his arm and waved his tail and stared at him.

"*Eaahrneyyy.*"

Earny's smile broadened. "You've been practicing, eh? I'm prou-dovya, I am. By the time we get back to Ms. Jana, you'll be readin' outta books, wager a thumb. Never been so proud ova thing in my life."

Ruti batted his wings excitedly.

"You ready fer some rest? Don't know about you, but this has felt like the longest day in tha history o' days and I'm about to pass out."

Ruti drew up, his scales flexing outwards as they tended to do, and nodded again.

"You've been tha best friend I ever had in this miserable life. Short of my wife, Keeper Bless her," said Earny. He felt tears in his good eye again, but held them back so the Root Dragon would not see.

The sadness gave way at length and he smiled, content, and closed his eye, trying for sleep. When he drifted off at last, his dreams were full of monsters and Blood Demons and worse, but Ruti was there and so it was all right and the little dragon proved a valuable ally in the ethereal boundlessness of his unconscious.

A best friend if ever there was one.

As Earny drifted off to sleep, Ruti pressed closer still and stared out the window at the slow silver spin of the night sky, remaining awake, as though savoring something ineluctable, as if he did not want to miss one precious moment before it was gone forever.

3

The day had not yet broken when Earny woke.

He rose and rubbed his eye and scanned the dim light of Tomson's home. He could hear Tomson and Mary still breathing, deep and even, in their room. There was no one else about.

Ruti was gone.

Earny rose and raked his fingers through his hair and stroked his chin stubble (he meant to shave come downtime from all this madness), searching the dark for his boots. He found them after a moment and pulled them on.

"Ruti? Ya there?"

If the Root Dragon was around, he was not answering. Earny rose, his concern growing. He whispered into the darkness, as if by repetition he might make things true that were not. "Come on. Answer me. We still got a bit to sleep 'fore we press off."

Nothing moved in the shadows. Earny sighed. "Ruti?"

Then he heard a flutter and it was outside. He thought he glimpsed movement through the fretwork, the vague silhouette of his tiny friend, and he hurried after it. "Wait, where're ya goin'?"

By the time he was to the door, Ruti was down the hill and gliding towards town. Earny watched him go and considered leaving his friend to his own business. *Last thing anyone in this world wants is a nosey-knob.* He went so far as to close the door and head back to bed when something Donovan might have named his low voice told him to go back, that he must go back. He listened reluctantly, eased open Tomson's door and shut it silently behind him. Peering into the darkness, doubting himself still, he jogged down the hill.

He spotted his friend from a hundred paces. The Root Dragon was hovering over Donovan's body, small feet dangling, tongue flicking. From here he looked like a miniature miscolored dove, though doves could not hover far as Earnald Avers knew. He wanted to say something, but he knew the Swordsman had shared long, late nights with the Root Dragon and had confided in him in their dead language and whatever bond that had formed should be mourned. The ex-bandit squatted instead in the middle of the muddy cold and hugged his knees and watched as the small dragon lowered himself onto Donovan's chest.

For some reason then, shivering in the merciless chill, he recalled his family, vibrant and alive in some mundane moment his mind had chosen to store. Then he saw them after the sickness, halfway to the Black, rotting on the outside and the inside, and a deep pain ate through him.

Ruti was staring at the stars and did not seem to notice him, though he had a feeling few things on this earth could sneak up on his small, scaled companion. Overhead, fires burned and twinkled in the sky from distances incomprehensible, each flicker of light a reach through time by the very moments which had birthed the Root Dragon and times older still, when other men with other aims and far different minds had walked and ruled this place. They whirled overhead in a celestial pirouette, and below them, Ruti, who knew of such things by way of Memories according to Donovan, looked from the sky to the fog-shrouded town of Pleasantry, and then to the colorless complexion of the Swordsman.

A deep silence grew that stilled everything, even the thrum of Earny's heartbeat.

Then the light began.

It started as a single ember born from the Root Dragon's chest. It grew brighter soon, a shimmering star than which no fireball in the sky could feel fitter. It pulsed rhythmically, and from Earny's vantage Ruti's body seemed aglow with a gleaming white halation.

Earnald Avers was not considered a quick-witted man by even the kindliest of regards, and he wrinkled his brow and watched this spectacle and strained to discern what was happening. His mind searched with all its fallible resources his memory and his knowledge, for he dared not interrupt and ask his age-old companion.

And then, like a meteor, a single memory struck and left him stunned.

I've heard it said a Root Dragon can save a single flux of a man's breath and return it later, for a price, should he lose it.

It was Donovan's voice. Then Earny's eye opened wide and he understood. "Ruti! Ruti, no!"

The dragon looked at him at last, and even from this distance the once-bandit could spot the warmth in those tiny blue eyes as they regarded him. But something else was there too, more than warmth or caring; it was a sense of purpose, something which overrode all else, the look of a man or thing that subscribes to an ideal worth trading everything for.

Arms floundering, steps sottish, Earny hurried to reach his friend, as though his ineffectual hands might somehow stop a thing built of so many years and so many lives. Somewhere along this dash, he pondered whether Root Dragons had lived in secret among the old folks before the Shift; surely they had, so ancient was their race.

Ruti's tail wagged at the sight of his friend, and Earny thought that he glimpsed undersized tears wriggling over the Root Dragon's small cheeks, crystalline beneath the intense glare of the lifesource pulsing in his chest.

Earny slowed ten paces away and watched Ruti traverse Donovan's chest, inching, as though each movement was filled with anguish and it was only his will that drove him forward. When he reached Donovan's breathless lips, Earny saw the glittering light rise along the Root Dragon's neck, his entire body rendered phosphorescent now, his tail and his wings outstretched with the look of something fierce and ancient and of a nature the world knew not and would never see again. When the light settled, he bent slowly to Donovan, tongue flitting, opened his jaws, and let that luminous orb slip from his mouth to the Swordsman's, and there it vanished.

It reappeared moments later, expanding until it encompassed man and dragon, and Earny threw up his hands to shield himself. He swore he felt a rumble within the earth then, though he could not be sure, but imagined or not, something knocked him from his feet. He landed hard and struggled upright and now the light was flaring so brightly he feared it might burn his flesh.

When it extinguished at last and the rumbling—for there *had* been a rumbling—settled, he wiped his eye and looked upon the aftermath.

There was Ruti, limp now, laying upon Donovan's still black form.

Earny approached, a hard sob plugging his throat. As he came to Donovan's side, Ruti forced himself up onto unsteady legs, legs held up not by living strength but by the last clutch a dying thing keeps to its fading life.

"No. Please no…" said Earny, his voice breaking. But words could not undo such things and the ex-bandit knew it.

The Root Dragon crept close enough to flick his small black tongue across his friend's lips, and then whispered, "Eaahrrn-ey."

Then Ruti the Root Dragon, a survivor of the old world and the thousand years since, closed his eyes and exhaled deeply and died, and with him a thousand years of the Memories, for nothing, no *ai'che* or any other magic, could bring back what had been sacrificed this day.

4

When Donovan opened his eyes, the first thing he heard was sobbing. He sat up upon his funeral bier like a demon summoned from the Black, and when he moved his body was filled with acid and a low pulsing heat in his chest that pained him. When he looked down, he saw Earny sitting on the ground beside the bier, and cradled in his hands was the gray and lifeless body of the Root Dragon, the iridescent quality of his scales gone now, leaving a matte corpse devoid of any indication that it might once have lived.

The Swordsman eased his legs over the edge—they felt as though they had never been used, the oversized legs of some giant newborn—and settled them onto the ground. The flesh on his back felt stiff and sore but no comparison to what was; whatever magic had called him back from the Black must have knitted his flesh as well. Above him, the stars sang from the nether and the moon glowed on a jagged horizon and from everywhere came the sound of cricket song. Still, in the cellar of his mind, lay the Cold, dormant now, perhaps living its life parallel to his, taking respite from its constant barrage once its quarry was thought dead and lost.

Earny looked up at the Swordsman, and Donovan could barely see his singular blue gaze through its thick tears. Without a word, he sat beside the retired highwayman, and together they looked on the still form of their friend who would never move or fly or nuzzle or speak again, all so some greater good might come to this world.

As for what that good might be, Donovan Maltrese, who had spent years marching soulless and aimless but for his survival, was now certain, and he swore silently that when he called forth the souls of those left behind to lend him their strength, among them would be Ruti of the Root Stone.

And what a mighty strength it would be.

5

When the Swordsman entered Tomson's home, the mayor and his wife were awake and dressing. Upon sight of him, Tomson shrank back against the wall with his eyes wide and Mary let out a scream before withdrawing to the next room and peering back in through the doorway. "What devilry is this?" asked Tomson, jaw quivering.

"The last gift of a friend. And what would I not give for it to be otherwise," said Donovan. His voice was grim.

"I…" began the mayor of Pleasantry. "I don't believe it."

Donovan nodded, his mind already racing, his plan forming fast in the back of his mind. "You must believe, friend. I ask you now for one last favor. Would you hear it?"

The mayor looked him over with a deep frown. "What do you ask of me?"

Donovan crossed his arms and considered his words carefully.

* * * *

They were mounted by dawn, Brig and Mullville and Two-Shock as well. Earny came with them, and outside Tomson's house he brought Orin from its hiding spot and proffered it to the mounted Swordsman like an idol. Donovan took up his family blade, which felt long missed and sweet and familiar in his grasp, and he slung it across his shoulder and adjusted it so that it dug into his back just right.

As their procession headed towards the edge of town, the old man Grampy came before the Swordsman's horse, hobbling on his cane. He waved and the Swordsman waved back and reigned in as

485

Grampy reached into the folds of his robes and produced a small tin, offering it. Donovan took the gift; inside was a month's worth of Boon. "Yer friend Earny thar says yer fond o' the Boon. Not a thing wrong wit' tha like 'o that, Swordsman. Not a damned thing."

Donovan's smile broadened. He handed the tin back to Grampy and the old man's wrinkled hands shook as he grasped it. "You keep it. Smoke one for me now and then, if you would," said the Swordsman.

"Keeper save us, I'll smoke two fer ya and more often than I should," said Grampy, his old yellow teeth, a great many missing, bared in a smile belonging to a much younger fellow.

Some townspeople gathered as before to watch them leave.

This time, not one spoke ill of the Swordsmen or his companions.

Then, together, the men rode out, though to what destiny Donovan had not yet revealed.

* * * *

They crossed the great plain, and here Donovan saw the disturbed earth and shattered trees marking the path of the Dwellers who had met their end in Pleasantry. He glanced at Earny, who was eyeing the ruined copses with a dark frown, and he reached for the saddened highwayman and touched his shoulder, finding a reluctant smile in response.

They rode through the creek, through the narrow defilement, and the way was much less treacherous without flesh-eating beasts snapping at their heels. Donovan once or twice glanced back at Tomson, whose knife was sheathed across his thigh and who looked a mountain of a man that no wind could topple. He wondered if he should tell him or any of the others of what had almost happened in Pleasantry: that his path had taken him so far towards darkness that only luck and fate and perhaps the arrogance of Shadow himself had saved them. He opened his mouth to say as much, and then closed it without a word and decided that all would be told in the end, should fate allow it.

By late day they had reached the Dweller holy place, ruined now by their battle. The body of the king was gone, but the crumbled remains of shattered walls and dolmens and the dry puddles and dapples of blood remained. The rest of the men waited near the entrance when Donovan rode in and he looked back and asked them why they did not follow. "I've risked my life once, Donovan. This is far as I go. Gotta keep a breath o' room to turn and run come need," said Brig, and the others agreed. In the end, only Earny followed Donovan in.

The Swordsman dismounted at the center of the great stone enclosure, and with a grimace reached into his pannier and produced the still dripping, still pulsing heart of the slain Dweller King. He held it overhead, and as he did he felt the ropy scar across his body stretch and ache. In the bottom of his mind, the Cold rose up.

(Still here, ever here, the same again and ever again...)

He ignored it, for though it felt strong and vengeful it was not as before and he could contain it for now. He climbed the center dolmen and looked on the shattered remains of the winged effigy, the head of which was still recognizable, the rest dust, and thrust the black heart into the air, roaring. The sound of his voice clambered about the distant jags and died there.

Earny dismounted and stood with one hand on his basilard, the other on the reigns of his spooked horse, and waited. When nothing appeared for a time, he asked Donovan, "Master Swordsman, sir. What're we doin here?"

"What we are doing and what I hope to do are not one same thing," he told Earny, much to his befuddlement. "Stay close and quiet and follow my lead."

This seemed good enough for Earny, who stood back to back with Donovan and did not lower his basilard.

Donovan looked back towards Tomson, and there were the men still outside the stone near the buttresses, fear in their eyes and their weapons ready. That was all right by the Swordsman's reckoning; this next exchange would be between the Dwellers and himself, and it was only his low voice that told him such was possible, a fleeting view of things more complex than he had first imagined, glimpsed initially at the Gestalt and its far shore.

They did not wait long. Minutes later the Mist appeared, first outside the stone enclosure, then within, faint initially, and then coalescing into a greater suffocating mass. As it did the horses whinnied and reared, and Earny grabbed them both by the reins and hushed them. Behind, Tomson and Brig exchanged words Donovan could not understand. He heard Brig's axe, still notched, slip from where it rested.

He watched the white sheet of the Mist, which was motionless now and did not creep like mere fog, and waited, his heart thumping but his mind set. He thought of his death, which had felt like no more than a dreamless sleep, and looked at his hands and realized no blood had flowed through them this time yesterday. The thought put a shiver in him.

Then the Mist receded, and there stood seven Dwellers in a semicircle before him, all with their swords still clamped to their backs, each clothed in the same impenetrable cowl hiding any feature, eyes or teeth or otherwise. Their tattered robes, sewn of some thick material, heavy wool maybe, wavered on a low breeze that swelled about them. Overhead, the clouds had regrouped and now worked to blot out the sun entire and were halfway successful.

Donovan watched them with the Dweller King's heart still held overhead, black tendrils of blood swirling down his bare forearms. Then the Dweller in the center came forward, noiseless, Mist curling like the ghosts of serpents before the stripped and fraying hem of its robe.

"*Anath moei kotaen*," he said to the Dweller, and he thought a wave of reaction swept through them but could not be sure.

They regarded him darkly, enigmatic specters so disparate from man as to render them inconceivable. Then the Dweller who had stepped forward reached for its sword. As one the men still mounted at the mouth of the enclosure readied their weapons; Donovan heard this and halted them with a sharp gesture of his hand. When he looked at the Dweller again, the great creature held its sword in salute, then returned it to its hold. Then a voice erupted, the sound of wet scraping rocks and rumbling quakes in the earth, of scuttling insects millions in number and of great, warping sheets of iron: "*BUELI KOMENTHANAKATAI. PEI FI MOETH SAO ELOI.*"

The ground trembled from the sound, and when the creature was done speaking Donovan looked at Earny and then the others and they were all of them staring open-mouthed and wide-eyed, unable to move or react, all thought of their weapons fled.

"*Uhi eui noai komenth*," Donovan said, and then leaped from the dolmen and approached with the Dweller King's heart held before him. He could smell the creature beneath the robes from here, the sweet yet acrid scent of a bonestrewn grave or a sickhouse or a butcher's store, the cloying tingle of something else, rotting and terrible, beneath it all. As the creature shifted and hunched with its huge claws opening, Donovan could hear the wet sound of its movements and wondered what horrors he might find behind those black garments, whether they be the dress of soldiers or religion or for some other purpose. The Dweller closed its taloned fingers gently around the black, dripping heart and took it from the Swordsman, then handed it off to another creature where it disappeared into the folds of its great black robe.

Donovan watched expectantly, his heart racing, and prayed this wager would succeed. If it did not, then Jana Hunter would surely be lost, for how else might a plan be mobilized so quickly? He feared magic mortally; only with dire need did he summon it, and nothing could be more dire now than saving the young girl whose show of courage had altered the course of his life and the lives of every soul in Pleasantry.

"We need your help," he told the Dweller, praying that things so unearthly and so ancient would know the tongues of man. For a moment he feared they might not, for the Dweller looked to its kin as though perplexed. Then it gazed on him again, though he could not see its eyes, and it nodded. Donovan took another step forward, his blood afire with something akin to battle blood but beyond it.

The feeling of doing what is just, perhaps...

"I was sent here by a man you know as the Cleric, but I know him as my once teacher and comrade. He says your kind have formed a pact with him, one that serves well for now. But he has sent me here with the purpose of slaying your King for aims I do not understand, dark though they surely are. What I do understand is this: whatever his designs for this world, your kind are no more a component of his mechanizations in the end than are mine. He required this piece of your ruler beneath the guise of curing an ailment which threatens me. I now think it more likely he is looking for a way to change you the way he has learned to change us."

The Dwellers exchanged looks, somehow worrisome despite their expressionlessness.

"You have come across what we humans call Blood Demons in your travels, no doubt, for there are thousands upon thousands of them and they spill into and from Pal Myrrah each day."

The Dweller nodded.

"The Cleric is a blight on our land. He seeks to replace all nature has wrought with his own creations by altering them through dark magic. He has learned to do so with humans, and all that bars his way is you and your fellows. He sent me here knowing that if I succeeded it could be kept secret who had performed this task, and that if I failed it was not bound to him for failure would surely mean my death. Your king was a great warrior and I regret what has taken place here where you worship."

He searched the ground for words, praying his conjecture was right, for even with the Dwellers as allies there was one final piece needed to save Jana Hunter's life.

"You travel by the Mist, do you not? That is how you move from place to place…"

The Dwellers exchanged silent council. At length, the one forward nodded.

Donovan stepped close and looked straight into the maw of that hood, Orin held at his side. "Does it carry only your kind? Or might you take us, humans, as well?"

The Dweller stared long and hard at the Swordsman for a moment that stretched forever, then retreated to his fellows where they formed a circle. Donovan watched as they deliberated, heard those same utterances, muted now, of slick and unearthly speech. He glanced at his companions, and all of them, even Earny, were gaping at him as though he was a madman.

When the Dwellers broke congress and approached, the one forefront now wore the crown fallen from his beheaded brethren, and Donovan bowed his head in respect.

"*Builoekuethi. Ueli, Ko'tai,*" it said to him.

If Donovan had expected to hear any words of the old tongue from this creature, those were not them.

His heart, pounding before, bounded up his throat and pulsed in his head, unbridled. He turned to the men who had ridden here with him. "Tomson, Brig, Earny. All of you. Come closer."

The men looked at him and then at each other, and one by one they acceded and rode into the center of the Dweller holy ground. The Swordsman grinned at them all.

"We are going for a ride," he told them.

6

The Swordsman called Vine was drunk, a common way for him as of late. He stumbled from the tavern, called Grumbling Bill's, which lay at the northeast corner of Rend, and walked a waving course over the dirt roadway with a pipe of Boon in one hand and a jug of stout dangling from the other.

He paused in the center of a square and struck a match on the fourth try and tried to light his pipe, but he could not. And of course not, for if the Keeper should let him enjoy a night's drinking alongside an hour or two of sweet Boon, then the Keeper might as well strike him dead where he stood, for to what greater pleasure in this life might he look forward? He immediately looked at the sky and bowed his head and reminded the Keeper that he did not truly wish to be struck down, if He minded the saying.

The streets of Rend were empty, most men snoring in their beds drunk or unconscious where their barfights had left them senseless or in bed with their wives or their whores, or fully armored and stationed about the walls staring into the utter black of the night, listening to the twinkling song of the Hunter, daydreaming about whatever it is young men dream of when they're primed for a war that never comes, for a siege that is never laid. Only a young man might lament that, Vine thought to himself. Never one who had seen war. Never one who had walked the smoldering remains of Kolendhar.

Most nights at this time he would venture into a darker quarter and find himself the warm embrace of a young woman—or several, for who among them would say no to a *Ko'tai*, a Swordsman? But tonight he veered left instead of right and walked the empty streets with his head hung low. Tonight Vine missed his wife, and these nights were the hardest. After all, his former commander, Donovan, was not the only Swordsman who had left loved ones in the destruction at the Tip of the Sword. Vine's younger, vengeful heart sought repayment for what had been lost there, but always his older voice, the one that had kept him alive across battles and plagues innumerable, rose to squash out such rashness.

He walked the cobbles of the market, only half-laid, what had once been small adobe huts replaced now with masonry and shingled roofs. There was the forge of Martin of Ley, a blacksmith who had left to sell his wares elsewhere and been successful and come home with food and spices and other traded goods, only to discover his village destroyed by Blood Demons. Killed one of them, too, the wily bastard, stabbed it to death with the only sword he hadn't sold, the one he still wore now no matter where he went.

Vine halted his drunken march and lay down his jug and set his fogged mind again to lighting his pipe. A wind blew just at that moment and the match flame winked and went out. Vine stood staring at the spiraling filament of smoke, then threw it to the ground and stomped on it with a curse. Never in this world could all things go right. The Keeper always saw to that. Always a monkey to be thrown your way, or however that old saying went.

That aside returned his thoughts to Kolendhar, as all paths in this life seemed to, and to the great library there, overflowing with tomes, some written by scholars alive still and of much repute, others recovered from old books so faded and cracked they would turn to powder if you moved a page the wrong way. Those books had been transcribed and rebound, though many pieces were missing, and Vine had spent long nights poring over them, imagining what fingers might first have scrawled those words and what the minds controlling them had thought, loved, lost.

He finished the last of his stout and tossed away the jug. Somewhere in the distance a rooster crowed, hours off its appointed watch, and elsewhere raucous laughter and the mew of an alley cat echoed into the night. Vine looked around at all the emptiness and felt a deep sadness. Nothing would ever replace home, he realized. But this place would have to do. This and no other. No sense lamenting the unchangeable, as Master always said. No sense at all.

He nearly headed home, but instead made for the high stone stairs leading to the battlements. He wished suddenly for another jug of stout, for the men atop those walls would be cold and could use warmth in their bellies even if it meant dulling their senses.

Bad idea and you know it, said his low voice. Or his high voice. Either way, it was bad.

He shambled up the steps, seeing triple of everything, and at the top, he was greeted by the night captain, Anders was his name. "How goes it?" Vine asked the man, who eyed the drunken Swordsman head to toe and then laughed.

"It goes as well as any night goes," said Anders.

Vine nodded, as such an offhand remark described succinctly his thoughts about life entire. He stepped to the crenel and looked out at the plain and sighed.

When the first call came, it echoed from the northeast corner of the wall and Vine did not respond right away, but merely gazed out into the darkness without focus, leaning on the crenel for balance.

Anders rose beside him and cupped his hands around his mouth. "What is it, man?" he called out.

"Mist, sir!"

Now Vine's attention snapped to focus, his battle blood already rising, his drunken mind fast removed of its dimness and replaced with a razor alacrity. He drew his sword and headed down the wall towards the guard, a small man with big owl's eyes who was peering into the dark beyond the city. Vine squinted, the wineink tattoos across his cheeks bunching, and followed his stare.

And there it was, in the center of all the blackness, just within the glow of the cressets outside the city: a wall of gathering Mist.

"Anders," he said, already wishing his prayers for action had not come true, not in this form, demonic and questionably mortal. "Wake the men. Get as many suited and ready as you can. Go now!"

"My lord," said the man who had spotted the Mist. "Look!" He pointed, and Vine again followed his sightline and slapped his face to sober himself completely. Dwellers, seven of them, marched outwards from the Mist, towering black silhouettes that with one good leap could grasp the ledge of the battlements and heave themselves over to devour the good people of Rend at will.

Well then. What way of finding the Black might be better or worse?

He held ready his sword and was about to call to Anders again when an oddity caught his eye. He slapped his face once more, thinking it may just be the Boon, but no, he had never managed to light his pipe…

As they drew closer, there could be no mistaking it.

There were *men* among the Dwellers, striding forth from the Mists with bold assuredness.

And at their center was Donovan Maltrese.

7

Earny watched the Swordsmen, three in number now where before his world had mostly known one (a near brush with death for the sake of identifying Donovan being the sole exception). They sat at a table overlaid with a hastily scrawled map. Along it were lines and calligraphy denoting the Ven, the Gestalt, the Wastes, and Pal Myrrah, which bore a tiny illustration of a fortress beneath a label Earny could not read until the Swordsman said the words aloud and pointed. The ex-bandit sat himself down, craving Boon or anything else that might dull the senses. Now and then his fingers reached for his pocket, hoping to find Ruti's outstretched neck eager for a stroke. This time, when he found only air, his entire spirit seemed to sit on its rump, slump forward and give up on everything at all.

Compared to the sensation of traveling with the Dwellers, that feeling was a small matter.

First, there had been Mist, suffocatingly thick, like someone had jammed wool into his ears and nose and mouth and left him gasping. Then came the sensation of falling, endless and always accelerating—what tumbling from the world's tallest mountain might feel like, but without the rush of air or other indication of movement; the mixed signals left the brain dazzled. Then they had glided through a nightmare landscape of shadows without detail, phosphorescent outlines of ridges and promontories and gullies profuse with tall patches of grass and copses of trees, all dead, featureless in the Stygian depths the Dwellers' power commanded. Then suddenly the sensation of movement reversed with a fluttering of the stomach, as though they had been launched from a catapult. Then solid ground appeared beneath their feet, spinning along with the rest of the world, and before them stood Rend in all its splendor. The city was not Pal Myrrah's equal, and no keep within its walls matched the Cleric's stronghold, but it was imposing nonetheless; that Kolendhar had been grander than either according to the Swordsman was beyond his imagining.

Donovan was mulling over the map now, propped above it on his hands, his hard eyes hidden by a thoughtful squint. Across from him sat Vine, Goesef, and three other men who had skipped Earny during their introductions once the initial chaos of the Dweller's arrival had subsided. The Dwellers, presumably still stationed outside the city gates—though where precisely none could say—had spawned a rush of panic which had culminated in arrows firing and the townsfolk who lived nearest the walls fleeing and stumbling over each other, seeking refuge in the inner fortress.

Now the townsfolk were home again but wary, many with sons or husbands set watch near the walls, keeping an eye out for those black horrors and their great swords that many had fled here to escape.

Earny twiddled his thumbs, his mind no more fixed in place than spit in a river, the only constant his worry for Jana and his impatience with this whole political to-do. He prayed that Rend, having been built by soldiers, might circumvent the usual plodding that plagued men into inaction.

"So here it lies. The crossroads of all. Pal Myrrah," said Donovan, his thin lips pressed tight. "I know not if the Cleric thinks me dead or alive. But my sense of him is lessened if not gone, and I'd take that as a sign he is unaware of our actions. This might be our only chance for surprise."

"If," began Goesef, "Your sense of any of this makes a difference."

"Donovan, my friend," said Vine, who sat arms folded with his boots up on the table as though this were his private living quarters. "I can't say I'm sad to see you arrive here since Goesef and I went hefts out of our way to invite you in the first place. But the last thing I hoped was for you to show up with those devils on your coattails claiming allegiance."

"After years upon years of hunting men and consuming them like you and I would scarf down a rabbit, now suddenly they're eager to be allies? I think they're apt to turn on us right there on the battlefield and gnaw our bones and lick their claws and laugh about it after with the Cleric. With Master…" said Goesef. His eyes, full of mirth when last Earny saw them, now turned downward and solemn.

"Theirs is a warrior's culture. That much I've surmised. They thought us food and nothing more, but something changed in Pleasantry. I slew their king and three others and to them that forges respect. They'll not turn on us," said Donovan.

"Says you," said Vine.

"Yes, I do," replied Donovan, leaning back with a harsh gleam in his eyes.

"What is your plan?" asked Goesef, tattooed arms crossed. His massive larger cousin to a claymore sat propped against the table, and Earny eyed it and wondered what kind of damage that might do to a man caught with a full swing. *The kind there's no sewing back together, I'm sure.*

"The Cleric is massing his Blood demons now—" began Donovan.

"Call him Master, for isn't that who he is?" said Vine.

Donovan shot the other Swordsman a look. "Morlin Sayre died in the Darklands. This man who faces us now is an abomination. Built of the same parts but to some other whole entirely."

Shadows on the Swordsmen's faces. Earny had expected these men to be all for the idea of charging forth with swords drawn and planting their blades into the thick of their troubles. Yet here in their eyes was nothing but hesitation.

"Soon the Blood Demons will number too great. They can create their own fellows and so can he and they are limited only by the folk they have ready to assimilate. Or perhaps not. Perhaps they procreate as well. What man can say?" Donovan paced behind the table, his hand holding lightly Orin's sheathed point. The crack of the fire threw orange light into his eyes that reflected outward brightly, and Earny thought of Demon Donovan's gaze with its smelting pot gleam and shivered.

When Donovan turned back to his fellows he looked angry. "I did not think I'd find this here."

"And what is that?" asked Vine.

"Apathy."

"Apathy, you say?" said Goesef, brow furrowed into dark lines of anger. "How about temperance, friend Donovan."

"Apathy, my friend. What think you? That we sit here within your fine walls, built by whom you're not quite sure, and wait for fifty thousand Blood Demons to march on you until you die screaming in the blood of your friends and loved ones and your children, or become one of them and crawl the world a mindless minion of the Cleric? For that is what will happen."

"We will fight them off. This is not Kolendhar."

"You're right," said Donovan evenly. "This is barely a shadow of Kolendhar. And see in its ashes what can fall in a single day beneath the might of this enemy."

"We can hold the city. We've learned from our mistakes," said Goesef. The wineink scrawls of his face gave him the look of a beast more than a man, and in the firelight this was intensified.

"We've not. Our mistake was not our defensive measures, my friends. If we have not learned to press any advantage available against this threat, then we are lost and that is all to be said of it." Donovan squared off with them. "You think you can hold supplies, wall up here. This will be no simple siege. The gates of Rend will shatter under the Cleric's sorcery before you even realize you've been invaded."

"If his power is so great," said Vine, leaning forward at last, "What makes you think we stand a chance taking the fight to them, on their own ground?"

Donovan smiled darkly; to Earny he looked like a lion. "The Shades. They are each of them thirty soldiers or more. And they'll not turn from the Blood Demon's toxin."

"And how do you know that?" asked Vine.

"Because the Cleric would not have sent me in search of the Dweller King's heart if they could, else his solution would have been obvious."

The men sat hushed then, some peering empty-eyed at their boots or the throbbing hearth, others exchanging looks of hesitancy.

Earny met Donovan's gaze and saw a radiant, untamable fervency there that heated his blood. The Swordsman faced his fellows again.

"In your doubt, I see a semblance of my own soul. Too long we've strayed from the Oath, lost in the troubles before our eyes and unable to mind those farther reaching, ones that define not just our fate but that of our species, whatever your feelings for its endless squabbling which Master oft lamented."

At this the Swordsmen looked up, seeming to respond to their former commander's words.

Donovan continued. "What is that emptiness you have felt? That consumes you even now? What has scoured your hearts and left you a husk from which all living stuff has been exhumed? What began when Master betrayed us and Kolendhar fell? It is not the loss of our home, or our records, or our friends, and pray the Keeper it is not our loved ones dead in the rubble. It is *us*. *We* have changed. It is the same folly that smote whatever greatness men achieved before our oldest recalled ancestors crawled this world, the constant infatuation with our own gain along a timeline far too short, within a scope far too narrow."

He drew Orin and discarded it on the table where it landed with a clang. The other Swordsmen withdrew, and to Earny they looked appalled.

"If this is what we've become, then I am ashamed to call myself *Ko'tai*. For what honor then are we beholden to but like other men to die upon the blades of our indifference?" He looked about to burst. Without warning, he lurched forward then and flipped the table and the map and the other Swordsmen withdrew in time but the rest were struck. Donovan paid their protestations no heed or apology. "My friends. If ever you were Swordsmen, if ever you knew my hand to be steady or my will true, then you know in your hearts the purity of this. This is right action. We can end something terrible now, right at the Cleric's gates. You tell me you hold five thousand trained soldiers within these walls, is that not true?"

One of the men who had not yet spoken nodded, his long greasy hair covering his face like some land-battered pilgrim. His long hauberk shone dully in the firelight.

"Raise them up and get them suited. By dawn tomorrow we can be afoot in the Wastes on the doorstep of Pal Myrrah."

"How?" asked Goesef. Already there was something new in his eyes and Earny saw it true. "How can we get there so fast?"

"The Dwellers are massing. As many of their kind as they can summon. They say they can move us all in one push."

"*Move* us?" said Vine. He looked equal parts inspired and terrified.

"By what power, I'll not tell you, but it is the same which brought us here. All I can say is eat light before you enter their circle or you'll hear of it from your stomach," said Donovan with his dark, odd smile.

"You're telling me," said Goesef, "that you want us to gather every good fighting man we have here in a lump out in the fields and let an army of Dwellers encircle them on the hunch that they'll somehow whisk us off to fight the good war against our master, Morlin Sayre that was?"

Donovan chuckled, perhaps at the absurdity of it all, but nodded and his gaze did not waver.

Goesef stared at him a good while, his wide jaw gritting, his eyebrow cocked. He looked at Earny suddenly and said, "What do you make of this, highwayman? You've not said three words since we met."

Earny's stomach somersaulted and he straightened suddenly as the attention of the room turned to him. "Me, yer lordship, sir?"

Goesef nodded.

"I'm far too simple for tha like of this sorta mulling."

The men all laughed save Donovan. Goesef took his sword across his lap and held it there. "I hear from Donovan you're an unexpected bearer of great wisdom. I'd hear it now, for sometimes those outside carry us the finest council, unclouded as they are."

Earnald Avers swallowed hard and stood with his hands first in his pockets and then crossed before him. *Fine show of it already, Earny. Fine, fine show.* Then he adjusted his eyepatch and said, "My take of it is…"

The men watched expectantly, but Earny could not find the words.

But yes, he could, couldn't he? They were right there all along.

"All I know is I promised Ms. Jana I'd be comin' fer her, with Donovan or you fine fellows and yer army or all by myself. Told myself I'd ride a Dweller clear across the Gestalt, come tha need.

Looks like I might be doin' somethin' akin to that after all, I wager. So the short and long of it is her. I lost one good friend already to these happenings. I don't aim to lose another. Nothing else matters to my mind."

He felt immediately foolish and wished he hadn't spoken, but when he looked up the Swordsmen were staring at him with grim realization. Vine and Goesef looked at each other, then at Earny, and finally at Donovan. "You were not jesting, Donovan. The last person I'd expect by look to show such honor would be this fellow before us," said Goesef.

Donovan nodded, still smiling his odd smile. "Indeed. And how such things have brought me before you this night."

Vine rose, and for a moment Earny thought the Swordsman meant to lash out. Instead, he offered his hand and Donovan took it. "We're all going to die doing this, mark me. But what a glorious death it will be."

"Vigilance to the end. Strength till the Black we find," said Goesef, and he, too, took Donovan's hand.

"Ready the men," said Goesef to the greasy-haired man, who looked uncertain but nodded and darted off. To Donovan he said, "Get your monster friends ready. We'll leave an hour before dawn."

The room emptied, leaving only Donovan and Earny.

The Swordsman touched the ex-highwayman's shoulder, not as a commander or a teacher or lord, but as a comrade-in-arms, and together they headed out into the city.

Twenty minutes later they were with the Dwellers.

* * * *

Great calls erupted from within the high city walls, the peculiar orchestra only the act of arming and armoring great multitudes can rouse, each resounding percussion a constituent of war itself, an echo of terror or glory or both in the heart of every man who had fled to Rend to discover security in numbers and who now fell into rank beneath the hard gaze of the Swordsmen to pay the price, behind-hand often but never absent, for such solace.

Out in the field, they massed beneath the unborn day, a great storm of gilt and guidon.

As women and children watched from the battlements, a ring of Mist began to materialize, enveloping the army until just the immense encroaching shapes of the Dwellers, hooded and monstrous, were visible around them, and then they too were hidden by those great billows, within which magic or science undiscoverable to men was being summoned.

8

Jana slipped into the hall and eased the door closed behind her. She looked both ways, straining for a sign of approaching soldiers, of Leto the gruff but kindly. When she heard nothing but the crackle of the torches, she set off, her food satchel full of a foul-smelling collection of goop now, looped in place near her hip. Water sloshed in its vase, which hung from her like a canteen, capped off with a patch of leather and sealed with rawhide. As she moved, she gripped her father's dirk, brought all the way here from the Hunter Estate, and it felt natural and satisfying in her hand. Her six-gun dangled from its rawhide cord on the opposite hip, bouncing with each step she took. It still made her nervous, feeling that cold metal tap her hipbone.

As she maneuvered the halls, sticking to her mental map despite its large blank spots, she thought of the Cleric. He had been so close to her she could smell his foul breath, and yet she hadn't been able to move enough to hold her nose, let alone kill the man—if a man he truly be. *What were you thinking, stupid, stupid girl? You thought you'd walk up to the one who trained the likes of Donovan, who had gone into the Maw headfirst and come out chuckling and stab him in the chest with your little knife?* Worst of it was that she *had* thought just that, and in naive young Jana Hunter's mind that plan had seemed fine and sound. But now her rage, the deep flame that had moved her towards revenge, was extinguished by a frigid wash of fear. The Cleric had come to visit her, and this time he had not taken his leave of her body, but maybe next time he would. Maybe he would and then the time after and the time after that, and who was to say he'd stop even when she was mad? Maybe she wouldn't care then, but her low voice told her she'd know in some deep way that frightened her more than anything else could, like being locked in a cage within a vast blackness, unable to respond in the physical world while the Cleric tortured her for all eternity. If the choice was that or dying alone in the Wastes, then the Wastes it would be.

She came to a concourse and men were walking by. She watched them in their plate mail and their boots with their maces at their sides, headed either to or from training grounds, she wagered. And where in all of this stone maze lay the pen for the Blood Demons? She knew they were here; Leto had let slip there were thousands kept ready for defense and other tasks, though who might attack Pal Myrrah and all its miserable remoteness she could not fathom.

She pressed into an alcove much like the one that led to the holding chamber where her chattels had been stored. Inside the door there she could hear murmuring, muted but almost intelligible. She had just stepped towards it to listen when sudden footsteps sounded from the hall behind her. She mashed to the wall, hoping the shadows were thick enough to hide her, and waited for the approaching men to appear. They were nearly upon her when the door beside her swung open just as suddenly, its aged hinges groaning and its ornamental straps flashing in the torchlight. It halted inches from Jana's face as a man stepped out from the room, separated from her by three inches of old oak and that was all. The men in the hall greeted the man exiting the door with an exchange of pleasantries while Jana stood beside them, her breath reflecting onto her face. Her heart drummed the inside of her ribs, the rush of battle blood burning the backs of her neck and arms.

This is it, I'm going to have to fight.

She tried to ready herself and prayed some of Donovan's lessons had stuck.

Then the men in the hall entered the room and the man exiting said his goodbyes and he was gone and the door closed and somehow no one saw her. She stood inanimate for a moment and prayed the Keeper, then kept moving.

Here the beige of the sandstone gave way to black tiles and things round and tall and columnar built into the walls, and Jana felt a sense of familiarity. She paused to climb a low ledge nearby and peer out a window there, and outside she could see the gates to the fortress, which were open. *It's as though the Cleric bathes in his impunity. He dares anyone in the world to come to his home and make a stink and see what happens.* That such impunity might allow the reverse to occur might not have crossed any of their dark brains. All the better for her.

When she leapt down from the ledge a soldier was standing there with his sword drawn; she could not tell for the life in her how he had approached so silently. "What're you doing there?" His voice attempted an air of command but without total success. She saw that he was young, a thin man perhaps a few years older than her. His hair was tied back in a tight ponytail and his leather armor marked him as an archer.

Jana smiled her best smile at him. "I've lost Leto. Have you seen him?"

"Leto?" said the young man, sizing her up. "I've not seen 'im all day." His eyes narrowed. "Wait, I know you. You're not allowed to go anyw—"

She drew her six-gun before she could think, and while the old Jana Hunter who had spent her childhood nights staring out the window with Stink waiting for Dad to come home from Market might have been reluctant to squash a fly, this Jana Hunter was soaked in desperation few knew or suffered outside war itself. The report was deafening in the small hallway, and a hole the size of an acorn opened up in the man's chest just above his heart. His eyes opened wide and he tottered over onto his back gasping and was still gargling his cries when she turned the corner at the end of the hall.

She ran then, all thought of stealth undone by that thundering echo. Everywhere she turned she saw that young man staring wide-eyed with his chest pouring blood. *You've done it now, haven't you? You wondered if you could pull the trigger when the business end was facing a man. Well, now you have your answer.*

She reached a set of large brass doors and there were no guards there. Somewhere in the stomach of the fortress, Jana could hear shouts and the footfalls of converging sentries, but they were far away and she decided she couldn't worry about them right now. She sprinted hard, stomach clenching, chest burning, her heart pumping fiercely.

Then she was in the black chamber where the albinos had purged Donovan of the Aspy poison, or one very much like it. She turned around, looking for any sign to guide her; in her panic, she had lost all bearing. She thought she spied daylight through the cracks of the double doors to her left and moved there on instinct. Outside lay the same long hall and stair that she remembered from their arrival. She felt relief as she moved through it, premature she realized, but she held onto the feeling anyway. The tiled walls and planked doors strapped with ornaments like those in other parts of the keep and the drum-like columns between them blurred by. With every breath her chest filled with the acrid smell of the Cleric's unending torchsmoke, another way for his magic to invade her body and just as insensate and with its own wicked purpose indifferent to hers.

The hall stretched on. All about her tapestries the color of that young man's blood wafted on a breeze that must come from the mouth of the corridor, for there were no windows in this place. Life-sized statues of men in armor and of other things watched her go by with the same impassivity with which they watched the dust on the floor otherwise.

Then at last she turned a curve and saw the gates she recalled from their entrance here. She wondered at how few soldiers had stood along her path thus far. *Maybe they don't need so many men. Maybe there's plenty of Blood Demons to account for their lack.* That those very Blood Demons might be waiting outside in some capacity crossed her mind, but she ignored it. It was too late to worry about that now. She'd save one bullet for her head come that choice.

As she approached the door she saw movement out of the corner of her eye and veered away, tripping headlong in the process. Her head cracked against the cold stone floor and split open the skin there and her vision exploded into a starfield. When she flipped belly-up, the vague motion she had spotted coalesced and loomed above her, and at first her mind would not accept what her eyes witnessed: a massive spider as tall, if not taller than a man.

She unfroze as it scurried forward, legs dressed in thick tufts of fur as long as a bear's, its myriad eyes watching with unblinking hunger, its pincers gesticulating, oozing a virescent venom that would no doubt paralyze her just long enough to be dragged underground to some nightmarish place where a web built of thread as thick as her arm would bind her until she could be eaten alive.

She dragged herself away with her elbows and armed the blood from her eyes and screamed as the spider bore down on her.

When no attack came, she peered over her shuddering fingertips and there was the spider, no larger than one she'd stomp in their shed before she had burned it down. She rose, shivering, no longer trusting her eyes. Before she could think better she aimed the six-gun and levered back the trigger and again that thunderous report and the spider exploded and so did the black marble it crawled. *Excessive, girl*, said Donovan in the back of her mind, and she could not help but smile as she recalled her dead and gone friend's condescending manner. Then she stole towards the big black doors ahead and did not stop until she was heaving them open with all her might.

Outside, the curving path leading to the front gates was soaked in a deep indigo, the hardiest stars battling just above the teeth of the world as the verging sunrise undermined the vast blackness of night.

She ran hard, the way she had run from the Dweller as it scarfed down the last chunks of her brother in that blood-soaked ravine somewhere in the Shodan. She ran past servants and soldiers, both of whom stopped and stared open-mouthed, as if the concept of a wanted prisoner fleeing this place had so little crossed their mind that the very notion rendered them paralyzed. She passed stone huts with windows sealed by fine fretwork and others with bars on them and some with no fixtures at all and just portholes into the open air. She passed dogs chained to a wall where they shared bones—bones so human in proportion she could not bring herself to think of it further.

Then came the calls from the walkways atop the walls.

As Jana flew through the smaller inner gate she saw in her periphery soldiers in full armor. They spotted her, struck with that same paralysis for a moment, then signaled to another company and now more of them came charging down the steps, violet plumes dancing, armor glinting in the swift approach of the new sun. Behind her the yells and curses of something miscommunicated and the gate grumbled shut as she passed through it, trapping the soldiers within.

They rapped their weapons angrily and shouted but they were at the mercy of the slow turn of the winch. The chain raising the portcullis groaned and clanked and she was halfway down the path when she heard the men come pounding after her.

More men espied her while she sprinted towards the front gate, these in the middle of eating or drinking or just waking, some in their undergarments and nothing else. One man watched her go by halfway through a swig of stout and afterwards he called to his fellows and threw down the jug and came running, shirtless, his gut swaying over too-tight boiled leather and chain trousers and his sword raised.

There was movement atop the front gate, those great black jaws, a flurry beneath the hoardings, and she saw men pointing and cressets burning that same sickly green. The men posted on the battlements were archers and they were surprised but took aim anyway and loosed. She ducked and hugged her arms close while arrows whined past and clattered on the stone behind her. The men trailing called for the archers to be careful, yet when they aimed again it was just as rashly and this time an arrow whizzed by close enough to disturb her hair.

Then she was through the gates, the broad spread of the Wastes before her, once perhaps a great lake but now a flat playa which terminated near the Ven.

She ran from Pal Myrrah as if the Reaper himself was on her heels (and wasn't he?). Overhead, stars still burned but the sun these days was anxious and it was already gaining in the distance where the desert swelled upwards in a great heave to obscure the mountains beyond, those ancient stone colossi she had fantasized of while captive and that now felt dreamlike, impossible to reach.

Beneath her moccasins, the dessert crumbled and sprayed and shifted and was uncertain. On most days she was nimble enough to give the Swordsman a good run come matters of footing and stealth, but fear and maybe madness had dulled her senses and dexterity and she slipped, not completely, but enough to slow her.

As she did, she heard the arrow.

It began as a low whoosh, and then like a fiddler's sliding note it increased in pitch, blooming into a whine. Something in her mind cried out in warning and she twisted away, judging its position by feeling alone. Then the whistle ceased and there was a sharp flame of pain in her upper back or shoulder. It spun her halfway around and she tried to scream but only managed a sharp exhale. She pivoted and fell hard in the dust and lay there writhing. When she tried to rise she couldn't and there was blood pouring from her wound, the arrow wagging in her flesh like a misplaced mutant tail, and all beneath her the blood seeped into the sand as if in some earthen reflection of the sky and the dawning light it absorbed.

Get up girl. Get up for the love in it!

But even the Mule was stunned by the agony. She felt as though something had its claws in her and was tearing her back open strip by strip. When she tried to stand her legs worked for a moment and then they didn't and she toppled and swallowed sand and choked on it. Still behind her were the men's calls and more arrows flew. They stuck in the ground beside her, black fletching winking in the desert wind, the archers who fired them nocking the next volley and drawing again and finding their range. She managed to turn onto her bottom and sat there bleeding. Ahead she saw men marching out from the gates.

She was struggling to rise when they halted suddenly.

She watched them and waited for one last arrow to fly, to bore through her throat and spare her the misery awaiting in the Wastes. She was disturbingly at peace with this idea; *any* end was finer than the coming madness, than the prison of endless dark within her shattered mind as the Cleric's pet.

She managed her feet as she first heard the rumble, and just outside the walls to the right of the front gate she saw a fissure groaning open. It was manmade, for it slid on invisible track and sand poured into the crevice afterwards, which was thirty paces across by her estimate. Inside dwelled a blackness that might swallow noonday sunlight in all its intensity should such light ever manage to shine here from the cloud-maligned sky.

Then a snarl, animal, savage, devoid of intelligence save that which its master deigned.

A figure shambled up a ramp through the opening and stood there with its elongated claws spread threateningly, its doughy flesh shining in the sunrise, its teeth cloaked in viscous slobber the color of urine. The Blood Demon roared and its eyes, blank but for the pupils, dripped the creature's namesake. It broke into a run, horribly fast, and Jana Hunter hurried away into the Wastes.

She ran over stony outcroppings, past a small esker and the long-forgotten bones of creatures newly bared by a searching wind, bones that would be covered again soon to lay outside the gaze of men or anything else until the earth ground them back to dust. The Blood Demon charged at her heels, snarling like a rabid dog, claws jangling with each pump of its disproportionate arms like they were steel and not bone. Once she chanced a glance back and the creature had halved the distance between them. Far behind, the men of Pal Myrrah watched and Jana imagined them chuckling amongst themselves and placing wagers on her survival. *The smart money's only going one way.* Then there existed only the notion of escape, as though she might somehow outrun this beast unnatural and bereft of mortal needs and limitations and no doubt exhaustion was among them.

A voice spilled through her head while she moved and it was not hers, nor was it the voice of madness. Quite the opposite.

It was her father's voice.

Stand and fight, Jana.

"I can't!" she cried with no self-consciousness.

Do it, girl. It's all you can do. Stand true.

But Jana did not want to stand true. She wanted to be home, in a time just as lost now as Donovan's life. She wanted to sit cross-legged before a fire with a stomach full of stew and her family and Dog beside her and no Cleric and no scar, no madness eating away at her. She wanted a life that was but could never be again, and she thought such a wish was to be the curse of men and women for all of time.

Then, just as suddenly, her desire for that wish died somewhere in the dark of her mind where there were no witnesses, and the Princess, Hunter'lue, was no more; only the woman Jana, who knew this world and knew her place and lived no further in denial, remained. That this occurred while her body traversed the grim reach of the Wastes with death seconds behind struck her as no more profound than if Earny had tripped in the woods. Where else better?

She stopped cold, whirling, looking some demon birthed of the desert herself. Her fingers found the cold grip of her six-gun with practiced precision. Ahead the Blood Demon charged, its claws dangling low and ready to skewer her, its great fangs gaping.

It's death. At least I get to see it coming. At least I get to shoot it in the chest a few times, too.

And then she opened fire.

The muzzle of the six-gun flared, volleying forth one, two, three bullets. The first missed. The next took the Blood Demon in the shoulder and blood geysered and the creature stumbled but did not slow. The third carved a wide notch in its neck, yet this wound, grievous enough to drop even a man like Donovan to his knees, did not faze the creature.

She stepped backwards, those snapping fangs so close she could smell the fetid stink of them, and aimed again carefully, the beast's head between those old iron sights. But when she squeezed off the next round the Blood Demon faded right suddenly and the bullet whirred into the mountainous distance beyond. Now she had only one charge left. The Cleric's creation was close enough to strike, its claws lashing out as soon as it was within reach, and it was only chance or maybe the battle blood like Donovan called it that kept her alive. Jana leaped backwards and the claws sliced the air where she had stood and she landed hard on her back with a groan.

The creature paused only to gather its balance, then it was after her again.

"Come on!" she called to the black slits in the center of its bloody eyes, loud enough to echo into the empty land around them.

It stared at her cries without understanding, nor did it require any. "COME ON!"

And it was coming, yes, for her, for her soul, for her flesh.

Jana Hunter put the six-gun Donovan had given her to her temple and held her breath, placed her finger on the trigger, and pulled.

Halfway into the rise of the hammer something bright flew from the unmeasured distance behind her and struck the Cleric's monstrosity in the breast. The creature paused its charge and stared dumbly at the blood pouring from where it had been struck, a long silver spike protruding there that glinted in the dawn as it burned brighter on the horizon. The creature looked at Jana, those black pupils swimming in blood, its fangs working and opening and closing and drenching the sand below with slaver, and then it lumbered on, disregarding self-preservation, obeying soullessly the will of its unseen Master.

Again a silver spike whistled and this one punctured the creature's throat. It fell to its knees, still scrambling. It was almost upon her, limp but battling to complete its mission, when a large black boot materialized from what seemed the very air itself and planted on the silver spike within the Blood Demon's neck and drove it deeper, severing its spine with an audible *snap*. The disembodied boot thrust away the creature and it sprawled in the sand and shivered and then lay still.

Jana peered up, the haze of her shock receding, and there stood who she least expected.

Donovan Maltrese rose above her, a towering black thing clawed free from the Maw or maybe reborn of some other dark place beyond man's reckoning. He stood there regarding the stone hold of Pal Myrrah, an eidolon of death made substantial, the thick oilcloth of his black duster billowing behind him on a great gust of hot desert air. A crescent moon drawn by the daylight curved above his head through the clearing sky, a primordial scythe wieldable by beings unknown and to what purpose none could say but perhaps the Keeper himself.

The Swordsman turned his gaze to her, a man walked clear of the Black by his own accord, as though his stubbornness was too great for even the universe to contend with. And when his thin lips parted in a familiar yet odd smile and his green eyes glittered in the newborn light, Jana felt no annoyance, no childish thing she refused to name yet allowed to steer her course; she felt only relief, enough to drown out, for now, the pain of her wounds.

Donovan reached with a soiled hand, dry and callused, and that hand, which had seen much death and dealt most of it, now offered just one thing. She took it and he helped her rise. "Good to see you again, too, girl," he said to her. "You were out of bullets anyway."

She looked at her pistol and saw that he was right. *I forgot the damned spider. Fine mess that would've been.*

She looked behind them, and there were the Swordsmen, Goesef and Vine, and others that bore swords like Donovan, twelve, thirteen of them in all. Jana watched them march with the sun on their backs towards her, their faces grim and determined and their hands ready on their namesake weapons. Behind them were soldiers, rows upon rows of serried men in full armor. Their chainmail boots crossed the sand of the Wastes in perfect time. Together their glistering spears and maces and bows and their helms and their cuirasses gave them the look of a singular steel animal unleashed from bowels of the earth itself, for where else could such a force have come from?

Behind them a smog of rising dust, but also something else, white, impenetrable before, now a fading remnant.

Mist?

Then the Mist solidified again—*yes, that must be what it was*—thick enough to blot out the sun. When it drew back Jana thought first that the contour of the Ven had somehow changed. Then she saw that the new shapes were Misties, hundreds of them, a row of black featureless cloaks and faceless hoods like monks associate to some tenebrous monastery where only giants worshipped. They marched towards Pal Myrrah as one being, and beneath them the earth trembled from the weight. Jana recalled her fear upon seeing a single Dweller by the Gestalt, and now the sight now of so many on Donovan's heels somehow filled her with joy.

Let's see your little monsters put up a fight now, she thought to the Cleric, hoping he could read her mind.

Among the men walked Tomson and also Brig and Mullville and a few others from Pleasantry. Jana rubbed her eyes, sure this must be some benign manifestation of the Cleric's madness. But it wasn't, because when Earny Avers appeared and adjusted his eyepatch and took her hands, the warmth in them was too tangible, too familiar to be mistrusted. He hugged her tight, careful to avoid the arrow still protruding from her shoulder. "Oh Keeper save us and every other thing worth savin' in tha world," he said, his voice brimming with relief and something else that she had never heard from him before.

When he pulled away there was a tear creeping from his good eye, and in that eye welled such relief that it stirred Jana to her core. Her own tears came, and this time she was not ashamed. "I said I'd come fer ya," he told her. "And this ol' Earny's word is strong as oak. Pray it very true."

Donovan looked at the arrow in her shoulder and frowned, said, "It didn't hit bone or artery, but I'd not remove it here. Stay to the rear. You'll be safe there."

She met his look, fierce as ever, turned and said, "Break it off." Earny looked concerned, but she silenced him with a gesture and stared at the Swordsman.

"I said break it off."

The Swordman's frown turned into his odd grin.

"Yes, Hunter'lue."

He grasped the arrow with his hard hand and broke it close to the skin and tossed it aside into the desert. Jana cringed but did not cry out as a fresh batch of pain flowered. Then she dropped her pistol and drew her father's dirk, and together she and her companions faced with their army the keep of Pal Myrrah.

Even from this distance, she could spot the brilliant white flash of the Cleric atop a balcony high in the trident towers of the fortress.

Out of the gates below him poured men in their violet-plumed armor, spears born skyward.

And then there were Blood Demons spilling forth from the earth by the thousands.

9

The Cleric, who once thought of himself as Morlin Sayre but nevermore, watched the black figure on the horizon and his army of men and Swordsmen and Dwellers. Fate was a creature of its own design; the whims of men did little to influence its course. A thousand variant outcomes he had witnessed in his endlessly calculating mind, yet this was never one. Perhaps such was a characteristic of inevitability. If so, then this was how it was meant to be, one final lesson before his inauguration into a higher awareness. In the end, what would it matter?

He turned from the balcony and entered the halls of Pal Myrrah, and as though the mutated bodies of the Blood Demons were the Cleric's own extremities, their collective minds told him Donovan's force was about to charge.

All well.

No creation might exist without its trials.

10

Donovan held his sword, Orin, overhead and it caught the burning sunrise on its acid-etched face and looked aflame, as if the spirits of the men who had died with their fingers enclosed on this same hilt now flooded the steel with something ethereal. He looked at Jana and he saw a young girl before, now a woman, the same fight in her eyes that had freed the Raistlinders from the bandits of the Shodan luminescent there now. He saw Earny Avers, his reformation complete, his basilard ready, his good eye smiling at Donovan as much as his twisted lips. And he saw his fellows, the Swordsmen survived of Kolendhar, with their family blades held before them awaiting his call, and it filled his heart. Somewhere, whether in the sky or his soul, he saw Rosaline, too, watching him with her soft smile, her indomitable yet fragile countenance warmer on him than any sun.

This is what I was meant for, Rosaline. Wherever you are, I hope you can forgive the road it took for me to arrive here.

Donovan of the Maltreses roared his family battlecry into the crisp morning air and, as one, townsman, bandit, Swordsman and Dweller charged the Wastes towards Pal Myrrah and the host of Blood Demons swarmed to meet them.

They closed the gap in seconds, them with their myriad blades aloft, their enemies a locust swarm of fangs and claws. The Dwellers enveloped the playa behind them in a tidal wave of blackness, utterly silent except for the thunderous metallic roar of their swords drawing in perfect synch. Those great black-cloaked creatures circled wide around the edge of the army and all of them met the Blood Demons in the center of this ancient stretch like a great pincer.

Donovan felt the battle blood take over as soon as a creature drew within reach, and with its guidance Orin cut the air and monstrous flesh with the same ease. The Swordsman felt his body flow without thought from one form to the next, some taught to him as a boy by his father or by Morlin Sayre himself, others of his own creation, and with each shift between those forms one of the Cleric's creations lay dead behind him with one or many parts removed. Every time his blade found flesh he felt a pang of guilt and wondered what farmhand, what loving mother, what soldier or peasant or bandit this one might have been before the Cleric's pollution. Could they be saved? If he and Jana, human still, were beyond the Cleric's aid, then these things with their souls ripped out of them would not be healed by any magic. The thought fueled his rage and he cut into the Blood Demons with a roar.

Beside him Earny lashed with his basilard, his one-eyed face speckled with blood. For a moment the sight of the ex-bandit broke Donovan from his bloodlust and he saw in that single eye, simple most times yet filled with profound, often accidental insight, the very fire his fellow Swordsmen carried. Donovan felt a smile creep across his face, then three Blood Demons charged him at once. Three cuts, face, gut, chest, and all of them lay dead or dying.

Across the mass of bodies he saw Dwellers flooding into the ranks of the Blood Demons, massive blades cutting them down in groups of fives and tens. Severed arms and heads and torsos, all deformed by unearthly magic, filled the air. Ten paces away a Dweller raised a Blood Demon clawing and snarling from the ground and ripped it in two as though it was a leaf. It hurled the limp upper body into more approaching creatures and bowled them down, its great sword retrieved again, already arcing towards new enemies.

The Swordsmen fought as Donovan did, each a honed machine with the sole purpose of dealing death. Vine ducked and wove between the creatures, claws slipping through the air a split second after he occupied it. His sword slid deep into a Blood Demon's chest and it swung its claws, snapping, blood gushing from its eyes and mouth. He kicked it free, sword curving behind him before plunging earthward to impale the creature's ruinous face. It chomped at the blade twice as though it might eat its way to the owner, then slid back, dead.

Goesef's blade, giant for a man but dwarfed by those of the Dwellers, whirled in massive arcs but still with the precision of his peers. He stepped on the neck of a writhing Blood Demon and split the bones there asunder with a pivot as two more threw their claws towards him. Both of those ghastly heads went tumbling with that next blow and then he was on to other foes.

Donovan heard the loosing of hundreds of arrows and the men of Rend who had stayed back with their yew bows filled the sky with shafts and feathers and steel heads. The arrows curved across the sky, which spread bright and igneous beneath the inferno of the aging dawn, and swooped like a flock of deadly birds, most finding throats and faces and limbs to impale as the rear ranks of the Blood Demons floundered and fell before they could even reach the battle.

Jana wielded her father's dirk well. Donovan stayed close as often as he could, and once he saved her from a rear attack; otherwise the girl was a torrent, slicing and thrusting, most blows not mortal but precise enough to slow or lame. Once she found a Blood Demon on its knees bleeding out from a Dweller's strike and planted the dirk in its throat and then pushed the abomination aside to die in the dust.

Brig and Tomson fought alongside the Swordsman, the former's axe, still notched from their skirmish with the Dweller King, searching the mass of malformed bodies. Tomson's knife carved a line through a Blood Demon's throat, enough to fell any mortal creature, but the undead thing kept its fervor and hammered Tomson from his feet. Instantly the battle blood spurred Donovan to action. With one deft spring, he mounted the arm of a nearby Dweller as it withdrew its blade from an annihilated foe. Beneath him the Blood Demon's claws swept downward, ready to shred Tomson's flesh and carve the life from his bowels. Donovan landed two paces behind them and Orin screamed skyward and the creature's accursed blood drained onto the mayor of Pleasantry but no harm befell him. Donovan offered his hand, but Tomson rose on his own and grinned and then charged bellowing back into the fray.

A cluster of soldiers from Rend were driven back by a hard push from the Blood Demons, the misshapen devils insane with hunger and with mindless zealotry for their master's will. Donovan saw one man pitch forward with eight claws through him and another man screaming into his own blood as his throat was carved open, and elsewhere soldiers stabbed and thrusted as the Swordsmen had taught them, but precision against the mindless rage of an animal is not always efficient and many of them died.

Donovan rushed to Goesef's side and the big tattooed warrior met his gaze and saw his gesture towards the rank of men which was about to break. Goesef nodded, and the Swordsmen charged as a single war machine and hacked at the whirling claws and sent many of them to the ground and their owners soon after.

Far across the field, two Dwellers surged and ebbed over and around one other as if they were weightless, silent but for when they killed. Blood Demons scaled their backs and sunk their fangs into those cloaked and hidden throats and other parts and sheathed their razor claws to the palms into their flesh, and some of the Dwellers arched their backs in agony and fought to reach their attackers but to no avail.

Donovan saw this as well, and while Goesef plowed over attackers—one of which had undone the meat of his arm and now blood was running—the former Swordmaster of Kolendhar raced for the archers of Rend. He found Mullville on the ground in their midst, clutching his gut. His face was bleached and his body quivering, but he smiled when he saw Donovan, who took up the fallen man's bow and quiver. "Just need me a minute," said the man from Pleasantry, and Donovan knew grimly that no stretch of time would heal that terrible wound.

A Dweller hunched before the Swordsman as it snapped away the head and shoulders of a Blood Demon, and Donovan took hold of those great rolls of black cloth and clambered up and shouted, "*Aloiu mueth koeam!*" The creature seemed to hear him, for it remained stationary as Donovan reached its massive shoulders, and from there he could survey the Blood Demons bestriding the other two Dwellers. The Swordsman aimed and fired his bow in rapid succession. Some arrows flew wide, but more found their marks and sent the Demons twisting and thrashing to the ground, and the Dwellers they had mounted sunk their hidden rows of teeth into those unnatural beasts and gorged on their entrails.

Below, Brig fought aside a Blood Demon's attack and sheared its gory face apart. It overturned, half-blind and damaged mortally, but its wanton savagery drove it on. Donovan watched this and called a warning, but the big man from Pleasantry did not hear him as the Blood Demon sank first one and then both sets of honed claws into his vertebral column and ripped them outward, disintegrating Brig's torso into a fine red mist. Donovan descended from the Dweller's shoulders and the last thing that Blood Demon saw was a flash of steel before Orin skewered it longways.

Here Swordsmen whirling, dealing death at each turn, one of them wielding two swords in a cyclone of ruin, blood drizzling about them like rain. There a Blood Demon assailing a Dweller's leg only to be crushed beneath another Dweller's great hide-bound foot.

Scores of arrows flurrying. Bows plying. Pauldrons and bassinets glowing like pinpricks of starlight above the milling flanks. Now the Dwellers surged forward, black blades sweeping over whole rows of Blood Demons at once. Another gale of arrows turned black against the morning sky, raining death across the Demon horde.

We're winning. Keeper save all of us, we're winning.

Then, as if in response to this thought, the Blood Demons suddenly withdrew.

They formed a rank a hundred feet out, their numbers decimated by a third. A few were still within reach of the Dwellers, and they swung their swords and obliterated many of them, then looked about almost quizzically while the battle slowed to a halt. Blood filled the playa now where once there had been water long ago, and Donovan's boots splashed in it. He stood beside Goesef with gore both human and demon crawling his face and soaking his clothes and watched as the Blood Demon army regathered.

Jana appeared beside him. Somehow she was unharmed except for the arrowhead still lodged in her shoulder. She looked like a demon herself, drenched in blood like that. There was an animal ferocity in her eyes and the Swordsman pitied any that might find this woman their enemy.

With a unified consciousness, the Blood Demons parted down the center, and the Swordsmen and the Dwellers and the rest turned to face them.

Then a lone white-clad figure approached the center of the battlefield, the curved blade of his staff heliographing, and Donovan Maltrese knew his ultimate destiny had arrived at last.

11

The Cleric stepped forth from his creatures, a soilless white beacon. The blood pools he stepped through parted centerwise on his approach and encircled his feet, only to fill back in as he passed. He stopped at last and placed both hands on his staff, his scarecrow body deceptively frail before the massive breadth of Pal Myrrah. Donovan saw men positioned along the great keep, archers and armored infantry bearing spears, but none had engaged in battle. And why would they? Their numbers might be two, three hundred?

"Donovan!" called the Cleric, and the voice that had once been Morlin Sayre's echoed into the Wastes.

Donovan breathed deeply, as if the air might provide added resolve.

Goesef took him by the arm as he began to move. "Donovan, old friend, you need not do this. We have the numbers…"

Donovan thought of Mullville, a man he had known for less than a week, dying in the mud with a smile on his lips. "Yes. I do."

Goesef watched his fellow Swordsman's eyes as if taking measure of what lay behind them, then withdrew his hand. "Whatever happens, you must not listen. Master was always fine at the roundabout."

Donovan nodded, more aware of this than any. Jana was looking at the Cleric with unbridled hate and he motioned for her to stay back. Then he marched to meet his old teacher, his limbs sore from battle but still charged with the remnants of the battle blood, ready to surge again at a moment's notice. When Donovan stood ten paces away the Cleric's smile gleamed. "My friend. Still alive. I saw your death and I despaired, for I had hoped no such thing might transpire without my aid."

"Do you offer terms?" Donovan said to him, a show if ever there was one.

"Is this all for the greatness of Donovan Maltrese? To rid yourself of the gift I've bestowed you?"

"This is to show that the greatness of men has not diminished, though it has been tried by these years," answered Donovan. Even now it was hard to look his Master in the eye; too many times as a boy had he seen those eyes flash in anger just before those hands doled punishment. "There is no cure for me or the girl, is there?"

The Cleric shook his head. "You cannot cure evolution, Donovan. We stand here and vie to make sense of the senseless with words that have meaning only because you and I are here to listen to them. That is why *they* are the old way." He pointed towards Donovan's army. "You know this in your heart. What I've given you is the gift of an existence that will make sense within the senselessness of eternity." His gaze fell on the rest of the Swordsmen, and Donovan saw that their once-master recognized each of them and those violet eyes turned away quickly.

"I do not want it," said Donovan, Orin grasped loosely, ready to be brought to bear.

The Cleric smiled, and in that smile the Swordsman saw the decaying flesh of thousands left in the wake of his machinations, each sacrificed in the pursuit of a world sought by none but for which the stuff of existence itself had been deranged. "Then you will have to give it back to me. No one may interfere."

Donovan felt an alien flutter of fear. Goesef and Vine were watching closely, and after Donovan's nod, they and the other Swordsmen lowered their weapons.

The Dwellers, perhaps sensing what was to pass or perhaps understanding their exchange, moved silently and formed a circle around the two combatants, their massive blades re-clamped, their faceless cowls conveying intense interest. Donovan watched the gray scaled hand of one Dweller vanish into the opposing sleeve and its brethren mirrored this and then stayed motionless.

"I loved you, my son," said the Cleric, the words twisted by his tone into something unrecognizable.

Then Donovan brought Orin to bear, felt beneath his fingers the marks of all who had lived before him since the birth of the Order, and he called into the nether for their strength as he charged his mortal enemy on this dead plain beneath the bitter gaze of the sun.

12

The Cleric did not move until Donovan's first swing came flashing down. When he sidestepped it was effortless, his staff brought about. Orin struck the curved blade at the head of the staff, neither spear nor scythe, a flash of blue sparks jetting from the point of impact into the cold air.

Donovan pressed his master, thinking Morlin's weakness, if it could be called that, was more likely to show during defense, a trait of his fighting style that none within the Order but Donovan would have noticed, and he only from long hours and days spent studying this man with his peculiar brand of obsessiveness. *Skill is built of obsession, Donovan. Men say the word as if it is something to be trifled or renounced, yet it is at the heart of mastery itself.* Such were the words of Morlin Sayre, former Swordmaster of Kolendhar, whose body Donovan fought now with every thread of ability he possessed.

Donovan moved and opened his mind to his low voice, to the battle blood pounding in his body and skull, his arms and legs ablaze with frightening energy. Again and again the Cleric parried blows that would have felled any of a thousand other men, ducking, leaning away, whirling his staff, redirecting thrusts and cuts with apparent ease. Donovan kept his balance, rage and frustration building. In his mind the phantom gaze of Rosaline's soul burned bright and unresolved, urging him forth. He thought of her sweet face, her skin, her laugh, her heat, all of it become moot from one touch of this man's evil magic. He roared and struck at the Cleric's neck then, for it seemed open. Yet it was not, and the Cleric stepped aside and that staff whipped about and opened the flesh in Donovan's temple and sent him stumbling backwards.

Somewhere Jana gasped and Donovan hoped the girl stayed put, for while she might harbor hatred that felt strong enough to slay this enemy, any attempt to do so would prove her naivety and little else. This foe was beyond her, beyond all the rest of them, perhaps beyond even himself.

Donovan waited for the world to stop spinning, for the throbbing in his head to dull, and then he pressed the offensive again. The Cleric moved in time with his blows as though they were predetermined, as if this was some dance the two of them had choreographed in advance and rehearsed until it became rote. The harsh peal of metal filled this place where the world had long retaken its hold after the fall of man's first claim to the earth with a sound undeniably divorced from nature. The Dwellers and the rest looked on as those weapons clashed and interweaved in fluid blurs, and all the while the Cleric's eyes never blinked.

Donovan felt his scar, which now had mutilated much of his body, throb and clench as though stimulated by proximity to its creator. Orin stabbed into empty air where the Cleric once stood and a spotless white boot pinned it there, and then Donovan's former master lashed out with a gaunt hand exuding a bloody halation, and that energy burst into Donovan's chest like a molten bolder and all the world turned red as he spun around and landed on his back, his vision dark, his chest afire.

Behind him, he heard Jana crying, heard her struggle to rush to his aid only to be held back.

When Donovan looked at his chest he saw it truly was on fire. The Cleric's magic had burned away patches of his chest plate and the cloth beneath, searing his skin, and now his scar was bared to the sky. He lay in agony for minutes before he could attempt to stand.

"It's not too late, Donovan," said the Cleric, unmoving now. "I'd not kill you if I don't have to, for from what materials might I create your like?"

Donovan thought that the Swordsman who had walked the Drudge with Jana Hunter, who had led the Dwellers to Pleasantry for the gamble of his salvation, might have agreed now, for the Cleric's tone sounded reasonable. But this Donovan Maltrese rose to a knee, his armor still smoldering, then to his feet, and raised Orin into an offensive stance instead. Then he charged, already plotting a variation in his strategy, and he prayed the Keeper it might work.

Two cuts and it seemed to have done just that. The Cleric was off-balance for a hair's breadth, and Donovan sliced downward and would have severed his staff—if it was made of earthly material that could be severed. Then the Cleric's arms unfurled and from the center of the staff a Swordsman's blade rang free in time to parry the attack. The Cleric held the bladed staff in his offhand like a scabbard, and there now as in their old lives stood two Swordsmen toe to toe with their ancient blades thrust before them.

"I thought you renounced your old life," said Donovan, unsteady, bleeding, his stomach and chest baking from the inside. "I thought it was the remnant of that which no longer suits this world."

The Cleric did not answer. Now it was his turn to press the offensive. Donovan moved and ducked and fell into every defensive form he had ever learned and some he imagined between moments here and now, yet it was all he could do to hold back the onslaught of his old master's fury.

The Cleric's sword fell again and again, the last time too fast, too precise, for it seemed to weave around Donovan's protective measures somehow and a sheet of white pain sheared across him as the tip of the Cleric's steel opened the skin on his stomach. He hobbled back, clutching his wound.

A cold wind rose about them while the Dwellers and the Blood Demons and the mountains themselves watched, and then that wind dispersed into the Wastes and died on the horizon, and still the two combatants measured each other. They clashed again at last, but Donovan's moves were sluggish now, his body debilitated, and the Cleric threw aside his student's attack and crushed the bladed sheath into the back of his head—the *occiput*, said his Studies in an insane flash. It was all Donovan could do to keep his hands and knees and not collapse face-first into the sand. He knelt rocking and watched blood pour from his head and stomach and saw the Cleric's boots nearby through a haze of pain.

"I taught you much, Donovan," said the Cleric. "But most important between men like us is this: always be able to kill your students." He paced in circles. Donovan looked for Jana but could not see her. Earny was beside Vine in the distance and, while the Swordsman watched, the once-highwayman fell to his knees.

"This is not some vague madness which approaches you over days and months from the shadows. This is your death, here and now, on the tip of my sword. I'd not see you slain, Donovan. But it is here you must choose."

Donovan looked at him and said nothing, and whatever the Cleric saw in his old pupil's eyes made him flinch almost imperceptibly.

"So be it, then."

His grim look belied no pleasure as the former Swordmaster set himself to deliver a killing blow. Donovan met his gaze, watching those depthless violet eyes that had once seemed to him the wisdom of all the ages made tangible, but now were demonic glass crypts interring within the pretense of a once-great man and the souls he had consumed along his journey.

And then, with inhuman precision, the Cleric whirled his blade towards Donovan's neck in a perfect, shining arc.

In that moment of death, Donovan glimpsed something; time itself perhaps. He saw back to the first seeds of his line and farther, to Ruti's forefathers, to a world no longer extant where men somewhere sometime on some lost battlefield had pushed their guts back into their bodies and risen and fought on regardless for an ideal worthy of any cost. From those men he found a seed of strength, indomitable, and that strength burned forward across the lines of time like gunpowder, reaching through the untold ages towards him in the span of a breath.

What makes you any different, Swordsman?

At last, he understood.

And so, between the moment the Cleric's swing began and the time it might have severed Donovan's head, some stockpile of strength surged, bred not of his body but somewhere else, maybe within the Cold, which now boiled in a hidden caldera inside him, its vile sense of self-preservation provoked. The Swordsman ducked sideways and the Cleric's blow scrawled a thin line into the sand where he had knelt, and then Donovan was on his feet with Orin in one hand and his stomach held together by the other.

Snarling, wolf-like, the Cleric pressed forward, sword flaring, and Donovan's arms were weak but some force drove his hand and he swept aside each strike as he fell back. He felt then the glow of his madness, familiar and dreaded, soak into his vision and cast the world in shades of blood. That light, brought to him by the Cleric from the Darklands or somewhere else just as infernal, overtook him like never before, both blinding and focusing. And yet the omnipresent chattering of the Cold, waiting in his depths beside his low voice, did not attempt to overtake him.

"You don't seem to understand, Donovan," said the Cleric, not sweating, his breathing even, his white cloak immaculate despite the swell of the wind and the debris it couriered. "This is what you give up. That no human might defeat you, just as none can defeat me."

The Cleric's sword whistled and that again should have been the killing stroke, the twin to those stopped short by that same hand countless times while sparring on the Din or within the walls of Kolendhar, the blow which was to remove Donovan's life. But this Donovan was no longer that boy, and he dodged deftly and the Cleric's second attack was delivered by the bladed scabbard, which Donovan sensed beforehand. The unknown flame still boiling behind his eyes, Donovan claimed the scabbard with a trembling fist and lurched downward and snapped it midway. With a spinning flourish, he swung Orin about, knocking aside the Cleric's defenses, and *there* was the moment, which his obsessive nature had noted as a boy, when Morlin Sayre would recenter his weapon after parrying in much the same trajectory every time. Still spinning, Donovan launched the broken end of the scabbard forward through the space of that motion and lodged it half-mast into the chest of his enemy.

The Cleric stared wide-eyed. No blood flowed from the wound. He clutched it with his thin fingers, then fell to his knees.

A quiet drew across the plains then, and Donovan, his last threads of strength driven from him, fell also to his knees and they sat there in the dirt.

The Cleric smiled a predatory smile. His fingers discovered his dropped sword. "We'll see the Maw together this time, Donovan. I should have taken you with me before."

The demon fire swept out of Donovan at his master's words then, just as suddenly as it had arrived, and with nothing to replace it he could not respond as he struggled to find Orin, which had fallen from his grasp.

Without rising, The Cleric drew back again to smite his once-student, and Donovan knew that this time there would be no last-minute evasion, no barely executed parry. This was his end. He hoped Rosaline would be proud of him at least. Proud that he had tried.

Two delicate hands drove downward an aged blade then, the steel shorter than its bearer's forearm, a blade forged who-knew-when-or-where, once wielded by a young man during his fighting days far south of here before he had given them up to raise children and become a farmer. Now the daughter of that slain man, the sole survivor of a family massacred by demons drawn by the Cleric's scent, her spirit blemished by his violation of her body and mind, plunged her father's blade through the top of her enemy's skull, and it did not crack or bleed but took the entire length of that old steel without resistance.

Donovan watched the Cleric's eyes roll back, then glaze, lifeless. His mouth levered open and blood did not pour out but rather some foul black fluid. Then he fell backwards with Jana's dirk protruding from his head and lay motionless.

Jana stood paralyzed over him for a long moment. "I interfered," she said, breathless, tears in her eyes.

Then the light erupted.

It birthed from the wound in the Cleric's chest with force enough to launch the broken scabbard spinning into the Wastes. A pulsing crimson aura flooded outward, blinding even in the full break of day. It swirled like smoke and grew and swallowed whole the Cleric's body.

Donovan fell back and threw up a hand to shield his eyes, but even closed the light still burned them. Then he saw something rising, maybe a product of the madness but maybe it was true, a face made of light and cloud, demonic and fanged and skeletal. It climbed from the Cleric's light-enshrouded body and hovered, gazing down at him with its borehole eyes gleaming. Then it dispersed like a plume of smoke and drifted away on the wind, immaterial as a dream.

The pain in Donovan's chest afterward was shocking. It pulsed and shredded through him like claws and he fell to his back screaming and heard Jana do the same. It crawled his chest, a centipede of agony, every foot laced in poison, stabbing into him. *It's the scar*, he realized. He felt his back arch and buckle and he screamed until his throat was raw and he could scream no more. Somewhere between consciousness he felt the scar rising, felt it moving like a living thing threatened. It was trying to peel away, trying to free itself from the prison of his body, but with the Cleric's governing power spent it no longer possessed the reserves to do so and, with a thunderclap that spread out from the plain in a shockwave, that ever-present weight lifted, and above him it too hovered and then dispersed. Nearby he witnessed Jana's scar wriggle through a tear in her shirt and slither onto the ground like some demonic worm, and then it vanished also.

Donovan pitched backwards as a second wave burst outward, and around him, men and Dwellers alike shrank back fearfully. The Blood Demons, now mindless drones without their Master, could do naught but stare, and they alone were struck by this force, this remnant power born of the Maw never meant for earthly appliance now unleashed in one malevolent bomb. The light tore through them and flooded over them like a million swords forged of lightning, and as one they were ripped asunder, shredded to a fine, fetid mist. With a chorus of inhuman screeches and howls each and every one of the Cleric's creations were hoisted into the air, some growling and screaming, others limp, and then the light died and so with it did their essences, and in the end nothing remained but the dead and the living men and their Dweller allies, all witness to something beyond their reckoning, all sure that what they had glimpsed here today was the end of this horrid chapter in a world of nightmares and perhaps the beginning of a new one.

Epilogue

S he stood alone atop the wall, which faced southeast, where the gates of Pal Myrrah emptied onto the wastes and where the fortune of the world had been battled for. She thought of the men who had died for this, and to her, the sacrifice seemed honored only if the world they hoped for now could overcome the very flaw which had brought them here.

And what is that, girl?

Perhaps it was as simple a thing as trusting in the man or woman beside you and them trusting in you.

Jana Hunter traced a finger across the exposed area of her chest, where for months upon months there had thrived an ever-present reminder of the man who had taken everything from her. Now there was only the smooth skin for which many eligible men in Pleasantry had come calling for, and that some who were not as eligible had come for, too.

The Cold was gone. It was over.

She thought of Brig, of Grampy, and others. She thought of Ruti, who now lay buried someplace near the foot of the Ven; Earny had been the soul attendant of that funeral. Jana remembered the last Root Dragon and wanted to weep for him, but she did not. The choosing of one's destiny, moving with your life the world towards what your heart knows is right should never be mourned.

She thought of the Cleric's men, who each and every one had surrendered and were now quartered within the keep, any sense of fight long drained from them.

She thought of her father, her mum, Stink, and now she could only smile.

I love you guys. I will remember you always.

At the foot of the stairs, she saw Donovan and Earny waiting for her.

She took one more look at the vast sunset painting the curve of the earth below in shades no artisan could hope to replicate. She saw the stars that managed to shine through from the void beyond with some undeniable vitality, their light everlasting and heedless of what had occurred here so far from the reach of their warmth.

Then she hurried down to her friends.

Earny was making faces and she was laughing as they made their way up the hill.

Donovan walked behind them, and when she turned he was smiling.

For once it did not look so odd.

THE END

About the Author

David McLeavy is an award-winning writer and TV commercial director. A native of upstate New York, he fancies himself a connoisseur of ginger ale, a reasonable replacement for IMDB, and spends as much time as possible boating with his wife and son. When he's not found writing, David can often be found on film sets, directing for companies such as Aquafina, Denny's, Comcast, Mercedes Benz and more. He currently resides in Pennsylvania with his family and their Samoyed.